PRAISE FOR *MULTIREAL*

"David Louis Edelman's vision of the future is so alive and full of energy the pages are practically buzzing. Wonderfully intricate with smart, satisfying complexity, *Infoquake* and its sequel, *MultiReal*, serve up a world where mindbending technologies promise a freedom nearly as endless as the Machiavellian ambitions of those who would control them."

Nick Sagan
author of *Idlewild, Edenborn*, and *Everfree*

"A thoroughly successful hybrid of *Neuromancer* and *Wall Street*, *MultiReal* is the kind of thought-experiment we need more of around here: rigorously backgrounded, tightly plotted, and built around one of the most intriguing neurotech conceits I've encountered in years. William Gibson once observed that the street finds its own uses for things. David Louis Edelman reminds us that both boardroom and back room do as well—and the people who lurk in those places are a *lot* scarier. . . ."

Peter Watts
Hugo Award–nominated author of *Blindsight*

"Just when we thought cyberpunk was dead, David Louis Edelman bursts on the scene with defibrillator paddles and shouts, 'Clear!' If there's any web more tangled than the World Wide one, it's the Byzantine networks of high finance; Edelman intermeshes them in a complex, compelling series. This DOES compute!"

Robert J. Sawyer
Hugo Award–winning author of *Rollback* and *Hominids*

PRAISE FOR *INFOQUAKE*:
VOLUME I OF THE JUMP 225 TRILOGY

Barnes & Noble's Science Fiction Book of the Year 2006
John W. Campbell Memorial Award Nominee for Best Novel 2006
#5 on Bookgasm's 5 Best Sci-Fi Books of 2006
John W. Campbell Best New Writer Award Nominee 2008

"David Louis Edelman's debut novel—the first installment of his Jump 225 trilogy—is equal parts corporate thriller, technophilic cautionary tale, and breathtakingly visionary science fiction adventure.... Brilliantly blending the cutthroat intrigues of the high-tech business world with revolutionary world building, Edelman could quite possibly be the love child of Donald Trump and Vernor Vinge. *Infoquake* is one of the most impressive science fiction debuts to come along in years—highly recommended."
Barnes & Noble Explorations

"Slick high-finance melodrama and dizzying technical speculation lift Edelman's SF debut, the first of a trilogy.... Natch's being a borderline sociopath makes him extremely creative in business tactics and personal manipulation (and thus fascinating to read about). The world in which he operates is also fascinating, with awesome personal powers being sold on a frantic open market. Edelman, who has a background in Web programming and marketing, gives his bizarre notions a convincing gloss of detail. Bursting with invention and panache, this novel will hook readers for the story's next installment."
Publishers Weekly

"In Web designer and programmer Edelman's first novel, he moves quickly from scene to scene, building suspense with believable characters and in-the-know technical expertise. This series opener belongs in most SF collections."
Library Journal

"A thought-provoking and terribly imaginative book... *Infoquake* is one of those books that hooks you into the story and makes you never want to put the book down. But once you have decided that you must get some sleep before work the next day, you put the book down and find yourself unable to stop thinking about the questions raised by the story."
L.A. Splash

"(5 Stars on Amazon.com) Libraries strong in speculative fiction will relish *Infoquake*.... A fast-paced, engrossing saga of social change."
    Midwest Book Review

FROM SCIENCE FICTION CRITICS

"The manner in which people who experienced *Dune* upon its publication speak about Herbert's opus is not dissimilar to the feeling *Infoquake* elicits—the genre might not be quite the same after this book.... *Infoquake* is a stunning debut novel by a lucid, precise, and talented new voice in the genre.... This may be THE science fiction book of the year."
    SFFWorld

"A high-speed, high-spirited tale of high-powered and low-minded capitalist skullduggery, corporate and media warfare, and virtual reality manipulation. It's the sort of thing that would make a perfect serial for *Wired* magazine.... Edelman seems to have convincing and convincingly detailed knowledge of the physiology and biochemistry of the human nervous system down to the molecular level. And [he] cares about making his fictional combination of molecular biology and nanotech credible."
    Norman Spinrad, *Asimov's Science Fiction*

"*Infoquake* is a triumph of speculation. Edelman has foreseen a nanotech future of warring corporations and stock markets of personal enhancement in which both the good and the bad of the present day are reflected with an even hand and startling clarity.... It's *Wall Street* meets *Neuromancer*.... *Infoquake* is a tech-heavy exercise in scientific speculation that combines economics, high technology, and business mechanics into an all-too-human story of greed, loss, and redemption."
    Bookgasm

"Edelman has one hell of a hoot taking high-tech marketing out to draw and quarter it with style and panache. *Infoquake* is a very funny and insightful novel of modern economics through a futuristic funhouse mirror.... It's the kind of book that deserves to be passed quietly from cubicle to cubicle in tech companies around the nation and indeed around the world. And it's the kind of novel that you want to be passing, the kind of novel you want to be reading.... Edelman, [Cory] Doctorow, and [Charles] Stross are, like all great science fiction writers, not really writing about the future. They're responding to the present.... Edelman's vision in this regard is particularly sharp and particularly on-point. There's a certain amount of satire going on here, but Edelman is quite serious about his world, which makes it all the easier to invest in his characters and settings."

The Agony Column

"If all novels were as chockfull of ideas as *Infoquake* is, then science fiction would never have to worry about a shortage of sense of wonder.... Edelman is like a more accessible [Charles] Stross; whereas Stross's fiction is about as dense as it can get and still be readable, Edelman's style is more inviting and, to me, more appealing. ... Few first novelists manage as assured a debut as *Infoquake*; almost all new authors stumble around a bit in their first novel, but Edelman comes off as a seasoned professional."

Orson Scott Card's Intergalactic Medicine Show

"The hyperbole surrounding this novel seems justified—drawing on cyberpunk and singularitarian themes, it boldly places a banner for what is arguably a new subgenre of science fiction.... As an engaging fictional mirror of the modern world, written from an angle rarely used, this novel definitely marks Edelman as a writer to keep an eye on."

Futurismic

"A brisk, well-told science fiction adventure set in the normally unadventurous world of business.... Edelman handles it all with considerable narrative drive.... A simple old-fashioned story, where incident crowds onto incident, where jeopardy makes us hold our breath, and rabbits are pulled from the hat only at the very last moment."

New York Review of Science Fiction

"There's always the risk that a complicated setting will overwhelm character and story, but Edelman avoids this pitfall, evoking a surprising amount of empathy for the amoral yet oddly charming Natch, and injecting a tremendous amount of suspense into what is essentially a saga of corporate politics.... The novel also addresses weighty themes: the destructive price of greed, the unchanging relentlessness of the human drive to innovate and to compete.... An entertaining and intelligent debut that should leave readers eager for more."

Fantasy Magazine

"(4½ stars) A very strong debut novel mixing a historically detailed timeline with an intriguing technological future. David Louis Edelman makes reading about corporate shenanigans fun.... *Infoquake* should appeal to just about any SF reader, but if you like [Frank] Herbert's *Dune* or any of [Charles] Stross's work, you should really enjoy this book."

SFSignal

"(Rating: 9 out of 10) This book was superb. I simply cannot believe that this is a debut novel, it reads so much more like the work of a seasoned writer.... This book however is anything but boring—it grips you from the start and leaves you at the end of the book wishing you had book two at hand."

The Eternal Night

"*Infoquake* is practically a cyberpunk novel, although unlike the works of William Gibson, author David Louis Edelman actually knows his subject and isn't prone to making errors.... Edelman has done an excellent job of bringing characters to life for a new writer. He even made business deals interesting. This is also very high-grade science fiction, using the trappings and then adding more."

SF Crowsnest

"An intense futuristic tale of business, intrigue, revenge, and technology.... This has the potential to be a terrific series filled with innovative concepts and enough double-dealing to keep the reader guessing."

Monsters and Critics

"Edelman has managed to capture the mania and obsession of Internet moguls nicely.... I found *Infoquake* interesting, and genuinely wanted to find out what happened next. The characters in the book are quite like people I've known in the world of international entrepreneurship."

SFRevu

"A study in drive and power, *Infoquake* shows the drive and need behind the rise of new corporations.... *Infoquake* remains a raw and fascinating novel, with a fast pace and nifty economic themes."

Prometheus, the newsletter of the Libertarian Futurist Society

"Edelman has created a fascinating world.... The interactions between Natch, Horvil, and Jara (who is both attracted to and disturbed by her boss) are volatile, complex, and very, very realistic. It is easy to believe in these people, and even feel like maybe this is a future that is not too far away.... It would be good to have a few months to ponder *Infoquake* before plunging into the next work, as I plan to do this summer, exploring more of this utopia/dystopia and enjoying a truly compelling tale."

Fast Forward TV

FROM AUTHORS

"So fresh and good I shamelessly stole an idea from it: the whole premise of a future corporate thriller.... Buy *Infoquake*, read it.... Give him the Philip K. Dick award."

Ian McDonald, author of *Brasyl*

"Inventive and provocative, with a surprisingly emotional kick. Read this book, and then argue about it."

Kate Elliott, author of *Crown of Stars*

"*Infoquake* is a rare beast: a future history that is simultaneously convincing and wondrous. David Louis Edelman takes no shortcuts to a destination quite unlike any visited before—and we are richer for it."

Sean Williams, author of *Saturn Returns*

"A fascinating glimpse into an all-too-possible future of business, software, wetware, and over-powerful technocrats."

Tobias Buckell, author of *Ragamuffin*

"My favourite SF novel of the year. A future of business and competition that we can all identify with, which neatly avoids apocalyptic cliché.... [*Infoquake*] stayed with me, kept on impressing me way after I'd finished it.... Its setting is something I haven't seen for a long time, a quite distant future that is nevertheless utterly plausible.... I have faith in this Mundane masterpiece."

Paul Cornell, novelist and screenwriter for *Doctor Who*

"David Louis Edelman's *Infoquake* may be a new subgenre unto itself: the science fiction business thriller. Set in a fully realized future world, the narrative is more interested in the economic impact of future technologies than in the technologies themselves. The suspense derives entirely from politics and economics, and the most exciting moments (and they are exciting!) surround new product launches. Edelman doesn't resort to any of the typical tricks to keep the reader turning pages, but I found that I still couldn't turn them fast enough."

Chris Roberson, author of *Set the Seas on Fire*

"If you like Charlie Stross, you'll like this book. If you wish you understood what everyone else is saying about Charlie Stross, you will really like this book."

Matthew Jarpe, author of *Radio Freefall*

FROM BLOGGERS

"*Infoquake* just might be THE Science Fiction novel of the year, if not the past five years. David Louis Edelman has done so many things right in this book, from the plausible next steps in human society to the characters, all the notes ring true."

Rob H. Bedford, Rob's Blog o' Stuff

"One of the best books I read in 2006 was *Infoquake* by David Louis Edelman."

Evo Terra, The Dragon Page and Podiobooks.com

"(Rating: 8 out of 10) Edelman has created a fully realized future with many parallels to the world we live in now. . . . But the real power of this novel is in the players. Natch is brilliantly intimidating and mysterious, and Edelman is at his best as he delves into Natch's past. . . . Edelman's first book is a wonderful debut and one of the best books released this year."

Ken Fergason, Neth Space

"David Louis Edelman's *Infoquake* just might be one of the very best science fiction debuts I have ever read. The book deserves all the praise it has garnered, and then some! . . . Had I read it when it was originally released, *Infoquake* would have trumped Scott Lynch's *The Lies of Locke Lamora*, Naomi Novik's *His Majesty's Dragon*, Brian Ruckley's *Winterbirth*, and Joe Abercrombie's *The Blade Itself*."

Pat's Fantasy Hotlist

"(5 Stars) The reason this futuristic science fiction seems plausible is the depth of detail interwoven into the cat-and-mouse story line, so much so that the audience will accept nanotechnology bio/logics as happening today.... In the first Jump 225 tale, David Louis Edelman writes an exciting thriller that grips the audience."

Harriet Klausner, Amazon's #1 Customer Reviewer

"David Louis Edelman keeps the action coming at a breakneck pace, and despite the lack of SFnal tropes such as interstellar travel and space battles, *Infoquake* never lacks in excitement.... *Infoquake* seems an obvious frontrunner in the race to win this year's Philip K. Dick Award.... Perhaps the best recent take on the dangers of widespread capitalism. A wondrous and scathing debut novel. It is the most successful attack on the future of mega-corporations and the inevitable failure of our current economic system thus far written...a must-read of 2006."

William Lexner, I Hope I Didn't Just Give Away the Ending

"(Rating: 9.3 out of 10 for science fiction fans) Some of the ideas Edelman bandies about here are insanely great enough to make your head pop right off your neck.... It's a great novel to be sure, an infinitely smart page-turner that will have your brain spinning for days afterward.... This dense story is literally a genre fan's dream; an entire universe with an entire glossary full of backstory, and even with an expansive Web site devoted to those who want to know more, allowing fans of such expansive universes to really wallow in the details of it all.... This fan-turned-professional delivers in spades everything a lover of smart science fiction would ever want."

Jason Pettus, Chicago Center for Literature and Photography

"A good and solid SF debut that should put Edelman in consideration for the Dick and Campbell awards.... Edelman has obviously paid attention during his own dot-com experience, and the result is a science fiction novel that has fully internalized the lessons of the past decade.... Fluent in the languages of business and information technology, *Infoquake* is a ride through a fresh future, a strong debut from a promising writer, and a proud representative of Pyr's early lineup."

Christian Suavé

"Despite a high-tech gleam and plausible hard science polish, [Edelman's] debut novel, *Infoquake*, is the sort of SF that non-SF readers can enjoy too.... It is SF, yes, but SF about cutthroat business practices and competitive programming (a way-cool concept of sorta programming in thin air), with an endearingly sociopathic protagonist, lotsa, lotsa nifty techno-supposings, and an interesting concept of

guild/spiritual family/religion/union groups in a technocracy.... Highly imaginative use of the current Zeitgeist."
   Paula Guran, DarkEcho Blog

"David Louis Edelman's postcyberpunk *Infoquake* is the imminent business thriller Richard Morgan wishes it could be."
   Chris Nakashima-Brown, No Fear of the Future

"Edelman has succeeded in making the world of the corporate boardroom into an adventure-filled narrative. What John Grisham has done with the legal thriller, Edelman has done with business.... The climax is fulfilling and exciting, yet it is only a speech, and a marketing one at that. Edelman has so well woven the elements of his plot together that Natch's simple speech has as much power and excitement to it as another science fiction story's destruction of a spaceship or a fantasy's evil overlord dying hideously at the hands of a hero. That takes skill to write, and Edelman has it in spades. I highly recommend this novel."
   Grasping for the Wind

"(Rating 8.5 out of 10) The book is fast paced from the start, although the action is much more cerebral than physical.... [Edelman] is clearly a master at fleshing out his concepts. The story drew me in from the start, and I'm eagerly anticipating the forthcoming volumes."
   Steve Spaulding, The Human Race

"The book is clever and imaginative, and Edelman, a Web programmer by trade, makes this far-future story feel completely contemporary, as though we were living in his invented world."
   David Pitt, Between the Lines

"Engaging and interesting.... As promised by other reviewers, the book was just bursting with new ideas and lots of fun. Besides, when the highlight of the book isn't killing people but is, instead, shipping a software project, it is pretty close to home."
   Al Billings, In Pursuit of Mysteries

"David Louis Edelman attacks the sci-fi genre and infuses it with his stunning vision of humanity's future.... This book carved a brand-new universe using alternate history, detailed imagination, and Edelman's computer programming background."
   Multiverse Reviews

"This biotech-based future is astonishingly believable. It's remarkable to have a novel that's packed with action, excitement, and tension when the action itself is more what you'd see in the *Financial Times* or the *Wall Street Journal*. With the sequel, *MultiReal*, out later in 2008, you'd be well advised to pick this one up and refresh your memory on one of 2006's great debuts."

Tomas L. Martin, blogger for Futurismic and reviewer for SFCrowsnest

"A truly compelling and unique future setting that mixes programming, bio-genetics (or bio/logics), and economic theory. It reads kinda like a libertarian capitalist *Dune*, if you swap out the Spice for the Market, replace the dueling Houses with mega-corporations, and think of Muad'Dib as less of a messiah and more of a cutthroat entrepreneur looking to make a lot of money."

From the Case Files

MULTIREAL

DAVID
LOUIS
EDELMAN

MULTIREAL

VOLUME 2 OF THE JUMP 225 TRILOGY

an imprint of Prometheus Books
Amherst, NY

Published 2008 by Pyr®, an imprint of Prometheus Books

Inquiries should be addressed to
Pyr
59 John Glenn Drive
Amherst, New York 14228–2119
VOICE: 716–691–0133, ext. 210
FAX: 716–691–0137
WWW.PYRSF.COM

12 11 10 09 08   5 4 3 2 1

Library of Congress Cataloging-in-Publication Data

Edelman, David Louis.
  MultiReal / by David Louis Edelman.
      p. cm. — (Jump 225 trilogy ; v. 2)
  ISBN 978–1–59102–647–1 (pbk.)
  1. Corporations—Fiction. I. Title.

PS3605.D445M85 2008
813'.6—dc22

2008021888

Printed in the United States of America on acid-free paper

CONTENTS

All goes onward and outward, nothing collapses,
And to die is different from what any one supposed, and luckier.
—Walt Whitman, "Song of Myself"

I

LESSONS LEARNED

(((|)))

Len Borda was dying.

Or so Marcus Surina told his twelve-year-old daughter, Margaret, one blustery winter morning, the two of them striding through the hoverbird docks, wind at full bore, the sun a frail pink thing cowering behind the clouds.

He won't die today, of course, said Marcus. His voice barely registered above the clanging of the cargo loaders and the yelling of the dock-workers. *Not this week or even this month. But the worries hang from the high executive's neck like lusterless pearls, Margaret. They weigh him down and break his will. I can see it.*

Margaret smiled uncomfortably but said nothing.

If the city of Andra Pradesh had a resident expert on untimely death, it was her father. Before he had accepted the Surina family mantle and assumed his birthright as head of the world's most prominent scientific dynasty, Marcus had wandered far and wide. He had teased the boundaries of human space, flirted with dangerous organizations in the orbital colonies. Death was a constant presence out there.

And yet, High Executive Borda seemed an unlikely candidate for the Null Current. He had been a hale and headstrong man upon his inauguration just weeks after Margaret was born. A NEW EXECUTIVE FOR A NEW CENTURY, the headlines had proclaimed. Some predicted that the troubles of the office would prove too daunting for the young high executive. They murmured that Borda had never been tested by hardship, that he had come of age in a time of plenty and had inherited the job uncontested. But his stature had only grown in the intervening decade. Try as she might, Margaret could find no lingering gaps on Borda's calendar, no telltale signs of weakness or indecision. As far as she was concerned, the high executive was on his way to becoming a fundament of the world, an eternal force like rock or gravity or time itself.

But Marcus Surina remained firm. *You develop a sixth sense out on the frontiers*, he said, examining the hoverbird manifest for the third time. *You begin to see things outside the visible spectrum of light. Patterns of human behavior, focal points of happenstance. Travel the orbital colonies long enough, and you learn to recognize the omens.*

Margaret stirred. *Omens?* A strange word coming from the lips of her father, the quintessential man of science.

The omens of death, continued Marcus. *Plans that wander from their steady paths. Appetites that suddenly grow cold. Thoughts that lose their ballast in midsentence and drift off to places unknown.* Her father stopped suddenly and turned his hyper-focus on a dented segment of the hoverbird wing no bigger than a finger. Three aides-de-camp hovered a meter away, anticipating a word of command or dismissal. *Some people, you can look in their eyes and see that the Null Current is about to pull them under, Margaret. You can see the inevitability. Just like you can see the stalk of wheat as the thresher approaches, and know that the time's come for a newer, stronger crop to bask in the sun.* Marcus made a gesture, and the aides scattered like duckpins.

Then he was striding off again, and it was all Margaret could do to keep up with him. She shivered as she ran, whether from the cold of encroaching winter or from the strangeness of the man before her she could not tell. Lusterless pearls? Wheat and threshers? His clattering metaphors made her teeth ache.

The girl resolved to be patient. In less than twelve hours, her father would be gone, off to the distant colony of Furtoid with the rest of the TeleCo board, and routine would slink out from the alcove where it had been hiding these past few days like a bruised animal.

She called him Father, but it was mostly an honorary title. Marcus had spent four years of the last twelve on the road, and here at Andra Pradesh he was constantly fenced in a protective thicket of apprentices, scientists, business associates, capitalmen, government officials, drudges, bankers, lawyers, and freethinkers that even a daughter could not penetrate. He would stop by her quarters unannounced, cloaked by the night, and quiz her on schoolwork like a proctor checking up on a promising student. Sometimes he would speechify as if Margaret were the warm-up audience for one of his scientific presentations. Other times he would assign her outlandish tasks and then vanish to some colloquium on Allowell or some board meeting in Cape Town.

Prove Prengal's universal law of physics for me, he told her once. It took Margaret three months, but she did.

Margaret had no doubt that she did not have a normal upbringing. But how far off-kilter things were she had no way of judging. The Surina compound was a cloistered and lonely place, despite the crowds. Her mother was dead, and she had no siblings. Instead she had distant cousins innumerable, and a team of handlers whose job it was to confine her life in a box and then call that order.

But there were some things the Surina family handlers could not shield her from. Lately Marcus's face had grown sterner, the lines on his forehead coagulating into a permanent state of anger and anxiety. Margaret suspected there were new developments in her father's battle with the Defense and Wellness Council. Len Borda wanted TeleCo. He wanted her father's teleportation technology either banned outright or conscripted for military purposes; nobody was sure which. And now, this past week, tensions seemed to be coming to a head.

Margaret couldn't quite comprehend what the fuss was about. She had watched a dozen trials of the teleportation process from unobtrusive corners, and it wasn't anything like the teleportation she had read about in stories. You couldn't zap someone instantaneously from one place to another. The procedure required two people of similar biochemical composition to be strapped into a metal container for hours on end while particle deconstructors transposed one body to the other, molecule by agonizing molecule. Margaret wondered why High Executive Borda found the whole idea so threatening. But whenever she asked one of the TeleCo researchers about it, he would simply smile and tell her not to make premature judgments. Marcus had big plans up his sleeve. Give the technology a chance to mature, they said—and generate much-needed revenue for the TeleCo coffers—and she would one day see wonders beyond her imagining. The world would change. Reality itself would buckle.

She took the TeleCo scientists at their word.

That look of inevitability, said Marcus, wrenching Margaret back to the present. They were taking the long, silent lift to the top of the Revelation Spire, where her father had his office. *That look of death. I've seen it, Margaret. I've seen it on Len Borda's face. The high executive knows that the thresher is coming for him.*

Margaret shook her head. *But he's not that old, is he? You're older than he is and—*

Age has nothing to do with it.

The girl wasn't quite sure what to do with that statement. How to make her father understand? How to pierce that veil of myopia and arrogance that kept Marcus Surina from the truth? *But—but—I was talking to Jayze, and Jayze said that you've got it all wrong. She said that the Council's coming for you. The high executive's going to bust down the gates to the compound any day now and take TeleCo away—*

Marcus Surina laughed, and the worry lines on his face broke like barricades of sand washing away with the tide. At that moment, they reached their destination, and the elevator doors opened. Marcus put one brawny arm around his daughter and led her to the window.

You see that? he said.

Margaret wasn't entirely sure what she was supposed to see. They stood on top of the world in a very visceral and literal sense. The Revelation Spire was the tallest building in human space, and built on a mountaintop, no less. Far below, she could see the Surina compound and a blue-green blob that could only be the Surina security forces conducting martial exercises. Sprawled in every direction outside the walls was the unfenceable polyglot mass of Andra Pradesh, city of the Surinas, now getting its first taste of the seasonal snow. Margaret could think of no safer place in the entire universe.

You see that? Marcus repeated. *It's winter. Everything is shrouded in snow, and the world seems bleak and hopeless, doesn't it?*

The girl nodded tentatively.

The gloom doesn't last, Margaret. It never lasts. Remember that.

But—

He gripped her shoulder firmly and turned her around to face him. Marcus Surina's eyes shone brilliant blue as sapphires, and she could smell the cinnamon of morning chai on his breath. *Listen,* he said quietly. *Don't breathe a word of this to anyone, especially your cousin Jayze. Len Borda's lost. Our sources in the Council say he's spent too much time and money coming after teleportation, and he's ready to move on.* That's *why the board's going to Furtoid. To negotiate a settlement. By this time next week, it'll all be over. Do you understand?* We've *won.*

The girl blinked. If the victory bells were ringing, she could not hear them.

Always remember this, Margaret. No matter how bad the winter, spring is always right around the corner.

The girl nodded, smiled, let Marcus Surina fold her in his arms for a last embrace. Better to leave him with this memory of hope at the top of the world than to shower him with cold truths. *Spring might always be right around the corner*, she thought. *But there's always another winter behind it.*

(((2)))

Lieutenant Magan Kai Lee stood at the window of a Falcon hoverbird and watched the Potomac scroll away until it was lost in the snow. December of 359 had proven an exceptionally good month for snow.

The pilot quietly veered off the established flight path, leaving the sparse morning traffic behind while they plowed through the mist a dozen meters above the river's froth and foam. Today, at least, the hoverbird's egg-white finish made decent camouflage.

Magan looked out the port window and saw the Shenandoah River slide into view. "Ulterior admission," he said quietly. *Full stop.*

It was a small craft, designed by Defense and Wellness Council engineers for first-response situations. Twelve could fit here with comfort, and today there were only three. The pilot could hear his superior officer's command just fine. "Impulse open and locked," he replied in acknowledgment. *Full stop.* Seconds later, Magan could hear the decrescendo of engines shutting down and the ethereal whir of antigrav kicking in. The hoverbird came to rest twenty meters above the treetops.

Within the space of a heartbeat, the illicit advertising began dribbling in to Magan's mental inbox. Guerrilla messages, automated, probably keyed in to the whoosh of the hoverbird's vapor exhaust.

COZY WINTER GETAWAYS on the SHENANDOAH:
Affordable Prices!
Hoverbird in Need of a Boost? Read Our Special Report
THE MAKERS OF CHAIQUOKE SALUTE THE SHENANDOAH COMMUTER

The hoverbird's third occupant blocked the flow with an irritated *tsk.*

Rey Gonerev, the Defense and Wellness Council's chief solicitor, rose from her seat and stood at Magan's side. She parted her long braided hair to reveal a thin face with skin of deepest cocoa. Magan could feel the neural tug of her ConfidentialWhisper request. "You sure we're not overdoing this?" she asked, her words appearing silently in his mind like adjuncts of his own thought process.

Magan ignored her and watched the skyline. His mind was sifting through combinatorial possibilities in preparation for their mission. Rey Gonerev had no place in his reflections at the moment.

The solicitor pursed her lips. "Lieutenant?" Receiving no response, she shrugged and retreated to her seat, keeping the Confidential-Whisper channel open just in case.

Magan turned his attention to the circular table that comprised most of the hoverbird's rear section. He waved his hand over the surface, causing a holographic map to blink into existence. It was an example of true Defense and Wellness Council austerity: the meeting of two rivers reduced to a handful of intersecting vectors, with the hoverbird itself nothing more than a triangle of canary yellow. As Magan studied the hilly terrain with a critical eye, four more yellow triangles arced into the display and halted in formation alongside them. He looked out the window and surveyed the line of sleek white hovercraft floating above the Shenandoah, silent as vultures. The lieutenant noted approvingly that the noses of the hoverbirds were in perfect alignment.

There was a momentary squawk of pilots confirming their rendezvous and their mission number. Then one craft broke off from the rest and took a vanguard position. A blue dot on the map indicated the presence of the team leader: Ridgello, a veteran from the Pharisee front lines and one of Magan's most trusted subordinates.

The team leader opened a voice channel to the rest of the troops. "Broad strokes imply a declension of purpose, and such things cannot be ascertained with present information," he said. *We commence operations in approximately six hundred seconds, after we receive the technical crew's signal. Any questions?*

"*My* question," said Rey to Magan over the ConfidentialWhisper channel, "is whether this whole thing is overkill."

The skepticism in her voice would have earned a swift reprimand had it come from anyone else. But Magan had learned long ago that kowtowing to superiors was simply not part of Rey Gonerev's nature. She would continue dropping little bombs of snarkiness all morning until he had answered her. "If you insist on observing," replied Magan over the 'Whisper channel, "the *least* you could do is follow standard procedure and use Council battle language."

The solicitor made a dismissive shrug. "This isn't a military issue," she stated icily. "It's a policy question, and you know it."

"This policy comes from High Executive Borda."

"But Magan—nineteen dartguns, six disruptors, and three technical crew, just for one unarmed man? You've taken out whole Pharisee outposts with fewer boots on the ground."

Lieutenant Lee gritted his teeth, perfectly aware that he had no cause to gainsay her. *You know she's right*, he told himself. *And there's nothing you can do about it.* He seethed momentarily with ire for the unsorted, for the unordered, for the chaotic and unplanned.

Magan turned and gave Rey Gonerev an appraising look. She had risen once again from her seat and was standing alongside the pilot watching the formation. Gonerev should have been the type of volatile element that Magan tried to suppress from the Council hierarchy. Instead he had worked hard to put Rey Gonerev in the chief solicitor's office, and it had taken him some time to realize why. It was precisely *because* she refused to kiss ass, because she was not Len Borda's toady and did not aspire to be Magan's either. Gonerev could always be counted on to cut through bureaucratic and organizational hypocrisy like a machete slicing through so many thin vines. It was no wonder the pundits had nicknamed her "the Blade."

Ridgello had just received final status reports from the other four hoverbird teams. "Perhaps we need to cover extremities and observe full zoning regulations," he said. *Commander Papizon will signal us when he's overridden the building's security and compression routines, and then it'll be time to move.*

"This man is not to be underestimated," Magan told the Blade. "He is as sly as a snake."

"But—"

"*Enough.* The high executive has made his decision. My duty—and *yours*—is to carry it out." Magan cut the 'Whisper channel with a curt swipe of one hand, and even the Blade knew that further argument was useless.

Ridgello concluded his preoperational briefing with a question for Magan Kai Lee. "South by southwest makes for a defensive maneuver," he said. *Anything to add, Lieutenant?*

Magan could feel the randomness algorithm hijack his thoughts and twist them into unrecognizable shapes designed to sow confusion among any eavesdropping enemy. "Keep pushing for higher ground, regardless of any spiking temperatures," he said. "It's a tribute to your preparedness that we have a robust strategy at all." He could imagine the same process at work in reverse in each of the soldiers' heads, realigning and reassembling his gibberish into something more comprehensible. *Remember that the subject is expected to be unarmed, and lethal force will not be required. If we encounter his apprentices, they are to be taken alive.*

Silence ensued. Magan watched the drifting snowflakes and tried to clear his mind. He could see the officers through the window of the next hoverbird polishing their dartguns, choosing which canisters of black code–laden needles to load. Rey Gonerev was making small talk with the pilot in plain speech, as if deliberately flaunting her defiance of military convention.

A little more than a month ago, Magan had never heard of this man, this fiefcorper who was the object of their mission. He had come from nowhere, really, a shameless entrepreneur who had clawed his way out of the bear pit of bio/logic programming. Nobody was quite sure how he had wormed his way into Margaret Surina's good graces, or how he had gained control of her MultiReal technology so quickly. Then he had showed up in Len Borda's chambers, mere hours ahead of a major product demo, looking to make a deal: the Council's protection from some group of assassins in black robes that had ambushed him on the streets of Shenandoah—protection from the black code swarming through his bloodstream even now like barracudas. In exchange: access to MultiReal.

The high executive had kept his word. He had raised his hand and sent three legions of his best troops scrambling for Andra Pradesh. The fiefcorper's product demo had gone off as planned.*

And what had the entrepreneur delivered in return? Nothing.

He had failed to show up for half a dozen scheduled meetings over the next week, leaving Magan and his underlings to sit alone in a series of conference rooms feeling foolish. Urgent messages and Confidential-Whispers had disappeared into the void, unacknowledged and unanswered. Threats had gone unheeded.

Borda had responded to this charade with the subtlety of someone conducting an orchestra in a suit of armor. He had sent white-robed Council officers to shadow the man twenty-four hours a day, then had those officers parade before the man's windows with dartguns drawn. When that had failed to apply the appropriate pressure, he had ordered the troops to accept no excuses and firmly escort the man to the Council's administrative offices in Melbourne. Still the fiefcorp master managed to elude them. He would disappear for days at a time right under the officers' noses—nobody knew where or how.

Two days ago, Len Borda's patience had reached its limit. He had called Magan Kai Lee to his chambers in the middle of the night, telling him to drop everything and bring the intractable fiefcorper back to the negotiating table, by force if necessary.

---

*For a more detailed synopsis of the events of *Infoquake*, book 1 of the Jump 225 Trilogy, see appendix A.

"In handcuffs?" Magan had asked.

"In chains," Borda had replied.

Lieutenant Lee had looked at that weathered face, that bald cap-stone of a head. The high executive had stared back at him with a gaze of acid. Magan felt his fingertips flex involuntarily, yearning to take hold of the dartgun holstered at his side and aim it at that caustic, lich-like countenance. Borda had merely sat there, defenseless but utterly without fear. He knew that Magan would not break their agreement.

And Borda was right. In the end, Magan Kai Lee had done what he was told. He had retreated back to his quarters, filing the impatience away in yet another mental side room that was full dangerously close to bursting. He had called up Papizon, and the two of them had sketched out this endeavor, with occasional input from the Blade. The next forty-eight hours had been a haze of architectural blueprints, supply requisitions, and scouting reports.

An incoming blip snapped Magan back to the now. It was time.

Go.

All at once, the Defense and Wellness Council hoverbirds blasted into motion. They quickly shifted into single file as they sped toward Shenandoah like a poison arrow, with Ridgello's hoverbird the barb and Magan's VIP ship the fletchings.

Magan took a parting glance at the crossing of the two rivers. He thought of the flow of illicit advertising and wondered what kind of societal parasite would resort to such a scheme.

Natch, he thought, *you brought this on yourself.*

• • •

Five hoverbirds darted out from behind the Blue Ridge Mountains, skirting close to the ground, where they blended in with the snow. Traffic was a farce this early in the morning. The sun hung close to the horizon, unsure of itself.

Papizon, what's your status? said Ridgello.

Even scrambled, the tactician's voice sounded serene and unhurried. *Security is under Council control*, he said. *We're decompressing the building now. Target apartment will be just inside the northwest entrance in ninety seconds.*

And Natch? asked the team leader.

We saw him enter the building last night at approximately ten o'clock local time. He's been active in MindSpace ever since. There are human and data agents watching every exit.

Magan and Gonerev exchanged looks of cautious optimism. So far, so good. Let the Blade call the plan overkill; once they had the fiefcorp master safely onboard a Council hoverbird en route to Melbourne, this whole operation would be yesterday's lessons learned.

Rey Gonerev joined Magan at the command console. The yellow triangles were rapidly converging on a blinking red star. A sixth triangle hunkered down beneath the building in the pipes of the city's underground transfer system. That would be Papizon and his technical crew.

Magan switched the rear windows of the hoverbird to battlefield display, blocking out the rapidly receding December landscape. Perspectives from six different soldiers filled the screens: here a man rubbing the barrel of his multi disruptor with a soft cloth, there a woman stretching her calves and muttering about the cold. Following regulations, Magan flipped through each of the twenty-five officers in turn to verify the connections. He found Ridgello calm and collected and not the least bit nervous; operations like this were his gruel.

The hoverbirds zipped over a large hill and went into a steep, nosebleed descent behind a copse of trees. The pilot cut the inertial cushioners to stifle the noise. Rey Gonerev grunted as her head bounced against the low hoverbird ceiling, but Magan remained composed. He thanked a thousand generations of Chinese heritage for making him too short to worry about such obstructions.

They touched down in the snow with a soft thud. All five yellow triangles were now clustered on a slope next to the blinking red star.

Seconds later, the doors whooshed open and the Defense and Wellness Council was on the move.

A disciplined sprint up a snow-covered slope, dartguns drawn. A building that curved atop the next hill like a natural extension of the landscape. Two dozen figures in white fatigues with muted yellow stars edging through a small huddle of fir trees. The fog of heavy breath.

About ten meters up, a door opened and spat forth a middle-aged woman holding a mug of steaming nitro. A black platform slid beneath her feet in the blink of an eye to serve as balcony. She yawned, stretched, cracked her knuckles.

Take her down, snapped the team leader.

Six pinpricks of light slid across the woman's torso. The dart-rifles sang. The woman collapsed, ceramic mug of nitro tumbling after.

Magan watched from his ship as Ridgello's team zipped across the snow and dashed through the building's northwest entrance. Rey flipped a window to focus on one of the three soldiers ascending the unconscious woman's balcony via magnetic cable. One of the officers glanced back over his shoulder at the copse of fir trees, which looked perfectly undisturbed. Ridgello was good. Magan felt confident that nobody inside the building had noticed anything unusual.

The interior hallway was brightly lit. Ridgello's team flew down the corridor, swift as ghosts, until they reached the first door on the left. Two officers lined up on either side of the door, dartguns drawn and needles loaded. Ridgello blasted the apartment security with a Defense and Wellness Council priority override, and the door slid open. A dozen troops swarmed into Natch's apartment.

Rey Gonerev let out a gasp.

The apartment was empty.

A half-eaten sandwich lay on the kitchen counter alongside a cold mug of nitro that had obviously been untouched for hours, perhaps days.

One of the viewscreens was broadcasting a spirited melee from a fencing tournament on 49th Heaven. A triangular blob of code rotated inside a MindSpace bubble in Natch's office with no hand there to rotate it. Even more telling, however, was the absence of the ubiquitous shoulder pack of bio/logic programming bars that fiefcorpers always kept within reach.

"You *said* he was here, Papizon," barked the Blade. "Where is he?"

A puzzled stammer came over the connection. "You mean, he—he's not *there?*"

"No, he fucking isn't."

"But the scope says . . . There's still . . . If Natch isn't there, then who's working in MindSpace?"

Ridgello, the only one still using battle language: *No sign of him, Lieutenant.*

The troops had relaxed their guard by now and were all casting dazed looks at one another. One of them scratched his beefy head with the barrel of his disruptor gun, against all weapons protocol. Officers were poking through closets and peeking under tables on the off chance that Natch might be cowering in some undiscovered corner. A woman standing behind the workbench in Natch's office turned to face one of the interior windows and was startled to read the text printed there in bold letters:

A PRIVATE MESSAGE FOR MAGAN KAI LEE

Back in the hoverbird, Magan blanched. Rey Gonerev's face showed some amalgam of disgust and amusement. *The snake knew we were coming*, thought Magan. *How could he possibly have known that?* Magan counted the people who had known the details of this operation ahead of time on three fingers: the Blade, Papizon, himself. Not even Ridgello had known what was going down until late last night.

The team leader had seen the text by now. *Do you want to read this, Lieutenant?* he said.

Magan felt his mind downshifting, looking for a more acceptable gear. The smart thing to do would be to ignore the message and get his people out of there as fast as possible. But wasn't that what Natch was expecting him to do? The message on the window was such a transparent ploy to get Magan into the apartment that the fiefcorp master must be counting on him to *not* take the bait. In which case . . . shouldn't he do the opposite? The lieutenant cursed silently. How difficult it was to use logic on a creature whose entire nature rejected the concept.

Magan opened the supply chest at his knee, grabbed a canister of black code darts, and snapped it onto the barrel of his dartgun. "You're not going in there, are you?" said the Blade incredulously.

"Shit," replied the Council lieutenant, striding for the door of the hoverbird. "I guess I am."

Within two minutes, he had made it up the hill to the tenement building's northwest entrance. Magan was approaching middle age and no longer possessed the feline agility of his younger troops, but he still doubted that any of the building's occupants had seen him. Magan glanced up at the balcony of the third-floor apartment, where the officer standing guard confirmed his assessment with the okay signal. Two other guards were escorting the unconscious woman back to her bed, where she would wake up in a few hours with a splitting headache. Even the dropped mug of nitro had disappeared back inside.

The yellow-starred officers in the apartment saw the look in Magan's eyes and gave him a wide berth. He walked into Natch's office, ushered the massive Nordic team leader out the door, and opened the message on the viewscreen with a gesture.

SMILE FOR THE CAMERAS.

Magan frowned. What kind of message was this?

Suddenly his eyes widened. "Out! Everybody out!" he snapped, unencrypted, startling the Council officers into a pell-mell gallop for the exit. "No, he knows we're here—southeast exit!" The group skidded to a halt and reversed directions. Rey Gonerev was yelling something in his ear, but Magan couldn't process it quickly enough. He managed to decipher the solicitor's words just as they burst into the southeast courtyard: "No, stay inside. The drudges, the drudges!"

Standing in the snow outside Natch's building was a pack of men and women whose eyes were lit with predatory glee. Magan recognized many of their faces on sight: the craggy visage of Sen Sivv Sor, the dandyish face of John Ridglee, the weasel smirk of V. T. Vel Osbiq.

The drudges.

Ridgello, clearly irritated, gave his troops the signal to sheathe their weapons. The Council lieutenant summoned PokerFace 85a to mask his own roiling emotions as the drudges formed a receiving line and began peppering the retreating officers with questions for their readers.

"Lieutenant, why has Len Borda decided to seize MultiReal by force?"

"Who approved this mission?"

"Has the Council consulted the Prime Committee about this?"

"What charges are you planning to bring against Natch?"

"Is this legal?"

Magan Kai Lee trudged through the courtyard, saying nothing, trying to figure out the exchange rate of this new situation. He could practically taste the bile in the back of his throat. "You see, Rey?" he said over ConfidentialWhisper. "*This* snake has fangs."

(((3)))

Natch stood at his workbench and waved his left hand. A shimmering bubble the size of a coin appeared in the air before him. The bubble quickly expanded until it encompassed most of the workbench, until it enveloped him entirely and blanketed the rest of the world in a translucent film.

MindSpace. An empty canvas, a barren universe. Anything was possible here.

With his right hand, Natch undid the clasps to the weather-beaten satchel that sat on the side table. The satchel flopped open to reveal its hidden treasure: twenty-six thin metal bars, branded with the letters of the Roman alphabet. Natch's fingers wandered blindly to the bar labeled F and slid it whisper-quiet from its sheath. As soon as the bio/logic programming bar passed the borders of MindSpace, spikes and finials burst from its sides like a butterfly's wings emerging from the cocoon. Natch swished the bar back and forth in front of him, and the butterfly took flight.

The fiefcorp master raised his left hand again and spread his fingers wide. The MindSpace bubble exploded with a sinuous curve of interlocking spheres, a virtual centipede in hues of purple and brown. The canvas was covered down to the last square centimeter, and yet still the shapes multiplied.

Too close in. Natch hitched his thumb back, zooming out to a better vantage point. The spheres only grew in density as they receded, until they became atomic particles in a solid block of gray. Farther out, the block was now merely one of thousands, a brick in the wall of an ominous castle of programming code. Natch, impatient, continued jabbing his thumb backward. Now even the castle was just one small portion of an immense oval-shaped structure. Parapets and walkways in aqua and silver swirled through the whole and made daring forays across the central void. A MindSpace megalopolis.

At last the entire structure lay visible before him. Natch could pan out no farther. He extended his left index finger and rotated his hand ninety degrees counterclockwise, causing a legend to appear atop the block of code.

POSSIBILITIES
Version: 0.76
Programmer: The Surina/Natch MultiReal Fiefcorp

Possibilities was the fiefcorp's brand name for MultiReal. Multi-Real: the product of sixteen years' isolation by one of the world's most brilliant scientists, with virtually unlimited resources at her disposal. MultiReal: the crowning achievement of an entire line of Surinas stretching back for generations.

And now the program belonged to Natch.

The entrepreneur hefted the spiky programming tool in his hand, testing its mass. He rotated the castle around and around, looking for just the right spot. . . . There. A soft place, a weakness in the virtual masonry. All at once, Natch raised the bar over his head and struck at the castle wall with furious strength.

Clang. The bar bounced off the castle and set his right hand vibrating.

Natch grabbed the bar again with both hands, wielding it like a crazed samurai. He began delivering savage blows to the structure before him. Again and again he struck, snarling with rage. Finally one of the blows smashed through the brick, and the castle wall shattered into a thousand pieces with a deafening crash.

Natch peered at the interior of the vanquished castle, expecting to see a skeleton of virtual boards, planks, and girders. But the structure was completely hollow and had no visible means of support. This was no mere emptiness, no simple absence-of-something-else; it was a yawning chasm of nothingness, a force of void that seemed to pull at him with intense gravity.

As the fiefcorp master stood, paralyzed with fear, the program began to crumble all around him. Blocks that had been anchored and secured by a thousand connections were buckling under the strain, pulling loose, succumbing to the Null Current. Soon objects across the room were sliding toward him; programming bars were making kamikaze leaps from his satchel; even dishes were somersaulting in from the kitchen to get swallowed by the growing darkness.

Natch felt the tug in his knees first. He struggled to get to the office door, thinking that if he could just shut out the nothingness, he would be all right. But soon the void was pulling at his entire body. He managed to hook his fingers around the doorjamb just as he lost his feet. For a minute, maybe two, he hung there with his heels in the air and his fingernails clawing for a handhold on the door. And then a chair slid in from the living room and bashed his knuckles. Natch lost his grip. He began tumbling end over end into the chill of the darkest night.

Nothingness.

He came to in a wintry patch of forest, a torch in his hand. A sickening smell that Natch identified as burning flesh wafted through the air.

Natch dashed through the trees. He was in a hurry, but he couldn't say why. Paths crisscrossed on the forest floor below his feet, but he didn't know where they had come from or where they were going; better to trust his instincts. And right now his instincts said to head west, toward the rapidly falling sun. He ran through the foliage as quickly as he could. Thorns and sharp branches lashed his face.

Then Natch heard the screaming.

Stop! Wait, stop! Don't! Don't! Don't! And then a long shriek of anguish and pain, underlined by the snarling of a confused and angry bear. The distant tumult of rushing feet through the leaves. The wet sound of human flesh ripping.

Natch could not move. The light from the torch sputtered and went out. In the split second before the dark enveloped him once again, Natch looked up and discovered he was no longer holding a torch—it was the bloody stump of a boy's arm.

Then he awoke.

● ● ●

Natch slowly lifted his eyelids and let the world soak into his consciousness one millimeter at a time.

He took inventory of his surroundings. It was a familiar setting. His hands lay palms-down on faux ivory armrests, and he could feel faux leather at his back. Sunlight tapped a staccato message on his face from behind a latticework of redwoods passing by at superhuman speed. Natch had practically memorized every twist and turn of this Seattle express tube over the years.

The entrepreneur took a closer look at the window. Something floated there in boldface awaiting his arousal from sleep.

COUNCIL STORMS NATCH'S APARTMENT
IN PLOY TO SEIZE MULTIREAL

Natch gave a tired nod. *So those fools took the bait after all.*

He skimmed through a few dozen drudge clippings, stacking them on the window like bricks. There was video from fifteen different angles, and some anonymous wit had given the whole thing a symphonic score. Natch summoned the baffled face of Magan Kai Lee and watched his entire walk of shame back to the hoverbird four times.

At last you have some breathing room, the fiefcorp master told himself. *Now you can stop running and go home again.*

Natch had woken up on a tube train every day this week. He had traveled the entire world over the past few weeks in an effort to skirt the Defense and Wellness Council. Yesterday he had seen the desert sands of old Texas territory, pausing for a brief multi foray to Shenandoah to set his trap; the night before, he had skimmed the surface of the Indian Ocean.

But there were a number of close calls. Natch could find only so much anonymity when his face had been burned into the public consciousness through a hundred interviews and drudge reports. A group of teenagers in São Paulo had seen right through his false public directory profile, and Natch had had to pawn off one of his new bio/logic programming bars just to keep them quiet. Counting the one he had flung at his black-robed pursuers in Shenandoah a few weeks ago, he was now two bars short of a complete set.

Then there was the disturbing incident with the crazy woman in central Europe. She had worn the bright blue uniform of a healer, but had reached the age when many abandoned curative treatments and sent in their applications to join the Prepared. The woman had walked up to him in plain view of three white-robed Council officers, indignant, demanding that Natch explain the "dirty tricks" he had performed at the demo in Andra Pradesh. Natch's mind had been gliding through some remote place, and he had nearly panicked. But suddenly people had stood up to defend him with voices raised and fists clenched. Soon a handful of L-PRACG security officers had gotten involved, and the Council officers had scurried over to investigate. A small-scale brawl had erupted between Natch's supporters and his detractors. Libertarians shouting *Down with Len Borda*, governmentalists bellowing *Respect the law*. Natch, dumbfounded, had offered no resistance when two libertarians calmly tugged him out the door and thrust him onto a tube running in the opposite direction. He had managed to escape before Len Borda's people realized exactly what was going on.

In a world of sixty billion people, simple mathematics dictated that Natch must have millions of sympathizers on the libertarian side of the political spectrum. A hundred million people probably supported his fight to keep MultiReal out of the Council's hands from sheer spite for Len Borda. But to discover that people had coalesced on this issue, that they were willing to stand up to *armed Council officers* . . . Natch simply didn't know how to process it.

Once aware of this undercurrent of libertarian sympathy, he began to see signs of it everywhere he went. Natch found posts of support on the Data Sea, speeches by L-PRACG activists, drudgic calls for embargoes against the central government. Suddenly he realized he had underestimated the number of his supporters by several orders of magnitude. A minority, perhaps, and still skulking in the shadows, but gaining strength every day.

And now the Council's raid on Natch's apartment building had altered the dynamics of the situation altogether. He called up Sen Sivv Sor's reportage on the window.

COUNCIL STORMS NATCH'S APARTMENT IN PLOY TO SEIZE MULTIREAL

I've said it before, and I'll say it again: Nobody is worse at bungling public relations than High Executive Len Borda.

In the three weeks since Natch's MultiReal demonstration at Andra Pradesh, the fiefcorp master has disappeared from the public eye. This morning, we found out why. Because Borda, in his supreme wisdom, has already decided to renege on his assurances of safety, and to seize Multi-Real from its rightful owners without provocation.

What else can we conclude from the dazzling display of stupidity executed by one of Borda's lieutenant executives, Magan Kai Lee, this morning? You all saw it right here, dear readers. If not for an anonymous tip-off to the drudge community early this morning, the Surina/Natch MultiReal Fiefcorp might have already been dissolved by now. And its fiefcorp master might be rotting away in some orbital Council prison.

It's astounding the lengths some will go to in order to preserve the vaunted status quo. Which is why—

Natch had read enough. He banished the potpourri of Data Sea ramblings from the window and let the redwoods show through once more.

Yes, Natch's clever MindSpace tricks had enabled him to reverse the tide of public opinion, if only for a day or two. Even the staunch governmentalist Mah Lo Vertiginous was grudgingly admitting that the Council had blundered today. Borda and Lee would not dare pull another stunt like that anytime soon.

Natch caught his reflection in the window. *So why are you still sitting on a tube train heading in the wrong direction?* he asked himself. *Why didn't you get off at the last stop and make your way home?*

He conjured a picture of the city of Shenandoah in his head. Home. But when he saw those undulating streets and shifting buildings, all he could think about was the mercenary precision of the black-robed figures who had ambushed him there. He could still feel the pinpricks of their black code darts and the icy rush of poisonous OCHREs suffusing his bloodstream. The void, the nothingness.

Natch stumbled upon an unexpected realization: he was afraid.

You find yourself capable of strange things when you run out of choices, Margaret Surina had told him last month.

Now Natch understood what the bodhisattva meant. For three weeks, he had been fleeing from the Council, catching the occasional update from Horvil or Serr Vigal over ConfidentialWhisper, taking quick glimpses at the evolving Possibilities program whenever he found a rented MindSpace workbench he could trust. Nobody had heard a syllable from Margaret in all that time. Nor had the Patel Brothers stirred from their lair to stop Lucas Sentinel and Bolliwar Tuban from thrashing them in the Primo's ratings.

And what about Brone? Natch blacked out the window and displayed the message he had received the other day in small, precise lettering.

Why is the vaunted master of the Surina/Natch MultiReal Fiefcorp running away? What does he think he will gain by fleeing from tube train to tube train? Does he think his enemies are just going to up and disappear?

How long before he realizes he needs additional allies to complete the MultiReal programming and bring the program to market? When will he finally accept the helping hand that an old enemy has held out to him? When will his need for funding, equipment, privacy, and security outweigh the irrational hatred he carries around his neck?

There was no trace of a sender or signature. Natch supposed he could use some arcane tools of the trade to track down the message's origin, but of course there was only one person who could have sent it.

A snippet of dream floated through Natch's head: a bear, screams, the bloody stump of an arm. Where was Brone? What was he doing? Certainly after all that had happened during the Shortest Initiation, after all the machinations Brone had gone through to put Natch in his debt, he wasn't planning to just sit on the sidelines. After all, he was the head of a major creed organization, the Thasselians, with vast stockpiles of credits and half a million anonymous devotees at his disposal. Opportunities for mischief were plentiful.

It was a time of suspended animation, of delayed choices. And now Natch's ruse against Magan Kai Lee had set things in motion once again.

You've faced challenges before, Natch told himself. *Brone, Captain Bolbund, the ROD coders, Figaro Fi, the Patels. What's different? What are you so afraid of now?*

It was the black code swimming through his veins. Somehow it had aged him in a way that none of his adversaries had managed to do before. He could practically feel it tinkering away inside of him, deconstructing his innards, disassembling his mind. Every day, Natch sensed that he was losing a small piece of this inner turf to the encroaching void, to the winter, to the nothingness.

The nothingness was coming to claim him. And Natch knew that all the battles he had fought before were merely the opening skirmishes of a much larger campaign against this nothingness. It was a campaign he could not afford to lose.

(((4)))

Magan spent the next four hours on three different hoverbirds, watching time and space drift by the window.

"Towards Perfection, Lieutenant Lee," chirped a voice from the cockpit as Magan stepped aboard the last hoverbird. Obviously the pilot had been too absorbed in the complex trigonometry of space flight preparation to catch the news. "Anything I can get you before we lift off? Commissary's got a nice batch of weedtea, straight from—"

Magan cut her off. "Nothing, Panja, thank you."

"How about—"

"To DWCR, please."

Panja quieted down. She had flown Magan to DWCR hundreds of times in the past few years—only a small number of pilots had clearance to fly there—so she had learned to read his emotions well. Something must have gone terribly wrong.

Magan took a seat in the back row of the hoverbird and strapped on his harness. The pilot conducted the ship's mechanical tests without a word, then set them on their way. Magan watched the clouds approach and fell into a light sleep until the ship alerted him that they were making the final approach into DWCR.

To those in the know, DWCR was the Defense and Wellness Council Root, Len Borda's center of operations—and those who could not define the acronym weren't aware of its existence anyway. But even most of those privileged enough to work at DWCR couldn't pinpoint it on a map. The location was highly classified, and officers like Panja had to withstand a battery of loyalty tests before they were admitted to the inner circle.

Magan himself had spent several years stepping on a red multi tile without knowing exactly where he was being projected. But he never minded such obfuscation, even when it served to block something in his path. A system with a hidden solution remained a system with a solution, after all; a welcome change from the centerless anarchy his life had been before enlisting in the Council twenty-five years ago. Magan knew that, with scrupulous planning, he could master any system that confronted him. He knew that time and chance were the only obstacles between him and the pinnacle of the Council hierarchy. Eventually the secrets of DWCR would be his.

Nearly ten thousand Council employees were not so confident. Magan saw them huddled in their offices week after week wasting hours in useless conjecture. Some believed the Root sat in one of the many unexplored crevices of Luna. Others favored the Pacific Islands or the Antarctic or the uninhabitable sectors of Furtoid as more likely candidates. But so far Len Borda's engineers had succeeded in keeping the Root impervious to any known positioning or tracing program, and prodigious sums of money were expended to ensure that the mystification would continue for years to come.

Nonetheless, Magan knew the secrecy could not last indefinitely. Secrets had a gravity of their own that sucked in the curious and the determined. Had the high executive planned for that contingency, or was he relying on the secrecy to last forever? The bodhisattva of Creed Bushido had the perfect aphorism to describe such closed-mindedness: *Short-term plans, long-term problems.*

In actuality, DWCR was a disk-shaped platter in orbit at the outermost reach of Earth's gravitational pull, only a slight rocket thrust away from either floating off into the aether or spiraling planetward to a fiery, cataclysmic doom. Lieutenant Lee watched out the port window now as the platter slid into view. A single observation tower jutted from the bottom with priapic majesty, as if waiting for something to impale.

Panja docked the hoverbird without a sound, and Magan stepped through the airlock as soon as DWCR had given them the all-clear.

Generals and military planners filed curt nods with Magan as he strode the Root's maze of twisty little passages, all alike. Without proper clearance, he could wander these shifting corridors of gunmetal gray for days. Someone had made an attempt to inject some color on the walls, but the smattering of pretentious landscapes and portraits of executives past did little to lighten the atmosphere.

Magan made his way to the observation tower and kept his ears open for the hallway gossip. He heard rumors of military deployments, complaints about research budgets, details of appropriations bills before the Prime Committee . . . but not a single comment about the failed raid early this morning. Magan frowned. The only thing worse than listening to officers chatter about the Council's failure was not hearing them chatter about it at all. He sighed as he reached the central elevator and cleared his mind.

The elevator did not head upward. Instead it dropped, leading Magan to a floor on the tip of the observation tower. Borda's private chambers.

When he emerged from the elevator, the Council lieutenant found himself standing on the deck of an ancient sloop-of-war. The ship swayed tipsily in the waves, sending the occasional spittle of SeeNaRee brine splashing on Magan's face. Still-smoking cannons on the deck spoke of a recent battle against some enemy hovering just out of sight in the fog.

Standing at the prow of the ship was High Executive Len Borda.

• • •

Borda listened to his lieutenant's version of events with rising ire, his back to the mast and his nose pointed out to sea. "Bloody drudges," he said in a rumbling basso that not even the waves could drown out. "If I wanted their opinion, trust me, they'd know it."

Some called the high executive *arrogant*, but that word seemed beside the point. After nearly sixty years running the world's military and intelligence affairs, Borda needed no tone of intimidation. He spoke with the timbre of a man who had been the final arbiter for so long that he had forgotten any other reality.

Magan watched Len Borda move to the railing and run his hand over the intricately carved wood. He seemed to be scanning the murky horizon for a sign of the enemy, which would be the French, if memory served. Why Borda devoted so much attention to this virtual playground, Magan could not fathom. He admitted that the SeeNaRee programmers had a terrific eye for detail and historical accuracy. But Borda was spending more time here than in the world of flesh and blood lately, and that was not a good sign.

"Today is December twenty-seventh," said the lieutenant after a long and uneasy silence.

Borda shrugged. "What of it?"

"The new year comes in four days. After what happened this morning, do you really think you can gain control of MultiReal in four days?"

One stony eyebrow lifted itself on Borda's forehead and then subsided, like a breaker on the SeeNaRee ocean. "Four days is a lifetime," he said. "I was willing to deal with Natch behind closed doors. He's the one who decided to bring this fight into the public eye." Borda scowled. "Let's see how he handles a full onslaught."

Magan clenched his fists into a tight ball behind his back, then slowly forced himself to stop, take a breath, unwind. Could Len Borda really be so foolish as to try the same thing again? Had his mind become so entrenched that he could do nothing but continuously loop through the same routine? "And what if this *onslaught* of yours fails?"

Borda was not nearly so successful at hiding his emotions, and he didn't bother with PokerFace programs either. The gritted teeth and the trembling jaw told Magan everything he needed to know.

The high executive was planning to break their agreement.

"Forget about the fiefcorp master for a moment," said Borda. "I need your help with something else." The high executive waved his hand and summoned a block of text to float against the gauzy gray sky. Magan pushed the anger aside and read the letter with a growing crease on his brow.

Congress of L-PRACGs
Office of the Speaker
Melbourne

In accordance with my duties as speaker, I am writing to inform the Defense and Wellness Council that the Congress has officially opened an inquiry into the causes of the computational anomalies known as "infoquakes."

Four such disruptions have occurred in the past month, leaving thousands dead and wounded. According to the sworn testimony of Congressional engineers, the severity of these disruptions is growing. It is my belief that the Council's measures to limit bandwidth on the Data Sea are no longer sufficient to contain this threat.

The Congress hereby charges all employees of the Defense and Wellness Council to answer any forthcoming subpoenas promptly and with the utmost discretion.

May you always move towards perfection,
Khann Frejohr, Speaker

"You assured me that Frejohr wouldn't be a problem," growled Borda. "You told me this libertarian uprising of his would die on the vine."

Magan Kai Lee banished the text with a hard blink of the eyes and stared glumly at the sea, which was barely visible through the thickening veil of fog. "So I thought, a month ago," he said.

"*So you thought*," replied Borda caustically. He bent to pick up a small chunk of wood, a splinter that must have been torn from the rail by French cannons. "Frejohr's only been in office for two weeks, and already he's got the Congress of L-PRACGs holding hearings."

"They're meaningless," said Magan. "The Congress has no authority over us."

"No, but the Prime Committee *does*. And these infoquakes give Frejohr the impetus to put ideas in their heads." Borda angrily threw the painted wood chip off into the mist, where the sea swallowed it without a sound.

"Papizon will find out what's causing the infoquakes," announced Magan. "It's only a matter of time."

"How much time?"

"I don't know."

The high executive snorted his contempt. "Papizon is usually not so vague."

Borda's pessimism was starting to grow tiresome. Magan thought the time had come for a quick knife thrust. "Papizon usually doesn't get distracted by your useless side projects."

Borda paced calmly across the deck of the ship. Magan noticed that the Ionic column of the high executive's body was immune to the rules of physics governing the rest of the SeeNaRee; instead of Borda swaying with the tide, the sea itself appeared to be rotating around the fulcrum of Borda.

"If you have something to say," rasped the high executive, "then say it."

Magan widened his stance, flaunting his lack of intimidation at Borda's presence. "You're going about this MultiReal situation all wrong," he said.

"Oh?"

"Natch thrives on anger. Every blow you strike against him only makes him stronger. So send another strike force to Shenandoah, start your *onslaught*. Not only will you fail to get control of MultiReal, you'll have the Congress in full-scale rebellion. You'll have people on the streets shouting their support for Natch and Margaret Surina."

Borda's face remained impassive, but the sea began tossing steep

breakers against the ship, as if trying to send Magan plummeting overboard. The fog thickened, further obscuring Magan's mental compass.
But the lieutenant executive had done plenty of time on Council naval
vessels and knew how to react to the choleric moods of the sea. He kept
his feet.

"You forget I've been through this before," said Borda in a voice
like molten rock. "I know how to deal with entrepreneurs. *And* with
Surinas." His words were punctuated by the crackle of cannon fire from
the enemy juggernaut still hidden somewhere off in the chop.

Magan recalled the iconic video footage that had swept across the
Data Sea almost fifty years ago, footage that could still be found just
about anywhere you looked. The smoking hulk of a shuttle half-buried
in the sands of Furtoid. A charred and mangled hand arching out of the
wreckage.

But then there was the other footage, the secret footage squirreled
away in the depths of the Defense and Wellness Council archives.
Marcus Surina, having miraculously survived the blast, blackened,
gasping, eking out the last fifteen minutes of his life on a Council
stretcher with Council dartguns aimed at his head and Council hoverbirds whirring in the background. Denied access to the soothing balms
of the Dr. Plugenpatch databases, lest someone discover he had not
perished instantly in the wreckage. Cursing Len Borda to the very end.

"He should have compromised," muttered the high executive,
gripping tightly onto the railing. Whether he was speaking to Magan
or to himself was unclear. "He didn't have to come to such an end. But
these Surinas, they're all the same. Too full of pride, too nearsighted to
see what's right in front of their noses. I tell you, it must be something
in the curry." He leaned on the railing and peered out to the sea, but
his attention was not on anything visible there. The British sloop
began to pick up speed, causing the few remaining hairs on Borda's
head to flap in the wind.

Magan stood his ground, icy silent, and made no reply.

"It was a choice I had to make!" yelled Len Borda suddenly, snapping his fingers and wheeling on his lieutenant executive. "What should I have done? Let Surina hand out teleportation to every man, woman, and child? Assassins zapping onto the floor of the Prime Committee! People teleporting into walls! Millions dead! Would *you* have that blood on your hands?" The high executive aimed one finger straight at Magan's chest. His voice was a thunderbolt, a primal and electric force of nature. "Consequences? Yes! There were consequences, Magan. Strong actions always have them. A new TeleCo board willing to listen to *reason*. A board *smart* enough to apply the appropriate safeguards. It was a necessary change. And if such a change required a—a market adjustment . . . then . . ."

Len Borda slipped into a troubled silence, which Magan Kai Lee made no effort to fill. The high executive was not blind. He had seen the millions wandering the streets for years with nothing but worthless TeleCo stock to their name. He had seen teleportation technology crawl back into the marketplace a stunted and crippled thing, too expensive for the masses to afford, too unreliable for the moneyed to trust.

And now Len Borda stood on the prow of his SeeNaRee ship, not just the most powerful man in the world, not just the master of the Council's invincible armies—but an old man with a fractured mind, a man who had sacrificed some crucial chunk of his mortality fifty years ago in a shuttle explosion on Furtoid.

Short-term plans, long-term problems.

Magan Kai Lee pressed his advantage. "You made a mistake," he said. "I can't allow you to make the same mistake again."

The high executive's voice was a croak. "And what say do you have in the matter?"

Magan steeled his spine and summoned all the repressed rage buried in his soul. "You gave me your word, Borda, and I intend to see that you keep it. You will announce your retirement from the Defense and Wellness Council in four days, and turn this crisis over to me. As we agreed two years ago." *When I stood here in this office with a loaded gun pressed to the back of your neck. When I swore to you that I would not be stung by an assassin's dart like the other lieutenant executives before me. When you convinced me that it would be better to take your seat as a chosen successor and not a mutineer.*

"You don't have the experience to handle this," scoffed Borda quietly. "Marcus Surina——"

"Marcus Surina was a buffoon. He hid behind his family name and his reputation with the drudges. But *this* man, this Natch—he has no family to lose. He has no reputation to uphold. This man will outthink and outplot your armies until the end, Borda. No, there is only one person capable of defeating Natch."

"And who is that?"

"Himself."

Len Borda slumped perceptibly and turned back to the sea, looking old and careworn—but not before Magan caught the briefest shimmer in the high executive's eye.

Magan felt a sudden nibble of doubt at his ankles. All his experience with Borda had taught him that the high executive was a creature of passion rather than forethought, a short-term planner. But why then did he occasionally see that knowing glimmer in Borda's eye? Was it just the nostalgia of the grizzled veteran watching the young protégé come into his own? Or could it be that Borda's ardor was merely artifice? Was that how Borda had bested all his would-be supplanters over the years?

The high executive stood for a long time without speaking. His ship had returned to calm seas, but the fog around them had only thickened. There was no sound but the soft, rhythmic lapping of oars on seawater, the distant cry of a gull.

Finally, Borda spoke. "I would like to offer you a compromise."

Magan said nothing.

"New Year's Day is just a convenient symbol," continued Borda, his voice disarmingly matter-of-fact. "We chose that day to protect the markets, didn't we? To cushion the financial impact of the announcement. But the *real* financial impact won't come until the new year's budget goes into effect on the fifteenth of January." The high executive stood up straight, brushed something off his collar. "So I'll give you two and a half weeks. Prove to me you can handle this crisis, Magan. Bring MultiReal under the Council's control by the fifteenth, and I will abide by our agreement."

Magan could feel his mind whirling like a difference engine, calculating odds, extrapolating possibilities. "And how do I know I can trust your word this time?" *How do I know I won't end up at the bottom of a river, like the last lieutenant executive who tried to bargain with you for succession?*

"What choice do you have?" said Borda.

"Don't delude yourself," said Magan, his voice keen and deadly as a razor. "This decision isn't yours to make, not anymore. You don't think I'm the only one eager to plant a black code dart in your skull, do you? The only reason you sit in the high executive's chair to this day is because *I* allow it."

For the first time in the conversation, Len Borda smiled. It was a horrid expression, the hungry grin of a carnivore. "Spare me the pity of Magan Kai Lee," mocked the high executive. "I don't need it."

And then, without warning, the SeeNaRee dissolved away. Magan found himself standing no longer on an ancient British sloop-of-war, but in a modern office arranged with the strictest military discipline. Two tables, a smattering of chairs, windows with a view of the globe below. Standing in a semicircle around him were four Defense and Wellness Council officers who had been hidden in the virtual mist. Their dartguns were drawn and aimed at Magan. As the lieutenant executive regarded them with a cool eye, he felt the barrel of another dartgun press into the back of his neck.

"I give you until the fifteenth of January to take possession of MultiReal," said Len Borda, his voice larded with triumph. "If you do, we have an agreement. If you don't . . ." The officer behind Magan pressed the dartgun barrel deeper into his flesh.

Magan kept his face neutral, determined to show no trace of emotion or hesitation. "You're not *giving* me anything, Borda. The Council will have control of MultiReal by the fifteenth, and you will relinquish the high executive's chair—one way or the other."

He turned without being asked, and the officer with the dartgun at his neck turned with him. Magan strode calmly to the elevator. Four of the officers sheathed their weapons as he passed, but the one at his back never let the nozzle of the dartgun stray from Magan's skin, even as he accompanied the lieutenant executive onto the lift.

When the doors closed and the elevator began its ascent to the main level, Magan fired off a secure ConfidentialWhisper to the man at his back. "Keep that dartgun right where it is until I'm off the elevator," he commanded. "Then send someone to find Papizon and Rey Gonerev. Tell them I need to see them."

Ridgello nodded. "As you wish, Lieutenant Executive."

(((5)))

On the way back to the hoverbird docks, Magan took a detour to see the statue of Tul Jabbor. The atrium where the statue resided was the one place in DWCR whose location never changed. The statue itself was a small-scale replica of the one standing in the center of the eponymously named Tul Jabbor Complex in Melbourne. A thick man with mahogany skin atop a tall pillar. No matter where you stood, some holographic trick caused Jabbor's gaze to always meet you head-on— and left you constantly standing in his shadow. This was as unsubtle an architectural metaphor as Magan had ever seen.

The founding father of the Defense and Wellness Council needed no caption, but bold block letters at his feet did pose a question.

DO YOU ACT IN JUSTICE?

The locution had always seemed peculiar to Magan. Acting *in* justice, not *for* or *with* justice. As if justice were merely a vehicle you might ride to a particular destination, and the terrain you trammeled to get there was nothing more than dirt under your wheels.

Certainly Tul Jabbor had treated justice that way. He had dramatically expanded the Council's power by going after erstwhile supporters like the OCHRE Corporation; some even suspected he had signed Henry Osterman's death warrant. Then again, Jabbor had come to power in a world without precedents, a world simultaneously drunk with the possibilities of bio/logics and desperate to avoid repeating the horrors of the Autonomous Revolt.

But Len Borda? Borda had two hundred years of Council history to guide him, with every manner of high executive from Par Padron the Just to Zetarysis the Mad as object lessons. He should have known better. Instead, Borda was ever willing to sacrifice principle for prag-matism, ever ready to steer justice down the muddy, unpaved path.

And you? the lieutenant executive asked himself, kneeling in silence before the statue of Tul Jabbor. *Are you forcing Borda to step down because he's made a mockery of Par Padron's ideals? Or are you just afraid to wake up at the bottom of a river?*

Magan Kai Lee was a man of reason and principle, or so he told himself. He had been drawn to the Defense and Wellness Council by its discipline, its rigidity, and its stability when compared to the life of the diss—or so he told himself. Now, after watching Len Borda use the Council as a blunt instrument of self-preservation for years, Magan was contemplating the ultimate move *against* the very discipline, rigidity, and stability that had brought him here in the first place. And that contradiction sat in his mind like a poisonous flower with ever-expanding roots.

But Magan couldn't allow Len Borda to repeat the mistakes he had made with Marcus Surina, could he? Wasn't there a higher principle at work here that needed defending?

Do you act in justice?

. . .

Papizon and Rey Gonerev caught up to him in the hallway, no simple feat in an orbital fortress whose constantly shifting corridors rendered geography meaningless.

"We spotted Natch an hour ago," said Papizon as he moved into step behind Magan like a hoverbird merging into traffic. "He's on a tube train, headed north out of Cisco."

The lieutenant executive ground his teeth together. "And you didn't think to look there *before* we raided his apartment?"

Papizon shook his head. He was immune to criticism. In fact, he seemed to have been inoculated against most forms of human expression altogether. Sometimes Magan wondered if Papizon was really some sublevel engineer's attempt to circumvent the harsh AI bans in place since the Autonomous Revolt. If so, one couldn't have picked a more peculiar vessel: lanky, storkish, brown eyes not quite symmetrical and permanently half-lidded.

Rey stepped up to Papizon's defense. "We *did* check there, Magan," she said. "We swept half the tube trains in the Americas yesterday. Natch was definitely not on that tube line."

Magan gave the Blade an appraising look. She had pointedly not fallen half a step behind him like Papizon, but walked at his side like an equal. A message meant not so much for him as for the other Council officers in the hallway—the ones she would be jousting with someday when it was Magan's turn to step down from the high executive's seat.

Papizon: "So are we going to try to pick him up again?"

"No," said Magan, shaking his head. "Just keep an eye on him for now—and make sure he knows we're doing it. Make his life unpleasant."

"Unpleasant," his subordinate echoed with a nod, then slipped down a side corridor and disappeared. Making Someone's Life Unpleasant had been honed to a science at the Defense and Wellness Council, and Papizon was a true authority on the subject. *Unpleasantness* meant snooping programs that left clear traces of their presence. It meant ghostly figures that followed you on the periphery of your vision. It meant a few unexplained transactions in your Vault account, too small to be of consequence yet too large to go unnoticed.

"And me?" said the Blade.

"You," replied Magan, "will be planning the main attack on this fiefcorp master. I don't care how much you spend—you have the coffers of the Defense and Wellness Council at your disposal. We need unprecedented coordination. Propaganda, logistics, regulatory, personnel, finance. This man has weaknesses, Rey. I want to know what they are, and I want your plan for exploiting them."

Gonerev nodded sagely with the look of someone taking notes in her mental log. "What about Margaret Surina?"

"Let her rot in her tower for now."

"And our time frame?"

"Two and a half weeks. MultiReal must be in our hands when the new year's budget goes into effect."

The Blade didn't blanch at the urgent timetable; if anything, she seemed to relish the challenge. Magan thought briefly about the day when he would find himself with Rey Gonerev's dartgun pressed into the back of his neck. That day would surely come, but it was still decades in the future. Would he go quietly? Or would he cling to power far beyond his time, resisting oblivion with every last breath in his body, like Len Borda? And if he resisted, how far would she be prepared to go to take him down?

2

THE NOTHINGNESS
AT THE CENTER
OF THE UNIVERSE

(((6)))

Geronimo: twenty-two years old, heterosexual, Caucasian, xpression board player for the Dregs of Nitro. A self-styled dissident, a philosopher, a poet, a lover. Or so his profile on the Sigh network claimed.

Jara wondered who he *really* was.

In the more prosaic world offline, the sullen man across the room wearing the CALL ME GERONIMO T-shirt might really be a diplomat or a black code junkie or a fugitive from the law. There was no way to tell for sure. Some sociologist had recently published a formula that purported to describe the ratio of truth to falsehood in Sigh profiles. Jara couldn't make heads or tails of it, but apparently the formula had something to do with Fibonacci numbers.

"Geronimo" spotted her and threw her a look. Jara could feel the incandescent knife of lust twisting in her abdomen. He rose from the purple couch and began strutting toward her through the crowd.

From a distance, the resemblance was uncanny. Average height, hair sandy and slightly tousled, physique trim yet not quite muscular. Eyes a vivid sapphire blue. If only science could provide a way for Jara to have him at a distance before he opened his mouth.

"Perfection," said Geronimo as he approached, in that incongruous half-lisp of his. "How you doin', Cassandra?" Of course, Jara didn't use her real name here on the Sigh; few people did. But at least she projected her own pixyish body onto the network instead of some idealized substitute, which was more than most could say.

"Towards Perfection yourself," Jara replied, standing on tiptoes to give Geronimo a hungry hello kiss. The kiss quickly evolved into a full-on tongue-dueling affair until the pain in her toes made her withdraw.

"So you get us a room?" grunted the youth, almost shattering the illusion. "How 'bout one-a those leather ones?"

The fiefcorp analyst winced. Jara didn't know whether this idiot was really dissident, philosopher, or poet, but one thing was certain—he definitely was *not* Natch. She hid her disappointment behind a coy smile. "Of *course* I got us a room. What, you think I'm some kind of amateur?"

Geronimo chuckled and brushed his knuckles across the side of her breast, an act that didn't require the slightest apology or explanation to the crowd. Not on *this* channel, at least. Jara could feel the knife twisting inside her, uncontrollable, setting everything it touched aflame. "Awright," mumbled Geronimo. "Let's get moving."

Please shut up, she thought. *Please, please, please.*

Jara and the boy walked arm in arm across the lounge, past columns of wriggling goldfish and green cushions nestled on the backs of porpoises. They saw twosomes and threesomes and moresomes of all genders and orientations flirting away the time between encounters. Jara noticed a trio of four-breasted mermaids rubbing fins. Geronimo goggled appreciatively at a woman who must have been three meters tall, locked in a passionate kiss with a man whose dangling equipment looked equal to the task. There were no fewer than three Len Bordas in the room. One of them had two heads.

They followed the data beacon around a long curved corridor, threading their way through gossiping bystanders. Geronimo was humming one of his atonal Dregs of Nitro songs. Finally, they reached a nondescript door and opened it to find an even more nondescript room. A low queen bed, a nightstand. Mirrors.

"What, you want *this?*" said the youth with a sneer.

"I thought I'd let you pick," said Jara.

"Oh," replied Geronimo, grinning goofily. "I get it. Well, lemme think for a minute. . . ."

Don't think too hard, Jara glowered silently. *You might damage something.*

Geronimo flipped through a number of exotic environments—

Amazonian jungle, Arabian harem, something called "The Twelve Rings of Zarquatt"—and finally settled on a pleasure den whose every surface was coated with black leather. Jara let out a small noise of exasperation. This was exactly the same motif Geronimo had selected for their *last* two encounters. Jara could already tell that this afternoon's tryst would solve nothing. That knife was wedged much too deep for a neophyte like Geronimo to reach.

The Natch look-alike was hopping on one foot, struggling to remove his pants. Jara thought about cutting her connection to the network right then and there, but decided to stay. She had paid good Vault credits for this room.

• • •

Jara had figured that three weeks away from Natch would cool her passion. She was wrong.

It's the eternal paradox of love, the drudge Kristella Krodor had written recently. *When he's at arm's length he's too far, but when he's in your arms he's too near.* Jara was ashamed to admit she read such tripe.

But the idea of using the Sigh as a therapeutic tool hadn't come from Kristella Krodor. It had come from an unexpected source: Bonneth, companion to her fellow apprentice Merri.

Jara had decided to open up to Merri a few nights after the demo at Andra Pradesh. As the fiefcorp's channel manager and resident truthteller, Merri spent hours every day in Natch's presence too, and sexual orientation was no barrier to the entrepreneur's charms. She would have to understand what Jara was going through, on some level. But Jara never got the chance to find out. Moments after Jara multied to her apartment, Merri rushed off to resolve some unexpected emergency with her beloved Creed Objectivv, leaving Jara and Bonneth alone.

The analyst felt as if she barely knew Merri, much less her quiet companion. But suddenly Jara found everything spilling out in one long, torturous flood. The proctor who took advantage of her, the two decades of professional frustration, the gullible years as Lucas Sentinel's apprentice, the stabbing desire for Natch that would not go away.

Bonneth listened intently from her well-padded chair. *I think I know how you feel*, she said. *Wanting something you just can't have, not being able to let go.* She raised her arms feebly and made a gesture at her brittle frame, twisted in what looked like a very uncomfortable position. Bonneth had Mai-Lo Syndrome, one of those rare instances of genetic engineering gone awry. The bones in her arms and legs were fragile as eggshells, beyond even the skill of bio/logics to repair.

When you've got multi and SeeNaRee and powered exoskeletons, it's not such a handicap, continued Bonneth. *But I'll admit . . . sometimes I just have to* know. *Late at night, after I've repeated all those Dr. Plugenpatch statistics to myself a million times . . . I just need to know what it's like, even for a couple of hours, and then I can go on again.*

So how do you do that? Jara asked.

That's easy, said Bonneth, with an impish smile. *The Sigh.*

Jara hardly knew where to start. She had taken plenty of practice laps around the shallow end of the Sigh when she was a teenager. But back then her options were limited by the boundaries of her parents' L-PRACG: no partners over eighteen, no extreme stuff. Now suddenly she was free to explore the three hundred thousand channels running on Sigh protocols—free to dive deep and explore the crevices and trenches, the scabrous surfaces, free to coax the hidden pearls from their shells. Most channels simply connected people of similar interests. There were other channels that specialized in every perversion humanity had dreamt up in the last hundred thousand years. Adventurous souls could dally with automated pleasure bots that had survived the long Darwinian slog through the competitive market of sexual programming. When the pleasure bots grew tiresome, there were channels that circumvented bodily mechanics altogether and delivered massive unadulterated doses of endorphins.

But how to exorcise this obsession with Natch? It wasn't as easy as it sounded.

The Sigh was not restrained by the same limits as the multi network, so it was simple enough to plaster someone else's face on your partner and be done with it. But while this subterfuge might suffice for the man living down the street or the faintly glimpsed woman on the tube, the illusion simply didn't work for an intimate acquaintance. Call it a failure of technology or psychology; virtual simulacra just could not fool the discerning human brain.

Enter the Doppelgänger channel.

Jara found a series of intriguing promos featuring celebrity impostors of stars like Juan Nguyen and Jeannie Q. Christina, all with ridiculously mundane names and occupations. *I'm Lester James, hover-bird repair technician*, said an Angel Palmero look-alike. *And I've been searching for you on Doppelgänger.*

It was a simple system. Point the interface to the Data Sea profile of your lust object. Doppelgänger proceeds to track down his unwitting twins spread throughout human space. Each twin is presented with an invitation to meet. Given a pool of sixty billion people to choose from, the odds were high that someone would accept the invitation. Frequently that someone was looking for a person just like *you*, which gave the arrangement a nice symmetry. The closer the match, the higher the fee.

Jara had fired off a Vault credit authorization to Doppelgänger, along with a video of Natch at his most beautiful and solipsistic. Two days later, Doppelgänger had led her to Geronimo.

The relationship worked very nicely for a week or so. Geronimo tried to fulfill Jara's fantasy of bedding her boss, and Jara tried to fulfill Geronimo's fantasy of bedding . . . who? A neighbor, a co-worker, some woman who had caught his eye in a Beijing night club? Jara didn't know and didn't care. This was the Sigh, after all, where mutual fulfillment was the decorum and questions were bad form.

Then that week turned into two and rounded the corner heading for three. Now, here she lay, thirty-seven minutes after her arrival in this leather SeeNaRee, and Geronimo was gone. Jara still had twenty minutes left on the account, and an additional two hours until the next fiefcorp meeting. She decided to loaf for a while.

Jara hated to chastise Bonneth for bad advice, but it was becoming pretty clear that this form of therapy just wasn't working. There was something intensely sexual about Natch. Yet he kept that virility under such iron control that Jara could not even tap into it through fantasy. What would Natch be like if he vented his passions in the bedroom? What if there were no bio/logic fiefcorps, no Primo's ratings, no MultiReal to distract him? Easier to imagine a bird without wings or a fish that could not swim.

The closer Jara got to possessing the fiefcorp master, the more he seemed to edge away. Achieving his lifetime goal of topping the Primo's bio/logic investment guide should have loosened him up a little, given him a sense of accomplishment. But instead, the entrepreneur was retreating farther and farther inside his shell.

How long would his sanity last?

It needed to last a while. Jara no longer had the consolation that this would all be over in eleven months when her apprenticeship expired. She had chosen to sign on to *another* apprenticeship, serving a brand-new company in a wholly untested market. Another few years wrestling with this peculiar crossbreed of loathing and lust.

Meanwhile, Horvil was out there somewhere. Sweet, innocent Horvil, who had opened up his heart on the floor of the Surina Center for Historic Appreciation while a thousand Council troops marched through the courtyard. They had managed to avoid being confined alone ever since. Jara could honestly say she had never thought of Horvil in a romantic light, and had no idea what to do. Her feelings were as easy to decipher as cuneiform.

Confused, emotionally knotted, exhausted, Jara finally logged off the Sigh and waited for the mediocrity of the real world to seep in again. There was a name for the haze of a mind switching between multi connections; why wasn't there a word for the postcoital letdown of logging off the Sigh?

Jara sat up in bed and looked at her still-white walls. In the living room sat the pitiful arrangement of daisies she had blown an inappropriately large chunk of her fiefcorp stipend on. She arose, walked into the breakfast nook, and had the building brew her up some hot nitro.

When did you lose yourself? the analyst asked her reflection in the window.

Was it at Andra Pradesh, when Len Borda's troops were swooping all around her? Or further back, when she had threatened to quit the fiefcorp after Natch's little black code stunt? Maybe there wasn't a single moment. Maybe it was a gradual eroding of self, a twenty-year process that had started long before she ever heard of Natch or Horvil. Everything that had happened in her adult life felt like one attenuated chain reaction to that moment in the hive when her proctor had settled his hand on her thigh, a few centimeters higher than propriety dictated, and Jara had tried to convince herself that she liked it there.

(((7)))

The familiar sight of his tenement curving around a Shenandoah hilltop put a smile on Natch's face that not even black code could dim. Natch had never felt a sentimental attachment to any of the places he had called home; he remembered walking out of the hive for initiation with barely a backward glance. But he had never savored the unique flavor of returning to a place he had fought to defend either.

The front doors swished open to greet him. Natch stepped into the atrium and nearly collided with Horvil.

The engineer's chubby face instantly sparked into a grin. "You're back!" he cried, folding the fiefcorp master into a bear hug. Natch could feel a turgid programming bar pressed against his back. The distinct smell of peanut butter drifted through the air.

"I'm back," agreed the entrepreneur.

"For real this time, right?" The engineer poked him in the collarbone with one grubby finger. "Not just another five-minute stop-by in multi?"

"For real."

"About time," grumbled a voice from the back of the atrium. Horvil shuffled aside to reveal his cousin Benyamin, who was rising from one of the stiff-backed chairs that lined the building's front hall. "Your apartment won't let us in," he said, stretching his arms up in the air with fingertips clasped.

"Well, that's not completely true," said Horvil with a frown. "Vigal, Jara, and me, we can all override the security just fine. But you never approved everyone else for emergency access."

"So *we've* been stuck working out *here*," continued Ben.

"At least the building management was nice about it," said Horvil. "They could've kicked us out. But they didn't. They even let us drag the workbench out here once or twice."

"You can thank *her* for that." The young apprentice tilted his head slightly to the left, indicating another roomier chair where the channel manager, Merri, had taken up residence. Merri struggled to stand, suppressed a yawn, then switched on a stim program to suffuse her with some energy.

Natch took in the blonde woman's disheveled dress and the backpack propped slantwise against the leg of an end table. Suddenly he realized that, unlike Benyamin, Merri was here in the flesh and probably hadn't been home since the demo at Andra Pradesh. "Why are you still *here?*" Natch asked incredulously. "Why didn't you go back home?"

Merri shrugged with embarrassment. "I know how expensive it is to teleport to Luna," she said. "It's just not worth wasting the company's money. And I'm not up to one of those long shuttle rides right now."

"Someone else would've put you up. Horvil's Aunt Berilla has a fancy estate in London. They must have a thousand spare bedrooms."

"It's not a big deal, Natch. The local Creed Objectivv hostel works just fine."

"But you've got a companion on Luna," Benyamin retorted. "Bonneth needs you, you said. She can barely get across the *apartment* by herself—"

"Bonneth," said Merri with an air of tired finality, "will be fine." Natch sensed undercurrents of tension between the two fiefcorpers, but decided this was something he could deal with another time. He shook his head, stepped around the pleasantly befuddled Horvil, and strode down the hall to his apartment with three apprentices in tow.

Jara seemed to have anticipated Natch's arrival before he even made it in the door. The tiny fiefcorp analyst was perched on the arm of Natch's sofa, contemplating an ornate holographic calendar floating in midair. "We need to talk scheduling, Natch," she announced without even looking up, as if continuing a conversation already in progress.

The fiefcorp master paused a moment and let the comfortable trappings of home flood his senses: the windows showing bar charts of the bio/logic markets, the workbench in his office with a trapezoidal structure bobbing above it in MindSpace, the sprightly patch of daisies in the apartment's precise geometric center. A cup of tea on the kitchen counter gave mute testimony to Serr Vigal's presence. "Where's Vigal?" asked Natch.

"Here I am," came the voice of the neural programmer as he wandered in from the balcony. Natch thought he spotted a few more gray hairs in his old guardian's goatee and an unusual amount of concern written on his wrinkled forehead. Serr Vigal surprised the both of them by taking Natch into a tight embrace.

"I'm glad you're back," mumbled Vigal.

"Me too," said Natch.

The moment was brief. There would be plenty of time later for sentimentality; right now Natch had business to attend to. He stepped free of the neural programmer's arms and began his normal hectic pace around the living room. Benyamin and Horvil hustled to find seats. "Everybody here? Someone's missing. Where's Quell?"

Merri settled into a quiet corner on the floor next to the balcony and sat with her legs crossed. "Quell went to get a bite to eat," she said. "He kept complaining about the food in your building, so we found him an Indian restaurant down the street. He should be back in a few minutes."

"Where's he been sleeping?"

The channel manager shrugged her shoulders. "I think he rented a room somewhere."

"Fine," said Natch with a flip of his hand. "Okay, Jara. Scheduling. Go."

"*This* was the day of our presentation at Andra Pradesh," said Jara, pointing to the holographic calendar. The square marked *Tuesday, December 6* popped off the calendar like a kernel of corn on the flame. "And here's today." December 28 leapt up, causing the previous three weeks to cascade off the surface of the holograph. "The public hasn't heard a peep out of us in three weeks. No press releases, no timetables, no demos, nothing."

"Natch's been a little busy," snorted Horvil, who had appropriated the chair-and-a-half for his ass and the matching ottoman for his feet.

"Granted," said Jara. "But the public doesn't know that. Three weeks is an eternity in bio/logics. It's a good thing the Council pulled that little stunt yesterday, because people were wondering if he was still *alive*."

"Don't even joke about that," muttered Vigal, balancing his cup of tea on one palm as he found a place on the couch between Ben and Jara.

"Magan Kai Lee swoops down here with dartguns blazing, and you call that a *little stunt?*" said Horvil. "If Natch hadn't warned us to stay clear, we could've all been killed."

Jara did not back down. "Come on, Horv," said the analyst. "The Council just wanted to scare him. They weren't planning on *killing* him."

Ben let out a harrumph. "How do you know that?"

"Because," replied the analyst as calmly as a proctor explaining arithmetic to a hive child. "Natch can't hand MultiReal over to the Council if he's dead, now can he?"

Benyamin's mouth clamped shut. Silence enveloped the apartment.

Jara continued. "Listen, Ben. We're talking about basic Data Sea networking principles. Len Borda can't just *steal* the MultiReal code from Natch. He needs core access, or Natch could just lock him out of the program whenever he felt like it. And core access on the Data Sea isn't something the Council can fake. They'd need the matching signatures tied up in Natch's OCHRE system. It's practically impossible to crack."

Serr Vigal nodded sagely. "She's right," he said. "Even the Defense and Wellness Council can't circumvent Data Sea access controls."

The young apprentice refused to give up. "They could get core access from Margaret."

"Sure," said Horvil, picking at a loose thread on his jacket. "But think of it this way. There're two people in the world with the master key to MultiReal. One of them's holed up in a tower with five thousand armed guards, and one of them's just hanging out in an apartment building. Who would *you* go after?"

"This is all beside the point," continued Jara. "Without Natch's cooperation—or Margaret's—Borda wouldn't even be able to *find* the code. You can't just trace subaether transmissions. He'd have to search every qubit on the Data Sea with pattern recognition algorithms. Even using the fastest computational engine in existence, that'd take . . ."

Arithmetic fluttered behind Horvil's closed eyelids as he yanked the string on his jacket free. "Two thousand one hundred twenty-nine years. No, wait. Maybe four hundred eighty-eight years. Or . . ."

Jara raised her eyebrows and extended an open palm in the engineer's direction. "A long time, at any rate."

"But if the Council couldn't find MultiReal, then *nobody* could find it," protested Ben. "It would just float on the Sea forever with all the other useless crap. If Len Borda's trying to get rid of MultiReal, wouldn't that suit him just fine? Get rid of Natch and Margaret, and then nobody has core access."

"Yes, but what if Borda wants to keep MultiReal for himself?" said Jara.

Benyamin leaned forward on the sofa and ran one hand through his inky black hair. "I must be missing something," he said. "This doesn't make any sense. If Borda can't take MultiReal away, and he can't kill Natch, then all he can do is threaten, right? What are we so worried about?"

Horvil put a hand on the young apprentice's shoulder. "Do I really need to spell it out for you, Ben?" he asked in a throaty whisper.

All conversation came to a halt. Bio/logics could do much to shield the human body from pain, but in the wrong hands it could also be used to cause pain. Over the years, unscrupulous groups had devised OCHREs that injected painful toxins directly into muscle and bone, nightmare SeeNaRees that tapped into their victims' darkest fears, and programs that directly stimulated the pain centers of the brain. Who could say which of these techniques the Council used?

Natch stopped midpace in front of the window, silhouetted by the Shenandoah morning. "The Patel Brothers are giving another demo this Sunday."

The rest of the company blinked in surprise. Nobody had noticed that Natch hadn't said anything for several minutes. Merri gulped uneasily and gave Horvil a sidelong glance. "I was going to mention that," she said. "How did you know, Natch? The Patels haven't even announced it yet."

"Well, how did *you* know?" asked Horvil.

"Robby Robby," replied the channel manager. "It's his business to know what's happening in the sales world. And it's *my* business to know what *he* knows."

Natch could feel the stares of his fellow fiefcorpers, but he paid them no mind. His eyes were locked on that pulsing square labeled *Tuesday, December 6*, hovering menacingly near Jara's fingers like an accusation. How was it possible for three weeks to slip through his fingers and vanish without a trace? Already those days on the tube were becoming ghostly, indistinct, something from a dream. Jara was right: three weeks was an eternity in bio/logics. What unspeakable malice had the black code inside him unleashed during those three weeks?

"Natch . . . ?" Vigal prodded gently.

The fiefcorp master blinked hard, trying to get his mind back into balance. He focused on the holographic calendar. How did he know about the Patel Brothers' demo? The same way he had known about Magan Kai Lee's failed incursion into his apartment building. Some might label it *intuition* or *foresight*, but to Natch it was simply algebra; all you needed to do was to churn through the variables and eliminate the cruft, and you would inevitably arrive at the solution. Couldn't they *see* the reddish aura surrounding that square labeled *January 1*? Couldn't they *tell* the Patel Brothers were giving a demo that day just by looking at it?

"So what did Robby find out about this demo?" Natch asked Merri. "Any indication what they're doing?"

"Not really. Just vague rumors. They've booked an auditorium at the Thassel Complex, but it's not one of the larger-capacity halls. We're guessing it's an industry-only event. Robby thinks he can get one of us in without too much trouble."

"I'll go," said Jara.

The fiefcorp master nodded and began to pace once more. "So how do we respond?"

Horvil did some mental extrapolation of his own, then dropped his face dramatically into the palms of his hands. "Shit," he said, nose poking through his thick fingers, "you're not gonna put us through all that crap again, are you, Natch? *Another* demo in less than seventy-two hours?"

Natch shook his head, and the rest of the fiefcorpers released their breath simultaneously. "There's no point," he said. "The demo at Andra Pradesh showed everyone that *we're* the standard bearers in this business now. If we scramble to beat Frederic and Petrucio to the punch again, it'll just look like we're being defensive. Better for us to schedule something on our own timetable. Take a little time to get this one right."

Jara gave a curt nod of agreement. "So, when?" She swept her hand across the calendar, causing entire rows of dates to ripple smoothly off the surface. Her fingers drifted down toward February in a transparent effort to bring Natch's attention to a later date.

Natch studied the chunks of time floating in the middle of the room and rubbed his chin. To Natch, each day had a unique flavor that he could roll on his tongue like wine. Few recognized the distinctions between weekdays and weekends anymore, and nobody but lawyers and accountants observed the new year. But there were a few days that seemed disturbingly rancid, for reasons he couldn't discern. January 15 stood out as a particularly bad day, and the whole following week tasted as bitter as ash.

"January 8," he said at length. "A week from Sunday."

More relieved sighs. Given what the fiefcorp had gone through for the last demo, eleven days felt like a century.

"It's too bloody quiet in here," came a gruff voice from the doorway. "Let's hear some more noise."

Quell strode in, his breath stinking of saffron and bay leaves. The Islander looked as if he could have curled the rest of the fiefcorp with one massive biceps. The thin copper collar around his neck feeding him the sights and sounds of the virtual world seemed more uncomfortable than ever.

"You're missing all the excitement," said Horvil to his fellow engineer. "It's demo time again."

"Fun," said the Islander, voice doused with sarcasm. "I can't wait." He walked over to Natch and enacted his peculiar Islander custom of clasping hands and shaking.

Natch stood before the window for a moment with his hands behind his back. Staring. "No, not a demo," he said. "An exposition."

Benyamin let out a skeptical *phfft*. "What's the difference?"

"A demo is a preview. An exposition is a celebration." The fiefcorp master's statement was greeted by a confused silence. He stepped back and spread his arms toward the window as if unveiling a marquee. "Picture this: a field of grass, a huge crowd. Two teams playing baseball, every single player using MultiReal."

Horvil gazed unblinkingly at the window. "Where are you going to get the other team?" he said. "You wanna invite the Patel Brothers?"

"No. We pick them at random. We pick *all* the players at random, both teams."

"We could hold some kind of public lottery," said Merri, her eyes glinting. "Then we could announce the winners at a big publicity event."

"I think this could work," put in Quell, rubbing his chin with his bear's paw. "Instead of holding MultiReal up on a stage, we give the audience a taste of it. So they'll know what it's really like to *use* the program. Makes it that much harder for Borda to take away."

"Aren't we beating this baseball thing to death?" said Jara. "People are going to think the only thing MultiReal's good for is hitting home runs."

Natch, unconcerned: "Then let's make it soccer. Or jai alai. Doesn't matter." He turned to face the rest of the fiefcorp and straightened his spine like a drill sergeant. "Listen, I know it feels like we have eons to put this together. But we've used up the element of novelty. People have been talking nonstop about MultiReal for a month now, and we can't just repeat what we did last time."

The analyst flipped dark curls of hair from her eyes, the better to face down a looming challenge. "I'm up to the task," she said. "But it's not me you have to worry about. Most of this is going to fall on Horvil's shoulders."

"Me and Quell, we've been pounding out all kinds of changes to the code in MindSpace," said the engineer with an insouciant air. "Possibilities is *humming*. It's like we turned some kind of corner. But still— doesn't mean it's gonna be easy. We have a lot of loose ends to tie up before we can sic this thing on five hundred million people again."

Natch: "So can you get the job done?"

Horvil's voice did not leak the smallest droplet of doubt. "Yeah, we'll get it done," he said. Quell gave a reinforcing nod of confidence. "Provided that Ben's assembly-line goons do *their* job."

"No worries," said Benyamin. "Greth Tar Griveth has the programming floor standing on notice."

"And I'll start working the sales channels with Robby Robby," put in Merri, standing up and brushing off her blouse.

Serr Vigal sat on the sofa, beaming quietly. His role in the fiefcorp was strictly an advisory one, but no one doubted that he would make himself available as needed.

Natch's pacing slowed as he surveyed the group arrayed before him. He could scarcely believe that a month ago, the Surina/Natch MultiReal Fiefcorp had been fumbling, awkward, and ready to quit. Now they had caught the same intoxicating scent of victory that Natch had been following since his first meeting with Margaret Surina. This was no hodgepodge of runners-up and also-rans Natch had assembled; this was a first-rate team.

The entrepreneur tried to conjure some words of inspiration, but for some reason the linguistic centers of his brain felt tangled and knotted. "All right," said the fiefcorp master, twirling one hand in the air. "Let's get to work."

(((8)))

Jara pledged to waste no more time with Geronimo until the Multi-Real exposition was over, at the earliest. There was too much to do. But she might as well have spent the next morning dabbling on the Sigh, for all she accomplished.

She began the day arguing with Merri over details of the MultiReal exposition. They agreed to have the lottery winners play soccer instead of baseball, but Merri insisted there should be twenty-three lottery winners instead of twenty-two.

"That's uneven," Jara complained. "Somebody's going to get an extra player."

"Yes, but think of the symbolism," said Merri. "One for each member of the Prime Committee. We could even choose one player from each Committee bailiwick."

Jara summoned a holographic bar chart that displayed the Committee bailiwicks in bright blues and purples. Across the Atlantic, Merri's window would be showing the same thing. "That means putting a bunch of central government employees on the field," she protested. Jara pointed to the column labeled MEME COOPERATIVE (3) and set it aglow. "Do you really want three Meme Cooperative officials nosing around backstage at *our* exposition?"

"That could be part of the gimmick. It's perfect, Jara! The Congress of L-PRACGs has twelve seats on the Committee, right? And all the other government and business interests put together have eleven. We can bill the game as 'the people versus the government.'"

"And the extra player?"

"I don't know. Maybe we can just rotate goalies. We'll figure something out."

But Jara was skeptical, and they decided to put off making any decisions until they had spoken with Natch at the afternoon fiefcorp meeting. *This sounds like one of his ideas*, thought the analyst. *He'll definitely take Merri's side, and that's just going to cause trouble.*

Frustrated, still itching with unscratchable desire, Jara decided to cut the conversation short and step out of her apartment for a change. Her next-door neighbors blinked in surprise when she passed them in the hallway, having given her up for dead weeks ago.

Jara emerged from the tenement into a glum, drizzly London afternoon. *So much for modern technology*, she thought. For thousands of years, the British Isles had been under the capricious grip of nature, and London had constantly wallowed in rain. Now, after two centuries of unparalleled technological progress, the weather was determined by the Environmental Control Board, the regional L-PRACGs, and a patchwork of smaller agencies—and still the city wallowed in rain.

The fiefcorp analyst made her way north, where the cobblestone turned to splotchy asphalt. She passed the farmers' market and the baseball stadium. Twenty minutes later, she found her destination: a small nitro bar nestled among the shops of New Downing. A familiar site, part haven and part hideaway. Jara could practically feel the warm nitro lathering her tongue as she walked in the door.

But as soon as she made it inside, she stopped short. The man standing in her path may have been wearing a loose green caftan instead of a white robe and yellow star, yet there was no mistaking Magan Kai Lee.

• • •

Jara could feel her animal instincts kick in. She made a quick pirouette, looking for the glint of Council dartguns, but all she could see was the quotidian assortment of nitro junkies and chintz-patterned sofas.

Jara had watched the video of Magan's failed raid on Natch's apartment at least a dozen times. She had gotten used to seeing him as a startled animal buffeted by a hailstorm of drudge questions. Now, standing in the nitro bar, the lieutenant executive was serene and confident, like a man who was either armed to the teeth or twice as large as everyone else in the room. But Magan bore no weapon that Jara could see, and even she topped his slight frame by a few centimeters.

"Towards Perfection, Jara," said Magan.

The analyst scowled. "What the fuck do you want?"

"Just to talk," said the lieutenant, sweeping one hand toward the side door with a magnanimous gesture.

Jara regarded the doorway with suspicion. "Talk," she said. "Right. How do I know you're not going to plug me with black code out there?"

The corners of Magan's lips rose a millimeter or two. A smile. "Surely if I can plug you with black code out there," he said, "I could do it in here just as easily."

Jara sighed, acknowledging the point. She had a passing familiarity with the waitstaff here, but she couldn't imagine any of them sticking their necks out for her. The initial shock of seeing Magan was wearing off, and she knew she needed to get out of there, fast. *Run, you fool*, she told herself. *Contact your L-PRACG security. Send a Confidential-Whisper to Natch. Go.*

But she did none of these things. Instead, she followed Magan out the side door.

There was no sudden barrage of black code darts, no ambush, nothing but the London drizzle. Jara exhaled in relief as Magan Kai Lee led her around the back of the building to a partially roofed courtyard decked with wrought-iron tables and chairs. The analyst had spent many weary afternoons out here nursing a chai or nitro with her loose circle of friends. But now, whether because of the rain or the Defense and Wellness Council, the courtyard was empty. Magan took a seat at an unassuming table set with a pair of steaming nitro mugs. Jara followed suit.

"All right, so here we are," said the analyst. "Now what do you want?"

"I want to introduce you to some people," said Magan simply.

"What people?"

"The people who have been following Natch around and scouring your fiefcorp's records."

Jara could feel her shoulder blades clench and her jaw tighten, the primitive reflexes of fear and flight. She quickly activated a pair of bio/logic programs to soothe her nerves as a line of Defense and Wellness Council officers marched into the courtyard from the alleyway. There were thirteen in all, each bearing a demeanor that could only be described as nonchalant.

"Allow me to introduce you to Commanders Papizon and Ridgello," said Magan. He indicated a tall flamingo of a man whose eyes did not quite line up, and a hulking blond mercenary who might even be a match for Quell in hand-to-hand combat. "Papizon and Ridgello are in charge of the security detail that has been following Natch's every move for the past forty-eight hours."

Papizon bowed awkwardly in Jara's direction, as if performing the act for the first time. Ridgello made an obscure gesture with one hand, causing seven more phantoms to step out of the shadows. Two or three looked vaguely familiar, faces Jara had seen in passing in Shenandoah and not given a second thought. Ridgello waited for her to get a good, long look. Then he signaled again, and the spooks melted back into the mist.

Jara reached somewhere deep inside herself for a bravado she did not feel. She tilted her head at the remaining Council officers. "So I guess *these* idiots must be the ones scouring the fiefcorp records," she said.

A lithe woman with dark mahogany skin stepped forward in response and gave a perfunctory bow. "You might recognize the woman I have put in charge of this team," said Lieutenant Executive Lee.

Jara let out a gasp before she could stop herself. "The Blade."

"See, Magan, she *does* follow the Council drudge gossip," said Rey

Gonerev, seeming well pleased. Her voice was a wasp's sting. "It's an honor to finally meet you, Jara. I've read so much about you in the Council files that I feel like I know you . . . *intimately*." The slant on the word was unmistakable.

Jara felt a flush rising from her toes and diffusing across her entire body. She had heard rumors about sketchy channels on the Sigh selling customer data, but never quite believed them. How much did the Council know? And how much had they seen? There was nothing illegal about her frolics with Geronimo, of course, but the fact that someone might actually *know* about them felt as intrusive as any molestation.

Magan made a disdainful frown, clearly signaling to the Blade that she had crossed the line. Whether he was genuinely irritated, or if this was just part of their good cop/bad cop routine, Jara couldn't tell.

Rey Gonerev was just getting started. She marched up and down the row of Council officers, introducing each in turn. More than one seemed to be quivering slightly at the Blade's presence, or Magan's, or both. "Clarissa here has been itemizing every Vault credit Natch has spent over the last ten years," said Gonerev. "Refaru Gil Motivan is collecting every word he's ever spoken in public and every scrap of text he's ever posted on the Data Sea. William Teg has been keeping tabs on Serr Vigal, while Larakolia is in charge of analyzing your company's programs. . . ."

The flush in Jara's skin quickly turned to nausea. Police intimidation: it was a ritual as old as time, invented by the ancients with their primitive firearms and consecrated in a million crime dramas ever since. Jara felt like she could recite every line before it was uttered, but the familiarity did not stop her knees from shaking.

She didn't even hear what nefarious deeds the last few were up to. "Why are you showing me this?" she said quietly when the Council solicitor had finished her little presentation. "Am I supposed to be scared that you're following Natch around? Don't you think he already knows that?"

Magan gave the row of officers an almost imperceptible nod. One by one, the team disintegrated into the multivoid until just four members of the Council remained—Papizon, Ridgello, Rey Gonerev, and Magan Kai Lee.

"I'm showing you this to deliver a message," said Magan. His demeanor was almost polite, his hands folded on the table like an ordinary plebeian at teatime. "MultiReal is the Defense and Wellness Council's top priority. As long as Natch refuses to cooperate with us, the Surina/Natch MultiReal Fiefcorp is *my* top priority."

"I don't understand why you're hassling *us*," Jara said, pinching her temples in an effort to stanch the ache. "You want access to MultiReal? Go talk to Frederic and Petrucio Patel. I'm sure they'd be happy to sell you all the access you need."

Magan shook his head. "You know that the Patel Brothers are only licensees, Jara. Limited access. I suppose we could learn a lot from someone with master engineering privileges, like your friend Horvil. But what good would that do when Natch could lock us out of the program without notice? No, I'm afraid only Natch and Margaret Surina can give us what we need."

"Listen, I don't know who you think you're dealing with, but Natch is more than capable of st—"

"No," said Magan, cutting her off without raising his voice. "Don't be naive. Your fiefcorp master is canny and resourceful—I'll give him that. He caught us off guard the other day. But there are only seven of you. The Defense and Wellness Council has millions of officers at our beck and call. We have unlimited resources. *We will bury Natch.*"

"And those foolish enough to stand with him," added Gonerev. Unlike Magan, she appeared to be enjoying herself.

Again the slight disapproving grimace from the lieutenant executive. "Len Borda's agents are tailing Natch day and night," he said. "We are exploring every transaction your fiefcorp has ever done, every piece of code you've ever launched onto the Data Sea. This MultiReal exposition you are so diligently preparing for *will not happen.*"

The analyst slouched down in her chair, wishing she could slip between the cracks and disappear unnoticed. After everything Magan had revealed, why should it be a surprise that the Council knew about the MultiReal exposition? But it hadn't even been twenty-four hours since Natch came up with the idea, and as far as Jara knew, nobody had said a word about it to anyone outside the fiefcorp yet.

Jara looked to the steaming mugs on the table for relief. The drizzle had found its way under the awning to the side of her face, but it hadn't done much damage to the nitro yet. She reached for the closer mug and took a quick gulp, hoping that her beverage wasn't poisoned. *They ordered my nitro just the way I like it*, Jara thought with a shudder. *Extra dark, extra bitters.*

The Blade came close and crouched down until she was almost whispering in Jara's ear. Jara could have gotten lost in those long braids of ebony hair. "You don't think Natch is the *only* one Papizon and Ridgello are following, do you?" said Gonerev.

Commander Papizon merely stood there, squinting at the rain. Ridgello might have been a carven effigy.

She knew from watching the dramas that this was the point when she was supposed to crack. But somehow the thought of Council goons tailing her on the street helped Jara rally her courage. "This little act of yours is getting old," snapped the analyst. "If you were really so confident you could *bury Natch*, you wouldn't be sitting here playing these little games. You'd just go ahead and *do* it."

Again the insignificant raising of the lips on Magan's face. "And if *you* were so confident in Natch, you wouldn't be sitting here listening to us."

Jara said nothing. Rey Gonerev retreated to stand beside Papizon, her task done.

Magan rose from his seat and turned in profile to face the advancing clouds. Jara knew that even a lieutenant executive of the Defense and Wellness Council was not exempt from the dictates of the weather, but he seemed strangely untouched by the rain.

"What do you want from me?" asked Jara.

"I've studied your record very carefully," said the Council lieutenant. "I've seen the people you've worked for over the years; I've seen the quality and integrity of your work. You can't possibly be pleased with the direction Natch is steering this fiefcorp. Dirty tricks, sabotage, rumor, innuendo—this isn't *you*, Jara. I know what you really want: you want *out* of this miserable apprenticeship. You want to wipe the slate clean and strike out on your own.

"The Defense and Wellness Council can give you this.

"Do we want something from you in return? Of course. We want your cooperation. The more cooperation we get from you, the fewer public resources we have to waste, the quicker we can move on, and the easier it will be for Natch."

Magan turned and focused the full intensity of his glare on the fiefcorp analyst. It was not an unkind look, but rather a look full of hidden trapdoors and secret caches of information. In many ways, Lieutenant Executive Lee was Natch's antithesis: a man of hyperrationality, a man who scrupulously choreographed everything that happened in his presence.

"Jara, I can compensate you for any shares you lose. Not only that, but I can set you up with your own company. A proper company, one run in accordance with the laws of the Meme Cooperative. A company that can earn the number one slot on Primo's *honestly*, through hard work.

"Natch won't survive this, Jara. You can't change that. What you *can* change is whether you go down with him."

With that, Lieutenant Executive Magan Kai Lee gave a bow and strode off into the fog. He seemed small enough to be swept away by the rainstorm. Rey Gonerev, Ridgello, and Papizon followed seconds later, leaving Jara sitting alone in the courtyard with a mug of tepid nitro. It was only after several minutes of doleful reflection that Jara realized Magan had not actually asked her to do . . . anything.

(((9)))

Soccer was mainly an indoor sport in the Mid-Atlantic, especially during the wintertime. The regional L-PRACGs had a longstanding deal with the Environmental Control Board to accept the bulk of the season's snowfall in exchange for mild spring rains, and none of the politicians were willing to jeopardize that just to play soccer outdoors.

Still, finding an indoor field to use for practice and demonstration was more difficult than Natch had anticipated. The eastern seaboard was awash in soccer stadiums large and small and all sizes in between, but few of them had a secure MindSpace workbench on the premises. As luck would have it, Natch found one a short tube ride away in Harper. He strode on to the field with Quell, Horvil, and Benyamin close behind. Then he stood for a moment in the center of the field, hearing the roar of a crowd that was still nine days in the future. Excited fans, stupefied drudges, indignant Patels: he could hear them all.

Quell, meanwhile, was busy removing the tight metal collar from around his neck, which Natch supposed was only prudent for a game of soccer. He wondered if he should keep an eye out for any Council officers who might cite the Islander for failing to wear the uncomfortable contraption while in connectible territory. But Quell seemed unconcerned. He pinned a small, coin-shaped device to his lapel. Natch remembered seeing the device once before—a functional replacement for the connectible collar, almost certainly illegal. Natch shrugged. They were all here in the flesh this morning, so there were no multi projections for the Islander to miss. Besides, why should Natch care if Quell chose to skirt stupid laws?

The Islander grabbed a ball from the cart and crouched in front of the Harper Bulldogs' net like a professional goalie. "Okay, Benyamin," he said. "Since you got the short end of the stick last time we tried this,

I'll let you be on the winning side." He tossed the ball underhanded at the younger apprentice, who had positioned himself for a penalty kick. "Possibilities loaded up?"

"Yeah," said Ben, a wicked gleam in his eye. "All ready to go."

"Then let's see what you've got."

The two fiefcorpers squared off for a moment. Ben spun the ball in his hands like a gyroscope while Quell gave him a fierce stare. Then suddenly, Benyamin let the black-and-white sphere drop and lashed out with his right foot. The ball rocketed through Quell's arms and hit the net with a solid *whuff*.

"Good shot!" shouted Horvil from a bench on the sidelines.

Quell, undeterred, flipped his long pale ponytail over one shoulder and tossed the ball back onto the field.

Natch stood at midfield watching like a dispassionate referee as Benyamin nailed shot after shot through the Islander's hands. Inept kicks, clumsy kicks, sophomoric head butts, all sailed effortlessly into the goal despite Quell's best efforts. Ben flushed with satisfaction. The Islander seemed to be enjoying himself too, in spite of the humiliation.

After a dozen such plays, the Islander finally tucked the ball in the crook of his elbow and stepped out from the net. "So that's pretty much the same demonstration we did before," said Quell. "A collaborative MultiReal process. Benyamin activates the Possibilities program, and we keep replaying the scene over and over again in our heads until Ben finds a scenario that's acceptable. He closes the choice cycle, outputs that 'reality' to his motor system, and it happens." Quell touched a massive finger to his temple. "The alternate memories up *here* get erased instantly, and the guy who isn't using MultiReal—in this case, me—never even realizes what's happening. Now here's where things start getting interesting."

The Islander threw the globe back to Benyamin. Ben palmed the soccer ball in his hands and prepared to score yet another goal. He pulled back his foot, let the ball slip through his fingers—

And then both Quell and Benyamin slumped to the ground, exhausted. Ben barely had the strength to keep his head from slamming into the grass. Meanwhile, the ball rebounded off Ben's shin and went rolling toward the sidelines.

"What happened?" said Natch.

"That time," said Quell, panting, "we were *both* using MultiReal."

Horvil's eyes did a full clockwise circuit as he sifted through the data points. "Okay, so you've got two MultiReal users working at cross-purposes," he said. "Benyamin keeps creating scenarios where he scores a goal. But as soon as he does, Quell takes *that* scenario and runs it over and over again until he blocks the kick. You get . . ." The engineer's jaw rocked back and forth in confusion as he tried to reconcile the equations in his head with the bizarre performance he had just witnessed.

"You get exhaustion," moaned Ben, still sprawled on the field trying to catch his breath.

"They're at an impasse," said Natch. "An infinite loop, until someone gives up . . . or his OCHREs run out."

Horvil pulled his cousin to his feet and gave him a vigorous *thwack* between the shoulder blades. "Eh, you'll be okay," said the engineer. "Ready to take on the Harper Bulldogs in no time. So what did it *feel* like?"

Benyamin bobbled his head and cracked his neck. Horvil's good-natured clap on the back actually seemed to have helped him recover his equilibrium. "Pretty much like you'd expect. Just the same thing over and over. And *over* and *over* and *over* . . ."

"How many times?" said Natch.

"I dunno. You lose track. Felt like hundreds, maybe even thousands. It's like an enormous grid that you scroll through in your head, but you have to expend this tiny bit of *effort* for every move. Doesn't seem that bad at first, but it adds up. I couldn't take it anymore. Finally just gave up and cut the whole process off."

Quell did not bother to pick himself up off the grass, but simply lay there with his head propped up on one elbow. He had to be packing at least twice as much mass as Ben, and yet he seemed just as winded. "So here's our challenge," he said. "You've seen two instances of Multi-Real running at the same time. But at our exposition, we're going to have *twenty-three*."

Horvil's head slumped to his chest. "Oooh," he moaned.

Natch stood with his arms folded. "Don't tell me that it never occurred to Margaret in the last sixteen years that something like this might happen."

"Of course it occurred to her," replied Quell calmly.

"And it's been tested?"

"Sure, it's been tested . . . just not with twenty-three people at the same time. Listen, Natch, don't get ahead of yourself. Let me show you the next demo. Horvil, take your programming bars over to the work-bench, go pull up the common tools library. . . ." A long and tortured series of mathematical formulas sprayed from his lips. Horvil soaked it all up, nodded, then dashed through a door in the stands to find the bio/logic workbench.

Natch paced slowly up and down the sidelines, kicking at the grass with one foot as they waited for Horvil to complete the program modifi-cations. He had been in possession of MultiReal for a month now, and yet he still knew so little about it. The most powerful work of bio/logics ever created, the pinnacle achievement of the Surinas. But there were still basic concepts about MultiReal he did not understand and simple questions he could not answer. Even Horvil had knowledge gaps large enough to pilot an OrbiCo space freighter through. Natch silently cursed Len Borda and Magan Kai Lee for keeping him on the defensive for the past few weeks, for keeping him on the run and away from MindSpace.

Ten minutes later, the engineer emerged from the bowels of the stadium brandishing his programming bar satchel like a trophy.

Quell arose and brushed himself off, then reached for the soccer ball that had rolled to a stop near his feet. "Again," he said, tossing the ball Benyamin's way.

The young apprentice did a few quick stretches, trying to psyche himself up, unsure whether to be prepared for victory or defeat. He wound up for the kick—

And found each kick thwarted by Quell's goaltending, time and time again.

"Something's . . . strange," said Ben, finally conceding defeat. "I'm using MultiReal, just like before—but it just *stops* at some point. It leaves me hanging there in midloop."

"Limited choice cycles!" cried Horvil, rushing onto the field before Quell could utter a single syllable. "I think I get this now. We put a limit on the number of reality loops Ben can do at one time—but *your* version of MultiReal still has no limits."

The Islander nodded. He strolled back to the cart with the ball clutched in one palm like another man might clutch an apple, then deposited it gently on the top of the stack. Apparently the demonstration was over.

"So why would anyone buy a MultiReal program with limited choice cycles?" complained Benyamin. "It's useless. If someone else can always trump you—"

"Not always," interrupted Horvil. "The other guy would only win if he's got MultiReal activated too—and if he's not running a limited version like yours. I suppose if you're both running limited versions, the person with the most choice cycles wins."

Natch made his way to the bleachers and gripped the cold metal railing with trembling fists. One of his last conversations with Margaret began to unroll in his mind, and for a moment he felt like he was back in Andra Pradesh watching the bodhisattva prepare for one of her dull presentations.

It had been an offhanded statement of Margaret's: *Frederic and Petrucio have a limited license. They can release MultiReal products, but they will be subordinate to yours.*

Natch, puzzled: *Subordinate how?*

The Patel products will have a limited number of choice cycles, Margaret had explained, *whereas yours will be infinite.*

He had nearly forgotten about that snippet of dialogue, given that it had taken place during an argument about how the bodhisattva had lied to him. Only now did he understand what had transpired there. Natch seethed. This was good news, to be sure—but how many more of these moments would he have to endure? How many elements of this MultiReal affair would become clear only weeks or months after the fact?

"So that's how Margaret decided to resolve conflicts among the MultiReal licensees," he said.

"Margaret explored a lot of different ways to deal with these conflicts," said Quell. "She spent years, but never came to any definite conclusions." The Islander walked to the sidelines and found a seat on the bench normally reserved for the visiting team. "Actually, that's not quite the right way to put it. Margaret came to the conclusion that she *shouldn't* come to any definite conclusions."

Ben frowned. "What does *that* mean?"

"That means she wanted to keep the options open. Give the owners and licensees every possible scenario, and let them sort it out for themselves. Margaret thought there might be different flavors of MultiReal available from different resellers. Maybe each company would come up with its own à la carte pricing. So she built every possible solution she could think of into the program and made it easy for an engineer to flip them on and off." The Islander threw one arm over the shoulder of the chief engineer, who had just planted his sizable ass on the bench. "Horvil's already demonstrated how easy it is to select the options. The *hard* part is deciding which ones to choose."

The engineer sat pensively, not speaking for a moment. "This exposition is going to be a nightmare unless we make some decisions before those lottery winners hit the field," he put in finally.

"Then why aren't we consulting Margaret?" asked Ben, ever ready to pin words on the silent questions in everyone else's mind. "She already knows all the pros and cons. She's been working on this for sixteen years. Why don't we ask her for advice?"

Horvil turned to Natch. He wanted to know the answer to this question too.

"I've tried to contact her," said the fiefcorp master with a frown. "She won't answer. Won't accept my multi requests. She's just sitting there on top of that bloody Revelation Spire, and she won't come down."

"Well, *somebody* has to be talking to her," continued Benyamin. "Quell? Don't tell me *you* haven't seen Margaret since the demo."

The Islander was busy removing his coin-shaped apparatus and replacing the burdensome collar around his neck. At Ben's question, his gaze instantly slid inward to some troublesome emotional vista. "Yeah, I've seen her," he mumbled. "A few times. She's . . . not doing well. You're not going to get a lot of help from Margaret."

"What's wrong with her?" asked Horvil.

Quell stood and shifted from one foot to the other, then back again. "She's ill," he said laconically.

Natch shook his head. "It's not Margaret's problem anymore," he said. "That's why I hired Merri and Jara, to work on these kinds of policy questions. *You* three need to concentrate on getting all those bugs ironed out so Possibilities doesn't choke in front of a billion people."

"This should be easier than last time though, right?" said Ben. "We had MultiReal interacting with hundreds of millions of people in that auditorium. This time it's only twenty-three."

"You're forgetting something," replied Horvil with a reprimanding finger wag. "At the demo, we really just did five hundred million one-on-one interactions in a row. Nothing complex about that. Heck, it was all rigged off a mathematical progression, so Natch didn't even have to *think* about it. But next week at the exposition, we could have twenty-three conflicting realities to work out. That's twenty-three times as bad—no, twenty-three times *exponentially* as bad."

Natch shrugged, already halfway to the door that would lead them back to the Harper tube station. He wasn't worried. If there was any bio/logic engineer in the world capable of hunting down such a challenge, it was Horvil. With nine days to go, his old hivemate would have twenty-three-way MultiReal conflicts mounted and stuffed on his mantel by the time the exposition was under way.

The fiefcorp master turned to make sure the others were following him and was confronted by the odd sight of Benyamin wriggling his arms and legs like a man trying to bring back the circulation. "What's with you?" he said.

Ben snapped his head up, embarrassed. "Sorry, Natch. Those MultiReal choice cycles can be exhausting—but it is such an incredible *rush*."

(((I O)))

Two days passed with a cyclone of activity. Impromptu meetings swept across the horizon and threw previously settled decisions up in the air again. Fiefcorpers breezed into Natch's apartment with no advance notice at all hours of the night, and there were no apologies offered or expected.

Jara couldn't sleep. Every time she lay in bed and felt herself sliding under, she would come thrashing awake with Natch's name on her lips and Magan Kai Lee's words buzzing in her ears:

As long as Natch refuses to cooperate with us, the Surina/Natch Multi-Real Fiefcorp is my top priority.

We are exploring every transaction your fiefcorp has ever done, every piece of code you've ever launched onto the Data Sea. This MultiReal exposition you are so diligently preparing for will not happen.

We will bury Natch.

Shouldn't she have warned Natch by now that the Defense and Wellness Council was still gunning for him? Wasn't that her duty as a fiefcorp apprentice? Then again, certainly this would not be news to Natch. He might have achieved a temporary triumph over the Council, but the entrepreneur knew better than to declare victory so soon. What more could Jara really tell him?

The internal argument raged as the night wore on. She composed a dozen messages to the fiefcorp master, discarded them, started again. The script for the MultiReal exposition, meanwhile, sat in a fetal state, shapeless and unformed.

Finally, at half past six, the analyst kicked off her blankets and summoned a view of the building's exterior on the viewscreen. She half expected to find a team of Defense and Wellness Council officers staring back at her taking notes. There were Council officers out there, all right, but they were far below, strolling placidly through the London mist along with everyone else. Was this a message in and of itself?

Jara collapsed back into her warren of pillows and tuned the viewscreen to the latest John Ridglee.

THE BOY WHO COULD DO NO WRONG

If the Prime Committee gives out civilian medals for bravery, then I propose somebody nominate Natch.

How convenient, thought Jara, stubbornly clinging to her midnight malaise. *We issue a press release, and all the drudges who hate Natch suddenly get amnesia.* She continued reading:

After Len Borda's aggressive posturing of late, the Surina/Natch Fiefcorp's announcement of a MultiReal exposition is not only brilliant, it's courageous. It puts Natch and his apprentices out in the open when a lesser man would seek the shadows. It's a bold and clear statement to the Defense and Wellness Council: we are not afraid of you.

And the symbolism of twenty-three lucky lottery winners playing MultiReal soccer shouldn't be lost on anyone either. Let's hope the twenty-three members of the Prime Committee are watching these soccer players carefully.

Sen Sivv Sor, meanwhile, was covering another promising development: the burgeoning membership of a creed called Libertas. The organization had been skulking around the periphery of the libertarian movement for years. But suddenly, with the election of Khann Frejohr as speaker of the Congress of L-PRACGs, the membership ranks of Creed Libertas were exploding. And the match that had set off the powder keg was nothing less than Magan Kai Lee's raid on Natch's apartment. In the past few days alone, the creed had pledged another fifteen to twenty million devotees.

There was plenty more, but Jara was suddenly interrupted by a multi request. Horvil.

She leapt out of bed, darted into the breakfast nook with the speed of a panther, and began a frenzied effort to straighten the countertop. *What are you doing?* the analyst scolded herself. *It's just Horvil.* She abandoned the breakfast nook to its sloppery ten seconds later and accepted Horvil's multi request. It had to be pretty important for the engineer to be up this early in the morning.

Horvil sidled in from the foyer, managing to look both furtive and transparent at the same time. His left hand was clenched tightly in his vest pocket, while his right nervously raked through rows of black hair. "I need to talk to you about something," he said.

Oh no, thought Jara, suddenly realizing why she had reacted the way she did. This was the first time the two of them had been alone since that awkward scene in the Center for Historic Appreciation. *All I care about is not losing you*, Horvil had told her as they crouched between the toes of the Sheldon Surina statue, waiting for their doom at the hands of the Defense and Wellness Council.

Jara looked in that chubby face now and auditioned a series of emotions—embarrassment, unease, gratification, reticence—but none of them seemed to fit the part. Finally she sat down in an easy chair and braced herself for whatever Horvil might have to say. "What is it?" she managed finally.

Horvil threw himself down on the couch opposite her and exhaled loudly from one side of his mouth. "It's—it's about Benyamin."

The analyst blinked rapidly in surprise. "Benyamin?"

"He's being blackmailed."

It took Jara a few seconds to refocus her mental lenses. Who could possibly be blackmailing Ben? The answer leapt into her mind after a moment's study. "That woman at Berilla's assembly-line shop. The one who manages the programming floor."

Horvil nodded ruefully. "Greth Tar Griveth," he said. "She's asking for credits. *Lots* of credits."

"Just to keep things quiet from your Aunt Berilla? This is ridiculous, Horv. After all that's happened in the past month, can't Ben just *tell* his mother he's hired her shop to do the assembly-line work on MultiReal? It's not like we won't pay her. Would she really shut down the programming floor?"

"You don't know her," replied the engineer with a sad shake of the head. "Berilla *hates* Natch. She's trying to mobilize that whole creed of hers to pass these official statements condemning him. If she finds out one of her shops is doing barwork for our fiefcorp—fuck yeah, she'll shut down the programming floor. In a heartbeat."

Jara made a dismissive gesture with the flick of a wrist. "Why are you even bothering me with this?" she said. "There's a thousand good assembly-line shops out there. Ben really shouldn't be contracting his mother's company anyway. Tell Ben to go solicit some competitive bids. He's still got a few days before we need to pass off the final templates. They're just doing low-level work right now. That should be plenty of time."

"He's tried. He put together three new deals, but they all fell through."

"Why?"

"Nobody's saying." Horvil's face devolved from melancholy to fullfledged misery. "The assembly-line managers just tell him that they're already running at capacity. But I think they're scared. Every time Ben shows up somewhere to talk business, a squad of Meme Cooperative officials shows up the next day and starts checking tax records. The word's gotten out."

Jara groaned. "Magan Kai Lee." She felt nervous even saying the lieutenant executive's name out loud, as if those words were a talisman to release some infernal warrior from imprisonment. Magan had so *many* arcane weapons at his disposal—taxes, regulations, laws, policies—and Natch had so many weaknesses. It just didn't seem fair. "So what's Greth asking for that's so ridiculous?" said Jara.

Horvil listed a number that ventured past the ludicrous into the realm of the obscene. The analyst whistled. "I don't know if Natch would fork over that many credits," said the engineer. "That's way too much. Besides, it's too big of a number for Ben to transfer without Aunt Berilla getting wind of it. Someone's bound to notice. Especially with the Council and the drudges hanging over everyone's shoulders."

Jara rapped her knuckles hard against the chair's nailhead trim. "Come on, Horvil, this Greth woman can't be *that* unreasonable. She's got to see that if she keeps behaving like this, she'll kill the goose that lays the golden eggs."

"That's the whole thing," said Horvil, slumping to a spine-cracking position in the couch. "Greth's *not* being reasonable. Either she's a loose cannon or she's just not very bright. She doesn't care about killing the goose that lays the golden eggs—she wants one *big* egg instead."

Jara sighed. She hated to admit it, but paying up was the only solution that made sense. Natch would authorize the bribe without thinking twice and find a way to carve it out of the woman's flesh later. That was simply his way of doing things.

The analyst was feeling the preliminary sorties of a massive headache and fired up Deuteron's Anodyne 88. "So what does Natch have to say about all this?"

Horvil flapped his lips in irritation. "Benyamin's afraid to tell him," he said, letting his head slump onto the back of the couch. "I kind of agree. Relying on that woman in the first place was a major fuck-up, and Ben knows it. He's convinced that Natch will kick him out of the fiefcorp for this. So I . . . I told him—"

"You told him you'd talk to me."

The engineer made a peculiar half-nod without actually taking his neck off the back of the couch. "You're the—the most level-headed one in the fiefcorp. You always keep your wits in these situations. I told Ben you'd know what to do."

Jara folded her arms over her chest and frowned. "If I'm the level-headed one," she grumbled, "then this fiefcorp is in bigger trouble than I thought." *Does Horvil have any idea how much time I've spent on the Sigh with that idiot Geronimo? Does he have any idea that Magan Kai Lee is recruiting me to betray Natch, and I haven't said no yet?*

"Listen, Jara," continued Horvil, "Ben *trusts* you. We all trust you. I mean, if it wasn't for you, I wouldn't be able to—"

Jara could sense a clumsy segue in the making, and she made a slicing gesture to cut him off. "Okay, fine," she sighed. "It's probably better not to pester Natch with this crap anyway. Here's what you tell Ben. Have him transfer a piece of the money from *our* accounts, the fiefcorp accounts. We've got it right now, and if we use the company money it won't get on your aunt's radar. Have him tell Greth Tar Griveth that this is all he could get on such short notice—but if she'll wait until after the exposition, he'll give her the rest *plus* an additional twenty percent."

Horvil gasped. *"Twenty percent?* I could buy a hoverbird with that additional twenty percent."

"It doesn't matter. She won't get it. Greth's leverage evaporates after the MultiReal exposition."

The engineer gave a judicious nod and rubbed his nose. "It sounds reasonable coming from you," he said, "but what if Greth doesn't buy it? She's going to suspect that Ben won't follow through."

"Not if she thinks this is all coming from Benyamin's head," replied the analyst. "No offense, Horv, but your cousin is kind of naive. Ben can sell it to Greth if *he* really thinks we're going to pay her after the exposition. Just tell him we don't have all that cash at the moment, and it's going to take a while to get it."

Horvil stood up from the chair, looking relieved and not a little sheepish. "Thanks, Jara," he said. "I think you might have saved Ben's job."

Jara smiled wanly and waved a farewell at Horvil before he disappeared. She felt that nothing short of an industrial decontamination chamber could wash away the stench of corruption oozing from her pores. She remembered Natch's words to her just last month. *Everyone who invests in bio/logics knows what's going on. Things like this happen all the time. Do you think the Patel Brothers got to the top without getting their hands dirty? Or Len Borda?*

Shaking her head, Jara arose and turned to take refuge in the bedroom. Suddenly she realized the window behind her was still tuned to a drudge clipping she had read the other day. It was a piece by one of the gossip drudges who made even Kristella Krodor seem like a paragon of substance. Jara looked at the headline and blushed furiously, realizing that Horvil must have seen it the whole time. If this ever got back to Natch, she didn't know how she could live with herself.

IS IT LOVE OR INFATUATION?
Our Foolproof Guide to Figuring Out How He Feels

• • •

After stepping off the multi tile, Horvil tried to bury his warped emotions in MindSpace, using his bio/logic programming bars as shovel.

His arms whirled in MindSpace, making and breaking data connections at blinding speed. Every few seconds, he would slip a bio/logic programming bar back into his satchel and slide another out to replace it with a single uninterrupted motion. Finally he chugged to a halt.

The engineer hitched back his thumb to survey the massive MultiReal castle before him. Horvil nodded and incremented the version number a fraction of a point. *It's ready*, he told himself. *But are you sure you want to do this?* He had been waiting for days to put the finishing touches on the latest iteration of Possibilities so he could conduct this experiment, but now he didn't feel so confident. Had anyone ever tried to run MultiReal nonstop to see what would happen? What if he got caught in some kind of unending choice cycle? Possibilities wasn't a typical bio/logic program that you could run through Dr. Plugenpatch to weed out the fatal errors.

Admit it, Horv. This shit is dangerous.

Then Jara's words came floating to the top of his consciousness. *If I'm the level-headed one, then this fiefcorp is in bigger trouble than I thought.* He couldn't keep going to Jara every time he faced a tough decision; he'd never get everything done in time for the exposition. Horvil flipped off MindSpace, activated Possibilities 0.812, and hustled out of the apartment before he could change his mind.

The first decision point came on the building's front steps. A large puddle of rainwater sat right at the intersection of stair and street; Horvil had been sloshing through it for days. But he could avoid soaking his shoes altogether if he could only vault over the side railing and land on that dry patch about a meter away—

Flash.

Horvil's consciousness slipped into a state of suspended animation as soon as he activated Possibilities. And then there was an indescribable *flash*, a mental widening of view. The image of himself hurdling onto the dry spot of concrete hung in his mind like a bead on a string, in limbo. Some hidden inner sense showed him a line of alternate realities that stretched out to eternity in each direction, Horvils leaping and bounding at every conceivable angle. He felt himself scrolling among them, looking for a better possibility, a future in which—

Flash.

—Horvil sprang over the railing and made an acrobatic landing just beyond the puddle of rainwater.

The fiefcorp engineer paused and ran an arm across his sweating forehead. He had barely made it out of the building, and already he felt giddy. *Not too late to turn back*, Horvil told himself.

He stood and thought for a moment. *Fuck that.* Then the engineer hooked a right and headed toward Centurion Market Square, a place that promised any number of interesting experiments.

Turned out the feeling was intoxicating, a high unlike any he had ever felt. Horvil spent two hours in the West London tube station alone, hopping on and off the trains. He made graceful sashays to avoid jostling into passersby. He made improbable darts and zips to catch the last free seat on the train. And in one ridiculous act of chutzpah, Horvil even made a flying leap across the tracks right in front of a speeding tube train. Possibilities made it all seem so easy.

But such appearances could be deceptive. Each contingency the program laid out was the product of Horvil's own probability engine, the old ROD they had hastily tacked on to the program like a postscript. And Horvil found out the hard way that his probability engine was not omniscient. He was making another preposterous leap over a metal railing when his hand lost its grip and he found himself tumbling head-first down a flight of stairs. Luckily the engineer was able to activate MultiReal again several times on the way down, and he came out of the tumble unbruised. When he climbed back up the stairs to investigate, Horvil noticed that the railing was slick with rainwater and almost completely covered in shadow. *Of course*, he thought. *MultiReal can only make calculations using the factors you give it. If you can't see that the railing's wet, MultiReal won't factor it in.* He thought back to his crazy leap across the tube tracks a few minutes ago. What if the train had suddenly picked up speed after he jumped? What if there had been a wire running across the gap that he hadn't been able to see? He shuddered.

And then dashed back down the stairs in search of more adventure.

Horvil had never had the time to just mess around with multiple realities before. When he was on deadline, every activation had a narrow and targeted purpose, to test this or that modification. Even when he wasn't on deadline, every activation was a calculated move to understand the product better. There was never any opportunity to gleefully splash in the program like a child in a wading pool. *Has it really only been a month since I first laid eyes on this thing?* he thought.

After a few hours, Horvil began to feel pangs of hunger, which were never that far away to begin with. He was rounding Centurion Market Square when he spotted a row of street vendors selling exotic foods. Horvil walked up to one at random and found an appetizing enough plate of rice and lentils. The proprietress, a girl scarcely old enough to qualify for an L-PRACG vending license, scanned the engineer up and down with the eye of a trained haggler. Then Horvil had a sudden inspiration.

Flash.

"How much?" he asked the girl.

"Thirty-two," she replied.

Flash.

"How much?" said Horvil.

"Thirty-two."

Flash.

"How much?"

"Thirty-two."

The exchange was not a vocal one. Instead it felt like a mighty abacus of alternate realities suspended in time. Horvil's questions, phrased in an infinite number of different inflections and intonations, served as the x-axis; the girl's responses, straight from her own unwitting subconscious, became the y-axis. Absurd and improbable realities branched off in new directions, realities where Horvil said something else entirely or gave her a rude gesture or flapped his arms like a madman. It was all one vast grid that stretched to eternity in every direction until it encompassed every action and response possible.

And Horvil was traversing that grid one node at a time, expending a small amount of willpower with each hop. Even in this state of null consciousness, the possibilities were sliding by as quickly as cards in a shuffled deck. Horvil could get a taste of each one as he passed, as if he were performing the same interaction over and over again; but at the same time, the memory of each alternate reality vanished almost as soon as Horvil passed it.

Finally, the engineer found the junction he was looking for.

Flash.

"How much?" said Horvil, back in real time.

"Thirty," replied the girl.

The engineer stuttered something unintelligible, paid the girl an even forty credits, and grabbed the plate she offered him. He felt dizzy. Aside from the slight crease of confusion on her forehead, she seemed completely ignorant of what had just transpired.

A conversation replayed itself in Horvil's head. Quell, standing on home plate of a SeeNaRee baseball diamond, explaining why Benyamin had such a hard time catching his pop flies. *For every missed catch, there were dozens of alternate reality scenarios played out inside our minds before they ever actually "happened." The whole sequence looped over and over again—dozens of my possible swings mapped out against dozens of possible catches—dozens of choice cycles—until I found a result I liked.*

Ben, sullen, defiant: *But I don't remember any of that happening.*

No. You wouldn't. Not without MultiReal.

The girl was now giving Horvil a strange look, and the engineer realized he hadn't moved since their transaction was completed. Horvil made an exaggerated smile, shoveled down a few spoonfuls of the gloppy mixture, and hustled away.

He should have realized this all along. If MultiReal worked on *physical* interactions—if it could cause an outfielder to live out that improbable reality where he dropped the ball every time—why wouldn't the same thing work on *mental* interactions? It made perfect sense. MultiReal trapped cognitive processes and applied computing logic to them before the body translated them into concrete action. And what was concrete action if not a cognitive process made flesh? Every word, every emotion, every breath you took was the product of a decision—and decisions could be altered.

Certainly if you try the same transaction a thousand times, thought Horvil, *you'll catch a time when the merchant sizes you up a different way and charges a lower price.*

He discarded the tepid plate of mush a few blocks away.

Later, Horvil wondered if that was the precise moment when the experience of constant Possibilities turned into a nightmare.

He continued to meander around London for hours, but the high was gone. In its place he felt the gambler's compulsion to ratchet things up further, to extend his lucky streak Just One More Time. He found life unspooling behind a constant two-second mental buffer as he analyzed and reanalyzed the movements of those around him. It became a craving, a hunger: the desire to avoid stepping on that broken piece of pavement, to dodge insects like bullets, to find the sweet spot in every crowd where the wind's bite wasn't quite so sharp.

Horvil finally staggered back to his apartment building many hours later and shut off Possibilities. His head felt like a weather-beaten old shoe, and his muscles felt like they had been stretched on a rack. Zipping through all those choice cycles did indeed take its toll after a while. On the way up, Horvil purposefully stomped through the rainwater puddle at the bottom of the steps. The moisture seeping through his socks felt good.

He stumbled into his apartment, flopped down onto the bed. He could barely move. Then he waved his hand at the nearest window and summoned the article he had been putting off reading all afternoon.

IS IT LOVE OR INFATUATION?
Our Foolproof Guide to Figuring Out How He Feels

$(((\mid \; \mid)))$

Fractal patterns pirouetted across the ceiling over Natch with schizo-
phrenic logic, darting this way and then that, expanding and then contracting. The colors spanned the entire rainbow and ventured briefly
outside the bounds of the visible spectrum.

"Too deep," said a familiar voice. Quell? "Can't see a fucking thing."

"Maybe you're just not used to looking at the mind of a genius."

"Quiet, Horvil."

Gradually Natch's senses reasserted themselves, and he began to
comprehend his surroundings once more. *This is my apartment. That's
my ceiling. The cushion underneath me is my couch. And the thing in my hand
is—is—*Natch looked sideways to find an unfamiliar object creeping
through the fingers of his clenched fist. It was something soft, something paper-thin and feather-light. He could feel his mind's engine
turning over but not catching.

A hand gently pressed his head back onto the couch. "You need to
relax," said a voice he recognized as Serr Vigal's. "We're going to read-
just the OCHRE probe and pull back the focus. Are you sure you don't
want to be sedated for this?"

"No," said the entrepreneur at once. "Absolutely not."

"It's gonna feel *weirrrrd*," warned the engineer in a child's singsong
voice.

"Try living with black code in your veins for a month," growled
Natch. The identity of the thing in his hand was dancing just beyond
the tip of his tongue. . . .

Vigal emitted an exasperated sigh. "Please, Horvil, can we put the
sarcastic remarks on hiatus for a few minutes? Quell's in enough of a
hurry as it is."

The Islander made some kind of phlegmy noise that might have been either an expression of amusement or one of dismissal. "Andra Pradesh'll still be standing in another few hours," he said. His face and bleached ponytail came into view directly over the fiefcorp master's head. He made some signal in the direction of the office. "Okay, Natch, hold on, you're about to feel a—"

Natch finally realized that the thing dribbling through his fingers was a crushed daisy from the garden. Then everything blanked out.

• • •

Time ceased to exist.

The feeling wasn't much different from the mental caesura of multivoid. Natch's senses had not diminished, but he could find no order in them. A flurry of lights, a jumble of glottal sounds, a softness pressing against his back—but what did it all *mean*? Patterned noise. Raw electrical activity without context.

Natch could not tell if he had lain there for two minutes or two years when full consciousness snapped back with the suddenness of a cartridge being loaded into a gun.

He sat up and took a swig from the water bottle on the table. Natch could feel a little bit of normalcy returning with every drop. He summoned a mental calendar and verified that he had indeed slid back into the normal groove of elapsing time. It was January 1, New Year's Day, and in forty-eight hours the fiefcorp would be announcing the winners of the MultiReal lottery. Five days after that was the exposition itself. He glanced at the ceiling, at the holographic fractal patterns that had been tormenting him, and realized he was looking at the standard OCHRE schematic of the human brain.

Vigal, Horvil, and Quell occupied three corners of the room, looking solemn and exhausted. It didn't escape Natch's attention that the Shenandoah sun was at a much different place in the sky than it had been before the probe began.

"Well?" asked Natch, brimming with impatience.

"We didn't find your black code," said Horvil hesitantly. All traces of the engineer's levity had slipped away while Natch was off in the netherworld of the OCHRE probe. "But—"

"But what?"

Horvil and Vigal's eyes swung instantly toward each other as if attracted by magnetic force. Quell folded his arms across his chest in consternation and turned to face the wall. "We found MultiReal," said Vigal under his breath.

"MultiReal? In my *head*?"

"Yes. It was . . . everywhere. All over your neural system."

"Not the whole program," said Horvil quickly. "Just bits and pieces. But they're definitely bits and pieces of MultiReal. I think I saw one of those structures in Possibilities just the other day."

"How do you know it's the same thing?" said Natch, delicately probing his skull with both hands as if it were a precious vase he might crack.

"We took a few samples from your head and plunked 'em into MindSpace. Then we did a side-by-side comparison with some of the structures from Possibilities. An exact match."

Natch could feel his hands trembling. "Show me."

They all walked into Natch's office and stood next to the workbench, over which Possibilities floated in a translucent bubble. The program looked ridiculous crammed in such a small space. "There," said his old hivemate. "Look at that right there." He dipped the end of a bio/logic programming bar into MindSpace, causing a beam of light to sweep across the bubble. Masses of MultiReal code turned transparent as the beam hit them. The light stopped on a yellow-and-black-striped module that looked like a mutant insect of some kind. A yellow jacket, maybe. "Now here's a copy of the same thing in your neural system. . . ." With a flick of the wrist, Horvil switched the display to a small chunk of Natch's OCHRE schematic. The resemblance was unmistakable.

The entrepreneur studied the two blocks of programming logic carefully. He switched back and forth several times. Horvil and Vigal had been correct; the chances of such a structure appearing in two disparate programs by accident were dangerously close to nil.

"So what is it?" asked Natch.

Vigal shrugged. "We're not entirely sure," he said. "It's a pretty obscure subroutine, buried quite a ways beneath the surface of the program. We can't seem to get inside. It's locked up somehow. I'm guessing this is just a library of logarithmic functions. I don't think it does anything important—Horvil just happened to recognize it, that's all."

"But if Horvil recognized *this* subroutine, there might be hundreds more in there that he *didn't*."

"I think the question we need to ask is how long that yellow jacket's been in your head," said a frustrated Horvil. "Was it there before those goons hit you with black code? Did it come from the black code darts? Or did it show up later?"

Natch noticed that he hadn't heard a peep from the Islander since he had woken up. He turned his focus on Quell, wishing he had a function that could see through people as easily as code. The Islander had removed himself to the doorway, where he was staring at the yellow jacket with arms folded and eyebrows furrowed.

Natch eyed him with sudden suspicion. "Is there anything you want to tell me?" he snarled.

Quell emitted a gruff *tssk* and shook his head. "Like what?"

"Were *you* behind that group in the black robes? Did you attack me in that alleyway and put MultiReal in my system?"

The Islander burst into laughter. "Don't be ridiculous! Why would I go to all that trouble when I could plug you right here in your apartment? And why would I do something like that in the first place?"

The fiefcorp master did not back down. "Margaret said the Patels sold out to the Defense and Wellness Council." He aimed one accusatory finger at the Islander. "Maybe you did too."

Quell clenched his fists and lowered them to his sides. All traces of humor were swept aside by a red rage swirling in his eyes. "You think I'm working for Len Borda?" he growled. "*Me* working for Len Borda." The Islander flexed his biceps again and studied Natch as if trying to determine the best way to eviscerate him. Horvil and Vigal backed slowly to opposite sides of the room, nervous, unsure what to do.

But the moment was brief. Quell soon bottled up his fury and stuck his hands in his pockets. "Do you want to know how my father died, Natch?" he said, his voice simmering down to a mumble. "The Council shot him. *Len Borda's* people shot him. The war of '34, skirmishes near Manila. I watched my father fall facedown in the sand with a pair of black code darts poking through his eyeball. Couldn't even—couldn't even get his *connectible collar* off before the Null Current took him." Quell let loose a few snorts, his thoughts directed inward. "I know you're under a lot of stress right now, Natch. But if you ever suggest I'm on the Council's payroll again, I'll crush your fucking windpipe."

Natch lowered his chin to his chest, conceding the argument. He still knew much too little about the Islander for his comfort, but he felt confident now that Quell was not working for Borda. Besides, the Islander had had ample opportunity to plant Natch with black code, or even slit his throat.

But if Quell hadn't put that yellow jacket inside him, then who had? Outside of the fiefcorp, the only ones who had access to Multi-Real were Quell, Margaret Surina, and the Patels. Pierre Loget had briefly been involved with the project before Frederic and Petrucio, but Margaret hadn't made it clear whether he had even actually *seen* the code. Still, why would Loget ambush him in the street like that? Or Margaret, for that matter? The Patels had plenty of motive, but Petrucio had disclaimed any knowledge of a black code attack while under the Objectivv truth-telling oath. That left Frederic Patel—though Natch's gut told him that an ambush wasn't quite Frederic's style.

"So what the fuck is going on?" said Natch, throwing his hands up at the ceiling.

More uneasy silence.

"All right," grunted the fiefcorp master after a few moments. "I'm not going to just sit here and let this MultiReal code run rampant. Start that OCHRE probe again. Get that fucking thing *out* of there."

Quell shook his head. "Natch, that yellow jacket is *everywhere*. See?" He walked over to the workbench and stuck his hand in the MindSpace bubble. Natch noticed for the first time that Quell's fingers were adorned with his Islander programming rings, allowing him to manipulate the virtual blueprint without metal bars. He panned the schematic to a few key intersections where globules of code hung unobtrusively like parasites. "We could spend a year hunting those snippets down and still not find them all," said Quell. "And if we try to just yank everything out without taking precautions—*serious* precautions—it could be catastrophic."

"Maybe and maybe not," said Natch, eyeing the black-and-yellow blob. "We need to crack that son of a bitch open."

"I've tried," moaned Horvil. "Believe me."

"Yeah, but did *he* try it?" Natch reached out, grabbed the Islander's wrist, and held his hand up in the air. The programming rings twinkled. "With these?"

Horvil merely shrugged. He extended his open palm toward the workbench as if to say, *Be my guest.*

The Islander eyed the bubble warily and removed himself from Natch's grasp. Then he plunged his hands into the bubble and began weaving a peculiar cat's cradle with the diffuse strands of data. His face flushed with concentration.

Natch gritted his teeth and clutched the windowsill, expecting another blackout at any moment. He felt a hand on his shoulder. "Maybe you should . . . sit down?" said Serr Vigal. Natch shook his head.

He watched Quell's fingers with a vulture eye, trying to translate the Islander's finger phrases into the programming bar idioms he knew so intimately. Some of the moves looked familiar, but others were completely alien. Natch reminded himself that Sheldon Surina and the original bio/logic programmers had coded this way—though they had used a much smaller set of rings and a rudimentary form of MindSpace that hardly deserved the name. Surina had built the foundations of bio/logics using such primitive tools. Certainly, it seemed to Natch, the best way to break into code locked by the Surinas was to use the same methods they had used to seal it.

The diagram panned out, swiveled, and changed colors many times. Yet despite Quell's best efforts, the mutant yellow jacket remained sealed.

"Maybe we should try to find a different subroutine from Multi-Real to crack into," offered Horvil, who had crept closer to the workbench to watch Quell's performance. "We might have better luck." No one answered.

Natch could feel his mind revving up, blasting pistons at a phenomenal rate. Something was hovering just beyond his perception. An arcane destination, off the main road—something peculiar—

"Quell," he snapped. "Give me those rings."

The Islander stepped back. "My rings? What—"

"Just *do* it."

Quell looked to his fellow engineer, dumbfounded, but Horvil didn't have any better idea what Natch was up to. Finally Quell shrugged, slid the gold bands off one by one, and handed them to the fiefcorp master.

Natch slipped the still-warm rings onto his fingers. He hadn't realized quite how large Quell's hands were. When he finished donning the programming rings, he felt like a child playing dress-up with his mother's jewelry. Even the notoriously thickset Islanders couldn't have standard ring sizes this big.

Natch stepped up to the workbench and raised his hands. The code floating in MindSpace seemed to exert a slight magnetic pull on his fingers, much as it did on a set of programming bars.

As Quell, Horvil, and Vigal looked on, Natch began conducting a data symphony with his digits. It started as a delicate tune that hovered in the middle registers. But as the fiefcorp master gradually gained confidence in his technique, he began to make more daring moves. Sudden staccato bursts all over the imaginary orchestra, glissando stretches from one end of the scale to the other.

After fifteen minutes, Horvil began to grow restless. "If you don't need me," he said, "I think I'll get back to work. . . ."

"Not yet," barked Natch. The engineer stayed put. Serr Vigal retreated to the chair in the corner and parked himself anxiously upon it.

Natch zoomed in on the peculiar bee-shaped structure and began twisting at it with his fingers, over and over again. The coil spun around like a lump of clay under the hands of a skilled potter. Every few spins, Natch would stab at the coil with his fourth finger.

"What's he *doing*?" mumbled Horvil, leaning in until his face was neatly bisected by the edge of MindSpace and took on a pinkish glow.

Quell squinted at the bubble dubiously. "Are you sure you know what you're doing?" he said. "If you keep doing that, you might—"

"Break it?" Natch grinned like a demon and made one final stab with four fingers at once.

And then the darkness spilled out.

• • •

Natch didn't know how long he lay there before the refreshingly prosaic voice of Horvil came meandering out of the blackness. "I can look after him for a bit, Vigal. You really need to get some sleep."

He tried to sit up, to respond, but his eyelids felt tied down and he could not open them. His body simply would not respond to his commands.

"I'm not leaving until I know he's okay," said Vigal. The neural programmer was almost within arm's reach. "When is Quell leaving?"

"Dunno. I keep telling him he should go to Andra Pradesh already if he's going to go, but you know how stubborn he is. I think he's trying to put it off." Horvil emitted a long, rattling noise of impatience through his sinuses.

Natch attacked the thorny thicket around his eyelids with every gram of strength he had. Pain flooded down his spinal cord and then abruptly subsided. He bolted upright to find the concerned faces of Horvil and Serr Vigal staring down at him on the living room sofa. Vigal's expression was clouded with gloom, while Horvil looked like he had aged a year. Natch noticed that the sun had almost disappeared behind the jagged Shenandoah skyline. How long had he been under?

"You okay?" said Vigal gently.

The fiefcorp master struggled with the snares around his tongue. After a few minutes, he managed to croak out a reply. "I don't think I'll be doing *that* again for a while."

Horvil plopped down on the chair-and-a-half. "I'm sorry, Natch," he muttered. "We were hoping to find some answers about the black code. But looks like we just made things more complicated."

"Complicated doesn't bother me," said Natch, stretching his neck muscles in an effort to unstiffen them. "I don't mind a complicated answer, as long as I have the answer. Is MultiReal the black code? Or are they separate programs?"

Horvil shook his head despondently and said nothing.

"Come on, Horv!" yelled Natch. "No clues? Nothing at all? Vigal, *you* know neural programming. You have to have some idea."

His old mentor frowned from the kitchen, where he was running his finger aimlessly across the countertop. Natch noticed the remains of a dinner that the three of them must have eaten while he was unconscious. "I don't think they're the same thing. I think there's another illicit program hidden in your OCHRE system. But that's just an opinion."

Natch, petulant: "So how did the MultiReal code get there?"

"I don't know," replied Vigal.

"Then what's it doing?"

Vigal rubbed his chin and stared at the wall, pensive. "Well, we know that it can put you to sleep for several days. . . ."

"There's *got* to be more than that!" shouted Natch, pounding his fist on one of the couch's throw pillows. "Why would someone put together a strike team just to slip me a sleeping pill? If all they wanted to do was prevent me from delivering that demo at Andra Pradesh, the fucking code would have self-destructed by now."

Serr Vigal slid into a weary silence.

Natch lurched to his feet, balancing himself against the edge of the sofa until he was confident he would not fall down. Vigal and Horvil both offered him a helping hand, but the fiefcorp master waved them away. "Where's Quell?" he grunted.

Horvil pointed wordlessly toward the balcony door. Natch clasped his hands behind his back and strode in that direction. The balcony door swished open as he approached.

Quell the Islander stood outside with his hands firmly clenching the railing, as if he were about to rip it loose and hurl it into space. His gaze was fixed on a small group of Council officers standing across the road, exchanging hand signals with other teams in the vicinity. They were clearly watching Natch's apartment, or at least pretending to. One of the officers went so far as to brandish a dart-rifle ostentatiously in Quell's direction, as if he might fire it at any moment. His fellows laughed.

"Sorry," said the Islander to Natch under his breath. "I know you want answers. But I don't have them."

Natch shrugged. "I believe you." He lifted his right hand up, waving the glinting programming rings under Quell's nose. "Mind if I keep these for a while?"

The Islander rubbed his chin for a moment, and Natch could see he was trying to decide if he should ask why. Finally he nodded. "Go ahead. I've got another set back at Andra Pradesh." He reached into the pocket of his breeches and withdrew a small black felt bag, which he handed to Natch. Natch deposited the rings one by one in the bag and then cinched its drawstring closed.

"Listen, Natch, I need to make something clear," continued Quell, lowering his voice. "Everyone in this fiefcorp seems to think I understand everything about MultiReal. But I don't. Of course, I know a lot more than you do . . . but even sixteen years ago, MultiReal was already bigger than any piece of bio/logic programming on the market. Some of the pieces of that program are over *a hundred years old*, Natch. I've seen routines in there dating back to Prengal Surina. I wouldn't be surprised to find shit written by Sheldon Surina. The Surinas, they *invented* bio/logic programming. One family, unlimited resources, three hundred sixty years. Does anyone really know what they're capable of?"

Quell shook his head, angry at everything and nothing at once. The taunting of the Council officer across the street caught his eye once again. The Islander hefted an imaginary dart-rifle to his shoulder and fired off a single round, with a *click* of his tongue as sound effect. His white-robed adversary rattled his very real dart-rifle in the air and shouted something insulting, unintelligible at this distance.

"You have to understand, Natch," continued Quell with more than a little bitterness in his voice. "Those Surinas, they don't let you in. Not even *me*, not even after twenty years."

Natch frowned. He knew the feeling all too well. Sometimes it seemed like the entire world was nothing but a vast edifice designed to keep him out. He caught a quick glimpse of Horvil and Vigal out of his peripheral vision, still deep in conversation.

"Listen, Quell," said Natch. "I need answers *soon*. This can't wait. The MultiReal exposition's a week from today, and I've still got Magan Kai Lee breathing down my neck." He made an angry gesture at the squads of Council officers below.

"So what are you going to do?" asked Quell.

"You're going to Andra Pradesh to see Margaret?"

The Islander nodded.

"Then I'm coming with you. No, don't say it—I've already tried to multi there half a dozen times. Her idiotic security force won't even let me in the compound. But if I show up there in person, with *you*, they'll let me in. Then you're going to take me to the top of the Revelation Spire, and I'm going to get some answers from Margaret."

"What if Margaret still refuses to see you?"

"Oh, she'll see me," replied Natch, his voice venom. "She'll see me, or I'll tear that whole bloody compound down brick by brick."

(((1 2)))

Jara strode through the crooked hallways of the Kordez Thassel Complex cursing the chill. *The Thasselians did this on purpose*, she thought bitterly, wondering if some fiefcorp with a warmth-generating program had thrown the creed a few credits to lower the thermostat. *I don't care if it* is *January in the Twin Cities—there's no excuse.*

The analyst closed her eyes and tried to clear her mind. Fiefcorp greed was a fruit that ripened in all seasons and could be found by the bushel anywhere you looked. She needed to stay focused on the subject at hand: the Patel Brothers.

Jara couldn't figure out what kind of playbook Frederic and Petrucio were working from. Obviously they had shifted tactics since their first MultiReal demo, which even the most Natchophobic of drudges called an overproduced, underimagined failure. Today's demo was an industry-only event. No creed officials or L-PRACG bureaucrats or curious onlookers would be on hand to provide distractions; not even the drudges were invited, unless they specifically covered the bio/logic programming beat.

What mischief were the Patels up to now? Were they really in league with the Defense and Wellness Council, as Margaret suspected?

Jara followed Robby Robby's beacon, which led her from the Thassel Complex's gateway zone through a drunken loop of frigid hallways and finally to a small clump of people outside the auditorium entrance. She hung back for a moment, checking Data Sea profiles. You never knew who was on the Council's payroll, and after her London encounter with Magan Kai Lee, there was no level of paranoia to which Jara would not sink.

The slick, square-jawed individual blathering away in the group's epicenter was, of course, Robby Robby. He had abandoned his cubed hairdo at some point this past week for a frizzy style that would have looked at home on a clown or a cultist. Next to Robby stood Phrancoliape, one of the Data Sea's most respected channelers, his distinguished white beard making a vibrant contrast with his rich African skin. Three quick pings to the public directory tagged the youths standing in Phrancoliape's shadow as his junior apprentices. So far, so good. Then Jara spotted the last member of the group and nearly bolted for the exit. Xi Xong, the Patel Brothers' dowager channeler extraordinaire.

Jara hadn't quite decided what to do when Robby Robby spotted her. "Watch out, Twin Cities!" bellowed the channeler in a voice loud enough to warp time and space. "The official Surina/Natch delegation is now assembled!"

Her cover blown, Jara walked up and gave a polite bow to the group. "Keep it down, Robby. I'm not supposed to be here, remember?"

"Eh, don't worry your pretty little head," replied Robby. "'Trucio knows you're here, and he doesn't care. Right, Xi?"

Xi Xong's face was painted as heavily as a Kabuki mask. "Of course, darling," she said in that faux high-society accent of hers. "The Patels always keep things aboveboard and out in the open. Not like *Jara's* boss." She turned toward the analyst with a vicious smile that revealed too many teeth. "Speaking of which . . . tell me, how *is* Lucas Sentinel these days?"

Jara could feel the blood flowing to her face unbidden. "I—I work for Natch now, Xi," she stuttered. "I haven't had anything to do with Lucas for, what, almost five years." *And you know it, too.*

The Patels' channeler emitted a whooping crane laugh. "I'm sorry, dear, you're right. I *always* get those two confused. Natch, Lucas. They're *so* much alike, don't you think?" Robby bobbed his head idiotically, always on the lookout for a stray opinion to agree with. One of Phrancoliape's apprentices chuckled. "Well, duty calls," said Xong.

"Perfection to you all." And then she whirled around on one knobbed stalk of leg and disappeared into the auditorium.

Jara bristled. How long were people going to browbeat her about her association with Lucas Sentinel? And what did she have to be ashamed about anyway? Lucas had been the one who demolished their working relationship with his fumbling attempts at seduction. All Jara had done was spurn his advances. So why did it still feel like a moral failure on her part?

Trying to regain her equilibrium, she turned to Phrancoliape. "So who're you shilling for these days, Phranc?"

"Oh, Pierre Loget, same as always," replied the channeler in a warm baritone. He either did not notice the tangled barbs on Xi's words or was purposefully ignoring them. "Now that you and the Patels have stopped worrying about Primo's, *somebody* has to keep Lucas and Bolliwar out of the top spot." The latter referring to Bolliwar Tuban, whose reputation for nastiness was on par with Natch's.

"So where is Pierre these days?" said Jara. "I read something about him on the drudge circuit the other day. John Ridglee says he's missing."

"Yeah, what do the drudges know?" one of Phranc's apprentices blurted out, a little too quickly.

The channeler himself let out a good-natured laugh. "*Your* boss has a tendency to disappear for weeks at a time too," he told Jara, waving his hand in dismissal. "Pierre likes his privacy, but the instant Sentinel gets within spitting distance of number one, he'll be back. Trust me."

And at that moment, a delicate *bong* echoed throughout the atrium of the Kordez Thassel auditorium, signaling the imminent start of the Patel Brothers' presentation. Phranc bowed to Jara and gave Robby Robby a comradely clap on the shoulder. Then he vanished along with his understudies.

Jara turned to Robby, who seemed blissfully ignorant of the entire concept of subtext. "You ready?"

Robby lit up like a sparkler. "As I'll ever be, Queen Jara!" he crackled.

Standard procedure at an event like this dictated that all multi projections should materialize inside the auditorium and stay there. But this crowd was evidently too small to bother with such rules. Jara turned to walk through the double doors and was assaulted by a garish billboard advertisement across the way.

CHILL GOT YOU DOWN?
Try WoolCoat 95 by the Bolliwar Tuban Fiefcorp

She scowled, and resigned herself to the cold.

Robby and Jara hustled through the crowd and found seats in the upper reaches of the auditorium, where they would be safely anonymous. Fearing another outburst from Robby, Jara covertly masked her lips with one palm in the manner of someone engaged in a ConfidentialWhisper. The channeler left her alone.

So the analyst sat and watched the audience file in. The carnival atmosphere that had plagued the first two MultiReal demos was distinctly absent today. This was an exclusive and drearily dressed gathering of bio/logic professionals: thirteen thousand of them, to be precise, crammed into a space that could have seated perhaps ten thousand live bodies. The crazies and the zealots were nowhere to be found— unless you counted the devotees of Creed Thassel, whose members were undoubtedly here under their cloak of secrecy.

And what about the officers of the Defense and Wellness Council, standing grim and barren of emotion? Jara didn't recognize any of the faces of the officers near her, but that didn't mean she wasn't being watched. After all, the Surina/Natch MultiReal Fiefcorp's big exposition was in seven days. When would Magan Kai Lee make his move? What was he waiting for?

After a few minutes, the lights dimmed and a hush settled on the crowd.

Smoke began to curl around the foot of the stage until it covered the entire floor. A soundtrack heavy on the bamboo flute echoed across the auditorium. The spotlight speared a circular platform that rose about a meter out of the smoke. Standing atop the platform was the jowly Frederic Patel, forehead furrowed, a pair of dartguns at hand. Seconds later, another platform rose on the opposite side of the stage carrying a similarly decked-out Petrucio. His waxed mustache practically glistened.

"This rivalry has gone on long enough," said the elder Patel with an exaggerated sneer.

"Yeah?" replied the younger. "I'd like to see you do something about it, 'Trucio."

"If you don't put down those guns, I will. I've been waiting for this a long time."

"You don't have the courage," snorted Frederic.

Jara felt Robby's elbow dig into her side. "*Phantom Distortions*," he said, sotto voce. For once, the analyst was glad for the interruption. She knew she recognized the Patel Brothers' banter from somewhere, but hadn't been able to place it. Jara had only seen *Phantom Distortions* once, several years ago, and thought it irritating and cliché-ridden. But the drama had won so many awards and penetrated so many strata of society that even she could recite its climactic scene from memory. This was the part where Juan Nguyen's character took careful aim at his traitorous brother and—

Petrucio fired the dartgun in his right hand. A sliver of poison vaulted across the stage and landed in the exact center of Frederic's belt buckle. "Aren't you glad I'm using SafeShores 1.0 by the Patel Brothers?" said Petrucio. And as Frederic stood there in slapstick dismay, the elder Patel proceeded to shoot a dozen more darts along his brother's belt line in quick succession.

The audience howled with laughter. It was a nice play on the real line: *Aren't you glad I don't have the courage?* delivered with maximum swagger. Jara allowed herself an appreciative smile. It looked like the Patel Brothers had finally figured out how to put together a decent marketing presentation, even if they were clinging to their lame "safe shores" motif with too much vigor.

Frederic made a cartoonish grunt of rage that seemed a little too convincing and then raised his own gun. "Well, so am I, *Brother*," he said. And let fire.

In the original *Phantom Distortions*, this was the moment where comedy mutated into pathos, where the brothers' long rivalry exploded into the open with ruinous consequences. But in the Patel Brothers' version, Petrucio was too quick on the draw. The dartgun in his left hand shot off with a reverberating *thwing*—and milliseconds later, there came the indescribable sound of two darts striking one another in midair and clattering to the stage.

Even Jara gasped. She had seen MultiReal's innards lying on a MindSpace workbench, and still Petrucio's feat hardly seemed possible.

Frederic continued firing with grim determination until the air grew hazy with darts. Each needle met its nemesis in midflight and ricocheted harmlessly off to the side. After a minute of this, Petrucio began to take the offensive, with similarly ineffectual results. Soon the brothers were fighting the kind of melee that only existed in the dramas: ridiculous amounts of ammunition, impossibly dexterous moves, and not a single hit on either side.

The muttering in the audience rose several decibels. Robby's tongue was flapping uselessly back and forth in his mouth.

Jara loaded up a mental imaging program and took a snapshot of the projectiles the Patels were blasting at one another. She zoomed in and studied them carefully. These darts appeared to be much larger than the normal variety, and they were coated with a mirrored substance that made them easier to see. The Patels were not firing directly at one another, but at an oblique angle that helped the odds considerably. But even given all that, Jara could think of no ordinary piece of bio/logics that would account for such marksmanship. This could only be the work of MultiReal.

Finally, at some predetermined moment, Frederic tossed his gun to the stage, where it was sucked down into the fume. "All this bickering is pointless, 'Trucio," he said.

Petrucio nodded. "In a MultiReal-on-MultiReal fight, there's only one possible outcome."

"And that's a draw," said Frederic, hopping off the platform and waddling awkwardly toward his brother, who had also shed his weapons. Jara noticed that Frederic's acting abilities were noticeably strained when portraying emotions like remorse and reconciliation.

The two Patels locked arms and walked together toward the foot of the stage. Petrucio appeared to be so exhausted that he was almost limping, though he was doing his best to hide it. "After all," said the elder brother, "couldn't we all use more safe shores these days?" Jara could have sworn he was deliberately looking in her direction.

• • •

"But it doesn't fucking *work* that way," Benyamin complained. "You didn't see Quell on that soccer field. When two people with MultiReal go up against each other, it all gets resolved like *that*." He snapped. "Instantly. In your head. If they were really having a MultiReal-on-MultiReal fight, then the winner would have hit the loser."

Jara stretched her neck and luxuriated in the SeeNaRee breeze. It was nice to be back in a virtual environment at the Surina Enterprise Facility, even if she had to put up with Benyamin's whining. She wasn't sure which beach this was supposed to be, or perhaps it was an amalgam of several. What did it matter? Jara could feel muscles in her neck unknotting and sluggish nerve endings in her fingers tingle with warmth from the SeeNaRee sun. She wondered fleetingly what had happened to Greth Tar Griveth's petty blackmail scheme. Jara assumed that the lack of updates meant the situation was under control.

"I know that's not how MultiReal works, Ben," she said. "And the

Patels do too. But what did you want them to do, get on stage and just stare at each other for an hour? I thought they did a pretty good job illustrating the concept. Besides, that wasn't the end of the show. Petrucio took a bunch of questions afterward, and he explained the whole thing in detail."

"Shooting down darts in midair," put in Merri from her spot nearby on the sand. "*We* should have thought of that." She sighed as the tide came trickling up the beach to lick her bare toes.

"Listen, we don't have time to worry about the Patels," said Jara. "Right now we need to be thinking about computational rules. We're going to have twenty-three people bouncing choice cycles all over the place in a week. It'll be a nightmare unless we make some decisions."

The blonde channel manager combed her fingers thoughtfully through the damp sand. "Why do we even need to worry about it?" she said. "Can't we just turn the whole MultiReal-against-MultiReal feature off?"

"You mean disallow competing choice cycles altogether?" said Jara.

Ben shook his head. "I don't think that's practical." He wanted nothing to do with the decadent SeeNaRee Jara's mood had conjured up, choosing to sit instead at a rigid oak conference table wedged incongruously in the middle of the sand. "If you don't have any competing choice cycles, you're defenseless against anyone who uses the program against you. That means the first person to activate MultiReal would always win. Right? Talk about a nightmare! People would flip on the program every two seconds, on the off chance that something important was about to happen."

"So then let's just deactivate competing realities for the exposition," said Merri. "We don't have to figure everything out today, do we?"

"Not everything," said Jara, "but we can't put these decisions off forever, Merri. Things are moving so quickly, we might not get another window like this. We need to make some decisions *today*."

Benyamin smacked his palm on the table and looked up with

inspiration gleaming through his pores. "What if we just let the market decide?"

Jara frowned skeptically. "How would that work?"

"The whole program's based on choice cycles. Every time you jump to another potential reality, you create another one. So why not just charge by the choice cycle? That way you wouldn't waste money using MultiReal to grab the last cracker on the buffet table—you'd save your choice cycles for the things that really matter. The things you're willing to pay for."

"A libertarian solution," mused Merri. Her circles in the sand grew wider and wider until the sea washed them away.

Jara leaned back on her elbows and let Ben's suggestion roam through her mental hallways for a minute. It seemed like a solution that Speaker Khann Frejohr would love. It seemed like a solution *Natch* would love. "I don't think that would work either," she said after a moment of reflection.

Ben was peeved. "Why *not*?"

"It wouldn't turn out the way you think. You're basically saying that the richest person in the room is always going to get what he wants. Do you really want to put a system like that in place?"

"But sometimes that's just the way the world works," the young apprentice retorted. "You make more money, you have more choices."

"This is totally different, Ben. Remember Horvil's story about haggling with that street vendor? We're not just talking about kicking soccer balls around here. Think about it—there must be a thousand Lunar tycoons with more money than half of Creed Élan put together. They'd get the upper hand on every deal. All they'd need to do is keep dishing out money for more choice cycles. It wouldn't be fair."

"Life would be pretty harsh for the diss, too," added Merri. "You'd literally get pushed around all day, and there'd be nothing you could do about it."

"And let's not forget the Islanders and the Pharisees," said Jara.

Benyamin rose from the table and began stomping to the edge of the water and back. "I can't believe I'm hearing this. *Not fair?*" He threw his hands up toward the sky. "This isn't a question of ethics, Jara. It's basic economics. If our product doesn't give customers unlimited choice cycles, then someone else's will. Do you think the Patels are going to sell *their* customers a limited product?"

"They don't have a say in it," said Merri. "Natch said that limited choice cycles are built into the Patel Brothers' licensing agreement. They can't run a product with unlimited choice cycles."

"I didn't realize that," said Ben, vindication sculpted into his face. "This is great—we're going to crush them in the marketplace. If *our* version of MultiReal gives you unlimited choice, and *theirs* just craps out at some point . . . who's going to buy from the Patel Brothers?"

Merri nodded hesitantly. Jara got to her feet and took a few steps toward the bay. She watched the tiny virtual sand crabs scurrying on the beach, jousting with each other in accordance with the SeeNaRee algorithms.

And suddenly she felt her thoughts line up like dominoes. Xi Xong telling Jara that Petrucio knew she was attending the presentation . . . The two Patels blazing away at one another fruitlessly . . . Frederic Patel discarding his weapon onto the stage . . . *All this bickering is pointless, 'Trucio. In a MultiReal-on-MultiReal fight, there's only one possible outcome. And that's a draw.*

"Wait a minute," said the analyst. "I understand now. The Patel Brothers. They were trying to tell us something with that demo."

Benyamin's mouth curled into a sallow frown. "Like what?"

"They're trying to tell us that there's another way," Jara continued. "A more egalitarian way. What if we give everyone, say, ten thousand choice cycles a month? Or fifty thousand? Whether you're a Lunar tycoon on Feynman or just some L-PRACG bureaucrat in Beijing— whether you bought Possibilities 1.0 from Surina/Natch or SafeShores 1.0 from the Patels—you get the same number of alternate realities as everyone else. And you can't buy any more, under any circumstances."

Ben wasn't mollified in the slightest. "So you're saying we should *handicap* our product so the Patels can compete with us?"

"I'm saying we should prevent MultiReal from turning into an endless arms race of who can stockpile the most choice cycles." Jara stubbornly folded her arms across her chest. "I suppose it works to Frederic and Petrucio's advantage. But that's not why we would do it."

"Natch isn't going to like this at all," said Ben, walking around the analyst to confront her face to face. "*I* don't like it. You're putting an artificial cap on a system that doesn't need one. That won't work. It never works."

Jara shook her head. "This isn't sociology class, Ben. MultiReal is dangerous. Haven't you figured that out yet? We can't afford to make a reckless decision here. People's lives could be at stake."

"Don't be so melodramatic," interrupted Ben, throwing up his hands. "I get the point already. But these things have a way of working themselves out. They always do. The Lunar tycoons would waste all their choice cycles trying to one-up each other. They wouldn't care what goes on down here."

Merri climbed to her feet and eyed the conflict between the two apprentices with unease. Ben and Jara were standing toe to toe now, glaring at one another with a hostility that the Patels had only pantomimed this morning. The SeeNaRee noticed the discord and hurled a strong wind along the shoreline, kicking up bits of sand and shell to nip at their ankles.

"This is just *wrong*," said Benyamin, a contentious frown on his face. "Crippling MultiReal won't help anyone. It'll only help Frederic and Petrucio drive us out of business. Once we're gone, the Patels will own the program outright and start selling unlimited choice cycles anyway."

"I don't think so," replied Jara. "You didn't see that presentation at the Kordez Thassel Complex. Frederic and Petrucio agree with me."

"What if the Patels only want you to *think* they agree? How do you know Magan Kai Lee didn't put them up to this?"

Jara's brow furrowed. The very mention of that name was enough to spike her blood pressure and make her sweat. "Why would he do that?"

Benyamin put a hand on her shoulder. "Because once we bring our version of MultiReal down to their level, the Council can use the Patels' version to get to us—and we won't be able to stop them."

Jara opened her mouth, nonplussed, but the pat response she was waiting for to leap to her rescue did not come. She was ashamed to admit that such a tactic had never even occurred to her. Everything always came back to the Council in the end, didn't it? "I guess that's just a chance we'll have to take," she said under her breath.

January 2: the day the fiefcorp was scheduled to unveil the winners of the MultiReal exposition lottery. The day that twenty-three lucky citizens would be given an appointment to experience the wonders of multiple realities firsthand.

The morning dawned blustery and brutish, with a fresh assault of hail in Shenandoah, a barrage of rain in London—and news of another infoquake in central Asia.

The Defense and Wellness Council managed to suppress the news for forty-eight hours. But even Len Borda's agents couldn't keep such a scoop hidden from the drudges forever. By midmorning, details were splashed across the headlines of every gossipmonger on the Data Sea. This infoquake was not nearly as severe as the last one, which had left hundreds dead and thousands wounded from Earth to the orbital colonies. The computational blizzard was centered in Tibet, though flurries were observed as far away as Andra Pradesh and Vladivostok. The death toll hovered at a mere two dozen—but the details of their demise were almost gruesome enough to eclipse the MultiReal exposition lottery. Drudges pounded the Council with questions about the cause of the infoquakes, but all the Council flaks could do was utter bureaucratic euphemisms for *we don't know*.

Forty thousand drudges, channelers, and capitalmen wedged themselves into a sunny São Paulo soccer stadium that morning to witness the lottery drawing. It was the same venue Natch had rented for the exposition itself, and with its newly reupholstered seats and dizzying array of giant viewscreens, the stadium made quite a spectacle. Merri worked the crowd with the help of Robby Robby's merry band of channelers, salting the cognoscenti with a heavy coating of marketing buzzwords. By midday, chatter about the latest infoquake had died down to a whisper, and the drudges were ready for Natch.

But Natch was not there.

Jara couldn't believe the entrepreneur would put everyone through this crap yet again. It had to be foul play, a clandestine strike by the Council, a mugging, black code. Then a flustered Serr Vigal rushed in at the last minute with news from Natch. He was on a tube train with Quell heading for Andra Pradesh and would not attend the drawing. A stunned Horvil spattered the freshly painted walls of the stadium's locker room with a mouthful of ChaiQuoke.

Panic had yet to set in when the apprentices received another surprise guest. Robby Robby oozed into the locker room, leading by the hand the world-renowned soccer star Wilson Refaris Ko. The man was rugged and handsome, with troll-sized hands and a chin the size of a graveyard shovel. "So where do I pick 'em?" grinned Ko.

"Pick them?" said Jara, feeling like her head was full of yarn. "Pick *what*?"

Ko, confused, scratching his ass: "There's usually a barrel with little plastic tags in it."

Horvil laughed. "You got a barrel that holds three billion plastic tags?"

"We've already got a program to pick the lottery winners," explained Jara. "All you need to do is read the names. Right?" She looked to the other fiefcorpers for backup, but nobody else had any idea what Ko was supposed to do. Jara shrugged. "Right. I'll go out there and introduce you, and you just read the names."

"Oh." The man was crestfallen.

Ko might not have had the keenest intellect, but what he lacked in brainpower he made up for in star kinetics. His panther strut caused men and women of all sexual orientations to drop their jaws, and his husky reed of a voice could mesmerize even the sourest drudge. Jara never knew for certain whether Natch had hired him directly or if his appearance was the work of Robby Robby, but it didn't really matter. When Ko walked onto the field, there was not a murmur to be heard from the crowd.

The soccer player cleared his throat and prepared to recite the names fed to him by Horvil's algorithms. Jara could sense a billion necks arching forward in front of viewscreens across the world. "And the winners of the Surina/Natch MultiReal lottery are . . ."

A leukocyte specialist from Dr. Plugenpatch. A mother of four pledged to Creed Bushido. An OrbiCo technician who spent most of his time jetting between the colonies of Allowell and Nova Ceti. A bio/logic programmer in Beijing . . .

The names rolled on. Jara breathed a sigh of relief, although she couldn't say why. You could tell precious little about someone from a name and job description; any one of those lottery winners could easily be on Len Borda's payroll. Or Khann Frejohr's, or Creed Thassel's, for that matter. But the names were *out* there now, and it was time to sit back and let the Data Sea journalists do their detective work.

• • •

His task completed, Wilson Refaris Ko cut his multi connection and vanished back to the Neverland of self-important celebrities. Merri took his place on the platform at the end of the field, smiling, her boldest Creed Objectivv pin riding high on her chest.

Ben tried to convince his cousin not to go out there, to wait until they had gotten Natch's explicit approval before announcing the exposition rules.

"You're really upset about this, aren't you?" said Horvil.

The young apprentice shoved his hands in his pockets and gave a sallow nod. "I'm not upset because I don't agree with the decision," he said. "If Natch decides we should give MultiReal users limited choice cycles, that's fine. It's just—Jara hasn't even *talked* to him about it. She made up her mind without consulting anybody."

"She consulted Merri and Vigal. They both agree."

"Do you?"

The engineer bobbed his head back and forth slowly like the pendulum of a fat grandfather clock. Did he believe that MultiReal should be released with limited or unlimited choice cycles? He didn't know. Usually Horvil was content to wallow in the numerology and let Natch make the policy decisions. But like a black hole, MultiReal warped the very moral and ethical dimensions around it. Horvil could feel the program's infinite density tugging at strings inside him that he had never realized he possessed. This program demanded that he abandon his neutrality and pick a side.

But not quite yet. "I dunno if I agree or not," Horvil said at length. "I think I do. But I haven't really given it enough thought."

Ben was clearly disappointed. "Well, Natch's opinion is the only one that counts, unless Margaret decides to come down from that tower. I wish he'd answer his fucking ConfidentialWhisper requests." The apprentice kicked an empty bottle on the locker room floor and watched it ricochet off the concrete wall. "Come on, Horvil. You know what Natch would say. You know what he's *going* to say when he hears about this. He'll agree that the market should set the number of choice cycles."

"Well, think of it this way. These rules are just for the exposition. We still have plenty of time to change our minds before we launch Possibilities on the Data Sea."

"That's not the point. The point is—"

Horvil rolled his eyes and reached out to pinch his cousin's lips shut. "The point is, Ben, Natch isn't here. Somebody needed to make a decision. Jara made it." And without waiting for a reaction, the engineer was out the locker room door and heading for the field.

• • •

Jara didn't want the haze of multivoid to end. She wanted to grab onto the nothingness and embrace it tightly. Some days she remained on the red tile in her hallway for several minutes, filtering out the sights and sounds of the apartment with a Cocoon program until she could bear to look at the world again. Today, she merely stood on the tile with eyes shut.

It's been a good day, she thought.

The drudges were well pleased with the lottery results. Her fellow fiefcorpers had performed admirably: Merri had looked stoic, Horvil knowledgeable, Vigal calm and unruffled. Benyamin had stayed out of the way. Best of all, Jara had already anticipated most of the drudges' questions, and so the fiefcorp was able to stay on script most of the afternoon.

Nobody paid much attention to what Merri labeled the Equitable Choice Cycle Model, but Jara had not expected them to. The public simply didn't have enough information about MultiReal to comprehend the issues at stake. But Jara knew that it was only a matter of time. The words she scripted would resonate long and loud for decades to come. All that mattered was that the Patel Brothers would understand. Frederic and Petrucio would get the message that the Surina/Natch MultiReal Fiefcorp was willing to be reasonable. (Still, Jara was careful to emphasize that the Equitable Choice Cycle Model would be in effect *only* for the exposition. She didn't want the Patel Brothers to get too comfortable.)

Six more days to the MultiReal exposition, she thought. *Six more days until the public gets a real taste of multiple realities. After that, there's no telling.*

She opened her eyes and absorbed the mundanity of her East London flat once more. Open surfaces, bare countertops, white walls. The first faint sketches of her future were drawn there, but the lines were still too indistinct for her to make out.

(((14)))

There were no redwoods on the long tube route that snaked halfway around the globe to Andra Pradesh. For most of the journey, there was nothing for Natch to look at but sea and sky—and the Council officers who had been tailing him since Shenandoah.

Watching Quell work the viewscreens on the window proved an interesting diversion. Natch didn't know if the Islander possessed the neural equipment necessary to give a window direct commands; his understanding was that the Islanders had most standard OCHRE machines implanted at birth but simply kept them turned off. How else could Quell run a program as complex as MultiReal? Whatever the reason, he was navigating the Data Sea with his fingertips via an onscreen maze of buttons. Natch fell into a light sleep wondering how many other systems had hidden unconnectible interfaces built into them.

"They're comparing you to Marcus Surina," said Quell a few hours later.

The QuasiSuspension program had Natch awake and alert before the Islander even finished the first syllable. He glanced out the window just in time to see the shores of Sicily hurtling past. "Who is?" said the fiefcorp master.

"The drudges at the MultiReal lottery." Quell gestured at the window, which was showing an opinion piece by some obscure pundit named Vermillion. "This guy says that if Marcus couldn't put together a feasible plan for teleportation, you won't do any better with Multi-Real. He thinks Marcus turned out to be mostly hype, and you're headed the same way."

Natch shrugged. "Doesn't matter. The drudges don't know anything. They're just blowing smoke." He scanned the first few paragraphs of the story, picking out the standard descriptors: *reckless, neurotic, maniacal*. Natch supposed he should give the article a closer look, make sure the lottery went off without any major gaffes. But right now the only things he could focus on were black code and MultiReal.

The entrepreneur settled back into his seat. "They could've chosen someone worse. Marcus Surina was the richest man in the world in his day."

Quell frowned. "Yeah, but he came to a bad end."

"Most good things do," said Natch as he drifted back into Quasi-Suspension.

• • •

From the moment the tube train pulled into Andra Pradesh, they could see that the Surina compound was in disarray—guards rushing everywhere, trash piling up, a little boy lost screaming for his mother and nobody giving him a second glance. The man checking identities at the bottom of the hill gave Natch and Quell no more than a cursory scan before admitting them through the gates.

Things did not improve when they climbed the hill and found their way to the compound's central courtyard. Figures in blue-and-green livery scurried around the square with little semblance of order, as if struggling to obey confusing or even contradictory orders. The entrances to the Center for Historic Appreciation and the Enterprise Facility were sparsely guarded, and a small platoon of Council officers could easily have snuck into the absurd castle that contained the Surina family residences. The security force was concentrated around the half-kilometer-high thorn known as the Revelation Spire. Margaret had exiled herself to the tip of that spire several weeks ago, when the Defense and Wellness Council marched in before Natch's last demo. And now, it seemed, she had decided to make it a permanent arrangement.

Quell pointed disdainfully at a pair of guards who were attempting to haul a disruptor cannon across the courtyard by the barrel. "I knew things were bad," growled the Islander, "but I didn't know they were *this* bad."

Natch shuddered. He had seen how effortlessly Len Borda's troops took control of the compound last month, when Surina security was still in relatively good shape. If Magan Kai Lee sent a few legions of his officers here today, what kind of resistance could the Surinas possibly offer?

The Islander snatched the arm of a passing officer. The woman yelped and reached for the dartgun in her holster. Then she saw who had seized her and let the free arm drop to her side. Apparently Quell's reputation still carried a lot of weight in this place. "You," he barked. "What's going on? Where's the security chief?"

"He—he left," stuttered the officer.

Quell yanked the woman's arm almost hard enough to dislocate her shoulder. "What do you mean, he *left?*"

"Suheil dismissed him," whimpered the guard. "Sent him home. The bodhisattva just . . . let it happen."

"So who's in charge here?"

The woman gave him such a pitiful look in response that Quell let her go. She tore across the travertine and disappeared into the Surina Enterprise Facility without a backward glance.

"Suheil," muttered the Islander, half to himself.

"Isn't that Margaret's cousin?" said Natch.

"Second cousin. Or third, I can never remember which. I should've known. . . . Suheil and Jayze probably started taking advantage of her the instant I left."

"Taking advantage? Taking advantage how?"

Quell pursed his lips, and Natch got the impression he had said more than he intended. "I shouldn't have brought you here. This is insane. I don't think you're going to get what you came for."

Natch folded his arms across his chest. "I just wasted half a day on a tube train to get here," he said. "You're not going to scare me away.

I came to get some answers from Margaret, and I'm not leaving until I get them."

The Islander tilted his head back and let his gaze wander up the slim shaft of the Revelation Spire to the summit, hidden high in the clouds. "You won't like what you see."

Natch made a noncommittal noise, squared his shoulders, and headed for the entrance to the Revelation Spire. After a moment, Quell sighed and followed.

The guards who had barred Natch's entrance to the Spire before were still in evidence today, but this time they let him pass. Quell's influence, no doubt. The Islander thrust open the large set of double doors at the tower's base and strode through them.

The inside of the Revelation Spire did not resemble the picture that had lodged in Natch's head all these years. He expected to see a utilitarian space filled with offices and Surina functionaries. Instead he saw a structure that served no useful purpose at all; an ornamentation, a gilded trophy.

The world's tallest building was almost completely hollow. A central column of air extended up through a jungle of structural supports to the limit of Natch's eyesight. Even using Bolliwar Tuban's Telescopics 89d, he could see no sign of the top. One long stairway made a dizzying spiral up the wall, interrupted at periodic intervals by wide platforms cantilevered off the side. Sculptures, statues, and paintings were strewn about everywhere with some avant-garde principle of decoration that eluded Natch. In the middle of it all stood a very lifelike marble representation of Marcus Surina, pointing confidently up into the aether.

So it's a museum then, thought Natch. But if it was a museum, why weren't there any civilians within eyeshot? Why were there only Surina security guards by the dozen, with dartguns drawn and ready? This was a different breed of guard altogether than the ones fumbling around the courtyard; these troops would fire first and ask questions later, if at all.

Quell had obviously been here a million times before and didn't give the pomp and pageantry a second glance. Natch followed him to the foot of the stairway. Half a dozen guards in blue and green blocked their path, and for a second Natch expected some of those dartguns to swivel in his direction. But the guards took a single look at the Islander and dutifully stepped aside. Natch allowed himself a slight sigh of relief.

Stair after stair disappeared behind them. Banners and ceremonial plaques and eclectic sculptures marched by. Natch assumed there had to be an elevator somewhere along the way; not even bio/logically enhanced legs could be expected to climb half a kilometer of stairs unaided.

It wasn't aching muscles that caused him to stop for a breather ten minutes later but the glacial cold permeating the soles of his feet. Natch supposed he should be grateful that the magic of modern architecture kept the Spire from turning into a giant wind tunnel. He scowled, not feeling grateful for anything today. "How do you stand the cold?" Natch complained.

"You get used to it," grunted Quell in response.

The fiefcorp master reached out to the Data Sea and located a program called NumbSoles 85. The program was prefaced with a lengthy warning about the dangers of nerve-enhancing software, which Natch ignored. He quickly revved up the bio/logic code until he could sense his toes again, and the two pressed on.

Finally, some ten stories up, Natch and Quell found themselves standing in front of a bank of elevators. Translucent shafts extended from the top of the elevators into the distance like the pipes of some massive organ. Natch couldn't begin to guess which one led to the Spire's summit, and the troops stationed nearby weren't volunteering any information. Quell strutted into the third elevator from the left without hesitation. Natch followed.

The ride up was a fifteen-minute exercise in tedium. After the first couple dozen floors, the building's architects had abandoned any pretext of utility; the upper levels of the Spire were all but empty, except for the occasional platform of troops aiming heavy weaponry out the windows.

Just when the monotony was growing unbearable, a sixth sense prompted Natch to look up. He saw a large gray mass approaching through the elevator's glass ceiling, a mass that could only be the underside of the Spire's top floor. Carved on that surface was an enormous basrelief sculpture showing an emaciated figure with impossibly long fingers clawing at the elevator shaft. Natch took in the supercilious stare and the hawkish nose, and realized that this was Sheldon Surina. THERE IS NO PROBLEM THAT CANNOT BE SOLVED BY SCIENTIFIC INNOVATION, read the inscription beneath him. Natch shivered as the elevator capsule slid between the talons of the father of bio/logics and came to a stop.

• • •

The door opened. Natch, overwhelmed, let out a gasp.

An enormous observation deck with space for perhaps sixty or seventy people. Sofas and divans spread languorously about the room. Several original Topes in all their psychedelic glory; the armless and legless torso that was the last remaining piece of the *Venus de Milo* perched precariously on a display table. Walls and ceiling made completely from flexible glass, giving the impression that the room floated in the clouds.

"Is he gone?" came a timorous voice from the other side of the room. "Is it safe?"

Margaret Surina.

Natch replayed their last encounter in his mind. It had been a month ago, shortly after the first infoquake and shortly before his runin with the black-robed assailants. He remembered the bodhisattva of Creed Surina as a nondescript woman with raven-black hair and fierce blue eyes. A bio/logic scion struggling to maintain her grace under pressure. But now—

Now Margaret, inventor of MultiReal and heir to the Surina fortune, huddled in a cavernous chair with a dart-rifle in her trembling hands. The gray that had been making slow inroads on her hair had become the dominant color. Her preternaturally large eyes loomed even larger through black rings of sleeplessness that tested the limits of OCHRE technology.

"Is who gone?" said Quell gently, threading his way across the room toward the bodhisattva.

Margaret double-checked that her rifle was cocked and loaded. "Borda," came her hoarse reply.

The fiefcorp master exploded. He could barely restrain himself from kicking a meticulously crafted vase that might have been ancient even in the days of the Autonomous Revolt. "Is he *gone*?" shouted Natch. "Len Borda's been gone for a fucking *month*, Margaret. If you would answer my messages, you'd know that. While *you've* been sitting up here doing nothing, *we've* been putting on demos and planning expositions and trying to appease everyone who's expecting a fully functioning product next week." He gestured wildly out the window at the somnambulant clouds. Their indolence seemed like part of a conspiracy against him. "Of course, it's not going to *be* a fully functioning product, is it? No. Because *I've* been dodging the Defense and Wellness Council for the past four weeks, and *you've* been up here, refusing to help us."

Quell reached Margaret's side and slowly untwined the bodhisattva's fingers from the rifle. The gun slipped to the floor and made a muffled thump on the Persian rug. "Are you okay?" he said in a low voice.

Margaret twitched her nose and blinked in confusion, as if she had been unaware of the Islander's presence until that exact moment. "Is it—is he—is everything okay?" she said, desperation mounting with every syllable. "Why did you come back? Tell me everything's fine. Please, Quell. Tell me he's okay."

The Islander clasped one of her hands between his gargantuan paws. Natch had never imagined that Quell was storing such tenderness inside that bricklike exterior. Once again, the fiefcorp master found himself wondering exactly what kind of relationship the Islander and the bodhisattva had shared for all those years. "Everything's fine," said Quell. "Everything's okay."

"You're—you're sure?"

"Yes." A pause. "Margaret . . . have Jayze and Suheil been up here?"

Margaret gave a hesitant nod. "Yes, they're—they're helping out. Just for a bit, until things . . . calm down."

Quell fired a murderous look out the window at the Indian sky, and Natch was very glad he wasn't Jayze or Suheil Surina at that moment.

But Natch had enough to worry about without getting ensnared in Surina family politics. A half-operational product, the high executive on his back, renegade MultiReal code in his head. He could spare no pity for this cowering shell of a woman. Natch marched across the room and grabbed a straight-backed chair. Then he dragged it in front of the bodhisattva and sat down. Quell shot him a look of disapproval, but Natch would not be deterred. He stared intently into Margaret's face. "I need some answers," he rasped.

Lucidity sparked in Margaret's face. "Natch," she replied evenly. "You're still—Borda hasn't taken control of MultiReal, has he?"

"No, of course not."

"He's going to put pressure on you. You know that, Natch, right?" Margaret's words were slow, methodical, as if she were struggling to remember how to use them. "He'll do to you what he did to my father. Or worse. Borda, he's on some kind of crusade against my family and everything we've touched . . . But Natch, you need to know this—he can't take MultiReal away from you. He *can't*. I've made sure of that."

Natch grabbed hold of himself, realizing that he was dangerously close to the point where rage overcomes reason. He switched on SootheIt 121.5 and waited a few seconds for the mild sedative to buff over his rough nerve endings. "I'm not afraid of Len Borda," he said. "I can handle him. But I need to know why there's MultiReal code in my *head*, Margaret. *I need to know what you did to me.*"

"That's what I'm trying to tell you." Margaret's hands were waving in the air in ever-widening circles. Quell watched those hands like a bird guarding its chick, ready to lash out the instant she got too close to the rifle on the floor. "MultiReal is becoming a part of you. You're not just its owner anymore, Natch—you're the guardian and the keeper."

"What the fuck are you talking about?"

The Islander clasped both of the bodhisattva's hands to his own. "You're afraid of something, Margaret. What is it?"

Margaret collapsed in on herself, despondent. "The nothingness at the center of the universe," she muttered. "The decisions I need to make. I—I'm afraid to make them."

The entrepreneur shot up and began pacing in tight concentric circles of his own, around the chair he had dragged across the room. Quell let go of her hands and made his way to the nearest window, where he glared at the outside world with scarcely concealed contempt. Every few seconds, he would turn back in Margaret's direction to make sure she hadn't picked up the rifle again.

"Listen," said Natch to the bodhisattva. "Let me explain something to you. I can't have mystery code hiding in MultiReal. If the program's interacting with something in my head, I need to know that. This is a *scientific discipline*, Margaret—we need to have the ground rules. You can't expect my engineers to ignore all these questions."

"But you'll have answers. You'll have access to all the answers, when you need them."

"What answers?"

Margaret's eyes were whirlpools spiraling down to an immeasurable depth. "Answers to help you make the crucial decisions."

Natch found a velvet couch nearby and folded himself into its welcoming embrace. Quell was right; this entire trip was a pointless exercise. Perhaps Serr Vigal could sift through Margaret's gibberish, if indeed there were any nuggets of sanity left to be panned from that muddy psyche, but Natch could make no sense of it. He resolved to simply collect her words and keep them handy for later analysis.

As for Quell, he seemed to have abandoned the mission of discovery he had undertaken the other day. His eyes were tinged with a peculiar mixture of concern, compassion, and incandescent rage. He retreated back to the bodhisattva's chair and sat on its arm. Margaret immediately collapsed against him like a mannequin.

But the bodhisattva had not finished her rambling. There was a struggle going on behind her eyes, a final wrenching effort at clarity. "Listen to me, Natch," she said. "You still have options. Don't let them tell you otherwise. The Council, your fiefcorp, anybody. MultiReal is *yours* now, Natch.

"I was foolish to have held on to it for so long. I am not my father. I'm not strong enough to make these decisions. But you . . .

"Natch, I picked you for a reason—because you'll resist Len Borda to your dying breath. You will resist the winter and the void. Understand this—something my father was trying to tell me. The world is new each day, every sunrise a spring and every sunset a winter. I know you'll understand this. You will stand alone in the end, and you will make the decisions that the world demands. The decisions I can't make. I know this. I know it."

There would be no more elucidation coming from Margaret Surina that afternoon, for as she finished the last word she slipped into a sudden fitful sleep. Quell cradled her in his arms, saying nothing. The fiefcorp master could see that the Islander comprehended no more than he did.

Natch stood once more and walked to the closest window. Far down below through the mist, he could see Andra Pradesh laid out before him like a chaotic playground of the gods, but from that quarter there were no answers forthcoming either.

(((15)))

The trouble began with a message in the early hours of the morning—early hours for Horvil, at least, who was still exhausted from yesterday's drudge onslaught and who even in the most lax of times would cross multiple time zones and hotel it to justify a few extra hours of sleep.

The engineer pulled his face from a cool crevice of the sofa and fluttered his eyelids to dispel the pixie dust. Bulky letters were hopping up and down impatiently on their serifs before Horvil's face.

HELP HELP HELP HELP HELP HELP

Horvil rolled onto his back, dropped his head into a net of interwoven fingers, and checked the signature. The message had come from . . . Prosteev Serly?

As an engineer in a highly visible fiefcorp, Horvil had met just about everyone in the Primo's top fifty. The entrepreneur Serly had bought him a few drinks last week on the pretext of fostering good relations among the competition. Never mind that Horvil no longer *was* the competition since MultiReal had come along. It soon became apparent that Serly was really after technical assistance with NiteFocus 51, which he had bought at auction when Natch liquidated the company's old programs. Horvil suspected that Natch wouldn't approve of such generosity to a former competitor, especially with the exposition looming so close. But free booze was free booze. Horvil and Serly spent a few hours in a Turkish bar discussing iterative functions and quantum dynamics and the conductive properties of the optic nerve. Prosteev took lots of notes and, more importantly, poured lots of drinks. The two had parted friends.

Horvil zapped off a ConfidentialWhisper. "How ya doing, Prosteev?"

Prosteev, panicked, teetering on the edge of violence: "What kind of shit did you put in that NiteFocus code, Horv? What's Natch trying to pull? I thought he was getting out of bio/logics, and now he does *this* to me—"

"Hold it, hold it, hold it," interrupted the engineer. "Start from the beginning. I have no idea what you're talking about."

"I'm talking about massive failures with NiteFocus. I'm talking about twelve *thousand* complaints in the past three hours, and more every minute. Now I've got the Meme Cooperative breathing down my neck, people demanding refunds, my analyst threatening to quit—"

Horvil calmed the man down the best he could and asked for temporary access to the MindSpace blueprints. He threw on a robe and shuffled to his workbench. Crumbs from yesterday's sandwich made lazy backflips off his sleeve. (*Read the contract*, he could hear his inner Natch griping. *You don't have to help Prosteev Serly. That sale was final the instant those credits changed hands.*)

Sifting through the soft blues and purples of the NiteFocus code was like catching up with an old friend. Horvil remembered the nimble swing of the programming bar that had created that parabola, the deft touch that had closed those loopholes. He briefly relived the evening when Natch had tested the program on his balcony and declared it unfit for public consumption. Soon Horvil was back in hyperfocus as he sifted through error reports and Plugenpatch specifications.

An hour and a half later, Horvil found the mistake: an improperly defined variable in one of the program's isolated ghettos. He swept through the logs and verified that the error was, in fact, *his* responsibility and not something tacked on later by Serly's engineers. It was a trivial mistake from those frantic nights before the NiteFocus 48 launch. Under normal conditions, such a flaw might go unnoticed for years without causing any trouble. Half the bio/logic programs on the Data Sea had failings like this that would only crop up in the most bizarre situations. Not even Primo's and Dr. Plugenpatch could find them all.

The engineer tossed his programming bar over one shoulder with a well-practiced motion, where it landed on a pillow and rolled to join several others on the floor. He called up bug reports and began cross-referencing the source of the errors. Billboard holographs, mostly, along with the occasional Data Sea news feed.

Horvil turned back to that insignificant thread drooping in Mind-Space like a flaccid phallus. What were the odds of twelve thousand specific calls to that strand in one morning? Astronomical. This was no coincidence. Someone had bought advertising space on those bill-boards and posted *just* the right image with *just* the right resolution at *just* the right time: a perfect storm of sabotage. But how had the sabo-teurs found the flaw? Unless they had stumbled on it by accident, which seemed unlikely, they would have had to reverse-engineer the whole thing from scratch. Not an easy task.

Horvil's mind triangulated with furious speed. Who could spare those kinds of resources? Who could afford to rent all that billboard space for those incriminating holographs? And who had the motive to muck with Horvil's code anyway?

Horvil silently tallied up all the bio/logic programs out there that bore his signature. Optical programs, mental process refiners, memory aids. Four dozen? Five? Certainly if one program was vulnerable to such attack, they all were.

• • •

The yellow jacket floated on the surface of the hoverbird window, life-less, inert. If Natch stared long enough, he could see it drift from side to side like a buoy bobbing on the ocean. There was a faint hum coming from some subterranean register as well. Natch knew it was just a trick of the hoverbird's audiovisual system, a way to hint at information that only a properly configured MindSpace workbench could provide. But until he arrived back in Shenandoah, this poor man's display would have to do.

He was still a few hours out from Shenandoah, closer than he would have been if he had taken the tube with Quell. But the Islander was so upset at the state of affairs in Andra Pradesh, he had decided to stay behind for another day to see what he could accomplish. Natch bristled, thinking of the MultiReal exposition in less than a week and the mountain of programming changes that needed to go to the assembly-line shop in the next forty-eight hours. But in the end he decided to give the Islander some leeway and just get himself home as fast as possible. Thus, a chartered flight, in a four-seater Falcon hoverbird. The pilot had never made any attempt to talk to him; she simply tuned the cockpit windows to a geosynchron weather report and lifted off.

As Andra Pradesh became a memory and Europe fled in the hoverbird's wake, Natch stared at the yellow jacket on the window, evidence of the MultiReal code in his head. *Who planted you there?* he asked the insect. *What are you doing? What relation do you have to the black code?*

What are you waiting for?

Natch was startled out of his reverie by a ConfidentialWhisper request. Horvil. The fiefcorp master waved the blob on the window away until it was nothing but a ghostly presence, a malicious idea. Many meters below, he could see the choppy waves of the English Channel. "What?" he snapped brusquely, shaking his head to jump-start his synapses.

The engineer's tone was tired and fatalistic. "We've got a problem, boss."

"Well? What is it?"

"The Council."

Natch felt a sudden nausea wash over him. It was the same primitive queasiness he had felt the night before initiation, when he had been outflanked and humiliated by Brone, and somehow he knew this was not just another petty harassment. "So what did they do this time?" said Natch, molars grinding.

Horvil let out a 'Whisper-audible sigh. "They sabotaged my programs," he said. "Twelve of 'em so far and counting. No, don't say I'm being paranoid—this has their fingerprints all over it. They figured out a way to generate all these complaints to the Meme Cooperative, and the Meme Cooperative's been funneling them to the Bio/Logic Engineering Guild. They're accusing me of—get this—*deceptive programming.*"

"So you've gotten some complaints. When has that ever—"

"Not just *some* complaints. More complaints than the Guild's ever received for one programmer." Horvil might have sounded amused if he didn't sound so exhausted. "Four million and counting. They're starting up a whole task force."

Natch blinked, hard. Four *million* complaints?

But before he had a chance to process this new datum, he was assaulted by a fresh ConfidentialWhisper request, also labeled urgent. Merri. "Natch," she moaned in a tone redolent of fresh sobbing. "They've—I've—"

Natch slumped down in his seat. "Let me guess. The Council."

Merri's nod was evident even through ConfidentialWhisper. "I don't know for certain—but it *has* to be them. Someone convinced Creed Objectivv to suspend my membership. Here, look." The fiefcorp master felt the neural twitch of an incoming message. He pointed at the hoverbird window and summoned a document whose quasi-mystical font could only have germinated in an Objectivv art department.

Horvil, still prattling on in the background: "I haven't heard anything from the Meme Cooperative yet, but the Engineering Guild is *pissed.* They've taken away my Guild card until this is all cleared up."

"I don't understand," said Natch. "Why would Magan Kai Lee care about some stupid trade guild?"

"It's political," replied the engineer. He seemed remarkably nonchalant, almost jocular, for someone whose career was under siege. "Lots of bad blood between the Guild and the Cooperative. Goes back twenty years. The Guild's been accusing the Co-op of coddling the business interests. So the Co-op keeps one-upping them lately, pushing the envelope. If the Guild takes away your card, then you can bet the Co-op's going to take away your license—"

Natch switched focus back to the channel manager. Labor politics always made him irritable, and all he really needed to know was that the Council was taking aim at Horvil's license to do business. He scrolled feverishly up and down the Creed Objectivv letter that Merri had received. There was only the typical bureaucratic obfuscation: all flourish and no content. "So what's going on, Merri?" he said. "Why did they suspend you?"

"My chapter manager says it's about . . . 'pledging under false pretenses.'"

The entrepreneur writhed under the neural miasma, wishing for the luxury of a molded tube seat instead of the Spartan practicality of this hoverbird chair. "Listen, I'm sorry to hear about this, but—"

"But what does it matter to the fiefcorp?" Merri sighed. "Well, the Objectivv truth-telling oath is a potent tool, Natch. Channelers who've pledged not to lie have a big advantage. So if the Meme Cooperative thinks we're gaming the system . . . If they think I joined the creed *specifically* so the fiefcorp could take advantage of the oath . . ."

"All right, I get it. Unfair competition. Customers filing lawsuits left and right: *I only bought their program because of the oath, and the oath is a sham.*" Perhaps not enough for any kind of conviction, but enough to get an investigation under way. Enough, maybe, to get Merri's license from the Meme Cooperative suspended.

Natch's heart raced. The contours of Magan Kai Lee's scheme were beginning to take shape. Not a military onslaught but a bureaucratic one, with the Cooperative as rifle and business licenses as ammunition. But why? What did Magan get out of suspended licenses?

Two more high-priority pings, almost simultaneous. Benyamin and Serr Vigal. Whatever else the Council was capable of, they had certainly mastered timing and coordination.

"It appears that the Vault has put me under investigation," muttered Vigal without preamble.

"My mother, Natch," said Benyamin, one beat away from abject terror. "She shut down the assembly-line floor."

"She *what?*"

"It was that programming floor manager, Greth Tar Griveth. She must have blabbed something to my mother—that's the only thing I can think of. The Council swooped in and opened an investigation. But that's not the worst part, Natch. My mother, she went into a rage when she found out. She actually ordered the floor to *roll back* the changes to MultiReal they made last month."

The hoverbird made a sudden shimmy from the turbulence. Natch's stomach lurched. "They're *rolling back*—?"

"—and even Primo's uses the Engineering Guild's routines to determine their rankings," continued Horvil, still operating under the assumption that he had the fiefcorp master's full attention. "That's what the rumor is anyway—"

Vigal: "I don't understand it, Natch. Some fool at the Vault has decided that I'm funneling money from my memecorp fund-raising into the fiefcorp. He says the receipts don't add up. The lawyer I talked to even accused me of slipping money to the Surinas, of all people . . ."

"I know what you're thinking, Natch." Merri. "You thought I took the Objectivv truth-telling oath years ago. But no, I only took the oath about nine months before I signed on with you. About the same time you started courting me for the job . . ."

Natch tried to parse through the confused babble streaming through his head, the overlapping ConfidentialWhispers, the worried moans. He tugged at the hoverbird harness as if preparing to stand up and pace off the built-up frustration. But there was no room to pace in this cramped vehicle. So instead he sat in his seat, paralyzed, as the avalanche of bad news came crashing down.

"We've got to do something, Natch. If we don't get to that factory floor *quick*, they could really mess things up. It might take us weeks to sort through it—"

"The Vault's put a hold on all my memecorp accounts. I tried to get on a shuttle to the cognitive processes conference this morning, and they wouldn't even let me board. . . ."

"The silver lining here is that the Guild doesn't have any power to block access to the MultiReal code. Cooperative doesn't either, really. So I can still get the program ready for the exposition, you just can't *pay* me for it. . . ."

"What should I do, Natch? The creed must be so disappointed in me. . . . I don't even know where to start. . . ."

"You know I've always been lazy about balancing the books, Natch, and it's just so complicated with money going in and out all over the place. You don't suppose that somewhere in the past few years I might have misplaced a few—"

"Horvil's going to *hate* me. . . ."

Natch turned to the window for a calming vision of the sea and saw only the illicit chunk of MultiReal code they had found in his head.

A ping. A text message, from Quell.

Be on your guard. We spotted a whole cluster of Council hoverbirds on the outskirts of Andra Pradesh a few hours ago, headed your way. Looks like they might be following you.

Natch sat back, activated a bio/logic routine to stanch the flow of sweat from his brow, and dialed the ConfidentialWhisper discussions down to a murmur. *Stop*, he told himself. *Calm down.*

He inhaled deeply and let the rarefied hoverbird oxygen rush into his lungs. *The Council wants you in a panic*, he thought. *They want you confused. They want you to make mistakes.* He found a snapshot of memory and held it up: a young boy, sullen and wild-eyed, threatening to report the capitalman Figaro Fi to the authorities. He had blown his chance at getting seed money for a fiefcorp and wasted several years of his life as a consequence. And why? Because he had been flummoxed by Brone.

But that's not going to happen again.

You can beat them.

Natch uncurled his fingers from their death grip on the armrest and slid into a straight and narrow mental groove. He watched himself coolly line up the fiefcorpers' wocs as if in spreadsheet columns. Horvil's termination from the Bio/Logic Engineering Guild. Merri's suspension from Creed Objectivv. Vigal's supposed financial improprieties. Ben's mother's attempt to roll back their MultiReal code. Quell's security issues at the Surina compound. Margaret's stupor. Jara's—

The panic lapped briefly over his mental seawalls, bolstered by exhaustion and doubt and black code. Why hadn't he received any word from Jara?

He tried pinging her. No response. Again, and again. Still nothing.

Stay focused, Natch admonished himself. *Think. What's the Council trying to do?* Magan Kai Lee had unleashed a torrent of suspensions, improprieties, and investigations on him, all scrupulously planned and nearly impossible to trace back to the Council. But what did it really add up to in the end? Clearly he was missing something. Where did *he* factor in? What catastrophe did Magan have waiting for him?

The last ConfidentialWhisper arrived from Robby Robby. "Bad news for ya, Natchster," said the channeler. He paused, waiting for some interjection from Natch that did not come. "Just tried to bring my team out to São Paulo for a look around the soccer stadium, and they wouldn't let us in. Told me the exposition's been canceled. Can you beat that? Jara's orders, they said. I tried to set them straight, but they—"

Robby's sentence was sliced off abruptly in midsyllable. But it wasn't just Robby—all of Natch's ConfidentialWhisper threads with his employees had been cut. He turned to the window, wondering if there was some kind of malfunction with the hoverbird, and discovered his connection to the MindSpace workbench in Shenandoah was gone too. In place of the yellow jacket was a Defense and Wellness Council hoverbird matching their course. Natch looked out the other window to find a second vehicle bracketing him in.

Raw and bloody anger. "What the fuck is going on?" he barked at the pilot.

The woman seemed unconcerned. She rapped her knuckles against the side of the hoverbird. "Don't bother trying to access the Data Sea," she said. "Nothing's getting through this hull unless we want it to get through."

"Where are you taking me?"

"The Twin Cities," she said, turning back to the weather reports and traffic chatter on the window. "Might as well get some sleep while you can. You're not going anywhere."

(((16)))

Natch didn't sleep for an instant.

The Council could have taken him just about anywhere in human space. He was powerless to stop them. Rumor posited the existence of hundreds of anonymous government compounds far from the civilized world that would be ideal places for interrogation and coercion.

So when the pilot began a familiar flight pattern toward the foggy lowlands of the Twin Cities, Natch couldn't help but expel a breath of relief. The Kordez Thassel Complex below was many things—libertarian gathering place, corporate Mecca, architectural perdition—but it certainly was not a Defense and Wellness Council stronghold. The Thasselians prided themselves on running a facility that was open and anonymous to all. This meant that Len Borda's lackeys had to go through the mundane process of filing a room request and shelling out a deposit, like the rest of the ants Natch could see milling around below. Somehow that comforted him.

Then Natch was ambushed by a brutal thought. Why *wouldn't* the Council take him to one of those secretive compounds, unless they had nothing to fear from him?

Natch thought it best to project an image of confidence. "You know the minute I leave this hoverbird, I'm going to summon John Ridglee and Sen Sivv Sor," he announced.

"Save your bandwidth," replied the pilot, yawning. "They've already been summoned. In two hours, this place is going to be crawling with drudges."

Natch let her finish her landing sequence in silence. At least he could console himself that the pilot was not setting down at the normal hoverbird dock across the creek, but at a more exclusive parking space in the rear of the building.

He expected to see an intimidating squad of armed Council officers when the hoverbird hatch opened. Instead, there stood a woman with wild braids of ebony hair. Natch felt a shock of cognitive dissonance as he recognized the face of Len Borda's chief solicitor, a face that should rightly be hugging the margins of some gossip column. The Blade. Standing behind her was a blond mercenary with the shoulders of an ogre and the demeanor to match.

"Towards Perfection," said Rey Gonerev, bowing smartly. "On behalf of High Executive Len B—"

Natch cut her off. "Jara," he said. "Where the fuck is Jara?"

Gonerev fluttered her eyelids rapidly. How long had it been since anyone had treated her like a petty obstacle? "She's inside with the rest of the fiefcorp," said the Blade, after a moment's hesitation.

"Good," said the entrepreneur. "Now *move*." The solicitor barely managed to scoot out of the way before Natch came barreling past.

Gonerev and the other Council officer struggled to keep up as he strode toward the closest door of the Thassel Complex. *I hate this place*, thought Natch as he walked through the doors and took in the deliberately crooked floors and the unevenly cut stone walls. He headed for a door at the far end of the hallway that was being guarded by a handful of men in white robes and yellow stars. Nobody made any move to correct his course.

Natch tried to think of some valiant act that could get him out of this predicament. Should he run? Should he call the Council's bluff and contact the drudges? But every path led to the same endpoint: he needed to see Jara. He needed to know what was going on. Indeed, as much as it chagrined him, Natch knew his best option at this point was to proceed as Rey Gonerev directed.

It was a relatively deserted wing of the complex, but still swarming with self-important businesspeople buzzing from meeting to meeting. One of the insects did not see him coming—a Vault employee, if the double balanced pyramids on his belt were any indication. Natch collided with the man, sending the two of them reeling in opposite directions. Enraged at everything and nothing at once, the fiefcorp master thrust his palms forward and shoved the bureaucrat flat onto his back. *When the universe pushes me, I push back!*

And then Natch was standing, immobilized, trying to calibrate a cerebral compass that was spinning wildly out of control. He lost sight of his whereabouts for a few seconds and felt himself slip into an extradimensional space between moments. The blankness of multivoid, the empty husk of the OCHRE probe in his apartment the other day.

The nothingness at the center of the universe.

Suddenly Natch caught sight of the Vault official sprawled on the floor, frozen as if caught in a basilisk's stare, and something inside him curdled. The blond mercenary was helping the man to his feet with the assistance of another Council officer, while Gonerev was staring at Natch with surprise and perhaps a little trepidation. He didn't stick around to apologize.

The white-robed men and women parted to let him through to the door. Natch paused, remembering the time he had come to the Thassel Complex to meet with his old hivemate Brone. The meeting had begun with an electrical shock from the door handle, followed by Brone's ghoulish laughter. Could this entire thing be a setup? Natch was fairly certain that the Council hoverbirds outside were real Council hoverbirds, and the Council officers here were real Council officers. But this facility was owned and operated by Creed Thassel, the creed Brone had purchased with his riches. The organization's membership rolls were secret. Who was to say these people couldn't be Council officers *and* Thasselian devotees?

He opened the door and walked inside.

Natch found himself standing on a stone slab atop a mist-shrouded alp, the Mount Olympus of some long-dead cultural imagination. The SeeNaRee was littered with broken columns and armless stone maidens that might once have held up the ceiling. Above him, impossibly muscular clouds were girding for battle against an otherwise gorgeous blue sky.

Sitting in the midst of the slab was an ordinary rectangular conference table. Benyamin, Jara, Horvil, Merri, and Serr Vigal lined the sides of the table looking alternately scared and defiant. There was no sign of Quell. Sitting at the head of the table was Lieutenant Executive Magan Kai Lee, flanked by a dozen Council guards with stony faces.

The fiefcorp master turned to Jara. "So I leave you alone for a couple of days, and you go to the *Council?*" cried Natch. "What were you *thinking?*"

Jara writhed uncomfortably in her seat for a few seconds, refusing to meet the entrepreneur's gaze. Her face reflected a troubled and self-loathing soul. "Fuck you," she growled. A miserable-looking Merri put her hand on Jara's shoulder, and the analyst fell back into an uneasy silence.

Magan's face was the very archetype of calm. He was wearing his formal uniform, complete with the gray smock that was the sign of his office. "Have a seat," he said on seeing the fiefcorp master. "Ridgello, make sure he doesn't leave my sight until this is finished." The fair-haired barbarian who had accompanied the Blade pulled out a chair at the table's foot and extended his hand in Natch's direction. Four of the officers behind Magan marched across the stone and made a confining semicircle around the chair.

Natch bottled up his rage and took a seat in the chair Ridgello had proffered him.

Magan Kai Lee sat up straight and folded his hands together calmly on the table. "Four weeks ago today, this company made a promise to the Defense and Wellness Council," he began, his voice matter-of-fact. "You promised High Executive Borda access to MultiReal in exchange for protection at your sales demo. The Council held up its end of the bargain. The Surina/Natch MultiReal Fiefcorp did not."

Natch found the lieutenant's declaration amusing. "So what are you going to do, arrest all of us? Throw us in your orbital prisons? Go right ahead, we're unarmed. Have fun explaining it to the drudges. Len Borda can't be *that* contemptuous of public opinion—especially now that the libertarians run the Congress of L-PRACGs."

"I have no intention of arresting you," said Magan.

"So why go after my apprentices' business licenses? Do you *really* think we care what the Meme Cooperative does to us? You might have slowed us down a little, but you aren't any closer to getting access to MultiReal."

Magan let out an almost-imperceptible sigh, as if Natch were hardly worth the effort of a response. "Go ahead, Rey," he said. "Let's just get this over with."

The Blade strode out from behind the fiefcorp master; Natch had forgotten that she was even back there. He felt an internal ping informing him that he had received a message of high importance. "What's this?" he sneered.

"That," said Gonerev, "is the brief my office filed yesterday charging you with a hundred and twenty violations of Meme Cooperative bylaws."

Natch opened the document and tried to skim its murky surface, but it was clouded with administrative doublespeak and he could make no sense of it. He fired up the Ripley Group's DeLegalese 235 and waited a few seconds for the program to filter out the unnecessary clauses and redundancies.

But Gonerev had already begun delivering a précis of her own as she strode around the edge of the stone slab like a prosecutor grandstanding before a particularly susceptible jury. "Failure to pay the Prime Committee tax to fund diss access to Dr. Plugenpatch," she announced. "Breach of contract against three different channeling firms in 356 and 357 . . . False advertising of a glare-reduction program marketed to three thousand different L-PRACGs in 358 . . . Failure to file proper work permits in Omaha . . ." The litany of

Natch's sins both great and small continued for several minutes, filling the SeeNaRee with a haze of regulatory vocabulary.

Natch let out a loud and ostentatious yawn. He didn't doubt that he was guilty of these complaints, and dozens more besides, but not even a niggling entity like the Meme Cooperative would waste its time on such trivia. The entrepreneur waved his hand and broadcast the document in large block capitals across the deep blue sky for all to read. "Please don't tell me you dragged us out here for *this*," he said. "I've been in front of the Cooperative arbitration boards a million times for shit like this. They never do anything."

"Oh, but they have this time." Rey Gonerev's voice was one big gloat as she leaned over the table next to Jara and placed her hands flat on the table. "Not only has the Meme Cooperative filed charges against you, but they've voted to suspend your license to operate a fiefcorp."

"Here," said the lieutenant executive, giving the slightest of nods, "is the notification you will be receiving from the Cooperative any moment now."

The entrepreneur opened Magan's message in private this time—though judging by the worried frowns percolating from the fiefcorpers' faces, they had all received copies anyway.

NOTIFICATION

In accordance with the bylaws and regulations of the MEME COOPERA-TIVE, incorporated in Year 177 of the Reawakening and given jurisdiction by the collective fiefcorps and memecorps to govern intra-business affairs, and which has been recognized as a lawful entity and given license by the PRIME COMMITTEE and the CONGRESS OF L-PRACGS, as of Tuesday, the 3rd of January in the 360th Year of the Reawakening, this body hereby suspends the business license for NATCH of the SURINA/NATCH MULTIREAL FIEFCORP for a period of no less than 30 days, pending review by the Cooperative's executive board, at which point further action may be undertaken.

This was a slightly more worrisome development. Natch should have figured that if the Council could find enough to soil his apprentices' reputations—if they could even dig something up on Merri and Serr Vigal—surely they could find the buried skeletons of the Meme Cooperative board too. A little push here and there, and a slap on the wrist becomes a bash with a shovel.

Natch leaned back in his chair and threw his arms behind his head, causing Ridgello to back up a step. "So you suspended our licenses," said the entrepreneur breezily. "That just puts MultiReal back where it started. On top of that spire in Andra Pradesh. Good luck getting in *there*."

"Maybe you've been too preoccupied to hear the news," replied the Blade, walking around the table once more. "Margaret has been declared mentally unfit. Procedures are under way to remove her as the head of Creed Surina, and the Meme Cooperative has acted to suspend her business license as well."

Natch hadn't realized how dire the situation in Andra Pradesh was; now he understood Quell's apprehension. Those slippery cousins of Margaret's must have finally tired of chafing under her mercurial leadership and taken action. With the Council's support, of course. It was barely worth mentioning that Islanders were nonentities to the Meme Cooperative; Quell could earn an apprentice's wages but was legally unable to make any binding decisions for the company.

Natch ran his hand over his forehead and rubbed a spot on the bridge of his nose. "You're stupider than I thought," he said, shaking his head. "Didn't you think this through? You can temporarily decapitate the fiefcorp. . . . You can convince those inbreeds at Andra Pradesh to push Margaret out of the way. . . . You can bribe my analyst to go along with a fat sheaf of credits." Jara leaned forward to make an objection, her expression confused and angry, but Natch didn't give her the chance to speak. "But you still don't have access to MultiReal. Don't you of all people know the *law*? Even if you throw us in prison, the Possibilities program stays in receivership. It just floats out there on the Data Sea for years until the courts have had their say. You can't touch it. Len Borda can't touch it. Meantime, the rest of us pay a two-thousand-credit fine to the Meme Cooperative, and we get our licenses back in thirty days."

Magan seemed utterly unfazed. Natch got the impression that he was still following the Council's preprepared script. "It's you who doesn't understand," said the lieutenant executive. "The Defense and Wellness Council has no intention of seizing MultiReal. The program rightfully belongs to the new master of the Surina/Natch MultiReal Fiefcorp—and there it will stay."

"*New* master?"

"The only member of the company whose business license hasn't been suspended. The Meme Cooperative has handed control of the fief-corp to your analyst, Jara."

• • •

Natch could feel the black code creeping across his flesh, biting, gnawing, envenoming him with each breath. He remembered feeling this way when he had discovered that Margaret had kept the Patels' MultiReal license secret from him. He had felt this way during the horror of the Shortest Initiation. But now, his emotions were amplified somehow by the black code inside him, or the MultiReal code inside him, or both.

Magan's face reflected a look of workmanlike satisfaction, like someone who had just completed a vexing puzzle. "You will be receiving an official notification from the Meme Cooperative at any moment," he said. "The Cooperative is compelling you to hand over core access to the MultiReal code to Jara."

"And if I refuse?" said Natch.

The lieutenant executive gestured at the troops surrounding Natch's chair, who were suddenly placing their hands on their dartgun holsters. "We are authorized to take you to an orbital Council prison until you comply," said Magan.

Along the sides of the table, the fiefcorpers were subtly recoiling from Jara. Horvil had a look of concentration as if he were factoring polynomials in his head. Had Jara really made a deal with the Council to seize control of the fiefcorp? Or was this just part of Magan Kai Lee's vicious game against them? Jara's emotions were hunkering down behind a perfect PokerFace, but her nervous fidgeting told Natch that she was tremendously conflicted.

Natch admitted that the Council's plot against him was indeed an elegant one. Rope off MultiReal, keep it in an isolated area where he could touch all he wanted but was unable to make a profit from it. Put the company in the hands of Jara, who was certainly much more pliable than Natch and predictable to a fault. Summon the drudges to a press conference and get the ball rolling right away.

And what could Natch do about it? He supposed he could use MultiReal to escape from the Kordez Thassel Complex. Would even MultiReal be enough to evade the dartguns of all the guards standing around here? But after that, he would be a fugitive. And escaping the Council's notice this time would be much more trying, since the Meme Cooperative had given them the legislative cover to freeze his Vault account, seize his apartment, even put a price on his head.

Yet there was something missing. If Magan was looking for an empty suit that Len Borda could intimidate into handing over Multi-Real, wouldn't Merri or Vigal have been better choices? He gazed across the table into the eyes of the Council lieutenant, chestnut-colored and mysterious. Natch knew the look of a man who had something to hide.

Within the cusp of an instant, Natch felt himself looking at the world from Magan Kai Lee's perspective. And in that moment he knew where Magan had made his crucial mistake.

The entrepreneur grinned, leaned farther back in his chair, and propped his feet up on the table. "Horvil," said Natch with a mad glint in his eye, "have you cleaned out the dock lately?"

The engineer looked around the mountaintop as if he expected to find another Horvil who would understand why his boss had abruptly switched gears. *The fiefcorp dock?* he mouthed silently. Benyamin offered him a perplexed shrug. So Horvil pursed his lips as he cast his mind out to the Data Sea and scanned the company's program launch space. "All clean now," he said.

"Good. Load Possibilities 1.0 on the dock. We're releasing it right now."

A cyclone of gasps came blustering across the table. Magan Kai Lee's jaw clenched, and Natch could almost hear the grinding of Rey Gonerev's teeth. Jara leaned over and grabbed Merri's arm out of instinct. Natch could feel the Council officers encircling him tense up and give one another looks of confusion.

"The Meme Cooperative voted to yank our licenses," said Natch. "But that notice says it doesn't take effect until January third."

"That's today," protested Horvil.

"Here it is. At the Meme Cooperative's offices in Melbourne, it is. But on the orbital colony of Patronell, at the *headquarters* of the Meme Cooperative, it's still January second, isn't it? It won't be the third for another"—Natch squinted his eyes and consulted the time—"two and a half hours. Which means I'm still the master of the fiefcorp until then. And *I* say we're releasing MultiReal now."

"But—"

"Merri, get ahold of Robby Robby. Use an emergency protocol if you have to. I'll bet he can sell at least a few hundred thousand copies of Possibilities in two hours."

Magan, Gonerev, and Ridgello appeared to be having a furious exchange over ConfidentialWhisper, punctuated by arching eyebrows and flaring nostrils. Seconds later, the Blade's right arm shot up in the air. "*Radium!*" she shouted, and a dozen dartguns snapped into Council hands in unison.

Ben let out a high-pitched wheeze. "Natch, we haven't run Possibilities through Dr. Plugenpatch yet. What—what if it doesn't *work?*"

"It worked just fine at that soccer stadium the other day."

"But my mother's assembly-line floor . . . The rollback . . ."

Natch laughed with a serenity he hadn't felt in weeks. "Running it through the Plugenpatch system won't do any good," he said. "There isn't a validator out there that knows how to deal with a program as radical as MultiReal. And don't worry about the rollback right now. They haven't had enough time to do any significant damage. The customers'll just have to take their chances. But just in case . . . Benyamin, you've got sixty seconds. Write me a quick disclaimer that basically says 'Buyer Beware.'"

"Launch that program," rasped Magan, "and it'll be the last thing you do." He was now completely thrown off his script and improvising wildly.

Natch ignored him, just as he ignored the ten Council officers who rushed into formation around his chair and bull's-eyed him with the barrels of their rifles. Merri was rubbing her knees and rocking back and forth, deeply entrenched in ConfidentialWhisper with Robby Robby. Vigal had one trembling hand raised as if waiting for a proctor to call on him, and Jara was simply dead to the world.

"Okay, Horv," said Natch, "I've put a fore and an aft on the Possibilities program. Version set at 1.0. Ben, got that disclaimer?"

Benyamin looked as serious as a scorpion. "Yeah, I found a good one in Billy Sterno's catalog. Should I—"

"Just throw it in the fore table. Horv, get ready to launch the program onto the Data Sea on my signal." Horvil sputtered something multisyllabic and unintelligible. "Well? What?" snapped Natch.

"Price?" whimpered the engineer.

"Eighty thousand Vault credits," said Natch without hesitation, choosing the first round number that floated into his head. "Unlimited choice cycles."

Merri slumped to the table like a discarded puppet. Eighty thousand was a gargantuan number, far beyond the reach of the average Data Sea pedestrian. It wasn't the highest price tag a bio/logic program had ever earned, but it certainly came close. "Robby wants to know who's going to buy it at that price," said the channel manager weakly.

Natch's grin broadened. "Everyone who can possibly get their hands on eighty thousand Vault credits. Lunar tycoons, L-PRACGs, creeds, capitalmen, you name it. Make sure Robby spreads the word that the Meme Cooperative is cutting off sales in two hours. Once people realize this might be their only chance to get a taste of Multi-Real, they'll spare no expense. Trust me, by the time dawn arrives on Patronell, people'll be stacking multiple realities up like bricks. And we'll all be so rich that we won't *care* what happens next."

The door burst open, and a dozen more white-robed officers swooped into the SeeNaRee with dartguns primed and ready. But they bypassed Natch altogether and headed straight for Serr Vigal. The neural programmer yelped and tumbled off his chair, finally ducking behind Horvil, who didn't exactly make inconspicuous cover. Above them, the clouds had conquered the azure sky and looked ready to rain down the fury of the gods.

"Y-you can't release that program," stammered the chief solicitor. "The Prime Committee gave the Council the authority to shut down any program on the Data Sea, just last month."

"Shut down?" said Natch. "Fine. Shut it down. Have you even *used* that authority yet? You have procedures in place for this? Think you can figure them out and cut through all the red tape in the next"—he consulted the time—"two hours and eighteen minutes?" It was a bluff, but it seemed to work. Was that actually *fear* in Rey Gonerev's eyes?

Benyamin started to say something, then stopped. Horvil stared down the guards and puffed up his chest with sudden bravado. Merri had gotten up from her chair and was backing toward the edge of the stone slab as if she might make a break for it. Magan Kai Lee's eyes were spotlights.

Natch raised a hand. "Everybody ready?"

Just at that moment, an improbably tall and gangly figure came rushing through the door, white robe flapping in the mountain gale. His eyes were saturated with sheer panic, but it wasn't a panic that concerned the fiefcorp master or MultiReal. The man bolted straight for Magan Kai Lee, grabbed his sleeve, and blasted some silent message in the lieutenant executive's face.

Seconds later, the dartguns of the Council officers dropped. A few rifles clattered noisily to the stone.

Without a word or a glance Natchward, Magan Kai Lee arose and made for the door, his face coated with some military flavor of a PokerFace program. He made a quick gesture with his right hand, causing the soldiers to abandon their aggressive positions around the fiefcorp. Ridgello and his officers formed a tight cordon around the lieutenant executive, and they all marched hurriedly out of the SeeNaRee.

Rey Gonerev was the last to leave. Natch leapt up from his seat and grabbed her shoulder. "Give me one reason I shouldn't launch MultiReal right now," he said.

The Blade's expression was distant, disconcerted. "Because," she said. "Margaret Surina is dead."

Natch had never seen a team shift tracks as quickly as the Defense and Wellness Council. A moment ago, the fiefcorpers had been surrounded by armed stormtroopers wearing the white robe and yellow star; now they were alone in the precipitous mountain SeeNaRee. Even the clouds had abandoned them.

Margaret Surina dead? Last month, Natch would have wondered how any assassin could possibly get to the top of that tower with all those guards around. But he had seen the condition of the Surina security forces not twelve hours ago. Penetrating that protective shell of troops around the Revelation Spire wasn't such a daunting task—especially if one had inside help.

Still, if someone could get to the bodhisattva of Creed Surina that easily, why didn't they come after Natch first?

Natch looked around the SeeNaRee and took in the stunned expressions flitting across the brows of his apprentices. Any thought of MultiReal and fiefcorp licenses had vanished from their faces. Natch didn't know whether to feel relieved to be free of the Council or frightened to be without their protection. What he wanted more than anything was to retreat home, or to Omaha, or to the redwoods. Safe places.

And then his thoughts came circling back to Andra Pradesh. Margaret, lying dead at the top of a heavily fortified building, surrounded by a large private security force. There *were* no safe places anymore.

"I'm going over there," he announced, rebelling against impulse.

A skeptical pause from the fiefcorp. "Where?" said Jara. It was the first word she had spoken since her abrupt curse when Natch arrived.

"Andra Pradesh," said Natch. "To find Quell. Find out what's going on."

"Are we sure there *is* anything going on?" said Serr Vigal. Everyone looked at him. "I mean, do we know Margaret's death was foul play?"

Jara snorted. "What do you think it was—'natural causes'?"

Horvil suddenly dashed over and gripped Natch by the elbow. "You can't go," he protested. "What if it's a trap? What if—what if the people who killed Margaret are still there?"

"Horvil's right," said Benyamin. He folded his arms across his chest. "How do we know the Blade was even telling the truth? Sounds like a perfect setup. Get everyone in a panic, lure you to Andra Pradesh, and then—"

Merri shook her head, despondent. "The bodhisattva of Creed Objectivv just issued a statement offering his condolences. Rey Gonerev wasn't lying." The channel manager stopped and parsed her thoughts carefully. "Well, she wasn't lying about *that*, at least."

The entrepreneur noticed that none of the fiefcorpers suspected Magan Kai Lee had dreamt this up on the spur of the moment, to prevent the release of MultiReal. But on further reflection, Natch realized that it didn't matter. Whether Margaret Surina was really dead or not, the news would completely overshadow everything else on the Data Sea within seconds. No amount of sales wizardry on Robby Robby's part would entice people to buy Possibilities in the next two hours.

"All right," said Natch. "Where's the closest multi facility?"

• • •

The multi gateway at the Surina compound was closed. The network dumped him at a public terminal a kilometer away instead. Natch hiked the rest of the way through the city, studying the compound on the mountain the whole time for any signs of violence. He saw none, although he did see a number of egg-white Council hoverbirds touching down. As for the citizens of Andra Pradesh, word of Margaret's death had obviously not reached them yet.

When he reached the iron gates at the base of the hill, Natch was surprised to find them already guarded by troops in white, not blue and green. A crowd of curious onlookers began to coalesce across the street. *What if they don't let me in?* Natch asked himself.

The Council officers gave the fiefcorp master a long, probing look, and then let him in. With an armed escort.

Natch couldn't remember if he had ever seen the Surina courtyard empty. Even in the early-morning hours, after the Center for Historic Appreciation shut its doors and Gandhi University wrapped up its academic semester, there were always people wandering around. Fiefcorpers liked to lounge here between midnight meetings in the Enterprise Facility, and there was always a pair of lovers or some forlorn poet staring reverently up at the Spire.

Now the only feet treading on the mountaintop belonged to Natch and his two Council escorts. The men were shaky and silent as junkies as they led the way to some unannounced destination; Natch could only hope they were going to the scene of the crime. *What happened to Surina security?* he wondered.

At that moment, as if responding to Natch's thoughts, the doors to the auditorium burst open and a gang of Surina officers came sprinting their way.

They were moving too quickly and chaotically for Natch to count, but he figured the number to be about twenty. Some of the Surina troops threw apprehensive looks over their shoulders, as if expecting an imminent pursuit. At the front of the blue-green wedge was a familiar figure.

Quell.

The Islander came to a halt mere centimeters from the Councilman on Natch's left. The man gulped audibly as he took in Quell's bulging chest and untamed ponytail. "We'll take those guns," declared the Islander, his voice gravel.

The Council lackey shot a glance at his compatriot. They

exchanged grim frowns of courage. "I'm sorry, Islander," he said. "We're not allowed to do that."

Quell made no signal to the crowd of security officers gathered behind him; nevertheless, their dartguns all leapt into their hands simultaneously. The Islander slowly unsheathed a metal bar of the darkest obsidian from his belt, a long nightstick sizzling with bottled lightning. "I said *we're taking those guns*."

The Council officers winced, and Natch did too. He had heard plenty of stories about Islander shock batons. A crack on the skull with one of those things could splatter the guards' brains all over the travertine, OCHREs or no OCHREs.

The men in white robes handed over their weapons.

"What's happening?" asked Natch as he trotted across the courtyard, trying to keep up with Quell's massive strides.

"I don't know," grunted the Islander. "The Council swooped in. Caught us all off guard. They started herding everyone into the auditorium like fucking sheep." He glanced behind him at Borda's lackeys, who were being muscled toward the Center for Historic Appreciation by a subset of the blue-and-green troops. "Jayze Surina just waved the Council in."

"What about—"

Quell cut him off with a snarl. "I said I *don't know*. But we're going to find out." Natch noticed that he had not sheathed his shock baton, opting to curl it like a barbell instead. That stick had to be pretty heavy to strain *Quell's* massive biceps.

Surina security officers began to trickle out the side doors of the auditorium and join the small group marching on the Revelation Spire. So far there was no sign of any Council reinforcements, but Natch knew it was only a matter of time. He could feel adrenaline spiking his veins and started to reach for a bio/logic tranquilizer, then decided to let his body chemistry handle itself.

The Surina troops flattened themselves against the base of the Spire and hid in shadow. Quell crept up to the double doors, then cracked them open and lobbed something into the atrium, grenade-style. There was a dull *fwump*. The Islander counted to three under his breath and then pushed inside, yanking Natch through the doors with him.

Natch saw white-robed figures lying all over the floor, hands clutched to their faces. A few were actually mewling in pain like puppies. It wasn't as large a contingent of Council officers as Natch had expected, but still more than enough to hold up the party of Surina troops until backup arrived. An egg-shaped device was rolling on the floor, not too far from the marble statue of Marcus Surina. The thing was burning heat circles in Natch's vision even now during its cooling cycle.

"Did you blind them?" cried the entrepreneur incredulously. He glanced at the pockets of Quell's jacket, wondering what other thaumaturgic surprises the Islander had stowed away there.

"For about ten more seconds," said Quell. "Hurry."

They weren't heading for the staircase Natch had ascended the other day. Instead, Quell was making for an inconspicuous side door behind one of the museum exhibits. THE AUTONOMOUS MINDS AND THEIR KEEPERS, read the holographic sign hovering over a group of mannequins in paisley uniforms. The nearby Council officers were just beginning to claw the floor for their dart-rifles when Quell, Natch, and a dozen other officers streaked through the side door and barricaded it behind them.

A narrow staircase, awash in the red glow of emergency lighting. Another door, invisible to the naked eye, that glided open at the touch of Quell's hand. A lift large enough to fit fourteen.

Nobody said a word during the long, drab climb up the interior of the spike. This clandestine elevator car didn't offer an interior view of the Spire's scaffolding like the one Natch had ridden the other day, so there was nothing to see but shuddering wall. Instead he watched the Surina officers slide new canisters of black code darts into their guns. Quell had chosen his crew well. These were hardened professionals, seemingly unafraid of a dustup with the Defense and Wellness Council.

What if this is all just an elaborate ruse to get me alone? thought Natch. *What if Magan Kai Lee is preparing to do me in here, away from the rest of the fiefcorp?*

The elevator slipped into its berth at the top of the shaft. Quell was snorting like an angry bull. The doors opened.

Natch had no idea what a real murder scene looked like. The entire concept belonged in the realm of things only seen on viewscreens. He half expected to see overturned furniture or shattered glass or copious amounts of blood, but nothing of the kind was in evidence. The room looked exactly as it had less than a day ago. The same elegantly cushioned seating bookended by priceless sculpture; the same windows letting in the glum cumulus of the Indian sky; the *Venus de Milo.*

Magan Kai Lee and several of his officers were there, along with a number of unarmed officials from different government agencies. They displayed no hint of surprise at seeing Quell and the rest of his party, and despite being outnumbered, Magan's face showed total unconcern. The tall, awkward officer who had interrupted them at the Kordez Thassel Complex was sniffing at the furniture like a bloodhound. A distraught woman in a serving uniform was being questioned at the far end of the room; Natch could only assume she was the one who had discovered the body. There was no sign of Rey Gonerev or Ridgello, or of Len Borda for that matter.

Quell stepped forward. His eyes blazed hot crazy. "You had no business forcing us into the auditorium like that," he said through gritted teeth.

One Council officer gave an inquiring look in Magan's direction and made the slightest of gestures toward his well-stocked rifle. The diminutive lieutenant shook his head. "I'm sorry," said Magan, though his face exhibited no such emotion. "We had to make sure the people who did this weren't still up here."

"What did you do with—?" Quell didn't finish his sentence. His jaw rocked back and forth uncontrollably as he caught sight of the desk across the room and the inert figure slumped in a chair before it.

Margaret Surina.

The Islander bounded to her on unsteady legs, letting his shock baton drag on the floor in the process. He slumped to his knees and buried his face in the dead woman's tunic. The bodhisattva's shoulder muffled his sobs.

Natch sidled toward the window and found an unobtrusive spot where he could observe the body. There was no sign of violence that Natch could see. It looked to him like Margaret had just slumped over in place with no provocation. Her luminous eyes of opal blue were still open and staring back as if across an unimaginably vast distance.

I was foolish to have held on to it for so long, she had told him. *I am not my father. I'm not strong enough to make these decisions. But you . . .*

The world is new each day, every sunrise a spring and every sunset a winter. I know you'll understand this. You will stand alone in the end, and you will make the decisions that the world demands. The decisions I can't make.

"Any sign of a dart, Papizon?" Magan asked the ungainly Council officer.

Papizon scuttled to the desk and leaned over to scrutinize Margaret's pale face. He seemed to either not notice Quell's anguish or not understand it. "No," he replied. "Not that I can see." He might well have been studying bacteria under a microscope.

"Dissolving dart?" one of the government officials chimed in.

Papizon narrowed his eyes and sniffed gingerly in the air. "Usually leaves a faint trace of sulfur. Could be, but I don't smell anything. The forensic team can verify when they get here."

"Everything locked down until then?" said Magan.

Natch had read something once about a special polymer the Council used to keep forensic evidence in place. It was supposed to be only molecules thick and practically invisible, some kind of miracle coating that kept every hair and dust mote from drifting off. That would explain why nobody was protesting Quell's handling of the body. "All locked down," confirmed Papizon, eyeing the Islander with suspicion.

Unsure what to do, the fiefcorp master took a seat next to the limbless *Venus de Milo*. Council officers fanned around the room with their noses to the ground, looking for evidence, but what they were hoping to find Natch didn't know. The Surina troops, meanwhile, had gathered near the window, where they were muttering to themselves.

Quell's tears continued unabated for several minutes, but despite Papizon's obvious concern for the sanctity of the evidence, nobody made any move to pry him away. Natch watched the Islander with amazement. Ever since that first tour of the Surina compound several weeks ago, he had known that Margaret and Quell were more than just master and apprentice. But he had never expected a display like *this*.

Magan Kai Lee clasped his hands behind his back and stepped to the window, where he confronted the enormity of Andra Pradesh laid out before him. From where he was sitting, Natch could see the lieutenant executive's face reflected in the glass. His expression was aggressively neutral, a study in forced calm.

"Don't worry," he said quietly. "We'll find out who did this." It was unclear who he was speaking to.

"*Find out?*" whispered Quell, raising his head slowly, dangerously. "We don't need to find anything out. We already know who murdered her." He gingerly laid the bodhisattva back down on the desk and got to his feet. Natch noticed that the shock baton had not left his grip. "Who had the most to gain by Margaret's death?" said Quell, voice steadily rising. "Len Borda. The man who'll stop at nothing to get his hands on MultiReal."

Lieutenant Executive Lee raised an eyebrow but said nothing. The other government officials began to slowly back toward the Council troops and their dartguns. Someone quickly escorted the serving woman to the elevator and sent her on her way.

"Don't give me that look," said Quell. He was addressing Natch, though Natch wasn't quite sure what look he was supposed to have given. "Do you really think Borda would *hesitate* to murder a Surina? Then you don't know your history." The Islander began swishing the bar back and forth, like a buccaneer testing the tensile strength of his blade. "Didn't you know? Len Borda killed *Marcus* Surina"—*swish*—"because Marcus refused to let the Council take control of teleportation." *Swish swish.* "You think a *ruptured fuel tank* blew up his shuttle? No." He came to a halt in front of Margaret's desk, brandishing the crackling baton before him with both hands. "That was Council sabotage. It was fucking *Len Borda*. And now . . . and now . . ."

The Islander slipped into a pause as Magan turned from the window to face him. Officers on both sides of the room were tensing up, sliding fingers uneasily into the triggers of their guns. Electricity from the baton flared up to the glass ceiling like a bolt of lightning in reverse.

It happened in an instant.

One of the bureaucrats backed up and stumbled into a vase. The vase shattered. A finger tensed, a muscle twitched, a Council dart came whizzing across the room.

Quell charged.

Natch saw a blur of motion streak past him, knocking over the *Venus de Milo* in the process. The entrepreneur reached out instinctively to catch the hunk of stone before it hit the ground. He watched as the sculpture passed through his virtual hands and landed on the Persian rug with a thunk.

The Islander was quick, but not quick enough. Magan Kai Lee dropped into a street fighter's crouch and lunged out of the way just as Quell came rushing in. The lieutenant executive did a clumsy roll on the ground and pulled himself up to his feet by the lip of an end table.

A canopy of dart fire covered the room. Natch ducked to the floor, forgetting momentarily that he was here in multi and these darts could not hurt him. Council officers slid into textbook military formations, while Surina troops huddled behind furniture with guerrilla instinct.

Quell and Magan Kai Lee were circling around each other in the center of the room, where the furniture was not so dense. By all rights, Magan should have been terrified. The Islander towered over him by more than half a meter. But Natch took one look at the cool detachment in Magan's face and the ferocious desperation in Quell's, and he knew this would not end well.

The rest of the guards quickly reached a détente. A handful of troops from each side lay paralyzed and twitching on the ground with needles protruding from their torsos. But the rest stood stock-still, eyes riveted on the confrontation in progress. Papizon had one finger suspended in the air, as if gesturing to some invisible third combatant, while the unarmed bureaucrats had fled to the safety of the elevators. Natch was on the floor behind the downed (yet intact) statue.

"Don't do it," said Magan. "It's not worth it."

"Worth it to *me*," roared Quell. And then he was in motion once again.

Darts streaked across the room from the Council officers' gun barrels, heading straight for the Islander's chest. Natch gaped in astonishment as Quell made an elegant pirouette and swatted the darts aside with two rapid swings of his truncheon. It looked as slick and effortless as a choreographed dance maneuver.

MultiReal.

For the second time in their brief acquaintance, Natch saw some distant relative of fear and uncertainty behind the Council executive's eyes. Magan scurried backward as fast as he could, tearing down pottery and knocking over chairs in an attempt to flee. Surina guards, meanwhile, started methodically taking out the Council troops, who were wasting their ammunition on the Islander. Poison needles littered the floor. One ricocheted off the Islander's club and passed straight through Natch's insubstantial forehead.

"Quell!" cried Natch, not sure if he was trying to encourage the big man or dissuade him.

The Islander pounced with a yell and struck Magan full in the chest with the baton. Sparks sparked through the air. The lieutenant went flying back against the window, where his head thumped against the glass. But Natch's cry must have penetrated the Islander's cloak of rage, because he had pulled the blow at the last possible instant.

In spite of the blood trickling from his nose and the visible indenture in his chest, Magan Kai Lee clearly realized he should be dead right now. "Fool," he croaked between ragged breaths, "don't you realize I'm the only one standing between you and Borda?"

The Islander hesitated. His eyes swiveled back and forth from Magan to the corpse of Margaret Surina, still lying on the desk where he had left it. He seemed to reach some decision. His shoulders quivered, then slackened. The shock baton slid from his fingers and hit the carpet.

And just at that moment, the elevator doors opened and two dozen officers in white robes and yellow stars swept into the room. They quickly formed a perimeter and relieved the remaining Surina officers of their weapons. Natch caught a movement from the corner of his eye, and whipped his head around to see a pair of military hoverbirds levitating right outside the window. He could only guess what their cannons were loaded with, but they were aimed right at him.

Magan Kai Lee slumped to the floor. He coughed, then spat blood. "Invest your forces in ultimate sacrifice," he said in the timbre of command, motioning toward Quell. "Make sure you've covered all reasonable supply requisitions." The lieutenant executive was obviously speaking in some kind of Defense and Wellness Council code, and he didn't appear to be in any mood for translations.

Natch climbed shakily to his feet, trying his best to ignore all the concentrated pandemonium in the room. The remaining Surina guards were dragging their limp comrades one by one to the elevator under the Council's watchful eyes. The officer named Papizon, meanwhile, was staring at the remnants of the battle with horror. Natch supposed that the destruction of priceless art meant less to him than the despoiling of precious evidence. Not even high-tech polymers could insulate from this kind of havoc.

Half a dozen Council officers wrestled the Islander to his knees, even though he was only offering token resistance. The MultiReal program had obviously sapped his strength to some degree, but more than that, he seemed to have lost the will to resist. One of the officers brutally wrenched the Islander's thin metal collar off his neck, leaving a shallow tributary of blood.

"I don't care," shouted Quell. "I'm never wearing one of those fucking things again. Do you hear me? Do you hear me?"

Magan Kai Lee simply shook his head. His breathing had already resumed something close to its normal rhythm, and the patch of blood on his chest was beginning to evanesce into the air. But this was one injury that would need more than OCHREs to heal. Magan gave Quell one last angry look and swiped an arm wildly toward the elevators. The Council officers dragged him away.

Natch stood as straight as his trembling knees allowed. He looked around and realized that all of the friendly forces were now gone. "So what are you going to do with me?" he said.

"You?" The question only seemed to irritate the lieutenant executive. "You are irrelevant. Go home."

And then Natch consulted the messages that had been piling up in his mental inbox. The citation from the Meme Cooperative suspending his business license was there, and it had taken effect a scant four minutes ago. Also present was the court order demanding that Natch transfer MultiReal core access to Jara.

Magan Kai Lee had delivered on his promises. The Surina/Natch MultiReal Fiefcorp was no longer under Natch's control.

3

VARIABLES IN FLUX

(((18)))

The World Economic Oversight Board sensed a disturbance in the marketplace.

And so the powers that moved the financial levers of the world sent their agents to a secure location to make some decisions. Everyone with a stake in the process was represented: the Congress of L-PRACGs, the big businesses, the Defense and Wellness Council, the labor organizations, the Meme Cooperative, the administrators of the Data Sea, the Prime Committee, all the thousands of institutions running Vault protocols.

It might have made for a cramped meeting had its participants been made of flesh and blood. But these were virtual entities, data agents stored as quark color changes on the Data Sea. One could find no purer representatives of organizational will, for strictly speaking these were not representatives at all but the things themselves, the essence as expressed in formulas and business logic.

The administrator of the World Economic Oversight Board gaveled the meeting to order, after a fashion. Roll was taken. Preliminary exchanges of information were made, micro-negotiations to determine place and order.

And then the administrator laid out the situation. A handful of unorthodox transactions had spiked the stock exchanges, causing ripples to flow far and wide across the economic spectrum, amplified in no small measure by sudden troop movements from the Islanders and the Defense and Wellness Council. VIP travel itineraries were fluctuating by the second. Information requests across the Data Sea were multiplying exponentially. Strange patterns abounded.

There was a flurry of conversation from the assembled crowd. Newly spawned data agents dashed across the Sea to fetch follow-up information and make detailed queries against private data stores. More micro-negotiations.

The administrator called for a status report. Like ants piling grain before their queen, agents of the world's financial institutions began depositing data points before the Oversight Board. Balance vacillations in key Vault accounts. Interest rates being charged by various lending institutions. The values of certain commodities in the global marketplace. Primo's ratings for a representative sample of bio/logic fiefcorps. The status of bellwether legislation wending through the various L-PRACGs. Each datum gave form and shape to the pile—a form that stretched through dimensions invisible to the human eye. Derivatives of derivatives of derivatives, probabilities and possibilities, vectors of analysis that stretched from the universe's putative beginning to its predicted end.

The administrator contemplated the shape arrayed before the assembly. The number of patterns stored in the Oversight Board's catalog was in the trillions of trillions, but this particular pattern fell into the sparse category of unknowns.

More information, commanded the administrator.

A second wave of data began accumulating on the pile, refining its shape. The presence of certain buzzwords and warning signs on public financial boards. The heart rates and blood pressures of the Prime Committee's voting members. Rainfall reports from the Environmental Control Board. OrbiCo shipping schedules, hoverbird flight patterns, TubeCo ridership figures. Membership and cancellation numbers from the Jamm and the Sigh. The throughput of quantum channels between the orbital colonies. Len Borda's cholesterol level and platelet count. The reported whereabouts of the bodhisattvas of the major creeds.

If the administrator knew anything about Margaret Surina, it knew her as a convergence point of data on the eternal sea of information. A confluence of trends both macro- and microeconomic.

If the administrator knew anything about death, it knew that death was a transformation, a final resolution of variables that had heretofore been in flux.

The general economic pattern might not have been comprehensible to the administrator, but certainly there were scattered fragments it could grasp. The sudden and unexpected death of a highly influential figure. Anger and distrust at governmental authority. Fear, agitation, change. The administrator took these fragments as it had been designed to do, analyzed them, cobbled them together like some mad virtual Frankenstein.

And now, what to do about it?

The administrator checked its core tables, the baseline values engraved in its memory by the Makers themselves. The goals were clear and succinct: preserve existing assets; encourage stasis; smooth the jagged edges of human activity into manageable probability curves.

The administrator began to put together a plan. Hurricanes could be ameliorated and tides could be manipulated. But so could human behavior, given enough time and sufficient data points.

Decision after decision flowed from the administrator to the full body of the Oversight Board, and each decision required the okay of the full board. Haggling erupted among the assembly as data agents darted from member to member, carrying proposals and counterproposals, modifications and amendments and official objections. Conflicting agendas laid themselves out like stones on a Go board, with the administrator holding the final token.

A few billionths of a second later, the plan was ratified.

Make it so, the administrator commanded.

● ● ●

And so the agents of the World Economic Oversight Board streamed across the Data Sea, where things were not so simple. Billions of programs sailed out there, many with aims in direct contradiction to those of the World Economic Oversight Board.

But the Board's agents were government troops on a sacrosanct mission. At every crossroads, priority credentials were presented and emergency overrides were given. In most cases, lesser programs stood down and gave the Board's emissaries the right of way. But there were countless holdouts and instances of stubborn resistance. Maverick programs eager to waylay the centralized government. Rebels. Spies. Proxies of monomaniacal self-interest. And at every juncture, the Board's emissaries had to decide where to fight and where to make exception. Where to call reinforcements. Where to brutally stamp out dissent.

The Board's edicts were quickly implemented across informational space. Banking programs that had been aggressively raising interest rates and trading shares were overridden by the implacable agents of the Vault. Transactions were actually reversed in a few isolated locations; other strategic crossroads were lined with transactional roadblocks to slow down the rate of exchange.

All was proceeding according to the administrator's plans. And then something unexpected happened: delays.

The trouble began on the Vault. They were only small delays at first, microscopic stutters in the fluid dialogue of economics—a picosecond of blank time where action did not meet with reaction. Soon there were phantom authorizations arising from nonexistent accounts and credits moving to places where logic dictated they could not go. In the deeper waters of the Data Sea outside of the Vault's shoals, such things could be dealt with. Messages could be recalled; contingency plans could be executed; holds could be placed. But the world of the Vault was a world without creative alternatives, a world where *a* must follow *b* without fail.

Delays snowballed into an avalanche of inefficiency.

Bio/logic systems that depended on a smoothly functioning financial engine queried the Vault for payment and received no response.

The appointed digital guardians of hearts and lungs were suddenly stranded, unable to obtain authorizations for their services. Without payment, dependent subroutines could not be invoked; third-party functions would not accept commands. One by one, the strands on the network of the bio/logic system began to fray.

The Prime Committee in its bureaucratic wisdom had long ago considered this possibility and passed legislation to deal with it. This legislation required every critical bio/logic system to have multiple redundancies, so that no failure of communication (or lack of credits) would ever stop a beating heart. So the bio/logic programs turned to governmentally mandated backup routines hardwired into the very OCHREs themselves. Routines that had not undergone the same rigorous real-world trials as the bio/logic programs themselves. Routines that had not received the same level of intense scrutiny from Primo's and the drudges. Routines that, despite the best Dr. Plugenpatch screening and verification, did not always function as advertised.

Routines that could fail when put to the test.

• • •

A boy in São Paulo was engaged in a vigorous game of pelota with his comrades. Suddenly he experienced a massive embolism and collapsed.

Within ten minutes, the infoquake had claimed a thousand lives.

(((19)))

The drudges edged as close to the tube tracks as they dared. One woman leaned her head out too far and tripped—or was pushed by a rival—directly into the path of the oncoming train. She stumbled, turned to face the juggernaut bearing down upon her, and let out a piercing shriek. The train car barreled forward without slowing. Half a second later, the multi network's automatic pain overrides cut the woman's connection.

Laughter trilled through the crowd.

"Animals," groaned Horvil from inside the train. He pulled his forehead off the window and used his shirtsleeve to wipe the oily smudge he had left there. "Barbarians. Philistines . . ."

"Drudges," concluded Benyamin from across the aisle.

As the tube slid to a quiet stop, Jara rose from her chair at the head of the car and surveyed her fellow fiefcorpers. Ben was slumped in his seat, picking sullenly at a rough edge on the armrest. Merri had been red-eyed and misty for most of the past hour. Serr Vigal was kneading his temples like a man trying to remember some vital piece of information he had forgotten twenty years ago. And Horvil, with his hair sprouting in twelve different directions like an ebony spider plant, simply looked confused.

I hope this wasn't a colossal mistake, thought Jara with a grimace. *But with Natch incommunicado, the drudges closing in on the Thassel Complex, and infoquakes happening left and right, we couldn't just stay there forever.*

The analyst puffed up her chest and spoke. "Okay, we need to pull ourselves together. We've gotta act like a *fiefcorp* here. Ben, stop that sneering."

Benyamin threw her a sour-apple look. "Do you really need me here for this stupid little pantomime?" he groused. "You want everyone to see us walking to my mother's estate. Fine, I understand that. But I don't need to walk there with you. My body's already *at* the estate. All I need to do is cut my multi connection."

"You look at that platform, and you tell me," replied Jara. She gestured out the window at the crowd of drudges eyeing the tube car like a giant flock of vultures. A flock of *agitated* vultures. "We all have to put in an appearance, Ben, even if it's just a quick appearance. Otherwise these people are going to crucify us. And what they say over the next twenty-four hours could very well affect your career—*all* of our careers—for at least a decade."

The young apprentice buried his chin in his chest and shook his black hair until it covered his forehead, mop-style. "I don't care what Magan Kai Lee says," he muttered. "You don't run this company."

For ten seconds, nobody took a breath.

Inside, Jara was trembling. She could hardly blame Benyamin for being suspicious. Everyone else in the fiefcorp was tangled in some government web, while Jara alone remained unblemished and untouched. And yet she was the one standing here giving orders. How could Jara explain that she didn't know any more than they did? How could she convince them she had made no deal with Magan Kai Lee, and this predicament had descended upon her as quickly and unexpectedly as it had upon *them*?

Merri leaned forward and put a consoling hand on the young apprentice's shoulder. "Benyamin," she said, "let's just . . . get indoors, get to a safe place. We can talk about this later."

Ben thought a moment, nodded, then stood.

Jara tried to give Merri a silent look of thanks, but the channel manager would not meet her gaze. Even Horvil was keeping his eyes glued to the floor. *I'm on your side!* she felt like screaming. *I'm one of you!* Instead, Jara locked her spine and activated the look of distress she had purchased twenty minutes ago off the Data Sea. Then she walked through the doors of the tube car.

And nearly collided with John Ridglee, who was hovering outside like a bird of prey.

"The last heir of Sheldon Surina is dead," said the drudge without even a *Towards Perfection*. "Four hundred years of noble scientific tradition is gone. Another devastating infoquake. Why choose *today* of all days to conduct a hostile takeover of your company, Jara?"

The analyst almost dropped her bereaved expression on the spot. "Uh—sorry, John," she said to Ridglee's hypnotically bobbing left eyebrow. "No comment." Then she walked into the crowd, hoping the others would follow.

But John Ridglee was only the first in a long line of drudges on the London tube platform, each squawking a more outrageous question than the last. Most of the questions were predictable ("How do you feel about Margaret Surina's death?" "Where's Natch?"), some were easy to ignore ("Did you kill Margaret?" "Who's getting fired next?" "Who are you fucking these days?"), but many were simply incomprehensible ("Have we atoned for the sins of Tobi Jae Witt and her Autonomous Minds?" "Can you name three chemical components unique to moon plants?"). Regardless, the analyst managed to keep her cool and say nothing but a quiet "No comment" to her interrogators.

Once Jara made it off the tube platform, she was in for another surprise: cheers. Standing on the opposite street corner was a crowd that straddled every major demographic. Men, women, old, young, Terran, colonist, rich, poor. Some of them bore a rising sun on their chests, insignia of Creed Libertas. "Don't be discouraged!" shouted a woman from the crowd. "Take heart!" cried another. Their words of support were so banal that they only added to the surrealism of the situation.

Rabid drudges, crazed creed devotees, sullen fiefcorp apprentices . . . Jara could only imagine the stack of messages she would find in her inbox when she stopped priving herself to the world. A flexible-glass bottle arced out of the sky and narrowly missed her head. She switched on Lucas Sentinel's Cocoon 33 and tuned it to a low setting that muted the noise but left her other senses intact.

Horvil pinged her on ConfidentialWhisper. "There's a guy here says he's from the Diss L-PRACG Movement. They're worried that we're headed for another Economic Plunge. Should I—"

"I don't care if he's Sheldon Surina," Jara said with mental teeth firmly gritted. *"Don't say a fucking word to anyone."*

The throng began to disperse as the fiefcorpers made their way toward the palatial estates lining the western bank of the Thames. The rabid libertarians stayed with them for a few blocks, but quickly lost interest after the drudge onslaught tapered off. Jara started to wonder if they had run this whole gauntlet for nothing, when she rounded the last corner and saw a fresh crowd camped at the gates to Berilla's estate. She allowed herself a sigh of relief.

The gates creaked open just wide enough to admit Horvil, Benyamin, Merri, and Vigal. Jara felt like she had wandered into an ancient painting as the others strode down a cobblestone path that looked like it had been built for automobile traffic, or even horse-drawn carriages. The path was lined with an exquisitely manicured hedge that served as boundary for a crisp and well-tended lawn. Jara's entire city block on the East End could have occupied that lawn, with room to spare. The house they were headed for stood an obscene distance back from the gates. It extended east to west in hand-laid brick like a Roman villa.

Jara waited patiently for the others to make it inside the gates before turning to face the pack in apparent afterthought.

"I'm really sorry," she said, her voice appropriately choked. "You've caught us all a bit unprepared. Give us—give us two or three hours, and someone will be back out here to deliver a statement, okay?" Then she gave a stiff bow and dashed up the walkway to join the rest of the fiefcorp.

"Thanks, everybody," Jara broadcast to the others over ConfidentialWhisper. "Well done. That should do the trick."

"Do *what* trick?" scowled Ben.

Jara could hear Horvil's snort from several paces away. "Don't be an idiot, Ben."

"But I don't see what—"

"All five of us, sitting in your mother's estate in West London. Two hundred drudges camped at the gates waiting for us to make a statement. It's probably the safest place in the entire universe right now."

• • •

Benyamin cut his multi connection as soon as the doors closed behind them.

Jara stood in the marbled atrium with the rest of the fiefcorp, simultaneously afraid to sit still and afraid to move. Just yesterday, the Surina/Natch MultiReal Fiefcorp had been headed for a triumphal exposition before billions of potential customers. Now the fiefcorp was—what? Under new management? On hiatus? Defunct?

Moments later, Ben emerged in the flesh from a side hallway and led the group to a large parlor in the house's west wing. Jara kept waiting for the infamous Aunt Berilla or one of her factotums to burst out of some antechamber, but not so much as a liveried attendant came to greet them. Horvil or Benyamin must have told Berilla they were coming. Either she didn't care enough about their presence to raise a fuss or she cared too much to give them the satisfaction.

The group stood in the parlor and stared at the carefully preserved trappings of an earlier age. Cherrywood furniture, stately purple curtains. Nobody said anything. Finally Jara stepped forward.

"Listen," she said, her voice low and husky. "I know . . . I know this is all very confusing. It's confusing to me too. I have no idea what's going on. I don't know what's happening with Natch or Margaret or the leadership of the fiefcorp or your contracts or—or anything. But here's what I suggest." She took a breath. "Let's just pretend that everything's normal right now. Until we have more information, let's just all . . . do the best we can." She trailed off lamely, hearing the razzes from Natch's imaginary audience in her head.

Hesitant nods from the rest of the fiefcorp. A shrug or two.

Within minutes, they were turning the stuffy parlor into a bona fide war room. Benyamin cleared the drapes off the windows and replaced them with Data Sea news feeds. Horvil converted an antediluvian rolltop desk into a bio/logic workbench with the press of a button. Jara and Merri went around picking up crystal knickknacks, while Vigal found enough seating to form a makeshift conference area.

"Someone get ahold of Robby Robby," said Jara when everyone had settled down. "Let's start working on that statement for the drudges. Merri?"

The channel manager crumpled onto a delicate chair next to the sideboard. "Sure," she replied in a hoarse whisper. "What are we going to say?"

Jara could feel her mind shift onto an express track. "Start with this: 'The Surina/Natch MultiReal Fiefcorp joins the entire world in expressing its sorrow at the passing of Margaret Surina. Margaret's brilliance, wisdom, and compassion set an example for all to follow.'"

"That's good shit," put in Horvil.

"Okay." Merri nodded. "I can work with that."

"The drudges are going to want more detail," said Serr Vigal, reclining on a plaid sofa so stiff it might never have actually contained a human being before. "They're going to ask about the dispensation of Margaret's shares, the work she left behind, what happens to Multi-Real, that sort of thing."

Jara shrugged. "It doesn't matter. All we can tell them is what we know, right? And we don't really *know* anything. So let's just keep it brief and bland."

"I'll do the best I can," said Merri, climbing slowly to her feet like one of the walking dead.

Jara gave her a perplexed look. The channel manager was not the type to bemoan her fate or engage in clumsy theatrics. "Don't worry," said Jara. "Robby can help you massage the wording. That's what we're paying him for. Take as long as you need—we've got to keep that crowd out there for a few hours, at least. Maybe longer."

The analyst swiveled around to face Horvil, who had already managed to unpack half of his bio/logic programming bars on an antique cherrywood hutch. "Horv, I need you to scour the dock for me. Make sure Natch didn't actually follow through on those threats and release Possibilities when we weren't looking."

The engineer blinked rapidly with his eyeballs tilted rafterward. "Nope."

"Good. Then why don't you do everything you can to *un*prepare that program for launch. Wipe the fore and aft tables, the pricing structure, everything. Put up as many barriers as you can to stop Natch from pulling that again. We don't want him just throwing MultiReal out to sixty billion people on a whim."

"Natch won't like that," said Benyamin with a grimace.

"No, he probably won't," replied Jara. "But look at it this way. We're not doing anything he can't undo later. We just need to . . . slow him *down* a bit."

"Why? If his license is suspended, he can't launch a bio/logic program on the Data Sea anyway. Or, at least, he can't charge for it."

Jara was growing very frustrated very quickly with Benyamin's contrarian attitude. "Not officially he can't," she said. "Not legally. But when has the law ever stopped Natch from doing anything?"

The young apprentice gave a grudging nod. Even *he* couldn't argue that point.

Horvil stood behind the desk and called up Possibilities in Mind-Space. Displayed on such an old workbench, the program looked positively minuscule. "You know, Pierre Loget has this great dock management routine I've always wanted to try," he said. "Lets you craft these sophisticated fore and aft tables, ties in with your accounting . . . puts all kinds of access controls on everything. I bet DockManage 35'd tie Natch's hands for a few hours."

"Go ahead," said Jara. "Ben, what's going on with your mother's assembly line? Are they still rolling back the MultiReal code?"

Benyamin shook his head. "They pretty much stopped doing that when the infoquakes started."

"Good. Let's cut off their access while we still can. Shouldn't be a big deal to just revert to the last functioning version before they started tinkering, should it?"

"If MultiReal was a normal program, no, it wouldn't be a big deal," interjected Horvil. "If Margaret had built it with standard workbenches and standard bio/logic programming bars from start to finish, no. As things stand . . . yes. It's going to be a real pain in the ass."

Jara sighed. "See what you can figure out, Ben. Ask some questions, but keep it quiet. Let's see if we can bring everything back to normal in the next couple days."

Serr Vigal leaned forward with his hands folded on his lap, looking small and fragile. "Is there something I can do to help?"

The analyst blinked. It suddenly occurred to her that the neural programmer had his own company to deal with. He would have been on a shuttle heading for that cognitive processes conference right now if all this chaos hadn't happened. "Why don't you help me go through the news coverage," she said. "We need to know what's going on out there, and we can't rely on InfoGathers to convey all the subtleties." Vigal nodded.

Jara stopped and took a look around. Aunt Berilla's sterile parlor had become a hive of activity, full of industrious hands and discreet conversations. *That's good*, thought the analyst. *We need to keep busy.* She moved next to Vigal on the sofa and began combing through Data Sea video feeds.

It didn't take long to track down footage from Andra Pradesh.

Drudges, videographers, and curiosity seekers by the hundreds were converging on the Surina compound. A privileged few had already been at the premises when the chaos began. As a result, there were hundreds of different viewpoints and conflicting spins to sort through.

After a few minutes, they located a feed from a tourist group that had been locked in the Center for Historic Appreciation by anxious Council guards. Jara felt the tug of some indefinable emotion when she saw the monolithic scientist statues in the atrium and remembered her own little epiphany there last month. Huddling scared at the feet of Sheldon Surina. Deciding to give the MultiReal demonstration in Natch's place, even if that meant confronting the Council. Horvil's unexpected declaration of affection. She cast a peripheral glance toward Horvil now, but the engineer had his nose buried in one of the rolltop desk's cubbyholes.

The tourists were all focusing their attention on the empty courtyard out the window, but nothing seemed to be happening. A few officers of the Defense and Wellness Council strode by, weapons at the ready. Surina security was nowhere to be seen.

Suddenly the doors to the Revelation Spire burst open and spat out a gaggle of Council officers. They were dragging along some colossal figure who was shackled in their midst. For a moment, it looked like the man might actually be trying to walk on his own power. Then one of the white-robed officers bashed the back of the giant's knee with a rifle butt, hard, and he slumped down again.

One of the observers zoomed in for a closer look.

Jara gasped. It was Quell.

Within moments, the gang of white-robed soldiers had muscled the Islander across the courtyard to their waiting hoverbirds. The view bobbed and weaved anxiously, searching in vain for an angle that would show what was happening. Minutes later, a trio of Council hoverbirds took flight and zipped away southward.

Jara turned around and discovered that not only had the other fief-corpers abandoned their individual projects and gathered behind her

chair to watch the video, but a cotton-headed Robby Robby had multied in at some point and was shaking his head theatrically at Jara's
elbow. She had completely forgotten he was coming here to help with
the drudge statement. Had he heard about the business license situation yet? If so, he was doing an excellent job of hiding it.

"The drudges are going to want an explanation for Quell's arrest,"
said Serr Vigal in a barely audible whisper. "We'd better include something in the statement."

"I don't think that's necessary," said Jara. "Nobody's going to
believe that Quell had anything to do with Margaret's death, will
they? Even the drudges can't be that dumb."

Horvil nuked the video display with a gesture. "Let's find out," he
said. A block of text appeared in the upper right corner of the window:

ZEITGEIST 29a
Another fine Billy Sterno program
Subject: *Was Quell involved in Margaret Surina's death?*

Boxes of words exploded on the screen like popcorn. Words clus-
tering together, forming associations, merging. *Pacific Islands. Unconnectible. Andra Pradesh.* Words spawning new meta-concepts,
branching off into new avenues. *Murder. Fiefcorp economics. MultiReal.*

Finally the frenetic activity began to subside. A graph superim-
posed itself atop the linguistic graffiti and began spontaneously popu-
lating itself with data.

Was Quell involved in Margaret Surina's death?

11%	Yes
18%	Leaning Yes
52%	Not Sure
12%	Leaning No
7%	No

The numbers wobbled up and down in ever-narrowing increments as the program gauged the currents of thought traversing the Data Sea. And then two small photographs blinked into existence next to the words *Leaning Yes:* Sen Sivv Sor and John Ridglee.

The atmosphere in the room grew gloomier by the second as the numbers quickly began to skew toward the affirmative answers. Jara finally shut the thing off when the numbers for *Leaning Yes* reached 40%.

Only Robby Robby seemed not to care. "These Zeitgeist numbers are totally meaningless, kids," he said, picking at his virtual mane with an equally virtual comb. "Ignore 'em. Take it from a professional."

Horvil pursed his lips with skepticism. "Zeitgeist has always been pretty accurate for me."

"Oh, I'm sure the numbers are *accurate*," said the channeler cryptically. "But they're still meaningless. What does Natch think?"

Jara frowned. "Where *is* Natch? Is he still in Andra Pradesh?"

"He multied over there," said Merri. "Vigal, didn't you follow him over to the multi facility?"

The neural programmer clapped a hand to his forehead. "You're right, I did. I had to make a quick stop in Omaha." He peered around the room, as if he expected the entrepreneur to materialize there at any moment. "Natch was standing right next to me when I opened my connection, but he definitely wasn't there when I closed it. I never even thought to look."

Jara gave a sidelong glance at Robby, wishing he wasn't around for this conversation but knowing there was nothing she could do about it now. She cast her mind out to the Data Sea. "Looks like some drudges saw him at the Thassel Complex earlier, but he managed to give them all the slip. How the heck does he *do* that?"

"One of these days," mumbled Horvil, "Natch is just going to disappear for good right under our noses, and we won't be able to do anything about it."

Vigal made an exhausted sigh. "He might prefer it that way."

(((20)))

The redwoods mocked him as the tube train hurtled through their midst, back and forth, back and forth without ceasing. Natch wondered how much human agency was actually required to run a tube route. Would this train still be plowing the dark between the trees a hundred thousand years after humanity had gone permanently fallow? Would some alien civilization stumble on this planet millions of years from now and find nothing but self-repairing trains caught in endless loops, transporting no one, serving nothing?

Natch focused on the curmudgeonly face staring back at him from the window. The letters beneath the man's chin instantly solidified into Prussian blocks of gray, obscuring Natch's view of the sequoias.

THE TRUTH WILL OUT
by Sen Sivv Sor

Am I the only one who remembers that the death of Margaret Surina also means the end of the Surinas?

Yes, readers, that venerable line of scientists, visionaries, and freethinkers founded by Sheldon Surina and continued by Prengal and Marcus has now seen its terminus with Margaret's death. There are other more distant relations still living at Andra Pradesh, but only Margaret could claim direct descent from all three of those great scientific pioneers.

The functionaries who will rise to fill the void in the Surina organizations are hardly worthy of the name. Jayze and Suheil Surina, the two most likely candidates, started tussling over the family riches as soon as Margaret disappeared to the top of the Revelation Spire. Suheil has spent ten years administering the Enterprise Facility—a cozy bit of nepotism if ever I've seen one—while Jayze has wasted decades meddling in local Indian politics. It's doubtful that either one of them could *spell* MultiReal, much less program it.

So what should the Council do with the man who has uprooted this great tree of wisdom?

It's no secret whom I'm talking about. I'm talking about the man with the audacity to hijack MultiReal right out from under Margaret's nose. The man accused of violating no less than one hundred twenty Meme Cooperative rules and regulations. The man who may have just ordered a hit on his erstwhile partner in the MultiReal business.

A premature judgment? Certainly. As the standard disclaimer for my column states, I'm no officer of the law, and I wouldn't presume to issue a final verdict before all the facts are in. All I can do is look at the evidence in the public eye.

But isn't it peculiar that Margaret was murdered right before the Meme Cooperative suspended Natch from the fiefcorp she founded? Isn't it peculiar that the Islander Quell—a man on Natch's payroll—was dragged out of the Revelation Spire by Len Borda's officers? Isn't it peculiar that Natch himself left the bodhisattva's side only hours before her body was discovered, and isn't it peculiar that he may have been the last one to see her alive?

I repeat: what should the Council do with this man?

Natch waved his hand and sent the drudge's words back to the netherworld of yellow journalism. He shouldn't have been surprised. The unholy trinity of Sen Sivv Sor, John Ridglee, and Mah Lo Vertiginous had long ago set aside all political differences to declare their hatred for Natch. Why should a worldwide tragedy change anything?

Nor should Natch have been surprised by the Council's reaction to the accusations against him exploding across the Data Sea like miniature starbursts: nothing. No statements, no admissions, no denials. Magan Kai Lee could dispel most of these accusations by revealing that Natch had been on a Council hoverbird at the time of Margaret's death, but instead he chose to drop out of public view. Nobody had seen or heard from High Executive Borda in days. Even Chief Solicitor

Rey Gonerev was maintaining complete radio silence, a remarkable achievement considering the amount of attention she normally received from the drudges.

The entrepreneur thought back to Quell's words atop that Spire, moments before his arrest. *Do you really think Borda would hesitate to murder a Surina? Then you don't know your history.*

Natch summoned the famous video of that burnt and twisted shuttle wreckage on Furtoid. Marcus Surina and all the progenitors of the stillborn teleportation industry had been in that shuttle. Now the vehicle looked like a brummagem sculpture, like a steaming turd left by some enormous metal beast. The camera panned over the wreckage in silence, and then lurched suddenly. Jutting from the bottom of the frame was a bloody severed *hand.* . . .

Had Len Borda ordered the death of Marcus Surina? Had the high executive set in motion the Economic Plunge that sent Natch's mother to the streets of Old Chicago? Was there any way to prove such a thing after almost fifty years?

And even if Borda had murdered Marcus Surina, did that necessarily mean he had murdered Margaret too?

Natch shook his head. These questions were too big for him; let politicians like Khann Frejohr tackle such matters. All Natch needed to know was who had planted MultiReal and black code in his skull and how to get his license back from the Meme Cooperative.

That fucking weasel Magan Kai Lee, he growled to himself. The lieutenant executive had found a way to neatly slice Natch off at the knees. It all looked so easy in hindsight. Take away Natch's license to sell bio/logic programs on the Data Sea, and you took away his ability to profit from MultiReal through any legitimate channel. Oh, there were plenty of Lunar tycoons outside the aegis of the Meme Cooperative who might stick him on their payroll, plenty of back avenues to making money he could explore. But Magan had judged him correctly. He knew that Natch wouldn't let go of MultiReal on any terms other than his own. And scavenging the dark corners of the marketplace for scraps, with the Council dogging his every move—that was tantamount to giving up.

Then there was the problem of Jara. Magan had put all the leverage in Jara's hands. If Natch obeyed the Meme Cooperative's order and granted her core access to MultiReal, she would have just as much control over the program as he did. Natch wasn't sure if she had the legal right to sell it off or give it away. But she would have the power to simply *move* the databases somewhere else on the Data Sea where nobody else would ever, ever find them. And yet, what alternatives did Natch have? He could always defy the Meme Cooperative's order, but then he would have to go on the run from the Council again, a prospect he dreaded.

Natch summoned a mental picture of the analyst and studied it intently. Jara was nobody's pushover. But she was also hopelessly naive and eminently predictable. How long would she last as Magan Kai Lee's puppet before either he or Len Borda did away with her?

Once that happened, MultiReal would be in the hands of the Defense and Wellness Council. And after that—

The nothingness at the center of the universe.

Natch would not give up.

Borda, he's on some kind of crusade against my family and everything we've touched, Margaret had told him. *But Natch, you need to know this— he can't take MultiReal away from you. He* can't. *I've made sure of that.*

Why shouldn't he believe it?

Jara had the advantage. She had the authorities on her side through whatever misguided deal she thought she was making with the Council. She had the legal rights to MultiReal while the rest of the fiefcorpers' fates were tangled up in Meme Cooperative jurisprudence. She would even have public opinion on her side, at least in the beginning.

But what did any of that matter? Natch knew how to *control* people. He knew how to disassemble them and find their weak spots.

Moreover, he possessed the ability to move the whole *world*, to put the bio/logics market in a panic with a few well-placed rumors and bits of black code, to change public opinion by cozying up to the drudges and the opinion makers. Who cared that the public suspected him of involvement in Margaret Surina's death? That was a temporary impression sown in panic and fed with unsubstantiated rumor. It would fade.

Natch knew what motivated Jara. He knew her better than the Council, no matter how long they had been following her and how many thousands of background documents they had uncovered.

He could handle Jara.

The entrepreneur nudged his eyelids open a fraction and took a surreptitious peek around the tube car. How long had he been sitting here debating himself with fists clenched? Time was a sieve. He looked at the three spies of the Defense and Wellness Council who had been following him since the Twin Cities—spies who stood out from the rest of the businesspeople, tourists, and layabouts like ants in a bowl of sugar. They gazed back at him and grinned cruelly.

Natch turned his attention back to the window, which had been recycling fiefcorp industry news for the past few hours. He could feel the black code inside him, a thousand vessels of doom just waiting to unload their toxic cargo on his OCHRE systems.

He could handle black code. He could handle the Defense and Wellness Council and the Meme Cooperative and the Patels, too. He could handle anything the world threw at him. The world might just depend on it.

(((21)))

Horvil reclined on the bed with arms held high in a position of surrender. His parents had long ago relinquished their piece of the estate to Aunt Berilla and moved on to warmer climes—the controlled heat domes of Nova Ceti, to be specific. Yet here his old room sat, unchanged, like a mausoleum for his teenage years. The same battered chair with nailhead trim still hunkered near the door. The same hearty ficus plant still towered over the southwest corner of the room, an embarrassment of fecundity. And the windows were still broadcasting raucous advertisements for Yarn Trip's reunion concert in Beijing, even though the concert had come and gone eight years ago, and the band had long since broken up again, re-reunited, then split (theoretically) for good.

Horvil remembered the day of that concert. He had stomped out of the house after an argument with Berilla and rented his own apartment the very same afternoon. But every time he came back here, his aunt rewound the window decorations to that same frozen instant. As if one day, Horvil might thaw the moment and resume life in the manor like nothing had changed.

He sensed an incoming ConfidentialWhisper. Aunt Berilla.

"You can't avoid me forever, Horvil," she said, voice properly petulant.

"Well, I'm right down the hall," replied the engineer. "Come on over. We can listen to Yarn Trip together. I always forget—were you into their molten lava phase or their mocha grind phase?"

An audible frown. "You know I've got a meeting to prepare for."

"Really? Sure you're not just afraid to face the fiefcorp after what you did? I mean, shutting down the programming floor's one thing, but actually trying to *roll back* the changes—"

"This isn't about the fiefcorp. It's about you. Why haven't you followed up with Marulana already?"

The engineer harrumphed. "Don't think I'm gonna take the job, that's why."

"But this isn't some dull bureaucratic position. Chief engineer for Creed Élan, Horvil! A position of responsibility. A job of consequence, for process' preservation! You'd have a staff. You'd have a budget and the best equipment. And you wouldn't have to put up with *him.*"

"Not that again. I don't want to hear it."

He could feel Berilla's frustration from all the way across the mansion. She abruptly changed course. "Listen, Horvil, you tell those people they're welcome to stay for a few more hours until everything blows over. But I won't have drudges camped at my gates forever! I will not have my household disrupted like this. Do you hear me?"

Horvil prived himself to Aunt Berilla's communications without a word. Then he closed his eyes, turned to face the wall, and played Yarn Trip's turbulent "Shitscape Symphony" on his internal sound system. Twice. Loud.

• • •

Jara found a study down the hall and appropriated it as a temporary office. The room looked like it might have lain untouched for several generations, or perhaps been transported here intact from antiquity through some subversion of time and space. There were a lot of rooms like that in the mansion. Jara looked at the treepaper books sitting on the shelves and shook her head at the ancient names filigreed on their spines. Coleridge, Toynbee, Kipling.

She lay down on the couch, draped one arm over her forehead, and cried for a good ten minutes.

What had happened to her career? How had she devolved from such a bright and promising student to a pariah in her own fiefcorp? Jara tried to retrace the winding path that had led her to this moment—the affair with the proctor, the years with Lucas Sentinel, the obsession with Natch, the dalliances with Geronimo—but it all seemed sickening and improbable.

You can't even say the fiefcorp situation is all Natch's fault, Jara told herself. *You're to blame almost as much as he is. You participated in Natch's lies and schemes for three years without saying anything. You even spread false black code rumors when Natch asked you to. Magan Kai Lee threatened the company right to your face, and you didn't do a thing about it.*

Jara felt a sudden urge to contact Geronimo again, but the urge came from a place far removed from lust. Then she pictured Rey Gonerev, reading a bureaucratic report about Jara's Sigh activities with a knowing smirk on her face. *I've read so much about you in the Council files that I feel like I know you . . . intimately*, the Blade had told her. So Jara restrained herself.

A knock sounded on the door, and in came Benyamin.

"I looked into the situation with the assembly-line floor," said the young apprentice, "and it's not good."

Jara felt like rolling over and telling Ben to go away. "Not good how?"

"Greth Tar Griveth—that woman who blackmailed me—she made a big mess." Benyamin flopped his arms aimlessly like limp dough, unable to muster the energy for a more emphatic gesture. "Turns out she was taking that money and using it to bribe some of *her* people. I don't know if Magan Kai Lee put her up to this or what. But Greth's people have been sabotaging the MultiReal code. Throwing in little surprises of their own."

Exhaustion had taken Jara's senses, and she couldn't quite get her mind to spark. "How bad is it?"

"Well, Greth only had limited access to the code in the first place. There's only so much damage she could do. But add the rollback on top of it, and you've got . . . Well, you've got a big mess."

"Does MultiReal still work?"

"Sure, it works just fine, for your basic one-on-one interactions. But we won't be able to do that twenty-three-way soccer game anytime soon."

Jara ran her hands through her hair and yanked hard at the roots in frustration. "And what does your mother think of all this? Is she ever going to come out of her office and *talk* to us? Come to think of it—why hasn't she kicked us out of her house yet?"

"I—I don't know."

The analyst lay quietly for a moment. A ray of sunshine poked through a slat in the blinds and jabbed her in the eye, prompting her to turn onto her right side and bury her nose in the couch's crook. She had no doubt that Horvil could weed through all the changes and restore MultiReal to full functionality. But with the program's creator dead and its chief engineer headed for some orbital prison, how much time would that take? Weeks? Months? He wouldn't even be able to use an assembly-line floor to do the heavy lifting.

"So are you going to do anything about it?" asked Benyamin, his voice suddenly querulous.

Jara shook her head. "I don't know, Ben. I don't know if there's anything else I *can* do. Let me mull this over for a while, okay?"

"But—"

"*Please.*"

Ben disappeared. Jara lay there and debated the merits of sleep. Not ten minutes later, Merri found her way into the study.

The people in this company sure aren't acting *like they're suspicious of me,* thought Jara. *Why can't everyone just leave me the fuck alone?* The blonde channel manager hesitated in the doorway for a full two minutes before Jara finally grew tired of waiting. "So what's the problem?" she said.

"It's my companion," squeaked Merri.

"Bonneth?" said Jara, taken aback. "Is she okay?"

"At the moment . . . yes. But when that last infoquake struck . . . Jara, she was totally cut off from Dr. Plugenpatch. For hours. She tried to keep me from finding out, but I could hear it in her voice." Merri's hands twisted at the hem of her blouse until Jara thought she might rend it in two. "This is all my fault. *I* was the one who insisted on moving to Luna in the first place, because I thought the artificial gravity would be better for her condition. If another one of those infoquakes hits up there . . ." Her sentence floated away into the thick wallpaper of books.

Comprehension dawned on Jara with a nauseating rush. She had assumed Merri's misery was a mixture of sorrow for Margaret Surina and apprehension about her own fate at Creed Objectivv. *I guess she deserves more credit than that*, thought the analyst. These infoquakes represented a real and immediate danger to countless millions like Bonneth with obscure diseases. OCHREs and Dr. Plugenpatch and bio/logic software formed a symbiotic triangle; remove one of the three, and the whole structure would collapse. To someone with Bonneth's condition, even a brief outage might very well be fatal.

Jara felt herself souring involuntarily. Did Merri think she was the only one who had these problems? Jara's mother lived on Luna too. Terraformers had made great progress on the moon in recent decades, but it still remained largely uninhabitable without bio/logics. If an infoquake delivered a catastrophic blow to the Data Sea, would Jara's mother be any better off than Bonneth?

"So what do you want *me* to do about it?" Jara croaked finally, rolling onto her back to face the ceiling and the skewering sunlight.

"I don't know," said Merri. "I just thought you might have some advice. . . ."

"Well, I don't," replied the analyst. "Why does everyone keep coming to me for advice about things I can't control? I have enough on my plate right now without worrying about hypotheticals. You're just going to have to tough it out. Do the best you can."

"Okay," managed the blonde woman, already shifting toward the door. "One more thing, though . . . We can't decide whether we should say anything in the drudge statement about Quell. . . ."

"I told you, talk with Robby! *You* figure something out for once!" Jara's voice strained and finally cracked. She regretted the words as soon as they escaped her mouth.

The channel manager let out another quiet "okay." Jara rested her forearm over her eyes to block the glare and waited for Merri to leave. Which, eventually, she did.

Seething with self-recrimination, Jara drifted off to an uneasy sleep.

• • •

Jara couldn't have said how long she slept. The sun was no longer burning a warm spot into her forearm, and the chattering of the apprentices down the hall had faded. She must have been out for a few hours, at least, but she didn't really want to know.

I'm not ready for this responsibility, she confided silently to the fates. The pit of her stomach felt hollow, acidic. *I'm not ready to run a fiefcorp. Please tell me I don't have to.*

As if in answer to her plea, Jara opened her eyes and saw a familiar face.

Natch.

The sight was so embedded in her consciousness it had almost become archetype: Natch making tracks across the carpet, arms clasped behind his back, muttering to himself. All the scene needed was an obscure piece of bio/logic code floating in MindSpace and a window full of share price histograms. "Good job," Natch said gruffly.

Jara had never felt so happy to receive a rude half-greeting in her life. She could feel her anxieties melting away. Natch would know how to handle the situation. He always did. "What did I do this time?" she replied.

"The statement to the drudges. Short and sweet, I like that." Natch tromped right over a green throw pillow that Jara must have knocked to the floor in her sleep.

The analyst propped herself up on one elbow; not satisfied, she clambered to a sitting position. A quick skim of her mental inbox revealed the finished drudge statement and about a hundred commentaries from across the Data Sea. Seemed like the statement had produced exactly the reaction Jara was hoping for: total indifference.

"We have a lot to do," continued Natch, talking to himself more than he was talking to Jara. "A *whole* lot. We've got to get that Multi-Real exposition back on track. That's critical. We need to time it carefully. Can't give people the impression that we're trying to profit from Margaret's death. But we can't let anyone forget about the exposition either. You've got a script ready?"

Jara nodded drowsily. After all that had happened in the past twenty-four hours, the exposition felt like it belonged in another universe altogether. "I do have a script," she said. And it was a pretty good script, too, she remembered. Easily digestible without being too gimmicky; a departure from the first baseball demo, but a departure to a familiar territory. "No worries on that score. But—"

Natch was in no mood for objections. "But what?" he snapped.

"Aren't you worried about our business licenses? We can't just keep going forward like nothing's happened. How's everyone going to get *paid*?"

Natch stopped, planted his hands in his pockets, and stared Jara directly in the face with such intensity it was almost surreal. "Don't worry about the licenses," he said. "It's all under control."

Jara could feel a throbbing current run from her abdomen to the back of her neck. Geronimo had utterly failed to spark that current in all his weeks of fumbling, and yet Natch could ignite her from halfway across the room. *Keep it together*, Jara admonished herself, turning away from those radiant blue eyes. *You're exhausted and you're not thinking clearly.* "What do you mean, it's 'under control'?" she said.

The entrepreneur got down on his haunches and reached out to steady himself momentarily with a hand on Jara's kneecap. "Follow the chain of command." His tone was low, conspiratorial. "Who pressured the Meme Cooperative to suspend our licenses? The Defense and Wellness Council. And what's the one governing body in the world that can put pressure on the Defense and Wellness Council? Who does Len Borda answer to?"

The answer was straight out of hive-level civics. "The Prime Committee," said Jara, trying to mentally will Natch's hand away from her knee.

"Exactly."

"But the Prime Committee's *afraid* of Len Borda. They're practically a rubber stamp for the Council. When was the last time they disagreed with Borda on . . . anything?"

"They'll disagree with him on this. Trust me." Natch had not so much as blinked in a minute, perhaps two.

Jara was starting to feel dizzy. Every time she got a handle on the situation, Natch would ratchet things up to some new plane with a totally different set of rules. He had jumped into fund-raising and product marketing and high-stakes mergers with great success, but did he know anything about politics? Jara didn't think so. In fact, she didn't know anyone who paid less attention to the ins and outs of government than Natch. How could he be so certain he knew how to influence the Prime Committee?

"Listen, Natch," she said. "I don't think you've thought this through. Even if the Committee is sympathetic to our cause, how are you going to get to them? There's only twenty-three of them, and sixty billion people clamoring for their attention. What are you going to do, just walk over to Melbourne and demand they focus on MultiReal?"

Natch was unfazed. "*I* won't. I'm going to get someone else to do it for me. Someone they'll listen to."

The analyst's brain flitted through the roster of governmental figures that paraded around the drudge reports. Natch's touch wasn't making things any easier. Most of the politicians she could name were either too beholden to the Defense and Wellness Council or too ineffectual to put up any resistance. Unless . . . yes, there *was* one person who didn't fall into either of those categories. "The speaker of Congress," said Jara. "Khann Frejohr."

Natch grinned crazily in affirmation and pushed himself to his feet, using Jara's knee as fulcrum. Then he began marching around the small room again like an automaton.

Not knowing what else to do, Jara straightened her spine and threw the results of an InfoGather 99 onto the window.

KHANN FREJOHR (280–)

Speaker of the Congress of L-PRACGs Khann Frejohr came into power at the end of 359, after a vote of no confidence toppled the previous speaker from office. Frejohr is the foremost representative of the libertarians, the political movement that seeks to shift power from the central government to the L-PRACGs.

As a youth, Frejohr was a well-known labor activist and vocal opponent of High Executive Len Borda. His career suffered a serious setback when he was accused of fomenting the Melbourne riots of 318. The atrocities committed there by angry rioters shocked the public, which had only recently endured the death of Marcus Surina and the collapse of the world economy. Many claim that these riots put the libertarian movement back twenty years.

Frejohr's role in inciting the riots was never proven, but he spent several years in a Defense and Wellness Council prison on related charges. He was subsequently pardoned by the Prime Committee in 326 under a general amnesty for political prisoners. Frejohr was first elected to the Congress of L-PRACGs in 332.

The analyst skimmed through a listing of the speaker's parliamentary maneuvers in a daze. Khann Frejohr started the *Melbourne riots*? Now that her attention had been drawn to this fact, Jara realized she had known it all along but simply forgotten. Her respect for the Congress's PR apparatus grew exponentially.

Jara found an image of the speaker and projected it into the middle of the room so he appeared to be standing on the coffee table. Khann Frejohr was rather short, with a shock of white hair and a single eyebrow forming a shelf of moral rectitude across his forehead. He had the look of a man who had been rakishly handsome decades ago. Hardly the type to lead an opposition to Len Borda.

Natch's hands were quivering, his voice a low rasp. "Don't you see the opportunity we have?" he said, stretching an arm through the holograph of Frejohr without appearing to notice. "Magan Kai Lee used the Meme Cooperative to *take away a fiefcorp* from its rightful master. How do you think the other fiefcorps are going to react to that? Do you think Lucas Sentinel and Pierre Loget and the Deuterons are going to sleep easy knowing Len Borda can shut down their businesses whenever he feels like it? No, of course not. They're scared to death.

"And they're not alone! The libertarians have just taken control of the Congress. They're putting up a united front and recruiting people to the movement left and right. That creed of theirs, Creed Libertas? You should see their new membership numbers. And guess what? You read that article by Sen Sivv Sor—people are flocking to Creed Libertas because of the Council's actions against *me*. I'm sure Margaret's death'll bring them a ton of converts too.

"Meanwhile, what's the Council doing? They're sending armed goons to break into my apartment! They're seizing businesses! They're marching on Andra Pradesh!" Natch's face was flushed and feverish now, his hands gesticulating wildly at the four corners of the room. "Don't you see? This is going to cause a tidal wave—the kind of wave that only comes along once in a generation. We can *ride* that wave, Jara."

The analyst shrank as far back into the couch as she could, teetering between fear and excitement, not wanting to let go of either. "I don't understand," she protested weakly. "You're going to use Khann Frejohr to get to the Prime Committee? But there are sixty billion people trying to get his attention too. What makes you think *Khann Frejohr* will talk to you?"

"The meeting's already been arranged," said Natch with a smirk. "Come on, Jara, I'm the face of the libertarian movement! Why wouldn't he talk to me?" His voice was completely lacking in irony.

"So you've got a meeting with Speaker Frejohr," said Jara. "But why would he stick his neck out for you? How are you going to convince him to confront the Prime Committee?"

Natch's face turned into one mad rictus of glee. Jara shuddered; she had seen that look before. It meant that once again, the entrepreneur was three steps ahead of everyone else on the planet.

And then he collapsed.

There was no swoon or gradual loss of consciousness. One moment Natch was striding around the room with his normal swagger, the next he was lying in a heap on the floor. He only missed banging his head on the sharp edge of the desk by centimeters. Jara was kneeling on the floor next to him in an instant.

Before she even had a chance to feel his forehead, the entrepreneur sprang up, flailing his arms to ward off some unseen terror. His elbow smacked Jara across the face, causing him to recoil and scurry back into a far corner. For a moment, she could see him bare and unmasked, a child in the dark.

Then Natch was back. Exhausted, confused, determined. A little embarrassed. "I'm sorry," he blurted out.

Jara shook her head. She rubbed her cheek where Natch had hit her. The fact that it was clearly an accident didn't make her feel any less uneasy. She sat on the floor with her back to the couch and waited for her pulse to slow to a manageable level. The hologram of Khann Frejohr stood placidly on the coffee table, forgotten.

"Listen," said the entrepreneur quietly after several minutes of awkward silence. He gazed intently at the carpet, searching for the right words. "This whole business with Magan Kai Lee and the Meme Cooperative. Putting you in charge of the fiefcorp. It's okay. It's not your fault."

The analyst blushed. "I should have told you," she muttered. "I should have let you know he was planning something." She hunched forward, planting her elbows on her thighs and her chin in her palms. "Natch, *you* know I didn't make any deal with the Council, don't you?"

Natch shrugged. "Of course." Jara couldn't help but let out a sigh of relief.

They sat silently, listening to the floorboards outside in the hallway creaking as the servants passed. Somewhere down the hall, servants were dragging furniture around in preparation for a group of Creed Élan do-gooders who Berilla had invited over, despite all the calamity of the past twenty-four hours. Jara tried to remember the last time she had been alone in a room with Natch for more than thirty seconds and came up empty.

"So what happens now?" Jara ventured after a few minutes.

Natch's eyes were suddenly suspicious. "What do you mean?"

"Well . . . technically, I'm your boss right now."

A tired smile crept over Natch's face, though Jara couldn't quite see the humor in the situation. "Let's just see how it goes," he said, making a dismissive motion with one hand as if he were tossing troubles over his shoulder. "I'm not worried. We can make some kind of arrangement until we figure out this whole license thing."

"An arrangement?"

"Well, *someone's* got to be in legal control of MultiReal. We can't have it floating out there in receivership. And we can't let Magan Kai Lee get ahold of it."

"No, I suppose not."

"So I sat down and thought about it for a while, and then I came to a decision." The entrepreneur took a deep breath. "I've decided to let things stand for now. The Meme Cooperative wants you to be the master of MultiReal? Fine. I've given you core access to the program."

Jara did her best not to gape in shock. Natch complying with a regulatory body's orders was like the wolf cozying up to the sheep.

Natch simply didn't do these kinds of things without ulterior motive. "Why?" she said.

"Because I need you to trust me," he replied. "I need you on my side."

The analyst stared into his eyes, trying to penetrate those depths the best she could. Jara had been working for Natch for several years now, and she had never felt like anything but a useful vessel for his ambitions. She had never felt like she *deserved* to be anything else. Now she was being entrusted with the most important thing in Natch's life: his business. Should she feel pleased or dejected that he would only do so grudgingly, after a deluge of threats from the government?

The important thing is that you've finally earned his respect, Jara told herself. She had thought she was looking for Natch's love, or maybe even his lust, but now she realized that what she was really after was just basic understanding and acceptance. She wanted parity. Did it really matter how she had achieved that?

"Now don't get *too* excited," said Natch with a laugh. For a second, Jara could see half a decade slough off his face like a shed skin. She remembered the day she had met him, in that tiny apartment in Angelos. The raw purpose. The intensity of him. "I'm not just doing this for *your* benefit. I'm also doing this because it's a good PR move that'll improve my hand with Khann Frejohr.

"And don't forget that obeying the Meme Cooperative is the last thing Magan Kai Lee expects me to do. It's going to drive him *crazy* wondering what I'm up to. It'll divert his attention.

"Look at it this way. The Council wasn't just out to yank our business licenses. They were out to divide the fiefcorp. To pit us against each other. So what's the smart move here? To confound their expectations by working *together*. And that's just what we're going to do."

Jara made a wary nod, unsure if she could trust this unfamiliar emotion. She thought she had been through psychological trauma, but Natch must have gone through ten times as much for him to make such a mental adjustment. The analyst exhaled sharply. Margaret Surina had said that MultiReal would change the world, but Jara had never expected that change so close to home.

"I just can't believe you'd give up MultiReal that easily," she said.

Natch grinned, and suddenly the wolf had returned. "The Meme Cooperative said I had to give you core access. They never said I needed to give up *mine*. Now come on, let's get to work. And that starts in Berilla's office."

(((2 2)))

Somewhere between the office door and the front atrium, Natch changed from cunning wolf to savage coyote. He strode through the hallway with head tilted forward like a battering ram as Jara struggled to keep up. He nearly ran over an old woman wearing the royal purple of Creed Élan and didn't react at all when a household domestic attempted to scold him for it.

They passed bedrooms, anterooms, and entertaining rooms beyond count, intersecting hallways that led to other wings of the house, puzzled servants, a multi chamber that could easily hold ten. Purple and red leapt out from every surface.

"So what's this going to accomplish?" asked the analyst.

"It's going to get Berilla off our backs," replied Natch.

"Is she *on* our backs? Berilla hasn't really bothered us since we arrived. I don't think she even knows you're here."

"She will."

Jara decided to just shut up and tag along for the ride. Natch knew what he was doing, didn't he? He *always* knew what he was doing, whereas Jara had never really done anything but flounder from circumstance to circumstance. She resolved to be patient. If Natch needed her assistance, he would let her know.

The hallway finally ended with a regal set of double doors that any member of the peerage would be proud to sit behind. Natch made no move to knock or announce himself first; instead, he firmly gripped the doors' brass handles and yanked.

"What on *Earth* . . ." came a high-pitched voice. The entrepreneur stepped through the doors, and the voice suddenly halted.

Berilla sat at a mahogany desk in the center of a cavernous room. Strange bric-a-brac cluttered the walls: beam and gunpowder weapons dating back to the Autonomous Revolt. The dedication plaque from an old hoverbird that had been decommissioned decades ago. An ancient replica of an even more ancient dartboard. A painting of a fox hunt being executed by pale white godlings in stiff tweed. Jara absorbed all this in awe, wondering what was authentic and what just clever mimicry.

The woman at the desk actually bore a much closer resemblance to her nephew Horvil than to her son. The same olive complexion and ebony hair, the same pear-shaped figure. But where Horvil's face had a permanent smile buried beneath his jowls, Berilla's face seemed to be entombed in a state of permanent disapproval.

"I see your manners haven't changed," Berilla sighed to Natch. She flipped her hand to extinguish a row of memos floating over the desk.

"Neither has your house," replied Natch without losing a beat. He took a seat unbidden in one of the sequined straight-backed chairs facing Berilla's desk. "You've kept the place just the way Wellington left it. Or was that Cromwell?"

"Are those supposed to be insults?" said Berilla, eyes drooping ponderously.

Natch shrugged.

Family matriarch and entrepreneur held a duel of blistering stares for over a minute without speaking. Jara wondered if she should bow and introduce herself, but since Berilla seemed to have no interest in her, she simply took the other chair and crossed her legs. The only sound in the room was the low *tick-tock* emanating from the rococo clock on the desk.

Berilla grew tired of their mental tug-of-war first. "So you've rudely pushed your way into my house without an invitation," she said finally. "I don't know how you managed to sneak past the household security and all those people out there, but I suppose it must be important. So what can I do for you, Natch?"

The entrepreneur touched his fingertips together in front of his face. "You can tell me why you halted production on my assembly line," he said.

"You mean *my* assembly line."

"Whatever. I paid good money for a programming floor. I expect to see results."

Jara tried to send Natch a ConfidentialWhisper, but he would not accept her requests. "They don't have access to the program anymore," she interjected, keeping her voice as low as possible. "We cut them off a few hours ago."

Berilla completely ignored her. "I didn't 'halt' anything, Natch. I simply instructed my people to work *backward*. The new floor supervisor was given strict orders to roll back every single connection we've made to your code. But don't worry—you'll be reimbursed for every credit you've spent, with interest. My accountants keep *meticulous* records."

"I don't give a fuck about the money. I care about the programming."

A part of Berilla was clearly hopping with joy. "Suit yourself."

Natch clawed at the arms of his chair as if psyching himself up to rip it to pieces. He worked at one for a moment, muscles knotted with exertion. "Don't you realize that anything you do to hurt *me* hurts Horvil and Ben too?" he said.

"I don't see it that way at all." The matriarch leaned back and crossed one ham-sized thigh over the other. If she minded Natch's mauling of her chair, she did not show it. "*You're* the one who's hurting Horvil and Benyamin. Every mistake you make puts them that much closer to giving up this ridiculous game of theirs." Berilla's frown deepened. "Playing at fiefcorps like children playing with toy soldiers. It's ridiculous."

Jara tried once more to insert herself into the conversation. "That's not fair," she said. "Nobody's forcing anyone to work for this fiefcorp. Horvil and Ben are adults. They understand the risks."

This caught Berilla's attention. She turned that froglike face toward the analyst. "Do they?"

"Of course they do," said Natch icily. "They're not risking anything that I'm not willing to risk myself."

The matriarch gave an exaggerated blink of amusement. "I don't know why I even bother arguing with you, Natch," she said. "You're risking—what exactly *is* it that you're risking? Your family? Your inheritance? Your ties to the community? No. You have none of these things. Excuse me for being so blunt, Natch—but you have nothing to lose. Horvil and Benyamin do.

"What does your business offer them?" she continued, steamrolling right over Jara's nascent protest. "Money? They *have* money. Prestige? Experience? Exposure? They can get all that working for Marulana at Creed Élan. They can get that working for me. They can get that working for tens of thousands of businesses out there that don't treat them like— like *raw meat*." She sat back, clearly satisfied with herself, and started straightening the desktop paraphernalia that didn't really need straightening: an antique letter opener, a quill pen jutting out of some hideous pot of ink, a plastic egg that looked like some kind of ancient computer appendage.

Natch kept robotically still during Berilla's little diatribe. "You don't understand," he rasped. "What you're offering them are jobs. What I'm offering them is a chance to change the world."

"I understand more than you think," scoffed Berilla, looking suddenly old and tired. "MultiReal might change the world—but do you know what you're changing it *to*?"

In response, the entrepreneur rose again and strode to the center of the faux bearskin rug that covered most of the floor. His face was sullen and pensive. "What," he said slowly, "do you want?"

Jara felt like she should ask Natch that question himself. She was starting to grow restless with this little meeting. What the fiefcorp had to gain by haranguing Berilla—and why Jara should be a part of it—she couldn't fathom.

Berilla let out a high-pitched cackle that ricocheted up the walls to the distant ceiling. "What do I want? What do I *want*? Natch, are you listening to anything I'm saying? Look around you! I already *have* everything I could possibly want. My main concern is making sure nobody throws it all away."

The entrepreneur stewed in place for a moment with his eyes wandering up and down the wall of knickknacks. His hands clenched and unclenched behind his back. "Everybody wants something, or they'd have no reason to get out of bed in the morning," said Natch after a moment. "Even you. You want stability. You want protection. For yourself and for your family."

Berilla let out a loud sigh. "What's your point?"

"My point is this: If anything were to happen to Horvil and Benyamin, you would be quite upset."

Jara could feel the bottom drop out of her stomach. She raised her hand and dropped it, unsure of what to say. Was Natch actually *threatening* his own apprentices? The matriarch's brow furrowed, and her chin rocked slowly back and forth as she caught the distress in the analyst's face.

And it was in that moment that Jara understood why she was here. What she had mistaken for desperate emotion on the entrepreneur's part was just a carefully choreographed act. Of *course* it was a carefully choreographed act—wasn't it always? But not only had Natch scripted his own part to the letter, he had scripted Jara's as well. He had specifically brought Jara to this meeting because he knew she would recoil from his suggestion. The fearful look in her eyes would prove to Berilla that Natch was serious. That he was perfectly capable of committing ruthless deeds.

"I don't see what you're insinuating," said Berilla, growing more disturbed by the second. "Don't try to scare me into thinking you'd actually hurt them. You don't have it in you."

"Hurt?" Natch smiled. "Who said anything about hurting anyone?" He began a slow walk around the bearskin rug, arms folded across his chest. "Let's not be melodramatic, Berilla. We're talking about protection here—protection from the Defense and Wellness Council." He came to a stop directly in front of the woman and laid his palms flat on the desktop. Jara could see a debate in Berilla's mind about whether to call household security. "The Council already found enough evidence to get Horvil's and Ben's business licenses suspended. But if they found out what your son and your nephew were *really* doing for me . . . Well, they wouldn't stop at just a fine or a suspension. Oh, no. They'd haul Ben and Horvil off to an orbital prison. A *Council* orbital prison."

A muddy speck of doubt clouded the icy green of Berilla's eyes. "This is absurd," she said. "You don't have anything on Horvil and Benyamin. Even *you* couldn't have that bad of an influence on them."

"No?" Natch gave the slightest of nods toward the window, causing the placid British gardens to be replaced by the blocky letters of a memo. Jara squinted to read the type and then gasped.

It was an anonymous message addressed directly to the Defense and Wellness Council. But this was much more than just a message; it was practically a confession. A lengthy list of all the illegal and unethical actions that Horvil and Benyamin had participated in during their apprenticeships to Natch. Ben's list had to be grossly exaggerated, considering he had only been with the fiefcorp for a few weeks now. But Horvil's list appeared to be spot-on. Jara recognized everything from the engineer's ruses that had helped the company steal customers from Captain Bolbund to his role in the black code scare that allowed them to conquer Primo's. There were also a number of accusations Jara didn't recognize, accusations that explained inconsistencies that had been nagging her for years. How had the fiefcorp staved off Prosteev Serly's assault on their optical programs? Why had Lucas Sentinel failed to bid on a certain lucrative L-PRACG contract? Jara now knew.

Whether anything on this list was actually enough to convict Horvil and Ben of a crime was uncertain. But it didn't really matter. If this memo found its way into a drudge's hands, it would have a much greater effect on Horvil's and Ben's careers than any Meme Cooperative hand slapping.

Berilla read through the memo with mounting agitation and not a little sadness. A trickle of sweat worked its way down her neck. "Horvil's stood by you since you were a little boy," she protested. "He follows you around like a puppy, Natch. He lends you money. Have you *really* sunk that low?"

"*Only the one prepared to sacrifice anything can achieve everything*," said Natch, quoting Kordez Thassel. "You said it yourself—I really have nothing to lose, do I? I might already be heading for a Council prison."

"But—but—"

"What can you do to stop me from sending out this memo? I'll tell you what you're going to do." The entrepreneur found his way back to the straight-backed chair and sat on it like a king taking his throne. "You're going to start production on that assembly-line floor again. You're going to undo *every fucking change* your team made to the Multi-Real code. And then you're going to *finish* the job you started. In fact, you're going to put the entire floor on the project so they finish faster. And if I see the slightest bit of evidence you're holding out on me, Sen Sivv Sor and John Ridglee are going to see this memo within the hour. Do you understand me *now*?"

Time shuddered to a halt. For a moment, Jara found herself admiring the deviousness, the sheer audacity, of Natch's plan. It was the ultimate bluff: mutually assured career destruction. If Natch went down in ignominy, then his apprentices would go down with him. Or at least so Berilla was supposed to believe. He wouldn't *actually* do something so Machiavellian, would he?

Then Jara caught a glimpse of Natch's face, and she realized that he was utterly serious. He *would* sacrifice Horvil and Benyamin's careers—and quite possibly their liberty—to get what he wanted. And the prize if he succeeded: a top-notch assembly-line shop at his command, ready to finally complete the MultiReal coding. No small thing, considering that there was no other shop that would defy the Council's blacklist. If Berilla put the entire floor on the job, they might even get the job done in time for the MultiReal exposition.

So Natch was now using blatant threats to get his way. But why allow Jara to hear them, unless he was implicitly threatening *her* career too?

She could see the scene unfolding in her mind. Jara would sit quietly through the rest of the meeting and confront him later in private. Natch would blow her off at first, then finally capitulate. *Of course I wouldn't have really sent out that memo,* he would say, touching her shoulder to short-circuit her logical processes. *Of course I was bluffing. But it was a bluff you needed to see. I needed to gauge your determination to deal with the hard realities of running a fiefcorp. You have to be prepared to do these kinds of things, Jara—and I don't think you are.*

But the worst part was not Natch's callousness or his scheming nature; it was not the fact that he was manipulating her. Those things were givens. The worst part was that Natch already knew she would capitulate. She would fret and she would yell, but in the end she would accept his explanations and do nothing to intervene. Not only that, but she would actually *assist* him in perpetrating his plots, and she would make excuses for him to Horvil and Ben. Wasn't that what she always did? Jara had unwittingly acted out that scene too many times to count.

Natch had reduced Jara to her essence, and that essence was cowardice.

As she sat there in Berilla's office, half a decade of seductive touches and gruff admonitions abruptly came together to form a sinister picture in her mind. How could she have believed that Natch was starting to respect her? On the contrary, Jara had become nothing more than a crass calculation to him. So confident was Natch of his dominance that he could *rely* on her to ignore his threats to Horvil and Ben. He could hand over core access to MultiReal without worrying that she would betray him. He could depend on her to simply submit to his whims—even when Jara would suffer for them.

Jara rose from her seat, veins throbbing with fury at Natch, at herself.

"I've had enough of this," said the analyst. She waved her hand at the window and banished the display into digital limbo. "You're not going to send that memo anywhere."

Berilla snapped her head around as if noticing Jara's presence for the first time. Natch plastered a creepy grin on his face, but it had the look of an artificial emotion constructed with bio/logic programming. He fired a ConfidentialWhisper in her direction; now it was her turn to ignore his requests.

"Jara," said the entrepreneur, standing up straight and slipping into salesman mode. "Why don't—"

"No," she interrupted. "Don't start. You really think I'm going to sit here and listen to you make *threats* against your own apprentices? Against *Horvil*, after all he's done for you?"

"Why don't we talk about this back in—"

"No, we'll talk about it *now*. You want threats? I'll give you threats. You don't have anything on us that we don't have on you. Erase that memo, or I give the drudges a full report of all your dirty tricks."

The entrepreneur smirked. "Didn't the Blade already do that?" More ConfidentialWhisper requests, more denials.

Jara knew her bravado would not last long. Already she could see Natch reconfiguring his strategy, adjusting to circumstances. She needed to end this quickly and decisively. Jara felt a bluff of her own come bubbling to the front of her consciousness. "Erase that memo, or I'll end this whole thing right here and now. You know I'm sick of this whole business. I'll give Magan Kai Lee what he wants. I'll give him core access to MultiReal. I'm sure he'll pay handsomely for it."

All at once, Natch's carefully polished veneer shattered. He stormed to the far side of the room, his face caught up in a snarl. "You think you know how to run a business, Jara? You think you can stand up to the *Council*? Open your eyes!" He flailed his hands around in the air as if he might smash one of Berilla's precious artifacts at any moment. "You're going to give them core access to MultiReal? That's exactly what Magan Kai Lee wants! That's exactly why he put you in this position—so the Defense and Wellness Council can plow right through you and take MultiReal away. Can't you see *anything*? Are you fucking *blind*?"

Jara did not flinch. "You're not running this fiefcorp any longer," she said, carefully enunciating each syllable. "*I* am. And I'm not going to let you drive it into the ground. I'm not going to let you trash five years of my life on some meaningless crusade." She took a deep breath. "The arrangement is off. Get the fuck out of here. We don't want you here anymore."

Berilla's jaw gaped open as she recoiled in her seat. Her hand grasped the ink pen as if its quill were a magical talisman of protection.

Natch paced frenetically around the room in an ever-tightening spiral. "Useless!" he cried out of nowhere. He turned and jabbed a finger at the doorway and the fiefcorpers somewhere down the hall. "You're useless. You're *all* useless. I knew I shouldn't have bothered to come here. I won't let you hand my business over to the Council. They won't take MultiReal away from me. Margaret chose me. *Me*. She said I'm the guardian and the keeper. So do whatever you want. I don't care. From now on, I'm doing what I have to do, and I'm doing it *alone*."

Then Natch whirled on his heels and strode back out the double doors. The sound of some fragile knickknack shattering echoed through the west wing of the house, and then he was gone.

• • •

Vigal, Merri, and Benyamin were already seated at the provisional conference table in the parlor when Horvil arrived. Their faces were frozen in various stages of distraction and worry.

And who could blame them? They were holed up in a London estate, while outside infoquakes raged and the public angrily clamored to know who had killed Margaret Surina. There were articles from know-nothing pundits all over the Data Sea fulminating about Natch's culpability, his lack of ethics, his inherent sliminess. Nobody had anything to offer except vague conjecture, yet they all seemed quite certain of their opinions.

The drudges had even come up with something of a communal narrative to explain the circumstances behind the murder. According to this narrative, Quell had gotten in a big argument with Margaret— about what, nobody could say. This argument had left him vulnerable to Natch's job solicitations and offers for revenge. Natch had hired Quell away for his insider knowledge of the Surina operation, arranged a hostile takeover, and then brainwashed the Islander into murdering Margaret when the deal went sour.

Horvil wondered when the drudges would figure out that Natch was responsible for the Autonomous Revolt and the death of Henry Osterman too.

Unfortunately, the Data Sea was full of persuasive, if anecdotal, evidence. There was a video that showed Quell being dragged away by Council officers. There was the complaint by the Meme Cooperative. Jayze Surina had leaked the fact that Natch might have been the last person to see Margaret alive. On top of all this, Creed Surina had announced a big public funeral for Margaret next week at Andra Pradesh. Whether such a spectacle would tamp down the flames of innuendo or fan them to new heights was anyone's guess.

Jara arrived at that moment, looking pale and angry. Her fists were clenched. Horvil, Merri, Vigal, and Benyamin stared at her without saying a thing.

"We've got to move in a new direction," announced the analyst. "Natch has been trying the same thing in this fiefcorp for—what? Four, five years now. Stirring up chaos. Pushing toward something that's always right over the next hill. Well, I'm *sick* of it."

Only Benyamin had the gumption to ask the obvious question. "So what does Natch think?"

Jara gathered up her courage and then looked the apprentice squarely in the eye. "Natch is gone. For good. I kicked him out."

Serr Vigal nearly fell off his chair in shock. Horvil tried to hold back his gaping stare, but failed miserably. In his peripheral vision, he could see Ben and Merri grip the table as if waiting for a hurricane to pass through.

"What happened?" said Merri in a timorous voice.

Jara pointedly ignored the question. "Listen, the Council's in disarray right now, with Margaret's death and the infoquakes and the public uproar. Those drudges will stay out there for a while in hopes of catching a glimpse of Natch. In the meantime, we'll have a few days to gather our wits. The Surinas are holding a funeral for Margaret next week. We'll have at least until then, maybe even a few days after that.

"So here's what we need to do.

"We need to spend that time repairing the company's image. The Surina/Natch MultiReal Fiefcorp has a *huge* image problem, and it won't just go away. We can't just sweep it under the rug. We keep fighting this same battle for dignity over and over again, day after day, and it's got to stop. The strongest hand we have to play now is public trust—and we don't have any.

"So how do we repair our image? We hold a press conference as soon as possible like any normal, ethical company would. Tell the world we have nothing to hide. Once that's done, we get to work clearing up these charges from the Meme Cooperative. Settle them, plead guilty to a few if we have to, it doesn't matter—just get everything *resolved* as quickly as possible so we can move on.

"The most important thing is to postpone this MultiReal exposition indefinitely. We can say we're doing it out of respect for Margaret Surina so we don't completely lose face. We just need to back *off* and let things simmer down. Then, in a few weeks—when we have a better hand—we sit down with Magan Kai Lee again and start the dialogue in earnest.

"So who's with me?"

Nobody answered. A confused silence hung over the parlor like smoke for several minutes. Finally Jara pursed her lips, walked back down the hall to the room she had appropriated as an office, and shut the door behind her.

(((23)))

Friday began with a death threat and only degenerated from there.

Jara received the message only minutes after confirming her reservation for an auditorium at the Surina Enterprise Facility. The threat was written in a hackneyed Cyrillic font that only the uneducated or imbecilic would find sinister.

Come to Creed Surina and ШЄ ШILL KILL ЧOU
Just like ЧOU killed Маяаdяет

The analyst sighed and beseeched Berilla's ceiling for deliverance from craven anonymity. She knew the wise course was to ignore the message altogether and let Surina security deal with any errant assassins. Isn't that what Natch would do? Instead, Jara lay on the vinyl couch and ruminated on the issue for twenty minutes. Was it in poor taste to discuss the dispensation of Margaret Surina's business in her own auditorium? Or was it a fitting tribute? Jara couldn't tell.

She decided to cancel the reservation and move the press conference to a Creed Objectivv auditorium instead. It was her first real decision as de facto master of the Surina/Natch MultiReal Fiefcorp. Already she felt like a failure.

Jara stretched, corralled her wayward hair the best she could, then shambled down the hall in search of food. The servants she passed gave her curt nods, but none of her etiquette training had prepared her for how to respond. *We're crashing in someone's house without permission because our company's founder has been murdered and our company itself is on the rocks. Should we be grateful that Berilla hasn't kicked us out yet, or irritated that she hasn't been more welcoming?* Jara decided on the former and quickly scoured the Data Sea for an appropriately humble expression to throw on her face.

But if dealing with the household staff was awkward, that was nothing compared to dealing with her own staff.

When Jara finally stumbled into the kitchen, she found Horvil, Merri, Benyamin, and Vigal already assembled and sporting looks of weary fortitude. They all clammed up the instant she rounded the corner. She supposed they were trying to make sense of the scene in the parlor yesterday, trying to figure out why Natch had made such an abrupt departure and whether he was really gone for good. But what could she say? What could she tell them that wouldn't sound petty and self-serving?

Jara poured a cup of nitro from the carafe on the counter. "All right," she said. "Let's get started. Let's *fix* some things."

Nobody responded. Four pairs of eyes watched her and waited.

Willing herself to be calm, Jara took her nitro over to a barstool and sat. "First things first. Has anybody tried to track down Quell yet?"

"Council still isn't saying anything," said Horvil glumly. "They've probably taken him to the orbital prisons by now."

"Well, we're going to need him. Try again. See if you can find out where he is."

The engineer leaned back in his chair and wedged one chubby knee against the edge of the table. "How?" he said. "You think Len Borda'll answer a ConfidentialWhisper?"

"Not today, please, Horv," sighed Jara, chugging down her cup of nitro and immediately getting up for a refill. "*I* have no idea what happened to Quell. But the Defense and Wellness Council has to have a public relations liaison or something who can point you in the right direction. If all else fails, just follow the drudges."

Horvil nodded. Jara wasn't sure she could trust him to find anything—he hadn't exactly pulled out all the stops to locate Natch after his disappearance a few weeks ago—but she couldn't afford to spend any more of her mental reserve worrying about it. She moved on.

"So can we still work on MultiReal?" continued Jara. "Did Quell or Margaret leave any documentation behind?"

The engineer pursed his lips. "Technically. But if you think *my* notes are hard to follow, you should see *theirs*. Might take me years to wade through all that crap."

"Well, do the best you can. Ben, where are we with the rollback issue?"

"Handled," said the young apprentice, trying his best to avoid looking Jara in the eye. "Well, it'll be handled soon. I called in a few favors on the floor, and it looks like the 'sabotage' was a little overblown. A few pranks here and there. I think we'll have everything back to normal in about a week."

"And . . . your mother?"

Ben shrugged. "She's not interfering."

Jara exhaled in relief. A lack of interference from Berilla was about the best she could hope for at this point. She remembered the puzzled and fearful look the matriarch had given her yesterday after Natch stormed out of her office. Jara could only guess what she had been thinking.

"Now . . . Merri and Vigal." The analyst turned to face the pair. "I'd like you two onstage during the press conference this afternoon. Otherwise it'll just be me and Robby Robby up there—not the most trustworthy people in the world right now." The two fiefcorpers nodded, their faces barren of emotion. Jara was trying to make a joke, but now she realized it hadn't come out like that.

"I can't believe you're actually going through with this stupid press conference," said Benyamin in characteristically high dudgeon. "We don't have a working product. We don't have a fiefcorp master. Shit, Jara, you're the only person with a business license from the Meme Cooperative right now. What are you going to say?"

"I'm not going to say much of anything, if I can help it," snapped Jara. "The point is not what I say. The point is that I'm going out there and *saying* it. I'm giving notice."

"Notice of what? That Natch is gone?"

"No, I don't want to spill that for a few more days, until things calm down a little. I'm just giving notice that the Surina/Natch Fief-corp has changed. That we're an *honest* company now."

"So . . . you're going to tell the drudges we're an honest company, and then you're going to mislead them by implying that Natch is still running it?"

The irony slapped Jara in the face and made her blush. She hadn't thought of it that way. Benyamin grimaced and shut up.

"Listen," said the analyst, her fingernails plowing long, tired rows on her scalp. "I'm not trying to get this business going again just as a matter of principle. Don't forget, while your business licenses are sus-pended, the fiefcorp can't *pay* you. Now Horvil and Benyamin might be able to weather a few thousand years without a fiefcorp stipend—"

"Presuming Aunt Berilla doesn't cut us off," muttered Horvil.

"—but I'm willing to bet Vigal and Merri can't. *I* certainly couldn't. So unless we get this business rolling soon, some of us could be in a real heap of trouble."

Jara guzzled down her third cup of nitro, well on her way to a per-sonal best. She discarded the cup on the counter and surveyed her fellow fiefcorpers. The room felt cloistered, devoid of oxygen, and the Surina/Natch MultiReal Fiefcorp felt more like a mythical entity than a viable business. *Why can't I inspire this company the way Natch does?* thought the analyst. *What am I doing wrong?*

"All right," she said finally, realizing that the rest of the fiefcorpers were waiting for a word of dismissal. "Let's get to it."

• • •

If the vibe at Berilla's estate was one of dejection, the vibe backstage at Creed Objectivv was more upbeat, thanks to Robby Robby's relentless optimism. The channeler was indeed a wonder. It seemed like some divine force had wound him up forty years ago and left him to cruise in a smooth, unbroken line ever since. Jara wondered if he'd ever experienced a moment of doubt, whether he'd ever had a cheating companion or a malicious boss or a friend who had lied to him.

Robby poked his head around the corner at the crowd of murmuring drudges in the auditorium. "Looking pretty grim out there, eh, Frizzy?" he said.

The channeler's young sidekick Frizitz Quo hung on his elbow like a purse. "I thought you said grim was your specialty, boss," he replied.

"It is!" grinned Robby, walking over to hook his other elbow with Jara's. "Give me a grim and uncooperative audience, Mistress Jara. I'll give you grim and uncooperative customers!"

Jara smiled weakly. With everything happening in the fiefcorp—not to mention the world—how could Robby and Friz still maintain the same smooth facade? Sure, their channeling firm had other horses in its stable. But Robby had to know that an opportunity like Multi-Real only came along once in a lifetime.

"Everybody ready?" said the channeler.

Merri and Serr Vigal walked up, their faces shellacked with bio/logically generated calm. "Sure," said Merri.

Jara looked at the apprentice's jacket pocket and saw nothing but fabric. "Aren't you going to wear your Objectivv pin?"

Merri shook her head. "I've been suspended from the creed, remember?"

The analyst felt the blood draining from her face. No, in fact, she had totally forgotten. She took a surreptitious peek around Robby's hair to the giant black-and-white swirl embossed on the stage just a few meters away. "I'm so sorry, Merri," she said, *sotto voce*. "Should we—do you want to—"

Merri cut her off with a brusque wave of the hand. "I'll be fine," she said.

"Time to go!" bellowed Robby, and before Jara could recover her composure, they were onstage.

As she stepped into the spotlight, Jara realized that she should have held this press conference at the Surina Enterprise Facility after all. Objectivv auditoriums were notoriously free of adornment, and this one was no exception. A stage, a podium, a few thousand seats: that was all. No subtle SeeNaRee effects, no soporific Jamm music in the background. Under ordinary circumstances, that would have suited Jara just fine. But there was a cloud of anger wafting through the crowd of three thousand drudges that didn't bode well for the presentation. Not even Robby's minions stationed around the auditorium were able to dispel the haze of distrust in the air.

Robby Robby took center stage, while Jara, Vigal, Merri, and Frizitz lined up dutifully behind him. Robby's previous expression of levity had been replaced by a look so solemn it approached the funereal.

"Towards Perfection to you all," said Robby to the crowd. "It's good to see so many of you here under such trying circumstances. We're still a little disorganized after the last infoquake—but heck, I guess it's been that way for everyone. We're going to do the best we can to give you some answers and just hope things aren't too rough around the edges.

"And now, without further ado, I'd like to turn the stage over to someone many of you have worked with before. I present Jara of the Surina/Natch MultiReal Fiefcorp."

The smattering of light applause hit Jara like birdshot. She took a deep breath, stepped into the spot Robby had just vacated, and clasped her hands together on the podium in what she hoped was the stance of an honest businesswoman. She looked at the crowd: women, men, frowns, grimaces, scowls.

"Towards Perfection," said Jara. "I stand before you today as a representative of the Surina/Natch MultiReal Fiefcorp, and I'm asking for your trust."

Light muttering, uncomfortable shifts from the audience. Someone tittered.

Jara felt her stomach lurch. It had sounded like a great beginning when she practiced it this morning at Berilla's estate. Jara immediately realized what was wrong: she had written a statement tailored for *Natch* to deliver. She scrolled madly up and down the little speech floating before her eyes, looking for something confident she could say in her own voice, and came up empty.

Five seconds passed. Ten. A ConfidentialWhisper from Robby: "Mistress Jara . . . ?"

Flustered, Jara segued into the more prosaic statement she had been holding for a backup. The Surina/Natch MultiReal Fiefcorp was deeply saddened by the news of Margaret Surina's death. Natch had heard the dreadful tidings directly from the Council's chief solicitor, but the fiefcorp didn't have any more information about the circumstances than anyone else. Margaret's contributions to science and humanity were incalculable. Doubtless she would be remembered as the greatest of the Surinas.

Jara paused, wishing she could call an end to the whole thing right there. "Any questions?" she said.

A florid Sen Sivv Sor stepped to the front of the crowd, and the crowd held its breath. Jara wondered what kind of wrangling and infighting and backroom deal-swapping the drudges used to determine their pecking order. She couldn't imagine any valuation system that would put carrion crows like Sen Sivv Sor and John Ridglee at the top. And yet, somehow, they always were.

Sor fixed Jara with a deadly stare. The red birthmark on his forehead glowered at her like an accusation. "Did Natch arrange to have Margaret Surina murdered?" he said, his voice a serrated blade.

Jara was prepared for the question, but not the vehemence of the questioner. "No, of course not," she replied. "Natch and Margaret always had a perfectly friendly and professional relationship. I can't imagine why Natch would have wanted to hurt her."

"Then where is he?" cried the drudge. "My sources tell me the Defense and Wellness Council arrested him."

"I'm sorry, but your sources have been misinformed. Natch was in London for a fiefcorp meeting yesterday. Since then, he's been taking inventory of our databases to make sure nothing was damaged in the infoquake. As far as I know, the Council hasn't named Natch as a suspect in any investigation."

Sor nodded, clearly not satisfied with Jara's answers but unwilling to press his first-questioner status any further. He bowed and stepped out of the way. Behind him, the line of angry questioners snaked far up into the audience. *One down*, thought Jara.

"What do you know about this Islander the Council dragged out of the Revelation Spire?" asked the next questioner, a man with a simian brow and low-dragging knuckles to match.

"The Islander Quell is a member of our fiefcorp and one of the principal engineers of MultiReal," said Jara. "He's been in Margaret's employ for years now, since—since the beginning." She reached inside her memory for a number to back her up and was surprised to discover that she had none. *Everything's happening much too fast*, the analyst thought. *Has anyone even had a chance to ask Quell how long he's been on the project? Long enough to gain Margaret's trust, of course—but how long is that? Two years? Ten? Twenty?* "Obviously we're not pleased with the way the Council treated him in Andra Pradesh," she continued. "It's pretty clear there's some misunderstanding going on, and we hope to have it resolved shortly."

"The rumor on the Data Sea," said the next drudge, "is that this Islander murdered Margaret and tried to take MultiReal for himself."

Jara had put together a perfectly innocuous laugh this morning in MindSpace, and now she let it loose on the crowd. "That's ridiculous," she said. She gave Robby a sidelong rolling of the eyes, which Robby returned on cue. "Quell's been a trusted member of Margaret's staff for years. He knows most of the Surina security force by name."

The laugh failed to appease the audience. In fact, it only seemed to inflame them further. Drudges began to step up in rapid succession and shoot questions at her, one after another like machine gun fire.

"If this Islander is so trustworthy, why did the Council arrest him?"

"Wasn't he just covering for *you* so you could execute a hostile takeover of the company?"

"Natch was already implicated in the murders of his hivemates during initiation. Why wouldn't he do it again?"

"Why did the Meme Cooperative suspend everyone's business license at the fiefcorp but yours?"

"How do we know *you* didn't have anything to do with Margaret's death?"

"What's going to happen to MultiReal? Did you sell it to the Council?"

"If you don't have anything to hide, why are you taking money under the table from Creed Thassel?"

Jara gaped at the last question. The Thasselians? How had *they* gotten involved in all this? She thought back to the bizarre fund-raising pitches Natch had undertaken last month when the fiefcorp was frantically trying to prepare for the unveiling of Margaret's then-mysterious Phoenix Project. Natch had made some elusive comments about borrowing money from an unnamed "third party," and Horvil later hinted that an old acquaintance from the hive had stepped forward with the cash. Jara had shrugged it off. Was Natch so desperate he would take funding from a discredited creed? And not just any creed, but a notoriously shady one with a secret membership roster?

The analyst flailed around in vain for an answer. She gave the subtlest of glances in Merri's direction, but the channel manager's mien was impenetrable. "I'm really not at liberty to discuss the company's finances right now," Jara replied lamely.

With a notoriously unethical creed as grease, the press conference began to slide down a dangerous slope toward the paranoid. The drudges began launching personal attacks on Natch's character, or personal attacks on Jara's character, or far-flung theories about MultiReal that bordered on the insane. It was all Jara could do to simply keep up with her canned responses. Someone even tried to pin the disappearances of Pierre Loget and Billy Sterno on Natch, to which Jara could only shake her head.

Just when it seemed like things couldn't get any worse and even Robby Robby was showing traces of unease, a misshapen lump of a man stepped to the front of the line. He had shifty eyes and an oily dab of mustache.

"A hundred and twenty violations of the Meme Cooperative bylaws!" squawked the man. "Isn't it convenient that in all the hullabaloo surrounding Margaret's death, everyone's forgotten about *that?*"

Jara stared at the drudge, certain she had seen him before. She lobbed his picture at the public directory, but his profile had been carefully scrubbed clean. Jara searched her memory and came up blank there too. "The Meme Cooperative gives out twenty thousand citations every year," she said. "If you read through the list, you'll see that ninety-five percent of them are politically motivated. Once Natch gets his day in front of the arbitration board, I'm sure he'll be vindicated for most of them."

"Most of them? *Most* of them?" The man emitted a squeal that might have passed for amusement and gave the woman behind him a conspiratorial elbow in the gut. Jara hoped the other drudges would hustle this odd person out of the queue so she could draw the conference to a close, but instead they were clearing a space for the man's grandstanding. "So what would you say if I told you I'm filing a whole new set of charges against the Surina/Natch MultiReal Fiefcorp for breach of contract?"

Jara was starting to get a major headache. "Breach of *whose* contract?"

"I'm glad you asked," said the man with a queer smile. Then he turned his back to the stage and lifted his hands with a flourish, like a prophet signaling to his people that they had arrived at the Promised Land.

A small band began to march through the crowd from the back of the auditorium. Amused smiles percolated across the faces of the drudges. Jara counted eighteen people in the group that came to a halt behind the grandstander. It was as random a group as one could possibly assemble, and Jara didn't recognize any of them.

"What are you *doing* up there?" came a frantic Confidential-Whisper from Benyamin. "Call security before this guy hijacks the whole press conference!"

Jara fidgeted and turned to look at an equally perplexed Robby Robby. What could she do?

"I give you Natch's latest victims!" brayed the lumpy man. "I give you the victims of the crass pyramid scheme called the MultiReal exposition lottery! Eighteen suffering souls who entered into a Faustian bargain with your boss Natch! Eighteen souls promised a chance at fame and fortune, under *legal contract*, mind you. A legal contract that was broken without a second glance by your scheming, manipulative fiefcorp master!"

That was when Jara finally placed him.

Captain Bolbund.

Something rancid and congealed in Jara's gut made an effort to creep back into her throat. It had been years since Natch's little altercation with Captain Bolbund in the ROD coding business, years since she had endured his putrid poetry. The last Jara remembered, Bolbund's business license had been suspended for impersonating a Meme Cooperative official. And yet here he stood, flaring his nostrils and stirring mischief. How long had this bottom feeder been festering in his anger, waiting for an opportunity at revenge? Was the list of Natch's enemies truly endless?

"Justice for the MultiReal exposition lottery winners!" thundered Bolbund, swinging his fist back and forth in an attempt to wrench the words into a rhythmic chant. "Justice for the MultiReal exposition lottery winners! Justice! Justice!"

Vigal openly buried his face in his hands, and Merri looked like she had been turned to stone. Robby and Frizitz were making clipped gestures to the channelers in the crowd, but what kind of message they were trying to send was unclear.

Jara made a few stumbling attempts at imposing order, but the genie would not be forced back into the bottle. Objectivv security officers rushed forward to apprehend the miscreant, but now he was darting through the crowd like a fat gremlin. Laughter spurted out of the drudges at the obscene spectacle. Someone even stuck a foot in front of the Objectivv officers, sending them crashing to the floor like a row of black-and-white-swirled dominoes.

The analyst rubbed her temples in frustration. A nightmare.

• • •

Jara wanted to bury her face in the soft refuge of her mother's belly. Berilla's couch made a poor substitute. The microfibers on the pillows wouldn't even absorb her tears, but left them to dribble down to the crook of the couch instead.

Someone tapped on the door. "Come in," said Jara softly.

The door slid open and admitted Horvil. He took in the analyst's misery and parked himself backward on a spindly chair. "You look upset," said the engineer, once again demonstrating his penchant for either stating the obvious or blundering right past it.

"I *am* upset," replied Jara. "I can't believe our own contest winners are suing us. On top of everything else going on right now."

Horvil made a sour face. "Bolbund," he said. "Never thought I'd see that idiot again. Don't worry about it. The whole exposition is yesterday's news. Those lottery winners'll just disappear into the woodwork, you'll see. If nothing else, that lawsuit's put more drudges at the front gates. There must be six hundred people out there now."

Jara craned her neck toward the window, but the couch's armrest blocked her view. "I should have listened to Ben," she said after a moment's reflection. "I shouldn't even have held that fucking press conference. You don't think I made things *worse* . . . do you?"

"All I know is that you stood up and did something," said Horvil. "Somebody needed to."

The headache that had begun during the press conference had now captured Jara's frontal lobes. She felt a masochistic urge to just let it rampage for a while. "Listen, Horvil, I . . . There's something I think you should know."

Horvil sniffed and shrugged at the same time. "If you're going to tell me about Natch's little threat to ruin my career, don't bother. Aunt Berilla already told me. It's not really anything to get upset over. I know he didn't mean it."

"Didn't *mean* it?" The pain lanced through the back of Jara's neck as she sat up abruptly. "How can you say that?"

"Hey, I'm not the one who just stood up and told a million drudges what an ethical businessman Natch is."

"That's for the good of the company. It's different."

Horvil nodded and slumped his chin down onto his folded arms. "Natch is stressed out, Jara. He's losing it. Have you noticed all that twitching, all those strange looks? I've—I've never seen him this bad before. That black code is tearing him up. He's running out of options. He wouldn't have made that threat to Aunt Berilla unless he had no other choice."

"I can't believe I'm hearing this," said Jara, aghast. "You're making excuses for him. Of course he had other choices."

"Really?" Horvil asked. "If someone put a gun to your head and said it's either you or Natch—what would *you* do?" The engineer rose and walked to the window, where he stood in plump silhouette against the moonlight. Jara could see that the drudges were definitely there, camped right outside the gates. She was glad she could see out the windows but they couldn't see in. "Natch didn't walk out just because of *me*, did he?" asked the engineer.

Jara shook her head. "No, it's much more complicated than that. You want to know the real reason Natch left?" She took a breath. "It's because of me," she said. "It's because of what I'm doing to the company."

Horvil pursed his lips skeptically. "What do you mean?"

"Listen, Horv . . . I haven't heard anything from Magan Kai Lee or Rey Gonerev since that meeting at the Kordez Thassel Complex. Not a single word. Why do you think that is?"

"Well, there's a lot going on right now," said Horvil. "Infoquakes popping up all over the place, Margaret's death. I hear that the Islanders are stepping up their border raids—"

"No, come on. That doesn't explain anything. Lee has more than enough people to deal with all that. . . . You want to know what I think? I think the Council's leaving me alone because I'm doing *exactly* what they want. Why did Magan Kai Lee arrange all this in the first place, Horv? Why did he give me control of MultiReal, and what was he preparing to do at the Thassel Complex?

"Natch knows exactly why. Magan Kai Lee put the program in my hands because he knows I'm easy to manipulate. I won't be able to take the pressure, and sooner or later I'll give in. I'll hand MultiReal right over to the Council. *That's* why Natch left when I told him to leave.

"So the question now is, who can destroy the fiefcorp faster—me or Natch?"

(((24)))

Natch's left hand was twitching.

He tried to convince himself that the spasms were just a paranoid delusion, the product of an overactive imagination. And for the past few days, that strategy had worked. The very act of asserting his will against the jittering allowed Natch to take control of it, and he began to wonder what other problems he might conquer with this method.

His victory was brief. By Friday, the twitches had returned with reinforcements. Now his hand fluttered even when he walked or carried something heavy like a satchel of bio/logic programming bars, and no act of will could stop it.

Black code, thought Natch miserably.

There was no other feasible explanation. The hammer and anvil of Dr. Plugenpatch and the OCHRE system had stamped out all but the most obscure neurological dysfunctions over the past hundred years—and those few that still resisted the powers of science were at least diagnosable. No, only human programming code could wreak such havoc.

Natch stayed indoors on Friday and watched the day waft by in slow motion. He spent hours in front of the mirror trying to figure out a way to hide his clenched fist behind his lapels, Napoleon-style. It wouldn't fool anybody in the long term, but it might be sufficient for short bursts of public exposure.

He received several messages from Serr Vigal and spent long minutes debating whether he should answer or even open them. Jara's betrayal he could deal with, but the prospect of Vigal's disapproval flared in his mind like a salted wound. It felt like the culmination of a long dialogue of failure and disappointment they had been conducting for the past twenty-five years. In the end, Natch filed Vigal's messages away unopened.

Numb to the world and unable to concentrate, he tuned in to Jara's press conference. He started flashing back to the confrontation in Berilla's office the other day. The huge mistake he had made giving Jara core access to MultiReal, thinking that would mollify her. A horror show of images echoed through his skull without context or explanation; not even the reappearance of Captain Bolbund on the viewscreen could rouse him from his stupor. He snapped back to sentience some hours later in a darkened apartment, wondering what he had missed.

Natch looked in the mirror at the quivering mess he had become. *What would Brone say if he saw you like this?* he thought.

• • •

Khann Frejohr wanted to hold the meeting at the Congress of L-PRACGs, but Natch wouldn't budge. "I'm not going to Melbourne," he told Frejohr's executive assistant over ConfidentialWhisper. "No way. The speaker will just have to come to Shenandoah."

"Perhaps you don't understand the protocol," said the assistant. "You don't just petition the speaker of the Congress of L-PRACGs for an audience and then insist that *he* come to *you*. . . ."

"Then tell him to find an office that's not right down the street from the Defense and Wellness Council."

The assistant emitted a strangled noise of exasperation. "If it's safety you're worried about . . . don't you think you'd be better off at a heavily guarded compound in Melbourne than at some apartment building in Shenandoah?"

"No," grunted Natch. "I know how to defend myself here."

There was an annoyed silence from the flunky's end of the connection as he went to consult a higher echelon of public servant. Natch realized he was being unreasonable; he also knew that he could ill afford the Congress's wrath on top of the Council's. But these were not times for mindlessly hewing to social niceties. With the shadow of the infoquake hanging over them all—five thousand people had died in the wake of the last one—Natch felt there was no paranoia too great.

Besides which, Frejohr needed him. The libertarian caucus had fallen into a peculiar schizophrenia after Margaret's death, veering between unfocused indignation at Len Borda one moment and mawkish nostalgia for the Surinas the next. Meanwhile, the markets were engaged in a mad dance of their own as second-tier fiefcorps began sabotaging each other left and right. The drudges were in a frenzy. And the number of Creed Libertas devotees had literally doubled again in the past forty-eight hours. Frejohr needed to take a strong stand in the MultiReal crisis, and he knew it. Natch might not have legal claim to the program at the moment, but he was still its public face.

The flunky returned to declare that the speaker would come to Shenandoah after all. In multi. Ordinarily, conducting an important meeting in multi would be considered an insult, but Natch knew there was no point harping about it now. These days he took his triumphs where he could.

Frejohr's security detail arrived late Saturday and spent an hour combing through the apartment with bulky metal instruments that looked like panpipes. They posted sentries in the hallway and on several neighboring balconies. One of the guards cast a suspicious look at Natch's clenched hand, and the entrepreneur was forced to hold the shaking lump of flesh out to prove he had nothing to hide.

Ten minutes later, Speaker Khann Frejohr materialized in Natch's foyer. The two exchanged polite bows.

"Let's just skip the Perfections," said the Congressional leader in a voice both gravelly and hypnotic. "I congratulate you on getting to number one on Primo's. You congratulate me on getting elected to the speaker's chair. Okay? Done."

"Fine with me," Natch shrugged. *A promising start.*

He sized up Len Borda's nemesis as they headed for opposite couches in the living room. Frejohr was older and shorter than the images on the Data Sea suggested, but he had a rough-edged charisma that contrasted well with Borda's stony diffidence. A man of the people, a leader even . . . but a violent revolutionary? It hardly seemed possible. Natch wondered what kind of displacements had occurred in Frejohr's mind since the Melbourne riots forty years ago. Was he still as hot-tempered and uncompromising as he had once been? Or had decades of government service mellowed him?

"The Council took my business away," Natch began, sitting on the edge of the sofa. "They threw a bunch of trumped-up charges at the Meme Cooperative and convinced them to suspend my license. And now MultiReal's in the hands of my—"

"Yes, yes," interrupted Frejohr with a wave of his hand. Although he had only just sat down on Natch's sofa, he already looked like he owned it. "I follow the news, believe it or not, so I'm fully aware of what's going on. And?"

"*And?*"

"Look, Natch," said the speaker with an air of impatience. "You know I've got no love for the Defense and Wellness Council. I'm sympathetic to what you're going through, believe me. But I'm not sure the Congress has any business getting involved. It's a big world, and the high executive has a million tentacles." He raised his bushy unified eyebrow in the direction of the window, indicating either the Council officers on the street or the Council hoverbirds in the sky or perhaps the totality of human space from here to Furtoid. "You can't just expect the Congress to intervene every time Len Borda forces someone's company out of business," continued the speaker. "We'd never get anything done. We have to pick our battles carefully."

The entrepreneur scowled. "So why did you agree to talk to me then?"

"I said I'm not sure if we should get involved," replied Frejohr, tired. "Which means, I'm not sure." Natch could sense calendar appointments and to-do items flitting behind the speaker's eyelids. He wouldn't be surprised if Frejohr was mentally dictating correspondence as they spoke.

Natch arose from the sofa and stalked over to the window, clutching his fist so it was invisible from the speaker's perspective. Jara had warned him he wasn't ready for the political spectrum, and he had ignored her. He could hear the accusatory barbs from an entirely different conversation on some subvocal register, a conversation not with Jara or Khann Frejohr, but with the universe itself. *Arriviste. Upstart. Nobody. Pretender . . .* How long would it be until someone took him seriously? Would he have to wait until the shadows of Borda's hoverbirds were darkening every doorstep, when it was too late to do anything about it . . . ?

Then he felt the speaker's hand on his shoulder. It was a firm yet avuncular grasp, the kind Serr Vigal gave when the mood struck him. Natch realized with a start that Frejohr hadn't used some stealth program to sneak up on him; it was he who had blanked out for an indeterminate length of time. He hoped it had only been a matter of seconds and not minutes.

"Come on," said the speaker, inclining his head toward the balcony door. "A little moonlight will do us both good."

• • •

The balcony whipped out from the side of the building in a heartbeat, yet Natch was hesitant to step onto it. Magan Kai Lee might have declared him "irrelevant," but he had made no move to recall the Defense and Wellness Council tails on the street. They didn't even bother to wear disguises anymore; they simply lingered in formation with fingers never more than a hair's breadth away from a dartgun or disruptor trigger. Khann Frejohr, however, seemed to have complete confidence in the bronze-robed men and women keeping watch from the neighboring balconies. So Natch muzzled his trepidation and followed the speaker outside.

The two stood at the railing for several moments and watched the city. Shenandoah was an important metropolis, but it was relatively small in size. Thus one could easily catch the mood of the entire metro area from the top of a building like Natch's. Right now the epicenter of pedestrian traffic was clearly downtown, where the Winter Baseball League was holding a three-game extravaganza. Natch and Frejohr silently watched the stadium gobble up space from neighboring office buildings that were compressing for the night.

"Len Borda killed Margaret, didn't he?" said Natch abruptly.

Frejohr pursed his lips, expressing some emotion that Natch didn't recognize. Reticence? "You're just guessing," said the speaker. "Unless you know something I don't."

"I know Borda's scared of MultiReal. I know he'll go to any lengths to get core access to it. And I think—I think he—" *I think he ordered a special ops team to dress in black robes and assault me in an alleyway.* "I think he wouldn't hesitate to kill someone of Margaret's stature to get his hands on it."

Frejohr closed his eyes and nodded. His white hair glared vibrantly in the moonlight. "That's obvious."

"Quell—the Islander who used to work for Margaret—he said something strange just before the Council carted him away," continued Natch. "He said that Borda killed Margaret's father."

"That's obvious too," said the speaker.

Natch felt as if a cold and many-legged insect had just wriggled up his spine. Could the high executive be so contemptuous of the Surinas that he would kill both Marcus *and* Margaret? Was even Len Borda ruthless enough to cut off the line of humanity's greatest benefactors in cold blood?

"How do you know?" the entrepreneur croaked, clenching the

railing almost hard enough to crack it. "If the Congress has evidence that Marcus Surina was murdered, why haven't you brought it forward?"

"It's the evidence we *don't* have," replied Frejohr. "A shuttle explodes in a distant region of Furtoid. Ruptured fuel tank, the whole executive board of TeleCo dies instantly. No surviving witnesses. No Council officers around for kilometers. No distress calls, no explanation for what Marcus Surina was doing out there in the first place. That's pretty convenient, isn't it?" The speaker winced as if probing the vestigial traces of an old pain in his gut. Natch had seen Vigal's hollow stare of loss whenever someone mentioned Marcus's death, and Vigal had never even met the man. Khann Frejohr had been involved in politics long enough to have worked with Marcus personally.

"Look, Natch," continued the speaker, "this is how the Defense and Wellness Council *does* things. It didn't start with Len Borda. This is part of the organizational culture going all the way back to Tul Jabbor. Someone opposes the Council; the Council tolerates it just long enough to avoid suspicion—then that someone ends up in a tragic and fatal 'accident.' It happened to Marcus Surina. It happened to Margaret Surina. Some of us even think it happened to Henry Osterman."

Natch said nothing for a moment. He tracked a group of white-robed officers on the street below as they made a tight circuit around the block. "So what's to stop Len Borda from getting away with it this time too?"

Frejohr retreated into the shadows and slid his hands into the pockets of his bronze robe. "I don't think he'll get away with anything," he said, "because I don't think Borda's responsible."

"So if the Council didn't kill her, then—"

"I said *Borda* isn't responsible. I didn't say anything about the Council."

Natch let out a long, ragged breath. The image of the slight lieutenant executive with the impenetrable stare knifed through his consciousness. *Fool*, he had told Quell. *Don't you realize I'm the only one standing between you and Borda?* "Magan Kai Lee," whispered the entrepreneur.

"There's a major rift in the Defense and Wellness Council right now," said Frejohr, his voice laced with bitter satisfaction. "Borda's old. The rumor is that he was planning to hand control of the Council over to Magan before this whole MultiReal crisis hit."

"Hand control over? How can he do that? The high executive is appointed by the Prime Committee."

"And the Committee is in Borda's pocket. It's a rubber stamp; they'll appoint whomever he tells them to appoint. But that's all irrelevant. Now that Borda's decided to stay for a while longer, we hear a lot of officers muttering about *speeding his retirement*." Frejohr let out a hoarse chuckle. "There's a euphemism for you, huh? *Speeding his retirement.* The top officers in the organization are choosing sides. Rey Gonerev is stirring up the ranks. There's talk of a coup."

"A *coup?*" Natch stepped back from the railing, away from the eyes of the Council officers. Such a thing belonged in the realm of the never-possible. A rebellion against the high executive of the Defense and Wellness Council? Just as easy to rebel against time or the rotation of the Earth. "So what makes you think Margaret's death has anything to do with it?"

"Imagine this," continued the speaker. "Magan Kai Lee orders Margaret Surina dead and arranges it to look like Borda's doing. Then he persuades the Prime Committee to throw the high executive out of office and install him in Borda's place. Or maybe he arranges to frame *you*—which gives him leverage to seize MultiReal. He arms his troops with the program, and *then* he makes his move against Borda. With Borda gone, the Committee appoints him high executive."

Lieutenant Executive Lee had never seemed like the type to work for his own self-aggrandizement. Natch had pegged him in the slot of the Organizational Creature and had based his assumptions accordingly. But what if he was wrong about Magan? A whole new set of sickening possibilities was coming to light. What if Magan had purposefully *not* seized control of MultiReal to prevent Borda from getting his hands on it? Was that why he had arranged to give it to Jara?

The frightening thing was that it didn't really matter in the end. Whether Magan Kai Lee or Len Borda ultimately held control of MultiReal was irrelevant. Either outcome spelled certain doom for Natch's aspirations, and probably the world's civil liberties too.

"Now you see why I wanted to meet," said Natch. "The situation's getting out of control. You have to stop this before it's too late."

Frejohr shrugged. He was inexplicably vacating the conversation and moving on to the next item on his itinerary. "And how would you suggest I do that?"

"Get the Prime Committee to intervene. Get them to start their own investigation into the murder of Margaret Surina." Natch could feel his legs growing restless and started to pace back and forth across the narrow patch of balcony. Finding that too constrictive, he reached out to the tenement and upped his allotted balcony space, causing an additional length of metal walkway to slide out from the building.

"This isn't just about Margaret," Natch went on. "It's not just about *me*. It's about government intrusion into private business. It's about the Council bullying and threatening other government agencies. It's about Len Borda and Magan Kai Lee turning MultiReal into a weapon."

Frejohr was too smooth to allow Natch's badgering to upset his equanimity. "I wasn't sure the Congress should get involved when I arrived here," he said coolly. "And now I'm even *less* sure. Have you ever heard the saying *Nothing's less persuasive than a government committee?* If you work on this alone, you've got a chance, Natch. The public's on your side—or at least they will be once they stop blaming you for Margaret's death. If the Congress of L-PRACGs gets involved, the whole thing's going to turn into a partisan battle. Governmentalists versus libertarians. The minute that happens, you're going to lose half the public's support, and the Council will clamp down on you even more."

Natch's nostrils flared. His left hand was twitching too violently to keep it a secret from the speaker much longer. "What's *your* strategy then?"

"We wait. We let the Defense and Wellness Council weaken itself with internal politics." Frejohr rubbed his eyes, clearly exhausted. With all the infoquakes and the chaos going on, his week must have been even more stressful than Natch's. "And while the Council tears itself apart, there's a groundswell of support from the grass roots that's only going to get stronger. We're starting to see serious movement in the poll numbers. We've got a shot at turning the Prime Committee libertarian in next year's elections—and if that happens, the whole equation will change."

Natch grimaced. This was not the man the libertarian public relations machine claimed he was. Khann Frejohr might once have been a revolutionary, but now he had succumbed to the Melbourne mind-set, where all things revolve around the next set of elections. There simply was no time for dithering. Natch thought of the Council officers on the street below, the Patel Brothers in the Council's pocket, Jara dancing to the Council's strings with core access to MultiReal. He needed to take command of this conversation, and he needed to do it quickly, or Frejohr would be back in his office drafting obscure legislation within the hour.

"You want to sit around and wait for all of Len Borda's enemies to get their act together?" he said. "You want to wait for *elections*? Fine, go ahead. Go on inside and show me these great poll numbers on the viewscreen. If you can."

Frejohr blanched. "What do you mean, *if I can*?"

"Go ahead and try it."

The entrepreneur reached out with his mind to the Possibilities interface. It lay there in the fiefcorp data stores like an extension of his own anatomy. Natch switched on the program and felt its hum in his bones as he tried to recall the specific instructions Horvil had given him.

Flash.

Flash.

Flash.

Natch's mind skated along Feynman pathways, collating alternate realities at ludicrous speeds, selecting the one possibility out of a million that suited him, over and over again. Khann Frejohr's eyebrow writhed up and down in concentration. The speaker's expression took a slow journey from doubt to discomfort, and then dipped momentarily into fear.

Flash.

Flash.

Flash.

After several long seconds had passed, a single droplet of sweat trickled down the speaker's forehead and came to a rest on the tip of his nose. Frejohr had not budged from the railing.

"I—I can't move," he said.

Natch nodded with grim satisfaction as he shut off the program. He had never tried this particular MultiReal trick before, and he hadn't known if it would work or not. Manipulating a street vendor into giving a two-credit discount on lunch was one thing; thwarting the will of the speaker of the Congress of L-PRACGs was another. It was tremendously empowering. And yet, as Horvil had warned him, it wasn't without cost. Expending all that mental energy left him quivering like a junkie, just a few heartbeats away from total collapse. He switched on an adrenaline program to keep himself upright.

"Do you know *why* you can't move?" said Natch in a menacing whisper.

Khann Frejohr shook his head.

"Because when we run the simulation over and over in our minds, your brain tells me there's a possibility that you'll decide *not* to move. It might be remote. It might be insignificant. It might take me a million iterations to get to. But with MultiReal, *I can find that possibility.*

"And if *I* can find it—what could Len Borda find if he digs deep enough? The desire to obey authority? The desire to confess all your secrets, all the *Congress's* secrets?" Natch walked up to the speaker and leaned in close. "Maybe even the desire to stand still in the crosshairs of a Council multi disruptor?"

They peered over the railing at the group of Council officers below. One of them was actually checking the scope on his shoulder-mounted disruptor cannon; he could have aimed and fired at Frejohr in the blink of an eye. Nobody knew for sure whether the Council had the ability to pass black code through a disruptor beam, but judging by Frejohr's wide eyes and sweat-mottled forehead, the speaker didn't relish taking that chance.

"I don't think you understand the urgency," said the entrepreneur. "Once the Council gets ahold of MultiReal, *that will be the end of libertarianism.* That's it. Who could possibly fight against an army of Council officers armed with that program? Nobody. It would be the end of the Congress, the end of freedom as we know it for hundreds or thousands of years. It all comes down to this: if Len Borda or Magan Kai Lee seizes MultiReal, your speakership will vanish, and you'll be forgotten. Wiped out of history without a trace. Is that how you want to end your career?"

Natch could see the fear behind Frejohr's eyes ignite a spark of anger. For a brief moment, the man standing before him looked like the man in the history files. It was the sign Natch had been waiting for, an indication that the speaker could indeed prove useful.

Yet still there was hesitation. "I don't think you understand the politics involved here, Natch," said Frejohr. "I've only been speaker for a month. I'm barely holding on to a slim libertarian majority in the Congress as it is. You can't just expect the libertarian members to start pushing on the Prime Committee so soon."

Natch snorted. "I don't really care *what* they do. I didn't call this meeting to talk to the Khann Frejohr who's the speaker of the Congress of L-PRACGs. I wanted to talk to the Khann Frejohr who has contacts in the libertarian movement, the labor unions, the creeds. I wanted to talk to the Khann Frejohr who stages *insurrections*."

(((25)))

The politicos filed in from the foyer, nine in all, each more smug and self-satisfied than the last. Natch disliked them immediately.

It was a motley group. A labor boss who had led a violent strike against OrbiCo, simultaneously causing a handful of deaths and a plunge in the company's stock price. A pair of tycoons who had bought large swaths of real estate on Luna and turned them into indulgent playgrounds for the wealthy. A few L-PRACG politicians who dangled from the shadier fringes of the libertarian movement. The bodhisattva of Creed Libertas, looking quite regal with her long black hair and her robe marked with the insignia of the rising sun. A tiny bronze-skinned woman whose connectible collar tagged her as an Islander. And finally, of course, Khann Frejohr.

The interesting thing about the libertarian movement, Natch reflected as he watched the group jockey for seats in his living room, was that neither rich nor poor could claim ownership of it. The instinct to keep the centralized government out of one's business didn't just cross boundaries, it obliterated them.

Natch wished he could be somewhere else entirely. The MultiReal stunt he had performed on Khann Frejohr yesterday had taken more out of him than he thought possible; a palpable sense of uncleanliness seeped through his pores, as if his OCHREs were limping along near burnout. And that on top of the corrosive black code in his veins, the MultiReal programming in his skull, and the throbbing of his arm. If only he could jettison all these people from the apartment and just . . . *sleep.* How long had it been?

Frejohr waited until the labor boss had parked himself on Natch's favorite work stool and everyone had taken the prudent step of priving themselves to outside communication. Then the speaker brought the meeting to order.

"My friends," began Frejohr. "Comrades. We live in dangerous times. We're standing on the precipice of a very steep cliff. We're looking over the edge, and we can see that it's a long, long way down."

Natch had found a place near the front door where he could observe the proceedings without intruding. Listening to Frejohr now, he understood why this man had risen so far in the ranks of the libertarian movement, why he had become the symbol of opposition to Len Borda. The voice that had sounded like a tired mumble yesterday had metamorphosed into a hypnotic purr in the presence of his peers. The politicos were transfixed. Natch's exhaustion was quickly forgotten.

"Len Borda has single-handedly ruled the Defense and Wellness Council for almost sixty years," continued the speaker, beginning a slow stroll around the perimeter of the garden. "And what's the high executive given us in that sixty years? An unprecedented military buildup. A state of constant warfare with the Islanders and the Pharisees. The erosion of the people's power base and civil liberties. Just last month, the Prime Committee gave him the legal authority to shut down any program on the Data Sea, at any time.

"And now the Council is in a state of disarray. Within Len Borda's own organization, we hear, a rebellion may be brewing. A rebellion that could decide the fate of the world.

"Yes, the world! I'm not exaggerating. Because now the ultimate weapon has been thrown into the mix, and it's called MultiReal." Frejohr stopped, gave a particularly intense stare at the daisy patch in the middle of the room. "I assume you all heard about Natch's little . . . *demonstration* yesterday?"

The politicians turned toward Natch with something resembling awe, as if he himself were the weapon Borda was seeking. Natch thought he could detect a few trembling knees in the group, and he wondered if the politicos were going to demand their own demonstration. Thankfully, no one did. *I'd rather jump off the balcony than do that again*, he thought.

"MultiReal," continued Frejohr. "A weapon that can warp the will and control realities. A weapon that the Council could use to reduce the Islands and the Pharisee Territories to rubble.

"Now the creator of this weapon is dead. Its principal engineer's been dragged off to prison. And its owner"—he made a gesture toward Natch—"its owner has been stripped unlawfully of his property. All that stands between the Council and this deadly technology? A single fiefcorp analyst.

"So I've called a meeting with you, the power brokers of the libertarian movement. The forces on the street, the ones who were there during the troubles in Melbourne in 318." Natch saw a few nods from the group, including the bodhisattva and the labor leader. "The ones who did their part then, and the ones who will do their part when the next opportunity arises.

"My friends, the time for delay is over. The time has come to *act*."

The speaker stepped into the corner and bowed his head with what was less an ending to his oration than an indefinite pause. It was a good speech, Natch decided; short on substance, long on passion. The libertarians sat for a full three minutes staring at the carpet.

"So this fiefcorp analyst," said the labor boss, breaking the uneasy silence. He had perhaps the widest head Natch had ever seen. "What's her name again?"

"Jara," said Frejohr.

"This Jara—where is she? Shouldn't we go get her and hide her away somewhere?"

"Not as easy as it sounds," replied the speaker. "She's still holed up at that estate in West London, and the place is surrounded by drudges. There are a hundred Council officers right around the corner, just waiting for someone to make a move."

The Islander clasped her head in her hands. "So what's stopping them? The Council could raid that estate right now. They could torture her and force her to hand over MultiReal while we're sitting here."

"She's being watched," said the bodhisattva of Creed Libertas, stroking her hair like a cat grooming its fur. "We have devotees inside the estate keeping an eye on her twenty-four hours a day. If the Council tries anything—either faction, Borda's or Lee's—then we'll have some notice. We'll be ready."

Natch remembered the spontaneous protest on the tube that had saved him from those Council officers a couple of weeks ago. Antigovernment activists couldn't stand up to the officers of the Council in an open fight, of course. But if there were indeed sympathizers among the staff at Berilla's estate, they had a chance of spiriting Jara away from such a confrontation. They could keep her and MultiReal safe, for a little while.

"This is all moot," put in Frejohr. "With all the chaos surrounding Margaret's death and the infoquakes, the Council won't risk another raid. They'd have open rebellion on their hands."

"It's going to come to that anyway," said the Islander, with a mysterious glint in her eye.

"Maybe," grunted the speaker, reticent. "Maybe not." It seemed to Natch that Frejohr was very purposefully not looking in his direction.

"If the Council doesn't release Quell soon, you know exactly what's going to happen," said the Islander. "You know how Josiah is."

Natch had no idea who Josiah was or what he was threatening, but this insiders' conversation was growing tiresome. "You're both missing something obvious," he said with a scowl. Heads swiveled around, as if the politicians had forgotten all about him. "Why would the Council want to conduct another raid? They *put* Jara in this position. Magan Kai Lee did, at least. If he plays his cards right, Jara will just hand it over to him."

"How do you know?" asked one of the L-PRACG representatives. "What if—"

"What if what?" Natch barked. "Jara doesn't want the responsibility. She doesn't want MultiReal, and the Council knows that. Don't you understand? Lee and Borda are going to convince her that it's in her best interest to work with them. They'll grease the way so that giving the databases over is the easiest and most logical thing for her to do. She's very easy to manipulate."

"But can't you prevent that?" said a Lunar tycoon. "Just use Multi-Real against her. She won't be *able* to hand the program over."

Natch flung a withering look in the tycoon's direction. "That's the stupidest idea I've ever heard. What if Jara's using MultiReal too? Besides—just because I can stop her from giving it away *once* doesn't mean I can stop her from trying again. Do you want me to stand guard over her for the rest of my life?" He remembered his mental tug-of-war with Khann Frejohr out on the balcony. The thought of another pro-tracted neural battle so soon after the last one made his knees weak. "Listen, this thing isn't *hypnotism*. It's not magic. You can't just use MultiReal to permanently change someone's mind. If that was the case, don't you think I would've used it on Len Borda already? Don't you think I would have . . . have . . ." The sentence wandered off, seemingly of its own volition.

The conversation lost its momentum at that point, leaving the lib-ertarians to stare gloomily at the Tope paintings on the windows. Natch felt an irrational urge to just abandon them there and sneak out the front door. *No, it's too late for that*, he told himself. *Get ahold of your-self. You set this up, and now you need to see it through.*

Frejohr spoke. "Then I think it's clear what needs to be done," he said, his voice muscular with purpose. The speaker crossed his arms in front of his chest. "If it's inevitable that Jara's going to hand MultiReal over to the Council, we need to do it first."

● ● ●

Everyone gaped at the speaker, Natch included. "Have you gone com-pletely offline?" sputtered the bodhisattva of Creed Libertas.

Khann Frejohr appeared to be enjoying the surprise in his colleagues' faces, and Natch recognized the glee of a fellow showman in midperformance. "This is what it all comes down to, isn't it?" he said. "This is what it's *always* come down to, since the beginning. You still have access to the MultiReal code, don't you, Natch?"

"Of course I do. She said . . . she said it couldn't be taken away from me."

"Jara said that?" asked the labor leader, perplexed.

"No, not Jara. *Margaret.*" Nach felt his emotions rear up at the thought of the bodhisattva, at the thought of the MultiReal code inside his head and the crisis she had brought upon him. He closed his eyes for a moment, temporarily overwhelmed, and tried to mold his emotions into sentences. "She said I was the guardian and the keeper. It can't be taken away. The nothingness at the center of the universe. Why don't you *understand?*"

He opened his eyes and saw the labor leader swallow and sit back, obviously understanding nothing.

Frejohr was unmoved. "We need to let Len Borda have MultiReal. Let Magan Kai Lee have MultiReal. Let the creeds have it, the fiefcorps, the drudges, the Meme Cooperative." The speaker stretched his arm out to the balcony, which was facing the snow-engulfed eastern courtyard at the moment. "Release the code and the specs onto the Data Sea, Natch. Everything. Give everyone in the world access."

The room was starting to spin, and Natch could feel himself sliding down into the mental quicksand once more. *No, not now, not now!* He gave himself a bio/logic boost of adrenaline and assaulted the nothingness until it released its grip on him. His eyes shot open, and he noticed that the L-PRACG politicians who were standing nearby had quietly scooted farther away. "Let me get this straight. You're telling me I should take the most revolutionary product of our time— maybe the most revolutionary product in *history*—and just *give it away?*"

Frejohr was unrepentant. His silver hair glistened in the reflected sunlight from the window. "That's exactly what I'm saying."

"Why the fuck would I do that?"

"Studies show that free bio/logics products are more functional and secure," insisted one of the Lunar tycoons, sliding into lecture mode with one finger in the air.

"Plus free bio/logics creates demand," the other tycoon chimed in. "In fact, that's actually how I made my first—"

"I'm not an *idiot*," yelled Natch, causing the tycoons to shut up instantly. "Don't try to teach me hive-level economics. I know it backward and forward. Why would I open up the MultiReal code? To create demand? To speed adoption? Ridiculous. My product's got one hundred percent demand. Everyone in the solar system is going to be using MultiReal a month after we release it. You think opening up the program will make it more functional and secure? That's laughable. There's subroutines in this program that could kill you in a *second* if they're mishandled. People can't deal with that kind of freedom."

The entrepreneur found himself alone on the other side of the garden, though he didn't remember walking there. Khann Frejohr stood across the room with his libertarian posse clustered in their chairs behind him. Suddenly Natch scanned the eyes of the Lunar tycoons and realized that Frejohr had planned this. He had brought the libertarians to Natch's apartment for the specific purpose of convincing him to release MultiReal on the Data Sea. The thought gave Natch a perverse sort of amusement. Some of them had obviously known the agenda ahead of time, while others, like the bodhisattva, were just now coming around to the idea.

Speaker Frejohr stepped slowly around the daisies and put his hand on Natch's shoulder with another one of those Vigalish touches. "We need to release MultiReal so people can *defend* themselves," he said, voice low and sinuous. "With all that manpower at the Defense and Wellness Council—Natch, once they get ahold of it, this might be our only chance."

Natch sniffed. "Don't worry, they won't get ahold of it. Not once we've executed my plan."

"What plan?" said Frejohr suspiciously.

A grin spread across Natch's face like a malignant creeper. "I'm glad you asked."

• • •

The program hung in MindSpace, a spiky pyramid the color of a poisoned apple. Natch dimmed the lights in his office, causing a greenish hue to suffuse the room and reflect off every forehead.

"Black code," somebody whispered.

The entrepreneur didn't respond. Of *course* it was black code. Form didn't necessarily follow function in the bio/logics world—Natch had worked on plenty of innocuous routines that looked like fairy tale horrors in MindSpace—but the fact that this program exhibited no name or pedigree was indicator enough.

One of the L-PRACG politicians scratched her head. "So what does it *do*?" she asked. The rest of the politicians hung back near the door and peered over her shoulder, afraid to get any closer.

"It communicates," replied Natch.

"With whom?"

"With everyone. Every single person from here to Furtoid, if you want. If the Council lets it run that long." The entrepreneur reached inside the MindSpace bubble with a bio/logic programming bar, hooked the nameless black code on its tip, and swirled it around like a magician trying to summon something verminous from his hat. "But the ability to send a message *to* anyone isn't that special. It's the ability to send a message *from* anyone—individual, business, government."

"A forgery machine," said the speaker pensively, nudging the L-PRACG politician to the side so he could get a closer look.

"*The* forgery machine," said Natch. "The best one there is. It's not foolproof, of course—it's next to impossible to get foolproof forgery on the Data Sea anymore—but this is about as close as you can get." He spun the program around with the bar until it was nothing but a rotating blur.

"You've used this program before," said the bodhisattva.

Natch parsed his words carefully. "Let's just say I've seen it in action."

"So could we forge a message from the Council with this?" said the Islander with a little too much eagerness. "Could we report false troop movements, or—or—"

Natch cut the woman off before she short-circuited. "No. The program's not *that* good. The Council doesn't use normal Data Sea communications protocols."

Speaker Frejohr walked up to the gyrating blob and scrutinized it as the virtual friction of MindSpace began to slow its spin. How much the speaker knew about the intricacies of bio/logics, Natch had no idea. But at the very least, he was staring at the program's important junctures and not at its distracting ornamentations. "So you've got the ultimate forgery machine," he said in a dubious tone of voice. "What do you propose to do with it?"

"Let's start at the beginning," said Natch coyly, stepping back from MindSpace. He tossed his programming bar on the side table and began circumnavigating the workbench. "All those tens of thousands of people at the Defense and Wellness Council. All those officers in that hidden fortress of theirs. What do you think they *do* all day?"

No one answered. Natch could feel the impatience radiating off them like heat waves.

"They analyze," he continued. "They plot, they strategize. They conduct war games. Right?

"So somewhere in the Council databases, there has to be a whole collection of memos about the MultiReal situation. Plans for how the Council can take hold of MultiReal. Plans for what the Council should do *after* they've taken hold of MultiReal. Far-fetched scenarios. Hardline scenarios. Apocalyptic scenarios. What would these memos say?

"Let's pretend there's a memo that says, *We need to use MultiReal quickly to subdue our enemies.*

"Who are the Council's enemies? The libertarian L-PRACGs. The Islanders. The Lunar tycoons who've been chafing against central government regulation. The creed that's been stirring public sentiment against the Council." Natch looked over each political representative in turn, fixing them with a stare that was almost accusatory. "Once Len Borda gets his hands on MultiReal, he's going to go after each and every one of you. Or so the memo says."

The Islander frowned and shook her head, clearly disappointed that Natch didn't have anything more substantial up his sleeve. "So we leak this memo to the drudges, and the public goes berserk," she said. "Isn't the Council going to deny it?"

Natch smiled. "Of *course* they're going to deny it. Of *course* they'll call it a forgery. But isn't that exactly what they'd do if it were a real memo in the first place? Their denials are meaningless. Besides, the brave soul who risks his life to leak this memo isn't going to just use his own signature, is he? He absolutely *won't* pass it on through traceable communications protocols. No, he'll do his best to anonymize the memo.

"So we've got a memo of dubious authenticity. Nobody's going to believe the Council. The Prime Committee gives Borda his marching orders—in theory—so they'll stay out of it. Who's left? Guess who the public will look to for validation?"

Everyone turned to Khann Frejohr, who had stepped to the office window with a faraway look, as if reading small type on a distant viewscreen. His posture signaled his irritation that the meeting had taken such a detour. "And you expect the Congress of L-PRACGs to authenticate this message for you?" he asked with a sigh.

"Absolutely not," said Natch. "Come on, don't you know how this works? You tell the drudges you don't know the first thing about this memo. Who can tell if it's real. All you know is that nobody's seen any plan from the Council about what they intend to do with MultiReal once they get their claws on it. If *this* isn't the real memo . . . then where the fuck is it? Why hasn't Len Borda told anyone what he intends to do with MultiReal? What does he have to hide?

"As for the rest—well, that's easy. The public's primed and ready. They're *waiting* for someone to stand up to Len Borda. So you all fan the flames, stir up your constituencies, call for boycotts. The reaction to this memo is going to be explosive. With the public in a frenzy, and the Congress of L-PRACGs locked in a battle of words with the Defense and Wellness Council, who's going to step in to calm things down? Who's *got* to step in eventually?"

"The Prime Committee," offered the Islander.

The entrepreneur gave the most pedantic nod in his repertoire. "Exactly. The Prime Committee will intervene. Hopefully they'll call for some kind of special session to deal with the MultiReal issue. But we can't coerce them. They need to come up with the idea on their own, or it won't happen."

The bodhisattva of Creed Libertas was shaking her head in vehement objection. "You're jumping to too many conclusions. How do you know what the public's going to think? You have no idea how people will react to that memo."

"Sure I do," said Natch. "It's going to be an explosive reaction because we have a catalyst."

"Which is?"

"Margaret Surina's funeral, about eighteen hours from now."

Silence engulfed the apartment.

Natch looked around his office at the politicos who had multied to his foyer so smug and self-satisfied. Now they all looked defensive, unsure if Natch's plan would work and unsure if it would be a good thing if it did. Funeral ceremonies for the unexpectedly deceased—the unPrepared—were melancholy affairs and exceptionally rare. The funeral ceremony for the richest and most revered woman in the world would be even more so. Natch could see the mental calculations going on around the room: was it *right* to hijack such an event for political purposes?

Frejohr's reaction was really the only one that mattered. Behind those eyes, Natch could see a wrestling match going on between predilection and pragmatism. He didn't know what had really happened during those Melbourne riots back in 318. He didn't know if the speaker was actually responsible for those atrocities or not. What Natch did know was that Frejohr had not felt the full impact of the MultiReal situation until just a few minutes ago; even Natch's mind control trick on the balcony yesterday hadn't jolted him so hard. This was a crisis every bit as portentous as the Melbourne riots, and what he decided here today would have just as much impact on the libertarian movement—not to mention on his career.

"I can't participate in this," said Frejohr after several moments of silence. "I won't see Margaret Surina's funeral turned into a circus. I stand by what I said earlier. You need to release the MultiReal code on the Data Sea, Natch—every last gigabyte. That's the only way."

Natch gave them all a wry smile, then shut down the MindSpace bubble. He grabbed a bio/logic programming bar from the side table and began tossing it up and down nonchalantly. "Well, it's too late," he said. "The memo's already out there."

Another poisonous silence. "What do you mean?" whispered the labor leader.

"I mean I sent it to the drudges about two hours ago, shortly before you all arrived. But wait—I wouldn't be in too much of a hurry to cut your multi connections. The drudges know you're here. In fact, they think you've gathered here to discuss how to respond to this memo."

"And why do they think that?" thundered Frejohr indignantly, looking as if he might throw something.

"Well, *I* told them, obviously," replied Natch, matter-of-fact. He flipped the programming bar in the air and let it make a full three rotations before catching it again. "I'm sure they've noticed all those Congressional security officers hanging around outside anyway."

The labor leader stepped forward and planted his clenched fists on the workbench with a thump, but Natch did not flinch. "So what happens when someone finds out this memo is a fake?"

"Oh, someone will figure it out eventually, and the Council will probably shut the program down for good. But by then, it'll be too late. I'll already have had my day in front of the Prime Committee. And don't worry, no one'll be able to trace it here. I'm positive of that."

"And if they *do*?"

The entrepreneur shrugged and plopped into the chair next to the side table where Horvil usually resided. "Then tell them the truth. Hang me out to dry, it won't matter. The memo's not signed, it's not attributed *to* any particular person on the Council, and *I'm* not the one that's trumpeting it to the skies. What would I be guilty of? Nasty rumors? Conducting a thought experiment?" He grinned. "They can add that infraction to the hundred and twenty I've already got."

Natch could practically see the turbines whirring inside their minds. The politicos would have to make a choice when they cut their multi connections and stopped priving themselves to the world: to go along with the ruse or to deny it. If they intended to deny it, then the clock was ticking. Every minute elapsed was another minute they would have to explain away. Besides which, revealing the nature of the plan was tantamount to revealing that they had been duped. In the hard-knuckle world of libertarian politics, such an admission could be highly damaging.

And what was the alternative? Natch had already made it perfectly clear he didn't expect anyone to confirm the memo's authenticity—in fact, he expected them to do the exact opposite, to cast doubt, to stir up suspicion. They would reap the benefits in the end without taking much of the risk. Wasn't that the easier course?

Khann Frejohr was clearly incensed. He had not moved from the window, preferring to glare outside with palpable rage on his face. He had come to this apartment to strong-arm Natch into releasing the MultiReal specs on the Data Sea. Instead, *he* was being strong-armed into convincing the Prime Committee to put their foot down.

"Listen," Natch told the speaker. "You've got to understand. What you're suggesting—releasing the MultiReal code on the Data Sea—it wouldn't work."

"And why not?" growled Frejohr.

"Let's say I do what you're asking. Let's say I release the technical specs to MultiReal on the Data Sea. Don't you think the Council is going to be waiting right there with a thousand engineers to weaponize it? Two hours after I release those specs, Len Borda or Magan Kai Lee will be back with ten thousand troops that you won't be able to run away from. Do you really think you can out-engineer the Council? No, I'm sorry, Khann. The Council can't get hold of those technical specs. They can't *ever* get hold of them. MultiReal has to stay in private hands."

The libertarians shuffled back into the living room and began holding quiet discussions about how to respond to the inevitable drudge onslaught. Natch obliged them by plastering the memo on the windows to analyze. They were muttering to themselves, dissatisfied but willing to make do. After all, they were getting what they wanted—confrontation with the Defense and Wellness Council on a level playing field. All that was required was a little bit of clever dissembling to the drudges, and nobody would be the wiser. Natch knew they would see things his way eventually. Already he could hear one of the tycoons saying that Len Borda probably *did* have a memo just like this one in his files anyway.

Khann Frejohr took Natch aside, back into the office. "So let's say you get the Prime Committee to intervene and call a special session—what then?" said the speaker bitterly. "You think you can persuade them to overrule Len Borda? He's had the Committee in his pocket for twenty years."

"I don't know. One step at a time."

"And what happens if they overrule you instead? What if after all this they decide to seize MultiReal and put it in the Council's hands anyway? What *then?*"

Natch frowned and stared intently at the space where the black code had been floating just moments earlier. "Then I'll *make* them vote my way," he said. "I've got MultiReal, remember?"

Jara surveyed the list of the fiefcorp's high-priority issues. She had inscribed each item on a virtual block and used the blocks to form a giant skeletal structure on Berilla's couch. It looked disconcertingly like a vulture.

The analyst reached out and caressed a block near the vulture's feet. RETURN HOME, it read.

I'm tired of this fucking room, she thought, casting spiteful glances at the rococo furniture in the study. *I'm tired of Berilla. I'm tired of hanging out in the hallways with all the servants staring at us.* She tuned the window to the front gates and the small pack of drudges still holding camp there. *Just keep Len Borda out of here until Margaret's funeral*, she thought. *Just two more days. And then we can all go home.* She pinched the corner of the block between her index finger and thumb, then dragged it down to the base of the structure, upgrading it to priority one. The remaining blocks silently cascaded into new positions.

Jara arose from the couch and forced herself to make one more trip to the great room. Nobody in the fiefcorp was quite ready to abandon ship—not yet—but the failed press conference had certainly sprung new leaks in their confidence. Merri was going out of her way to avoid everyone; Benyamin's glower could be sensed from rooms away; Horvil seemed more distant and distractible than ever; and Serr Vigal was reduced to drifting about like an empty bottle on a windless sea.

Horvil was the only one in the great room. He was idling on a sofa, reading Primo's reports with programming bar in hand. Jara suddenly realized that she had never thought to ask where everyone else had been camping these past few nights. Horvil and Ben already had rooms in the estate, of course, but what about Merri and Vigal? She supposed they must have claimed a spare nook somewhere.

"So how bad is it?" Jara asked, settling on the chair with the fleur-de-lis motif carved into its back. "Where are we on Primo's?"

Horvil let his eyebrows float slowly northward. "Last time I checked? Two hundred thirty-something."

"Two hundred thirty—!" Jara couldn't even finish her exclamation.

"Primo's moves fast," said the engineer, his face displaying total unconcern. "We haven't launched anything since . . . since . . . well, I don't know when. Back before we took on MultiReal, I guess. The surprising thing is that we still rank at all. We sold all the products that got us to number one. So we should be off the charts altogether." He twirled his programming bar in the air like a majorette and whistled.

Jara took a minute to study the engineer. Horvil was persevering under exceedingly difficult conditions, and he was doing it with a smile on his face. If anything, he seemed more grounded now than before this whole MultiReal crisis started. Who else could claim that? Certainly not Natch. Certainly not Jara.

"So what are the other fiefcorps up to?" said Jara after a moment.

"Well, you know Pierre Loget and Billy Sterno have gone AWOL, and the Patels aren't paying much attention to the ratings either. Counting Natch, that makes four of the Primo's top ten suddenly gone. People are sensing this is the time to make a move. It's a land grab out there."

"Loget and Sterno . . . where are they?"

Horvil threw his hands up high, almost sending his programming bar into the ceiling. "Ridglee thinks they're on Patronell. Or Allowell. Can't remember which."

"Well, that's Ridglee. He probably thinks *we're* on Allowell. I wonder what they're up to."

Benyamin happened to be returning from the kitchen at that moment, sandwich in hand. "It doesn't really matter what those guys are up to," he said. "The question is, what's *Natch* up to?"

Jara nodded. It was the big variable in her calculations, the unknown that could torpedo all her plans. They could be performing miracles here in London, but that would all come to naught if Natch was working at cross-purposes—or, perfection postponed, actually *sabotaging* them. Robby Robby had promised to alert the fiefcorpers if he heard anything, and Horvil had put some feelers out to his engineering contacts. So far, nothing. The best they could tell, the entrepreneur remained sequestered at his Shenandoah apartment, accessing Multi-Real from time to time but not modifying it.

Jara knew this charade could only last so long. Already Robby was growing suspicious, and the drudges were making progressively wilder accusations. Pretending that the fiefcorp was still working together in harmony undermined Jara's whole effort to remake the company's image. Sooner or later, they would have to admit publicly that Natch had abandoned the fiefcorp, and they would have to concoct some plausible story to explain it.

Ben took an angry bite of his sandwich and ground it to a pulp with his molars. "Do you think we should . . . cut Natch off from the MultiReal databases?"

Horvil gave his cousin a stunned look. "What would *that* accomplish?"

"It would keep him from doing something irretrievably stupid, that's what."

"I'm not sure you appreciate—"

Jara cut him off. "It's a moot point," she said. "I've already tried."

Horvil simply stared at her.

The analyst sighed and kicked at a scrunched-up section of the Persian rug caused by shifting furniture. "Don't give me that look, Horv—I just wanted to see if we *could* lock him out. Turns out we can't. The Data Sea says he shouldn't be able to access the program, but he's getting in there anyway. I even tried moving the MultiReal databases to another location. Remember Horvil's calculation? The chances of him finding those databases are practically nil—but it's not even slowing him down. There's no explanation for it that I can think of."

Horvil grimaced. "I think I know the explanation."

"What?" said Jara, eyebrows arched.

The engineer explained to them about the rogue MultiReal code lurking in Natch's neural system and Natch's futile attempts to remove it. "That must be what the code is," he continued. "A back door. A way of tying him to the databases and circumnavigating the standard Data Sea access controls."

"How's that even possible?" objected Benyamin through bits of lettuce and cheese.

"Well, who created MultiReal?"

"Margaret Surina."

"And who invented the Data Sea access controls?"

"Sheldon Surina. Or maybe it was Prengal. One of the Surinas, at any rate."

Horvil extended an empty hand into the air as if to say, *Case closed.*

The question of what Natch was doing haunted Jara the rest of the day and into the night. Had Natch managed to get his meeting with Khann Frejohr? Was Natch cooking up some ruinous plan that would destroy everything Jara was fighting for? He had already duped her too many times to count. Despite everything she knew about Natch, she had actually *believed* he had made a sacrifice by handing her core access to MultiReal. He must have known already that it would make little difference. What other deceptions did he have in store?

Anchored by doubt, Jara couldn't seem to launch herself in motion. Meanwhile, the fiefcorpers spent hours drifting through the estate, conducting aimless MultiReal experiments that had little bearing on their business. That night, Natch visited Jara's dreams and did a slow striptease for her, only to reveal the smooth, sexless torso of a marionette underneath his clothes.

You can't keep this up, thought Jara. *Go ahead and* do *something, for fuck's sake.*

So Jara yanked herself out of bed the next morning at an industrious hour when the sun was just a faint red smudge in the east. She fetched a bracing cup of nitro, sat back in her makeshift desk, and spent an hour absorbing the drudge vibes from Sor, Ridglee, and Vertiginous. Something resembling the old electricity began to spark in her fingertips. By the time Vigal came tottering past the door in search of his morning tea, the analyst had already hurled a score of messages onto the Data Sea and made half a dozen appointments.

Jara sat back and allowed herself a slight smile. The anonymous ancient Britons on the wall regarded her with approval from beneath their ridiculous epaulets and brass buttons. She stared back at them, wondering who they were.

Only one more day until Margaret's funeral, Jara thought. *After that, those drudges will be gone, and Magan Kai Lee will be here looking for answers. This fiefcorp has got to be ready.*

• • •

The purple bottle had finger-sized grooves that would have been more at home on the grip of a dartgun than on a commercial beverage sold at sporting events.

"Go ahead, squeeze it," said Petrucio Patel with a mild grin.

Jara eyed the container skeptically as if it might jump up and bite her. She squeezed, causing the bottle to give way under pressure and coagulate into the jagged lightning-bolt symbol of ChaiQuoke. The cloudy liquid inside bubbled like molten lava.

"Not just flexible glass," said Petrucio. "*Ultra* flexible glass. Finally cheap enough to mass produce. Pretty impressive, eh?"

Jara managed a half-smile. "Sure, I guess."

"I tell you, we could all learn a thing or two from those ChaiQuoke marketing people," said the programmer. He took the bottle from Jara's hand and began enthusiastically molding it into a variety of obscure and occasionally obscene shapes. "They really know how to invigorate a brand identity over there. Xi Xong got a look at their new spring campaign and it's just brilliant, brilliant."

The analyst nodded, wondering how long she could keep up this pantomime of politeness before she grabbed the ChaiQuoke bottle and started bludgeoning Petrucio over the head with it. Here in this meeting space within the bowels of the Kordez Thassel Complex, she couldn't distract herself with the surroundings either. The curved chrome walls and semireflective table might have been designed by some government task force for unimaginative SeeNaRee. Jara found herself casting sympathetic side glances at the boorish Frederic Patel, who seemed just as exasperated with his brother's prattling but was nowhere near as proficient at hiding it.

"So I suppose you're wondering why we're sitting here," said Jara finally, when Petrucio's shtick had lurched to a halt.

The Patel brothers gave each other opaque looks across the table. "Of course," said Petrucio. "But I'm not sure I really want to know, to tell the truth."

"Funny you should mention *truth*," said Jara, inhaling deeply. "It's truth that brings me out here. Fairness. Justice."

Petrucio rolled his eyes. "So I guess Natch told you that I pledged to Creed Objectivv," he said, seeming irritated but not particularly surprised. "I didn't really want everybody from here to Furtoid to know about it."

Jara leaned forward and placed her hands on the table, palms down. "The Defense and Wellness Council is trying to destroy our business, 'Trucio. They're going around intimidating our friends and business partners. We need to take a stand against this. We *all* do— everyone in the bio/logics industry. We need to show Len Borda and Magan Kai Lee that they can't just get away with this."

Frederic chewed his nails apathetically. Petrucio's face had dissolved back into the normal vacant smile. "And how do 'we all' do that?" said Petrucio.

"You can do your part," said Jara, shoring up her foundering courage as best she could, "by testifying to the Creeds Coalition on Merri's behalf. Help her get reinstated as an Objectivv and clear up this nonsense about her pledging under false pretenses. I don't know what lies the Blade has been spreading around, but—"

"Please, Jara. *Please*." The elder Patel vented his frustration with a vigorous tug of his mustache. "Stop mangling the creed philosophy. It's just painful. You're almost as bad as *him*." He indicated the portly Frederic with a hitch of his thumb, causing Frederic to erupt into a toothy grin. "The Bodhisattva's definition of *truth* has nothing to do with *fairness* or *justice*. They're entirely different concepts. The Bodhisattva said that *truth is as heavy as a club and as sharp as a knife*. I pledged to tell the truth, but that doesn't mean I have to go around spreading peace and love. I'm under no obligation to spread truths that negatively impact my business."

"But we're talking about another Objectivv devotee here," protested Jara. "It doesn't bother you that she's been suspended from the creed because of a lie?"

Petrucio shook his head. "I don't care for Merri. She's too pious. It gets irritating after a while."

Jara removed her hands from the table, sat back, and rubbed her haunches. Her raised eyebrows asked the question *So what does that have to do with anything?*

Frederic was thumping his fingers on the tabletop, a mad pianist practicing scales in a discordant key. "Don't forget, there's *two* Patels in this fiefcorp," he said. "Maybe Merri's suspension from the creed works to our advantage. Maybe we *like* seeing your company go under. Ever think of that?"

"In the short term, sure," replied Jara without missing a beat. "For the next few months, you'll have all the momentum. But come on, follow the logic, Frederic. You don't have to be clairvoyant to see what happens if the Surina/Natch MultiReal Fiefcorp goes under. Len Borda will sic the Meme Cooperative on *you* too."

"Doubt it," grunted Frederic. "We got plenty of protection from the Meme Cooperative."

"But do you have protection against an army with white robes and dartguns?"

The younger Patel's protest withered and died on his lips.

Petrucio gave his bottle of ChaiQuoke a dexterous double-squeeze, causing it to form the shape of an arrow. He held it before him and aimed the tip at Jara's nose. "So answer me one question," he said slyly. "What do you think Natch would do if the tables were turned?"

"For process' preservation," snapped Jara, her patience a brittle vessel with deepening cracks. "Do I even need to answer that? He wouldn't help you, not in a million years." She took a deep breath and decided to just take that perilous leap before she lost her nerve. "But Natch isn't in charge of the fiefcorp anymore, Trucio. *I* am. Natch has left the company for good. And in case you haven't noticed, I'm not him."

Neither Patel appeared particularly surprised at Jara's declaration. In fact, something about her statement struck Frederic as humorous. His nose emitted a shrill whistle of amusement. "I think I'm starting to like this woman," he said.

"Good," said Jara, turning to face the younger, fleshier Patel. "Because I have something to ask *you* too. I want you to stand up for Horvil in front of the Bio/Logic Engineering Board next week. I want your help clearing his name and getting his credentials restored."

Frederic seemed much more amenable to this suggestion. "Now what they did to Horvil, *that's* a real shame," he said, chin balanced on one hand. "Everyone knows Horvil does good work. He was framed, plain and simple. If he wasn't working for that asshole—"

"He's not," Jara retorted. "Let me say this one more time. Horvil doesn't work for Natch. He works for *me*." She furrowed her brow and clasped her fingers together on the table, careful not to make it seem like a gesture of supplication. She fired up Earnest Xpression 35 and dialed it to a low setting. "Listen. Both of you. I'm not asking you to give up your business. All I'm asking is that, as a personal favor to me, you go to Melbourne in person and make a couple of quick statements. *Merri has integrity; I've never seen her lie; the charges against her are obviously untrue. Horvil's one of the best bio/logic engineers in the business; he was framed.* It'll take you a few hours, and I'll pay for the hoverbird fare. We'll both get good publicity out of it.

"Come on, Frederic . . . Petrucio . . . I don't know what kind of arrangement you made with the Defense and Wellness Council. But this is a brand-new world. Margaret's gone. Natch is out of the picture. *I'm* running the Surina/Natch MultiReal Fiefcorp now. It's just our two companies in the MultiReal space, and we don't have to play by the old rules anymore. Sixty billion potential customers. We don't need to go at each other with guns blazing all the time."

The Patels sat quietly for a few minutes, engaged in an urgent ConfidentialWhisper discussion. Frederic's finger pounding grew in intensity, while Petrucio gripped the ends of his mustache with great ferocity. Finally she could see the two come to some sort of consensus. Jara looked into Petrucio's eyes and tried to parse his thoughts. Was he gearing up to employ the patented pretzel logic of the Creed Objectivv truthteller, twisting some minor fabrication until it resembled truth?

"I'm sorry, Jara," the elder Patel said finally. "We can't do it." There was no artifice in his expression; he really did look sorry, and Frederic did too to a lesser extent.

The analyst summoned her most desperate stare and concentrated on the ChaiQuoke bottle for a moment. "You don't understand how badly we need this," she said.

"I understand," said Petrucio. "I'm sympathetic. I really am. But we can't just do something like this as a personal favor."

Jara ruminated on this for a minute, her legs twitching with irritation. "What if I put something else on the table?"

Frederic grabbed the ChaiQuoke bottle and choked it until it popped into a liquid boomerang. "This better be good," he grumbled.

"You remember the Equitable Choice Cycle Model we announced for the MultiReal exposition? Limited choice cycles for everyone?"

"Yesss," said Petrucio hesitantly.

"We'll put it into effect the day we release the product, for a trial period of six months. Everyone gets the same limited number of choice cycles per month. That way, whenever one of *our* customers gets into a MultiReal-versus-MultiReal conflict with one of *your* customers . . . ours won't be able to shell out an infinite number of choice cycles to win."

The mustached brothers blanched, their mouths agape. "How many choice cycles are we talking about here?" asked Petrucio.

"I have no idea. What number makes sense?"

Jara, Frederic, and Petrucio all stared at the wall for several seconds.

"Well, I guess we'll have to *pick* one," said Jara. "It has to be a fairly big number—enough that you could use it all day doing any number of things without noticing the limitation. It would only come into play when you're involved in a MultiReal conflict."

Frederic leaned back and grabbed a number out of the air. "A hundred thousand?"

"A hundred thousand choice cycles per day?"

"Yeah."

"Too many. How about fifty thousand?" put in Petrucio.

Jara extended her hands out to her sides. "Sounds good to me. Except . . ." She paused and tapped her foot in thought. "If I'm going to put your products on a parity with mine, I'm going to need your *full* cooperation in getting the whole fiefcorp's business licenses back. That means testifying in front of the Meme Cooperative, Creed Objectivv, the Engineering Board, L-PRACG courts—whatever it takes."

Another urgent ConfidentialWhisper conversation between the Patel brothers ensued. Fifteen seconds later, Petrucio gave a strenuous nod. "You've got a deal," he said, his voice hoarse with repressed excitement.

"Good, it's settled," said Jara. She smiled and stood up from her seat. "I'll draw up a quick contract and have Horvil put it into effect as soon as it's signed."

Jara almost broke out into a cheer herself. No reason to tell the Patels that she had already made this decision days ago. She would have set Possibilities to limited choice cycles for all no matter how the negotiations went today. Jara felt properly devious and Natchlike. She had convinced the Patel Brothers to help her bring the fiefcorp back to full legality, and she had given up nothing for it. Moreover, the Patels seemed pleased too. Win-win.

The analyst brushed off her robe and prepared to cut her multi connection. Her next stop: an independent assembly-line programming shop that had given her every indication that they were willing to take on the fiefcorp's business.

"One more thing," said Jara to the Patels as an afterthought. "You don't mind keeping that information about Natch under your hat for a few more days, do you?"

• • •

Horvil and Serr Vigal were both enthusiastic about the deal.

"Nobody should have that kind of power," said the engineer, lounging on the couch in what Jara had come to call her study. "Now everybody'll be on an equal footing."

"I agree," nodded Vigal. "And—call me crazy—but I think Natch would agree too. Eventually."

Jara stood at the window and watched the dwindling group of drudges keeping vigil at the gates. All but a few had given up on catching a glimpse of Natch emerging from the front doors. Everyone else had left to prepare for Margaret Surina's funeral in Andra Pradesh tomorrow morning. Jara had given the fiefcorp notice that they were all expected to attend as well.

And where was Natch? Would he show up at the funeral? And if so, what was he planning? Now she knew what the Defense and Wellness Council must have been feeling for the past several weeks. Natch was out there, he was relentless, and he was beyond anyone's control. Who's to say that he couldn't use that back door of his to sabotage her agreement with the Patel Brothers?

The analyst felt a sudden shiver take over her spine. It seemed to originate from some primordial portion of her brain, some center of animal instinct locked off from higher reasoning. "Horv," she said, "you remember that trick you did with DockManage 35? Tying up the system so Natch couldn't launch Possibilities onto the Data Sea at a moment's notice?"

"Yep," said the engineer.

"Can you do the same thing to the mechanism that controls the choice cycles?"

Horvil gazed at the floor for a moment as his mind receded into the alternate dimension of mathematics. "Well, not exactly . . . but there are other ways to accomplish the same thing. I think I could keep Natch from disabling the daily choice cycle limit in a hurry. It wouldn't be a permanent fix, but it should slow him down."

Jara nodded. "Then do it," she said. "And do it *quickly*."

(((27)))

"There's something I need to discuss with you, Jara," said Serr Vigal.

The analyst gave him a curious look. She had booked the whole fiefcorp on a hoverbird leaving for Andra Pradesh in less than an hour. They needed to get moving if they intended to make it to Margaret's funeral. But Vigal had prepped for more than a day trip. He had put on a semiformal robe and groomed his sparse hair and speckled goatee into respectability. Jara would have suspected he was heading off to a fund-raising pitch if his memecorp hadn't effectively been put in suspended animation by the Council's legal onslaught.

"Can we—can we talk about this in your office?" Vigal mumbled.

Jara winced. *Just yesterday it was my study, and already it's become my office?* They needed to get out of this miserable mansion before they started planting roots here. Thank goodness everyone would be going home shortly after the funeral. She led the neural programmer down the hallway to the study. Jara refused to sit down until Vigal had done so.

"What's up?" said the analyst in a halfhearted attempt at being chipper.

The neural programmer frowned, opened his mouth several times to start a sentence, then stopped. "I can't just abandon him, Jara," he said finally. "I've got to go to him."

Jara didn't need to ask who Serr Vigal was referring to. "Okay . . ."

"He needs my help. He can't do this alone." The neural programmer wiggled his fingers in the air, as if shaking off a particularly nasty spiderweb. "Everyone's working against him. The Council. The drudges. The Patels. Even . . . you. He needs someone on his side."

"I'm not *against* Natch. I've—"

Vigal waved Jara's objections aside. "Well, if you're not working *against* him, you're certainly not working *for* him either." He waited for a rebuttal, but she had none to give. The neural programmer didn't appear to be upset or even surprised. "I owe it to his mother, Jara. I promised him I would always be there. And so I need to go."

Jara scooted her chair closer and put one hand on his quivering shoulder. "Vigal, of course you need to go. I understand. Did you think I'd try to stop you?"

"Well, after you tried cutting off his access to MultiReal . . . I wasn't so sure. I hate to just abandon the company like this . . . but I can't very well help the fiefcorp and Natch at the same time. If there's a conflict of interest, my loyalties lie with—well, they lie with Natch." He exhaled a long, ragged breath. "I'm on your side, Jara. I'm on the fiefcorp's side. You just need to know that I'm on *Natch's* side first."

She couldn't imagine why the neural programmer was making such a big production of this declaration of loyalty. To be honest, Jara wasn't quite sure how Serr Vigal fit in to a post-Natch fiefcorp anyway. No doubt his intellect was prodigious, but it was of the unpredictable, scattershot variety, and Horvil more than filled that niche. Perhaps a sabbatical for Vigal from the fiefcorp would prove to be the best thing for everyone. In fact, it would probably make explaining Natch's departure to the public a little easier.

They both nodded and stared at the floor for a minute, then rose from their seats as a unit. An entirely new list of to-do items sprouted up in Jara's mental itinerary. She needed to solidify Vigal's extended leave of absence with a short agreement of some kind. She needed to prepare a statement for the press. For process' preservation, when had everything become so *complicated*?

"So how are you going to get in touch with him?" Jara asked. "He hasn't started answering his messages, has he?"

The neural programmer shook his head. "I don't want to approach him at the funeral, that's for sure. I suppose I'll just go over to his apartment after it's over. If he won't let me in, I'll start hitting him with messages until he finally opens one."

"And . . . what kind of help do you think you can give him?"

Serr Vigal shrugged, looking suddenly distracted and despondent. "I really don't know. Whatever help he needs."

They were interrupted by a loud and insistent knock. Five times, then another five in quick succession. Jara gestured at the door, and in spilled Merri, looking bleary-eyed and unrested.

"I think you need to see this," she blurted out.

Something about the channel manager's comportment set off a small whirlwind of panic in Jara's head. She hustled out of the study with Vigal and Merri in tow, nearly sideswiping one of Berilla's dour servants in the process. A minute later, Jara was standing in the great room reading a drudge headline on the window set in a point size usually reserved for wars and celebrity deaths.

WHAT DOES LEN BORDA HAVE IN STORE FOR YOU?
by V. T. Vel Osbiq

The crease in Jara's forehead widened like the fault in an earthquake as she read the article. Vel Osbiq was not exactly a household name, but she bore enough credibility in libertarian circles to ensure that the article would spread. "This isn't good," Jara muttered. "This isn't good at *all*."

Horvil materialized out of nowhere and poked his nose over Jara's shoulder. "What's not good?"

A minute later, he too was absorbed in the article and silent as a tomb.

They call us rabble-rousers. They call us troublemakers and rumormongers and other less savory names. But now we have tangible *proof*.

We now have a memo from the lieutenant executive of the Defense and Wellness Council himself that tells us just how far they're willing to go. We now have proof how irrelevant the Prime Committee has become, and how much contempt Len Borda holds for it.

Mass imprisonments! Seizure of TubeCo and declaration of martial law! A seal on the border with the Islander territories, and a system of "permanent rationing" for the Jamm and the Sigh! And worst of all: a suggestion that "harsh methods" might be necessary to deal with "the threat of the Surinas." This on the morning of Margaret Surina's *funeral*, less than a week after her *murder*. But don't take my word for it; go read the memo for yourself.

Horvil zoomed in on the words "read the memo for yourself" and pulled up a holographic copy of the document in question, then slunk over to the couch to read it. Jara continued with Vel Osbiq's piece on the window.

Does it matter that the Council is calling the memo a fraud? No. High Executive Borda's credibility is practically zero.

Does it matter that the proposals in the memo are just that: proposals? No. The Council has demonstrated plenty of times that they will always sink to the lowest common denominator.

Does it matter that the memo is of dubious origin? No. Consider this: if *you* wanted to leak classified memos from the leadership of the Defense and Wellness Council, would *you* risk sending them through normal channels? Or would you try to find the most anonymous way possible?

What *does* matter is that the libertarians in the Congress of L-PRACGs are keeping mum. Khann Frejohr's office issued a one-sentence response calling for more study. The bodhisattva of Creed Libertas has scheduled a rally—

Jara stepped away, reeling from a sudden rush of vertigo. This had the rank stench of one of Natch's media stunts. She risked a sidelong glance at the engineer on the couch, whose rapidly greening face was evidence enough that he had come to the same conclusion.

"That shit is all over the Data Sea," said Ben, shuffling into the great room with his hands in his pockets. "The whole libertarian population is up in arms about this. There's already talk of a walkout at TubeCo."

"I'm getting a headache," moaned Horvil, waving a hand through the poisonous memo floating before him.

"Well, it looks like one good thing has come out of this," said Merri from the side window. "It looks like the drudges have finally left the front gate. They've moved on."

"Of course they've moved on," groused Ben. "There are going to be *riots* for them to cover in a few hours."

Jara collapsed in place, with her back against the ancient rolltop desk. Somehow Natch had done it. He had connived Speaker Khann Frejohr into some rotten scheme to provoke public opinion against the Council. On the day of Margaret Surina's funeral, no less. Jara knew from bitter experience that Natch's public dramas were impeccably timed and that the appearance of this story today was no coincidence. What mad villainous deeds did Natch have in store for that funeral?

She hadn't thought Natch had been idle for these past few days since the confrontation in Berilla's office. Of course she had assumed that Natch must be working up some sinister batch of nastiness behind the scenes. But the *scope* . . . it defied belief. Jara had been tinkering with the mundane details of fiefcorpery, making fine adjustments to the dials of intercompany commerce. Natch, meanwhile, had been working on a truly Olympian scale, pulling giant levers that moved whole societies.

"I think it would be wise for us to skip the funeral after all," she said, her voice weary. "Why don't you all gather your stuff, and let's get *out* of here before that TubeCo walkout hits. I'm ready to go home."

• • •

Natch stands in the courtyard of the Surina complex and remembers his first Preparation ceremony.

It's a farewell for one of the proctors at the Proud Eagle, a centenarian with a face inscrutable and wrinkled as a bunched blanket. Friends, family, students, acquaintances line up in the great hall to offer unabashed praise for a well-ordered life. Enemies make amends. Food of the starchy and calorific variety is served, along with copious quantities of alcohol. The sun sets; the man stands on unsteady feet. And in one last futile attempt to impose structure on a life subverted by the anarchy of facts, the honoree delivers a final speech. Roads taken and not, lessons learned, regrets. Loves and losses. All sit quietly during the Last Minute and listen to the meandering responses of wind and tree. Finally the man turns. Attendants from the Order of the Prepared lock elbows with the old proctor and escort him through the gates of that compound, never to return.

But Natch is not here today for a Preparation ceremony. This is a funeral.

Today the sky over the Surina compound is cold and empty. A hundred creed banners undulate in the breeze on icy flagpoles. Zhunx's slow dirge "Mourning for the Forgotten" wends its way through every ear. The courtyard is packed so tightly that not a square meter of travertine is visible. Natch can't adjust his suit coat without butting into someone else.

Around him, he sees delegations from every creed he has ever heard of and many he has not: Objectivv, Élan, Conscientious, Surina, Dao, Enlighten, Bushido, Tzu, Autonomous. They are dressed in full creed regalia and standing side by side in an unprecedented display of solidarity. Two squat Africans Natch doesn't recognize wear the three parallel lines of Creed Thassel.

Government officials from every band on the political spectrum dot the courtyard as well. Natch takes note of the masters of the Vault, the keepers of the multi system, the judges, the L-PRACG officials, men and women in the garb of the Prime Committee and the Congress of L-PRACGs. Magan Kai Lee and Rey Gonerev are there representing the Defense and Wellness Council. Magan appears to have recovered completely from Quell's blow at the top of the Revelation Spire. Their faces have been scoured free of emotion, but security must be on their minds, as they've surrounded themselves with governmentalists. Len Borda is nowhere to be found.

Programmers, drudges, capitalmen, actors, philanthropists, healers. Lucas Sentinel, Prosteev Serly, Bolliwar Tuban, Frederic and Petrucio Patel. There are many Islanders, and some of them are in tears.

The blue-green uniforms of Surina compound security, augmented by private forces from Objectivv, Élan, and Dao. They're amped, clearly expecting trouble and ready for it if it comes.

The litter arrives to the monotonous drumbeat of Zhunx.

It's an ornately carved casket, gold with pearl inlay and the prominent fathers of the Surina dynasty in bas-relief. Sheldon Surina, magisterial and imperious, gazes directly into the eyes of the mourners. Prengal Surina has his nose buried in a book and a telescope held aloft in one hand. Marcus Surina stands in repose, shirtless like a Greek god, as if posing for the sculptor of this very casket. Dozens of other Surinas, great and small, are stacked in the open spaces as if holding the lid of the casket on their outstretched arms. Clearly this receptacle was a long time in the making, and Natch wonders how long and under what circumstances it was prepared.

Margaret Surina lies in the cushioned interior. She is dead but not at rest. Her once-raven black hair has now reached its final accommodation with the invading grayness.

The litter bearers reach the center of the courtyard and lay the casket on a raised platform. There is wailing and weeping from some, grim silence from others. Natch assumes the detached man immediately to the left of the platform must be Suheil Surina, while the glowering woman to the right could only be Jayze Surina. Their enmity for one another penetrates even through the fog of mourning; their indifference to the dead woman before them is harder to detect.

All stand and wait for a presence, a person of gravitas worthy of honoring the last daughter of the Surinas.

That person emerges from the gates of the Surina residences, following the path recently cleared by the pallbearers. He is a short man by Western standards, an African with a nose like a miniature fist. His skin is black enough that the folds on his black-and-white-swirled robe might be a form of camouflage, while his kink-curled hair is white enough to match. The crude metal scepter in his hand marks him as the bodhisattva of Creed Objectivv.

The bodhisattva makes his way to the platform containing the coffin. All present give him a wide and respectful berth. He bestows a beatific smile on the assembly and clears his throat to speak.

The world is clouded, but never more so than today. Today our tongues are confused, and we stand on queer geography. We are here to mourn this woman, Margaret Surina. This woman, this beacon. Seeker of truth, inventor of miracles. But today we are here to mourn something more. We mourn the Surinas, whose direct line ended a few days ago. The Surinas brought us not only science but enlightenment. Their coming heralded the dawn of a new age. Where do we go from here? To soar or to fall? Will their passing signal an end to the Reawakening? Will the human spirit slumber once more, or will it rise to glorious deeds?

Natch feels the words bounce off him like rubber. He cannot move or speak.

Standing before him is Margaret Surina, and she is alive.

She's ghostly, almost insubstantial. She floats through the bodies in the crowd and comes to rest a meter away, occupying nearly the same space as a fat man who wears the Plugenpatch uniform. Her hair is slightly darker than the corpse on the platform, but her eyes are as luminous as they ever were. She is staring at Natch; she is trying to speak. No words come from her mouth.

Natch closes his eyes and flees.

He feels himself sinking into the travertine. Sinking *through* it.

Passing down through the rock and soil of the mountain, the flesh of the Earth. There are civilizations down there in the rock, civilizations completely oblivious to the travails of the Surinas and Andra Pradesh, volcanic races of the almost-was and never-were. Natch passes through them.

Farther, farther down.

He emerges in an endless subterranean network of pipes. Pipes that form the core of the world. They are just tall enough for a man to stand in. Natch stands there in a crossroads, a nexus of pipes that extend in a million directions. Somehow he knows, he sees that these tunnels extend throughout the Earth. They extend into every city and every home, into the orbital colonies, through time and space, in universes alternate and improbable. And down here in the nexus, there is a hatch for each tunnel, clearly labeled with the names of every man, woman, and child who has ever, or will ever, live.

Spiderlike creatures scramble in the shadows. They have the hands and heads of men, which they use to dig, dig, dig. Always digging. They are constantly at work building these tunnels in a never-ending construction project. Natch hears them snickering at him.

He picks a hatch at random and draws it open, if only to escape the infernal laughter. The tube sucks at him like a pseudopod, and he flies through the roots of the world. Hours it seems he is flying. Then finally, an ending. A door. Natch opens the door.

It's a gathering. An L-PRACG building outside of Vladivostok, a center of civic activity and urban planning. There are raised voices. A memo floats in the air above the floor, its sentences underscored and highlighted by many different hands. The L-PRACG administrator stands and raises her fist in defiance, shouting the official government slogan over and over until the assembled lawmakers join her. A resolution is proposed calling for the immediate resignation of Len Borda from the Defense and Wellness Council; it passes unanimously.

Natch dives down and secures the hatch behind him. He travels many kilometers to another door (he hears the spiders' laughter) and opens that.

The financial exchange in Beijing. A man in a crisp gray suit sitting at a desk and examining a long string of facts and figures. There are distressing rumors, conflicting reports. The analysis programs and pattern-recognition algorithms he employs advise caution. He consults with his human partners, and they agree as well. *And if the memo really is a forgery?* he asks. *It doesn't matter,* answers his partner. *We get paid to safeguard our clients' money, not to play politics. If you think the company's headed for a fall tomorrow, it's headed for a fall tomorrow.* The man in the gray suit nods, sighs. Sells off a cornerstone of the portfolio with a wave of his hand.

Yet another door.

Transportation workers for TubeCo, underpaid, underutilized, their jobs insecure. Multi has become ubiquitous and taken away their livelihood. They stand in a tube train depot, yelling their displeasure at the labor boss who stands atop a parked tube car above them. *Is Len Borda going to seize the tube or isn't he?* one yells. *What's that mean for our jobs?* shouts another. The man atop the tube car makes placating gestures, urges calm. *Calm?* says the workers' resident agitator. *Fuck calm! You've got assurances from the company—but what if they're wrong? We could have a government takeover in a matter of days. If you're not going to do something about it—we will.* Moving as one, a large chunk of the uniformed workers marches out of the building.

An uneasy Defense and Wellness Council officer, patrolling the streets in the orbital colony of Allowell. A pack of private security guards following. Jeering. A tense confrontation in an alleyway. Darts fired—

Laughter.

Men and women in a station near São Paulo, donning the white robe and yellow star in a panic. Snatching loaded dartguns and disruptors off the racks, along with canisters of black code needles. Positioning themselves on the balcony in a phalanx and aiming weapons at the approaching mob—

An engineer on the underground transfer system lifting a metal wrench in the air, striking down at a hollow pipe that plummets into the bowels of the Earth. He strikes again and again until the pipe cracks. The conveyors shudder to a halt; a cheer arises from his colleagues—

Then Natch is back in the courtyard at Andra Pradesh.

The bodhisattva of Creed Objectivv is long gone now, and the litter carrying the dead woman has been taken to the ceremonial grave inside the Revelation Spire. The crowd is surging in every direction at once; the blue-and-green Surina security officers are on the move. A brawl has broken out somewhere, and the group of Islanders is at the center of it. A trio of white hoverbirds can be seen in the distance, heading this way.

Stones. There is a mob gathered outside the Center for Historic Appreciation, and they are throwing stones at the representatives of the Defense and Wellness Council. The Council contingent forms a tight phalanx and shoves its way toward the gates of the city.

Natch stifles a smile and runs for cover.

4

MADNESS
AND FREEDOM

(((28)))

January 12, Year 360 of the Reawakening

Natch,

I will try to make this message relatively brief, though you must be aware such a feat is beyond my means. Plan accordingly. One might suppose that during the course of a rigorous education in brain stem programming and engineering, a certain prestigious Lunar university might have endeavored to teach its pupils how to *write*—but alas, they did not.

However, I digress. (You smile knowingly. Perhaps fear of my digressions is what's caused you to ignore my messages for the past few days. Perhaps you will ignore this one as well. All I can do is press on and assume that I am reaching you on some level.)

Let me get my typical sententious blather out of the way first.

Natch, you have won many victories in your life. Digging yourself out of the troubles at initiation and climbing to number one on the Primo's bio/logic investment guide was quite an achievement. Arranging the transition of MultiReal from Margaret's fiefcorp to yours was another. Surely the popular outcry during the past few days over this disputed Defense and Wellness Council memo counts as a third.

(Yes, despite what the drudges have called "the largest spontaneous outbreak of public protest since the Melbourne riots" [John Ridglee, January 11], this unrest certainly does not seem spontaneous to me. It has not escaped my attention that the major events of this crisis—the street protests in Beijing, the government walkouts in Cape Town, the formal statements of dissent by the creeds and the L-PRACGs—were coordinated very closely with the drudge news cycles. Your new friend Khann Frejohr denied any involvement, of course, but his denial arrived just in time to make Sen Sivv Sor's evening report. Yet the most incriminatory piece of evidence is the fact that the tube line between Cisco and Seattle through the redwoods remains operational, despite an ongoing TubeCo operators' strike in North America. *Quod erat demonstrandum.*)

So you have won another victory. The Prime Committee has called for a special session to resolve the question of MultiReal and promises to debate the issue "for as long as it takes." They have issued subpoenas to you, the Council, and the Congress. The public, at least, seems willing to put its ire on hold for a few days and submit to the judgment of the Committee.

But like all your victories, Natch, this one brings you no resolution. It only qualifies you for a more intricate challenge.

I hardly need tell you the Defense and Wellness Council should not be underestimated in any circumstance, and especially not when they have been backed into a corner. You have already met Len Borda's chief solicitor, Rey Gonerev, but I'm afraid you have never seen her in front of an audience. I had the misfortune of witnessing a public hearing on orbital colony subsidies several months ago in which Gonerev proceeded to slash her opponent's sensible and practical arguments to shreds. There is a reason the drudges call her the Blade. The Prime Committee will allow Borda to choose someone to provide an opening statement for the governmentalist position, and I have no doubt that Rey Gonerev is the one whom the high executive will call.

Now I don't mean to sound defeatist—I have every confidence in your ability to sway a crowd—but you must be aware that you are fighting an uphill battle to regain control of this technology. In fact, matters may be more precarious than ever. The Prime Committee is effectively the final court of appeal, beyond which there are no more legal avenues to which you can turn. Moreover, I'm sure you know that the governmentalists still hold a substantial majority on the Committee, and governmentalists rarely contravene the word of High Executive Borda.

So it's an uphill battle, you tell yourself. *It's always been an uphill battle, from the very beginning.*

But there is no such thing as an ordinary battle for you. You tend to wrap your feelings of self-worth into your battles, Natch. I've observed you doing this ever since you were a child, and perhaps if I had been better schooled in the art of parenting I might have done something about it when I still could. You believe that the outcome of this fight for MultiReal will determine the success or failure of your entire life—just as you believed the same thing about your quest to achieve number one on Primo's, and your fight to win in the ROD coding market, and so on.

I know I risk sounding like a tedious public service announcement from Creed Conscientious when I say this, but I will say it anyway: you are not the work you do in life.

I shall repeat this and isolate it in a separate paragraph, like a professor emphasizing an important point before final exams. YOU ARE NOT THE WORK YOU DO IN LIFE.

We do not often get to declare victories, Natch, and most of them do not remain victories for very long. Ultimately when you reach my age you realize that victories are temporary, and in all the years of human history there is one final battle which nobody has ever won. Time has a way of changing the terms of your victories over the years, until you begin to wonder precisely what it was you fought for so viciously, so uncompromisingly. You begin to see that victory and defeat are but alternate reflections from the same prism. You see that the measure of a person really might be the integrity with which he fought his battles and not their ultimate dispensation, just like your elders have been telling you all along.

That old book of the Pharisees expresses it best: seasons come and seasons go, but the Earth remains forever. (Obviously Ecclesiastes had never heard of Hubble's law or gravitational singularities, but you get the picture.)

Again, I digress. (Cf. paragraph 2, above.) Let us move on to more practical matters.

I have spent many long hours pondering the challenge you face in swaying the Prime Committee, and I have concluded that what you need is a trusted voice. The Council will seek to put your face on the libertarian cause. They will highlight your admittedly uncompromising nature, your personal foibles, and your shortcomings; a vote for MultiReal is a vote for Natch, they'll say. You need the Committee to see your situation not as a conflict of brash personalities, but as an ideological struggle. You need someone to present the libertarian position on MultiReal in a measured, persuasive, and objective way.

It seems to me the ideal person to put forth such an argument to the Prime Committee is Speaker Khann Frejohr. And so—I hope you are not upset with me—I approached his office intending to convince him to speak on your behalf. Unfortunately, the speaker refused to see me, and his senior aides informed me that Frejohr would not make such a speech under any terms. I don't know what sort of disagreement you have with the speaker that would cause him to lie low in this conflict (his office laughably claims a desire to "maintain impartiality"), but he has indeed made that decision. Frejohr had assigned a midlevel Congressional solicitor to make the libertarians' opening statement. I made it my duty to observe the man in court, and the most charitable conclusion I can come to is that Khann Frejohr is not invested in your success.

So I offered to deliver the libertarian opening statement before the Prime Committee instead. The speaker's office agreed.

You gasp. You frown. I admit that I am no politician, and my speeches have been the butt of many jokes around the fiefcorp. It's true that I have no experience swaying government officials for their vote, and yet I *do* have decades (and decades) of experience swaying government officials for something even more precious and inseparable: their money.

My reputation has shown some tarnishing lately, as have all of ours in the fiefcorp. But I submit to you that I am still one of the world's preeminent authorities on brain stem programming and a much sought-after expert on neurotechnological issues. I have been stockpiling this reputation for many, many years, and at my age one begins to wonder exactly what one is stockpiling such a thing *for*. So now I offer this reputation to you in the hopes that it might be of some service.

You will, of course, get the opportunity to make your case before the Prime Committee in person. Nothing I do or say in my opening statement will change that. All I can hope to do is to make your task somewhat easier.

One last piece of business: Jara has informed me that she has also been called to testify before this hearing, or special session, or whatever the Prime Committee is calling it at this hour. She will be bringing the rest of the Surina/Natch MultiReal Fiefcorp with her. Since you have not been answering her messages either, Jara asked me to tell you that she does not see any benefit in broadcasting your differences to the world at such a perilous time. She has asked me to relay her assurances that her testimony will be both fair and impartial to the best of her ability.

And now I have succeeded in relaying her message, in this long-winded-even-by-my-own-standards way.

Rest assured, Natch, that wherever you choose to go or whatever you choose to do—and whatever becomes of this execrable MultiReal technology—from now until the moment they drag my creaky bones and aching joints off to join the Prepared, I will always, always be with you.

Sincerely,
Serr Vigal

(((29)))

Lucco Primo once said, *Size up your enemy by studying his approach.*

Defense and Wellness Council troops usually approached their enemies with the thunderclap of a hundred disruptors and the sonic boom of a hundred hoverbirds in their wake. Such was the Council's edge in technology that Len Borda's officers rarely needed the element of surprise, and their ghostly white robes openly mocked the idea of camouflage.

But when the Council unleashed its legal army, the standard rules of engagement did not apply.

None of the drudges had noticed any unusual activity at the Council's Terran headquarters recently. No streams of departing hoverbirds, no sudden influx of advisors. So when a torrent of white hoverbirds landed at the Melbourne facilities on the thirteenth of January and let loose a merciless tide of lawyers, the public was caught completely by surprise. Sen Sivv Sor and John Ridglee were among the drudges who could be seen dashing out of public multi gateways soon after the procession began. Even staunch governmentalists like Mah Lo Vertiginous were spotted in the crowd in various stages of dishabille or disarray.

The procession continued for over an hour. There were nearly two hundred attorneys, technical specialists, legal programmers, analysts, and researchers dressed in matching suits of crisp gray with a muted version of the five-pointed star embroidered on their chests. They fanned out across Melbourne's broadest boulevard and began a slow yet disciplined march toward the Defense and Wellness Council's administrative offices. Somewhere along the way, they picked up an accompanying scrim of military officers with dartguns drawn and disruptors charged. Half a dozen Council hoverbirds swooped over the street in perfect synchronization. (A dry run, some muttered, for the inevitable pogrom that awaited them all.)

By the time this bureaucratic army reached the Council's undistinguished slab of a building, a sizable crowd had gathered to witness the coming of history. Children sat on the shoulders of their parents. Politicians elbowed each other aside in a struggle for prime positioning. Vendors, advertisers, and salespeople fed off the crowd like leeches, while on the Data Sea, a menagerie of video feeds captured the Council's approach from every possible angle.

At the last minute, several libertarian activists emerged from the crowd and linked hands, cordoning off the steps leading to the Council building. A hush fell upon the crowd. There was a tense standoff between the commander of the white-robed officers and the leader of the libertarians. Several minutes passed, with their arguments growing more heated by the second. Finally, the irritated commander turned his back on the activists and made a gesture to his troops.

The officers shouldered their rifles as one and did not hesitate.

Murderers! cried a few strident voices. *Bloodthirsty tyrants!* But the Defense and Wellness Council's legal army continued up the steps with nary a pause and disappeared inside the building.

A few moments later, the libertarian activists struggled groggily to their feet, plucking darts from their torsos. They were dazed but otherwise all right.

• • •

The three fiefcorpers lined up against the wall of Jara's apartment like troops submitting to an inspection, their spines uncomfortably stiff and their eyes doggedly forward-facing. Jara marched down the aisle and bayoneted each one of them with a sharp stare. She insisted that Horvil comb his hair, that Merri stand up straight and project confidence, that Ben take control of his scowling or stay home.

Jara saw the reactions on their faces and almost backed off. Everyone was bone tired from the stress of the past few days—the disruptions in the tube lines, the demonstrations in the streets, the constant migraine of Council troops around every corner—and their attitudes toward Jara were beginning to slide from mild distrust to outright resentment. She was just a short hop away from breakdown herself.

Naturally, it was Benyamin who chose to speak up. "Can't you give it a rest for once, Jara?"

The analyst walked up to the young apprentice and stood within spitting distance. "I've had just about enough of you," she said with a grimace. "There could be ten billion people watching us tomorrow at that Prime Committee hearing. Do you understand that? *Literally* ten billion people. We need to look our best."

"They'll understand, Jara," said Merri, her voice stretched and hoarse. "Everyone's feeling a little surreal right now. The audience is going to be discombobulated too."

Horvil nodded. "She's right. We're not a theater troupe. You can't expect us to be onstage every day when we've got work to concentrate on. Do you realize how little we've gotten *done* this past month because of all this political crap?"

Jara stared at the engineer, momentarily speechless. His words might have been harsh, but his tone was mellow, almost supportive. She found her thoughts slipping, like fingers losing their grip on the rung of a ladder, falling back to that scene in the museum at Andra Pradesh. The feel of his chubby hand enclosing hers. The radiating concern. That warm, uncomplicated, perpetually adolescent face beaming at her with an emotion raw and undistilled. Who wouldn't feel embarrassed to be on the receiving end of such a look?

Ben cut through her reverie with a heavy sigh.

Jara only stopped herself from throttling Benyamin by a tremendous act of will. She flipped through her mental library and dusted off Grim-Face 202, one of the intense glares she had programmed for such an occasion. "Do you trust me?" she said. "All of you. Do you trust me?"

A pause. A few frowns. Merri, sheepish, answered. "Yes. Of course we trust you."

"Good." Jara walked up to Benyamin and stabbed his chest with the nail of her right index finger. "Then fucking *listen* and *do what I say.* All right?"

The fiefcorpers nodded and followed her out the door.

Jara berated herself for that petulant little outburst all the way to the tube station. *Isn't that exactly the kind of shit you criticized Natch for?* she thought. *Yelling at everybody for no reason. Refusing to explain yourself.* She was practically marinating in irony. *One week in charge of a major fief-corp, and all you can do is imitate Natch. Natch, the worst manager you've ever known. Pathetic.* She debated making some kind of apologetic gesture to the rest of the fiefcorpers all the way to the tube platform.

She still hadn't made a decision when the train arrived and everyone stepped aboard. Moments later, they were off.

The fiefcorp maintained complete silence for several hours after the train whooshed out of the station, and there was no one else in their part of the car to fill the void. So they kept watch out the windows. The dilapidated tunnels and debris-strewn lowlands of Britain, practically untouched since the Autonomous Revolt, soon made way for the comforting dull gray of the sea. After that, Africa. Sea became shore, shore became forest.

The silence was finally broken by the arrival of a freshly minted Latin accent during the stop at Cape Town. "Looks like the crew's all here!" said Robby Robby, oozing down the aisle with a jaunty grin.

"All the ones who aren't dead, accused of murder, or in prison," replied Horvil, deadpan.

Benyamin jabbed his cousin in the side. "What about Serr Vigal?"

"He works in a memecorp, doesn't he?" said Horvil. "I call that prison."

Jara allowed herself a smile. "Glad you could come," she told the channeler, and for once she meant it. If anyone knew how to whip up a dish of false confidence for the drudges, politicians, and pundits awaiting them, it was Robby. The fact that he had taken several days out of his schedule to come to Melbourne spoke volumes about his faith in the cause. The channeler took a seat next to Merri as the train got under way again. Soon he had sucked the fiefcorp apprentices into a low-stakes game of holo poker.

Jara found an empty section of train and tried to prepare a statement for her Prime Committee testimony, but it was hopeless. What did she have to say about MultiReal that hadn't been said a thousand times already? It was a powerful and potentially dangerous program. It could make her fiefcorp a lot of money. Didn't the whole world already know this? Jara stared glumly at the changing landscape, writing nothing, and hoped the Committee wouldn't actually need her testimony after all.

As for Serr Vigal—what was he *thinking?* Jara had no doubt the neural programmer's heart was in the right place. She had no doubt his opening statement before the Committee would be cogent and foursquare and thoroughly respectable. But Vigal just did not possess the gift of oratory. His politics were moderate. Having him usher in the libertarian side of the MultiReal debate with one of his dry, meandering speeches was an unmistakably bad idea.

But who else is there? thought the analyst. *Who else is going to stand up before ten billion people and testify that MultiReal belongs in Natch's hands?* There was Khann Frejohr, of course, except Frejohr had thoroughly rebuffed Serr Vigal's overtures. Jara wondered what Natch had done to antagonize him. She figured it had something to do with that obviously forged Council memo, but she decided she didn't want to know. She had already seen enough low-level forgery to last her a lifetime.

It only took Natch a week to make a powerful ally, use him, and then toss him aside, she thought, shaking her head. *That must be a new record.*

• • •

The track from Cape Town to Melbourne was one long stretch of undifferentiated seascape, punctuated by the occasional pit stop on dry land or artificial crossroads. Waves, sun, sky.

Jara didn't remember falling asleep, but suddenly she was being woken by a gentle hand on her shoulder. Horvil. "I thought you might want to see this," said the engineer.

The analyst sat up and rubbed her eyes. "Thought I'd want to see wha—"

Then she looked out the window.

The city of Melbourne lay sprawled out below them, a tapestry of neatly arranged buildings and flickering lights. The tube train sat suspended on a ridiculously high track over Port Phillip Bay, like a roller coaster of old, watching the city slide gracefully into dusk. Jara remembered reading about this; some arcane procedure involving military security, or underwater transfer conduits, or something. Many believed it was just a ruse by the Melbourne L-PRACGs to impress visitors with the majesty of the centralized government. Jara could buy that. From this angle, the city looked so orderly, so perpendicular with purpose, it might have been carefully laid there by some omnipotent force in an era long before human confusion.

Then the tube abruptly plunged into Melbourne at breakneck speed, and the illusion was shattered. The train came to a stop some five minutes later.

By the time Jara shouldered her bag and made it off the train, the rest of the fiefcorp was already waiting—as was a group of handlers in garish purple-and-red robes, courtesy of Creed Élan. Horvil and Benyamin seemed right at home in their midst. One of the men took Jara's bag with a deep, respectful bow, as if she had entrusted him with crown jewels rather than a few changes of clothing and assorted toiletries.

"Don't suppose anybody brought a thermos of nitro," grumbled the analyst with a yawn.

"There's plenty at the hostel," replied one of the creed handlers. "Lo-grade, hi-grade, you name it."

Jara nodded. "Then what are we waiting for?"

The purple delegation led the fiefcorpers through a vast maze of bureaucratic buildings, each more stodgy and architecturally unimaginative than the last. They passed the headquarters for OrbiCo, TeleCo, and GravCo, the offices of major lobbying firms and political parties, the Meme Cooperative's lone Earthside presence, creed bureaus, and drudge organizations.

There was something strange and out-of-place about the cityscape that Jara could sense but not name. Merri saw her perplexed look. "You notice it too?" she asked.

"I notice *something*," said Jara. "I'm just not sure what."

"The buildings—they're not moving."

That was it. Melbourne's governmental quarter was entirely devoid of collapsible buildings. At this hour, most downtowns would be exhibiting a conspicuous ripple as the skyline rearranged itself for the night shift. Melbourne did not budge. If Jara didn't know for a fact that the city had been substantially rebuilt after the riots of 318, she might have guessed it had been permanently frozen right before the Autonomous Revolt.

"Government buildings that don't move," said Horvil. "There's a metaphor if I've ever seen one."

Robby Robby's grin widened by a few degrees.

Jara felt the mental tug of an incoming ConfidentialWhisper. "Don't look now," said Ben, sounding clipped and nervous, "but I think we're being followed."

The analyst counted to ten, then took a casual glance around. The streets were crowded with security officers from a hundred different organizations striding this way and that, guarding every solid structure in sight. Pedestrians added a thousand more organizational insignias to the mix. Everyone in Melbourne, it seemed, had some kind of parliamentary affiliation.

And then she noticed them. Minions of the Defense and Wellness Council on every corner, following the fiefcorp's progress with great interest. Whenever the fiefcorpers lost sight of one group, another would inevitably turn up on the next block to track them.

Before Jara could formulate a coherent reaction, they came to a cul-de-sac and passed through an immense set of double doors—the Creed Élan hostel.

The place hardly fit Jara's definition of a hostel at all; it was enormous, richly furnished, and teeming with important-looking men and women in purple. Jara felt like she was back at Berilla's estate. The handlers who had met them at the tube station deposited their bags in a parlor fit for a high executive. Rugs and viewscreens obscured every surface, while flasks of wine sat on countertops for the taking. Benyamin ducked down the hall to pay his respects to the hostel administrator. Jara, meanwhile, found a thermos of piping nitro and began filling up a mug.

Merri sunk into a plush suede couch. "So does anyone know where Natch is staying?" she asked. Nobody answered. "Horvil?"

The engineer shrugged. "You know as much as I do," he said. "Natch hasn't shown his face in public for almost a week, and you all saw how strange he looked at the funeral. I don't know if he's up to testifying before the Prime Committee. Maybe . . . maybe they won't actually call him after all."

"Sure they will," said Robby, kicking off his shoes to reveal ten huge prehensile toes. "Natch is a symbol now. The libertarians are rallying around him. This unrest won't stop until he gets his say in front of the Committee."

"What about Vigal?" said Jara. "Where's he staying?"

Horvil: "With Natch, I presume."

"Do you think they're going to call on any of us to testify?" asked Merri.

Robby shrugged. "Anything's possible," he said, channeler-speak for *no*. He tucked his shoes under his arms and disappeared down the hall, presumably to freshen up.

"Who knows what they're going to do," said Horvil, taking a seat backward on a desk chair. "When was the last time the Prime Committee held a special session like this? Nobody even remembers the protocol anymore."

Merri craned her neck to face the engineer. "What is the protocol?"

"No idea. I don't know if there even is one. My guess is they'll just use some fancy version of *Let's call people up to testify until we've heard enough.* Ben's the one to ask about this stuff, not me." He stretched and groaned. "I just want this to be over already. I'm sick of the politics. I'm sick of the infoquakes. I'm sick of looking over my shoulder and seeing white robes everywhere. I just want to get back to the bloody *engineering.*"

Jara downed her second straight mug of nitro and took a seat in the corner. "If you don't want to see white robes, you're in the wrong place. Ben saw a bunch of them following us on the way here."

Benyamin returned at just that moment, his face pale as milk. "No," he said, his voice cracking. "That's not what I was telling you, Jara. Didn't you see? I wasn't warning you about the people in the *white* robes. I was warning you about the ones in the *black* robes."

(((30)))

Horvil and Benyamin voted to stay at the hostel and let Creed Élan security take care of them.

"We're just not getting *paid* enough for this shit," said Ben, his voice rising to a panicked squeak. "There's Council officers every five steps in this city. They've already taken Quell—has anybody even bothered to look for him? People are rioting and making death threats. Whoever killed Margaret Surina is still out there. And now we have to deal with these lunatics in black robes?" He sat down firmly on an ottoman and hugged his knees. "I don't even know why I came. I'm still—we're *all* still suspended from the fiefcorp. What's the point?"

Merri leaned over and put a placating hand on the young apprentice's shoulder. "We won't be suspended for long, Benyamin. Don't forget that Jara's arranged for the Patels to testify on our behalf—"

"The Patels. I forgot about the Patels." Ben tucked his chin down and huddled into the fetal position. "I'd rather chew my own leg off than trust *them*."

Jara knelt down on her haunches in front of the apprentice and fixed him with a no-nonsense stare. "Are you *sure* those people you saw were the same ones who hit Natch with black code?" she asked.

"There *are* a lot of groups that wear black," mused Merri as she walked back and forth across the parlor in slow-mo imitation of Natch's frenetic pace. "Creed Bushido's honor guard. The TeleCo board. I think there's a Pharisee group that wears black too. . . ."

Ben ignored her. "Of course I'm not sure they were the same people," he said. "Fuck, I wasn't sure if I really *believed* Natch's story until an hour ago. But these guys matched the description. Black robes, head to toe. Some kind of red Asian lettering running down the front."

"Didn't that look a little suspicious?" said Horvil skeptically. The engineer found a shadowy section of couch and slouched into it as far as possible, a poor man's attempt at subterfuge. "I mean, who walks around covered with a robe head to toe?"

"I don't—I don't know. I only caught a few quick glimpses of them. One guy was standing in a window as we walked by. Nobody else saw anything?"

The rest of the fiefcorpers remained silent. Jara was glad that Robby Robby wasn't here to see this. The less abject panic he saw, the less chance he would desert them and move on to some other, more stable business venture.

"I'm *not* making this up," sulked Benyamin.

"Nobody's accusing you of making it up," said Jara, placing her hands at her hips. "But even if those were the same people who attacked Natch, how is staying here going to help?"

"It'll keep us alive, for starters," muttered Horvil.

"You heard Robby," continued the young apprentice. "The Prime Committee's probably not going to call on any of *us* to testify. Why can't you just go and let us stay at the hostel?"

The analyst shook her head and gazed at the Pulgarti sketches on the viewscreen. The abstract geometric shapes and angry black lines reflected her mood. Her thoughts staggered back to a conversation last month when the MultiReal demo in Andra Pradesh was hours away and the fiefcorpers were being similarly irrational. *Don't we ever learn anything in this company?* she thought. *We just keep moving in circles. Around and around and nothing gained.*

"Listen," said Jara finally. "All of you, listen. You can't—we can't keep *doing* this."

Merri's attention had wavered to the mesmerizing Pulgarti on the viewscreen as well. "Doing what?" she asked.

"Hiding. Being . . . passive. Acting out of fear." The analyst waved a hand and blanked the viewscreen, snapping Merri back to the room at large. "Those people in the black robes—whoever they are—what's their objective? What are they trying to do? They're trying to scare us. Isn't that why they hit Natch with black code? They wanted to frighten him into calling off the MultiReal demo—or maybe to push him into the Council's arms, I don't know.

"The same thing goes with Len Borda and Magan Kai Lee. And the Patels, for that matter. The common thread here is that they're all employing scare tactics. They're trying to keep us off balance.

"And you know what? They succeeded—but they did too good a job. We're so scared that we realize there aren't any safe places left. Come on, Ben, Horvil—do you really think Creed Élan can protect us? Do you think Berilla's servants can protect us?" She gestured toward the bulky security guard down the hall, who seemed accustomed to ignoring guest conversations. "No and no. If we've learned anything these past few months, it's that *nobody* can protect us. The Defense and Wellness Council can march wherever they please. Assassins can get to Margaret Surina right in the middle of a heavily guarded compound. Magan Kai Lee can yank our business right out from under us with no warning. So what good is hiding going to do? No good at all."

Jara paused a moment to catch her breath. Merri and Ben were staring at the floor with solemn looks on their faces. Robby Robby had stepped back into the parlor just in time to give a vigorous nod of agreement. Horvil's expression had metamorphosed from a prunish frown into a goofy grin sometime in the past few minutes.

"Here's what I propose," continued Jara. "I propose we all get some rest, wake up early tomorrow, and have a nice big breakfast. Then I say we march over to that hearing in broad daylight, with our heads held high. We sit in the audience together, like a real company. I don't know what the Prime Committee's going to do about MultiReal. I don't know if we're going to get gunned down by a bunch of people in black robes tomorrow, or a bunch of people in *white* robes. But I'm not going to just sit here.

"Listen, I—I'm fighting for this fiefcorp. I really am. I know that some of you don't trust me, but there's nothing I can do about it right now. All I'm asking you to do right now is just hold on, stay with me. We'll get through this."

• • •

Jara half expected a greeting the next morning from Khann Frejohr. Sure, Frejohr had his issues with Natch, but they were all on the same side, weren't they? She figured at least one of the speaker's innumerable functionaries would take advantage of the lull in libertarian protests to bring the Congress's regards.

But when nine o'clock arrived with no word from anyone, Jara decided there was no reason to wait. She told the fiefcorp to gather in the atrium in thirty minutes.

Robby Robby was the first to arrive. He instantly sensed her frustration.

"Don't be too upset, Queen Jara," said the channeler, inexplicably filing his nails into sharp points suitable for a street fight. "I've been telling you all along not to trust the libertarians. Just because they hate Len Borda doesn't make them the good guys. They don't really care about Natch. They don't really care about *you*. Sure, they'll support you, but only when it suits their purposes, and only until they don't need you anymore."

"Yeah, I suppose you're right," said Jara with a sour face. "But I wasn't looking for flowers and a bottle of wine. I just wanted a few words of encouragement. And maybe some news about the big, dull speech that Serr Vigal's preparing."

"You don't give Vigal enough credit," replied Robby. "He's a smart guy. He knows what he's doing."

The analyst sulked against a pillar without answering. She was slowly coming to realize that the channeler was not the empty shell she had always assumed him to be. But a wise and sensible Robby Robby was more than Jara's worldview could bear at this point. She left him in the atrium and wandered back to the parlor for one last cup of nitro. By the time she made it back, Horvil, Benyamin, and Merri were standing there waiting.

The Surina/Natch MultiReal Fiefcorp looked like a pretty impressive company, Jara admitted to herself. The engineer was surprisingly dashing in his new Persian suit; the black-and-white swirls on Merri's dress subtly evoked the Objectivv logo without being too obvious about it; Benyamin, in his purple-and-red robes, might have passed for a junior bodhisattva of Creed Élan; and there had to be some constituency in the vast reaches of human space that would find Robby's Afro the epitome of style. Jara herself had chosen a vibrant green pantsuit that looked optimistically toward spring.

When the entire company was assembled, Jara opened the front door of the hostel and was greeted by a raucous noise.

Horvil grimaced. "What's that?"

Jara peeked nervously around the doorjamb and widened her eyes. "I guess it's the libertarian welcoming committee," she said.

The fiefcorpers emerged blinking into the Melbourne morning to the cheers of several hundred zealous demonstrators. People lined the entire cul-de-sac outside the Élan hostel, shouting, waving, beaming bold messages of solidarity in the air over their heads.

> LEN BORDA, Don't Take Our FREEDOMS
> *INFORMATION WANTS INDEPENDENCE!*
> THE *REAL* ISSUE IS THE RIGHT TO DO BUSINESS
> LIBERTARIAN RESISTANCE

There were a number of Libertas devotees bearing the insignia of the rising sun, and a smattering of Islanders to boot. An even larger pack of drudges hovered at the next intersection, watching and taking careful notes.

Robby Robby gave Jara a wry look and shrugged. She was amused to see that he was using his newly sharpened claws as a pick to fluff his already overfluffed Afro.

The libertarians were rambunctious, but they kept their distance as the fiefcorpers started down the street. So did the drudges. The crowd diminished as they made their way toward the city center, but did not disappear entirely. Downtown Melbourne was a constant carnival of protests and demonstrations, and it was difficult to tell where one sideshow ended and the next began. A core group escorted them the whole way, shouting righteous slogans for the drudges' benefit. Jara kept an eye out for menacing figures in black robes. She saw no sign of them, although the menacing figures in white robes and yellow stars were hard to miss.

And then they turned a corner and came face-to-face with the Tul Jabbor Complex, headquarters of the Prime Committee.

The building was gargantuan, dwarfing all other government structures in the city. It seemed to have been constructed for a much larger race of beings altogether. The windows stood impossibly high off the ground, while the doors could have comfortably admitted a tube train. The whole structure was slablike and boxy in shape, with a monolithic dome capping one end. From one of the hoverbirds streaming in and out of the adjacent dockyards, Jara supposed the building would look like a giant armless statue.

Horvil tapped her on the shoulder. "That's where we're going," he explained, pointing at the dome. "That's where—"

"Where the Prime Committee meets, yes, I know." The analyst smiled and tapped the side of her head. "I can access the Data Sea too, Horv." The engineer blushed.

The inside of the Tul Jabbor Complex was no less intimidating than the exterior. One broad corridor made a winding path through the center of the Complex like intestines. The sides of the corridor were six levels high and lined with an endless grid of office cubicles behind smoky glass. The corridor itself had no roof. Everywhere they could see public servants striding purposefully back and forth, sporting a hundred different uniforms.

Midway through the complex in a circular clearing stood an enormous hologram of High Executive Tul Jabbor, fifteen meters tall. The stern, Janus-like faces of the Defense and Wellness Council's first commander tracked the fiefcorpers mercilessly both as they approached and as they walked past. Jara shuddered and quickened her step until the curving corridor put Jabbor out of sight.

At long last, they reached the dome.

The analyst was suffering from sensory overload as she walked into the auditorium. Twenty-nine chairs of miserable black iron ringed a floor measuring some thirty-five meters in diameter. Behind and above this row of twenty-nine chairs sat another dozen concentric rings of normal, cushioned seats for the plebes. Each ring rested at an impossibly steep angle above the one in front of it, as if the rings were built for the hologram of Tul Jabbor to climb.

The analyst looked down at the floor and felt her heart curdle in fear. It was the most intimidating setting she could possibly imagine. Facing the entire Committee at once was impossible, and there were no chairs to sit on. From the floor, Jara supposed that the audience members must look like they were stacked on top of one another. Even an extraordinarily tall person would have to crane his neck at an uncomfortable angle to see them. There would be no multi tricks here, no abandoning of Cartesian space in the audience; whether out of security concerns or out of tradition, no multi projections were allowed in the Tul Jabbor Complex auditorium.

"What a nightmare!" said Ben—and then instantly clamped his hand to his mouth. The place was an acoustic disaster. Ben's exclamation bounced around the walls and quickly devolved into complete dissonance. Raising your voice only seemed to amplify the problem. Jara suddenly noticed that the place was rustling with the ghostly sound of a thousand whispers, which only added to the creepiness factor.

The fiefcorpers gave one another PokerFace glances and started down the narrow stairway. They headed for the petitioners' ring—the ring immediately above the Prime Committee, and the fiefcorp's new home until the MultiReal issue was resolved, one way or another.

• • •

Ten minutes later, Natch and Serr Vigal arrived. Jara stifled a gasp, then quickly looked around to make sure there were no drudges nearby.

Natch had not shown his face in public for nearly five days, but he might have aged fifteen years in that time. He seemed haggard and noticeably underfed. His left hand was thrust deep into his suit coat pocket as if weighted there by some dense object. Vigal, on the other hand, was so inwardly focused that he completely failed to notice the intimidating stage below. Jara wondered how the neural programmer had managed to reach Natch and whether the entrepreneur had helped Vigal prepare his speech. By the diffident way Natch was treating his old guardian, she suspected that he was hardly aware of Vigal's presence at all. The entrepreneur seemed momentarily confused as they reached the petitioners' ring, until Vigal's hand clutched his elbow and steered him toward a chair a quarter of the way around the ring from the fiefcorp.

"Something's wrong with Natch," said Merri.

"What do you mean, something's 'wrong' with him?" asked Horvil. "There's always been something wrong with him."

"Yes, but . . . his *eyes.*"

Jara noticed it too, even from this distance. The flesh around Natch's eye sockets looked as if it had been rouged with something dark and sinister. *Any half-decent OCHRE system should take care of that,* thought the analyst. *Natch, what's happening to you?*

A vein in her temple began to throb. She watched the neural programmer nod and mumble to himself like a student prepping for exams, while Natch simply stared straight ahead. Jara waited for him to glance around at the audience; he wouldn't have to tilt his head that far to the left to see the fiefcorp. But the entrepreneur did not avert his eyes from a spot of void hovering about three meters before his face. Jara slumped down in her seat. With Vigal delivering the libertarians' opening statement and Khann Frejohr lying low, she had pinned her hopes for this hearing on Natch. But Natch was obviously in no shape to persuade the Prime Committee of anything.

"How long do you have to go without sleep to get bloodshot eyes in this day and age?" mused Ben, half to himself.

Jara darted a glance at Robby Robby, but the channeler was either completely oblivious to their conversation or faking it well. She wondered if he was off shopping for hairdos on the Data Sea or holding a pep rally with his sales force.

Moments later, the delegation from the Congress of L-PRACGs arrived. It was the first time Jara had ever seen the legendary Speaker Khann Frejohr in person. He appeared calm and at ease in his bronze robe, looking every bit the wily and experienced politician. Frejohr and his accompanying band of libertarian activists found seats in the petitioners' ring toward Natch's side of the floor. Yet Jara couldn't help but notice that the speaker refused to look in the entrepreneur's direction, and he made no move to take the vacant chair on Natch's right.

Horvil shot her a ConfidentialWhisper. "He really pissed Frejohr off, didn't he?" Jara didn't answer.

And then the doors opened for the Defense and Wellness Council.

Lieutenant Executive Magan Kai Lee stood in the nucleus of a small pack of lawyers, administrators, and high-ranking Council officers. He looked almost Lilliputian in such an immense space. Jara recognized a few of the other lieutenant executives from drudge reports; she recognized Magan's flunky Papizon from personal experience. Jara felt a slight twitch of terror in her gut, remembering that Magan had unfinished business with her. She sneered it down.

"Don't tell me that Lieutenant Executive Lee is going to be delivering their opening statement?" said Benyamin.

Merri craned her neck forward. "Does anybody see any sign of—"

The doors slammed open once more, and Jara felt her heart sink. The Blade.

Rey Gonerev, the chief solicitor of the Defense and Wellness Council, strode through the doors with the confidence of a panther. Her long braids framed a face which mirrored that confidence. The Blade walked past the libertarian delegation, barely acknowledged Khann Frejohr's respectful nod, and headed for the governmentalist contingent on the opposite site of the auditorium. She was in her element here.

And yet, for all Gonerev's bluster and bravado, where was the Council's legal army? What had happened to the hundreds of lawyers, functionaries, and advisors who had marched confidently through the streets of Melbourne yesterday? Evidently that display had just been a show for public consumption, because few of them were present today.

Jara studied the twenty-nine empty chairs in the ring above hers— seats for the Prime Committee, the ultimate government authority, the people whose word superseded that of the L-PRACGs. Even the armed officers of the Defense and Wellness Council spread around the auditorium took their orders from the Committee, at least in theory. If anyone could give Natch a fair hearing, it was the people who would shortly be filling those chairs. But would they listen with open ears?

The analyst had a distressing thought. Did she *want* the government to give Natch a fair hearing? The Prime Committee had the power to overturn everything Magan Kai Lee had done and restore Natch to the head of his fiefcorp, to bring back the status quo and put MultiReal in his hands once more. Would that be a good thing?

At that moment, a more exclusive set of doors opened, and the Prime Committee entered.

(((31)))

The members of the Prime Committee might have been any random selection of pedestrians off the street. Their composition was about as polychromatic as any group of twenty-nine could be. There was a slight preponderance of females and people of Indian descent—what the sociologists glibly called "the Surina effect"—but nothing that could produce an obvious prejudice toward any one demographic. All were dressed in matching robes of dark blue, filigreed with elaborate gold tracing. The iron symbol of the black ring hung from their necks.

The members filed around the auditorium to find their seats. Jara noticed that the Committee members' row did not intersect with any of the main auditorium stairways. In fact, the steps from the petitioners' row to the floor actually ducked *under* the Committee members' seats with a flourish of architectural bravado.

As the men and women sat on the uncomfortable-looking black chairs, each person's representative organization flashed in hologram before them: The Vault. The Creeds Coalition. Dr. Plugenpatch. The Meme Cooperative. TeleCo. GravCo. Orbital Colonies. The Congress of L-PRACGS. True to their governing philosophy, none of the members' names were anywhere to be found.

"What do the italics mean?" said Horvil to nobody in particular. Jara took a closer look, and sure enough, some of the affiliations were displayed in a slightly smaller, italicized font: *Islanders. Data Sea Network Administrators. Pharisees. The Prepared. TubeCo.*

"Nonvoting member," replied Ben, pleased to be the resident expert on something. "Twenty-nine reps total, but only twenty-three get a vote."

"I thought TubeCo was a voting member," said Merri, scratching her head.

"They were. Got booted off last year, remember? It was—"

Jara waved them all to silence. "They're about to start."

Everyone in the Committee members' ring rose dutifully and bowed in unison. It was a stirring sight, something Jara had seen often in Data Sea videos but never in person. For a moment, she felt like she was suspended above Melbourne in the tube car again, watching the reasoned and orderly process of government at work.

The members of the Prime Committee remained standing as a blue light swept around the ring three times like a roulette wheel and finally stopped in front of a nondescript woman from the Meme Cooperative. Apparently this meant she would be the randomly selected moderator for the proceedings. All the other representatives took their seats again.

The woman spoke. Some feat of aural wizardry allowed her voice to boom across the dome without distortion or reverberation. "This special session of the Prime Committee, held here on the fourteenth of January in the three hundred and sixtieth year of the Reawakening, will now come to order."

There was a brief pause as the Committee members' assistants shuffled into place beside the representatives and held quick, whispered conversations. Spectators around the auditorium gradually took their seats, and Council officers took up their posts, though they seemed in little hurry to do so. Jara took a glance at Natch. The entrepreneur simply looked dazed, like a tottering tree that might crash to the floor at any moment.

The Committee moderator continued. Jara got the impression that her words had been prepared ahead of time, that they were only coming from her mouth instead of someone else's out of sheer happenstance.

"We are at an important crossroads in history," said the woman. "For the past two hundred years, libertarians and governmentalists have been debating what the proper role of government should be. What powers should reside with the citizenry and what powers should reside with their governments? Should these governments be centralized or decentralized? Elected or appointed? Where does personal liberty end and public welfare begin?

"The Prime Committee cannot pretend to be the final arbiter of these questions.

"Nor is that our job. Though we may be governmentalists or libertarians in our personal philosophies, here we are all simply members of the Prime Committee. We speak with one voice, and we represent every citizen of the Reawakening. We provide oversight; we provide law and structure; and in times of crisis, we provide stability and judgment.

"It is in that last capacity that we sit before you today. The world is in a crisis. Vortexes of information are causing death and destruction from Earth to Furtoid. One of the beloved icons of the Reawakening has died under mysterious circumstances. Activists have taken to the streets and jammed the gears of commerce. And at the center of everything lies a powerful new technology the likes of which the world has never seen.

"Government cannot simply stand by and watch matters unfold. For better or worse, government must take action.

"Let it not be said afterward that the Prime Committee had already made up its mind before these sessions had begun. *Truth walks through open doors*, the Bodhisattva once said. We come to this hearing as representatives of the public welfare with no preconceived agenda, and we ask the observers of this hearing to do the same.

"The Committee wishes to emphasize that this is not a trial. As such, we will follow no formal procedures other than simple parliamentary rules of order. The Committee will call witnesses as it sees fit, in the order it sees fit, for as long as it takes to satisfy the questions at hand. We hereby command these witnesses to speak truthfully, honestly, and without reservation.

"Such is the agenda of the Prime Committee. Let any objections be entered into the record now."

Jara peered around the audience, wondering who would have the temerity to speak out against such a high-minded opening. But, of course, objections there were—a representative of the diss, demanding a voice in the proceedings and a seat on the Committee; a robed and bejeweled member of the Pharisee tribes, questioning the legitimacy of the entire centralized government; the outlandishly dressed bodhisattva of Creed Null, proclaiming imminent doom for all and sundry. The woman assigned to be the Prime Committee administrator nodded without comment as each exception was entered into the record. Obviously they had all performed these steps in the dance many times before. The dissenters even had a small reserved section to themselves right behind the petitioners' ring.

When the formal objections were complete, the woman took her seat once again. "The Prime Committee hereby calls upon Serr Vigal of the Surina/Natch MultiReal Fiefcorp to make a statement on behalf of the Congress of L-PRACGs," she said.

• • •

Serr Vigal made his way down the stairs and through the passageway that ran beneath the Committee members' ring. The passage emerged at the edge of the floor and ended in a waist-high gate of frosted glass. Vigal walked through this gate and found the center of the floor. Then he promptly rotated in place and gave several polite bows to the Committee members.

"Distinguished members of the Prime Committee," said Vigal, his voice resonant with a calm that went beyond bio/logics. "I'm honored to be in your presence today. Usually when I stand before a government body, I'm there to ask for money. You'll be pleased to know that I plan on making no such appeals today—unless, I suppose, my speech goes very, very well."

A chuckle worked its way around the crowd, even levitating the lips of a few in the ruling circle. Jara had to admit that it was a promising beginning: disarmingly humble, homespun. She looked over and saw Khann Frejohr and his libertarian comrades displaying bland, pleasant smiles. Natch merely stared straight ahead.

Vigal continued. "So what better issue to begin my inaugural speech of political advocacy than the issue before the Committee today? I speak of the paramount right of humanity. The force that has guided and steered us for a hundred thousand years or more. I speak of *freedom*.

"Yes, on the surface, it might seem like the debate over MultiReal is a debate over government regulation or business practice or some other arcane matter. That is certainly what Len Borda wants you to think. The drudges would have you think that this is just a clash of forceful personalities. They would tell you that the issue is the stubbornness of one particular fiefcorp master present here today. Natch, stand up so everyone can see you."

A thousand pairs of eyeballs pivoted toward the entrepreneur, who had seemed not to be paying attention. But at Serr Vigal's call, Natch's face suddenly lit up with humanity as if he had received a charge of electric current. He rose and delivered as warm a smile to the crowd as Jara had ever seen him deliver. Across the floor, Jara could see Magan Kai Lee's icy glare and Rey Gonerev's dour frown.

Five seconds later, Natch was seated once more, his comportment robotic, his skin pale.

"I'm sure many of you have heard the tale that the drudges are spinning," said Vigal. "You've heard the rumors and innuendo that High Executive Borda has leaked on the Data Sea. You've read selective bits of Natch's personal history and the accusation that he is 'ethically challenged.'" The neural programmer made a flippant clicking noise with his tongue. "It is impossible for me to be objective about Natch's moral fitness—a topic that was my primary responsibility for eighteen years while I was his legal guardian—so I won't pretend otherwise. I also hold an advisory position in the Surina/Natch MultiReal Fiefcorp, so my subjectivity about the company is similarly compromised.

"But these rumors about Natch and his business practices are merely a distraction. A diversion from the real issue at hand. I propose we dispense with such irrelevancies and skip to the heart of the matter instead. The part Len Borda doesn't want you to talk about.

"What is the central issue here? As I said before, the central issue is freedom. Let me draw your attention to one of the adages of the first Bodhisattva of Creed Objectivv: *Knowledge wants to flow to freedom like rivers want to flow to the sea.*

"It's not for nothing that we call our vast compendium of knowledge the Data Sea. It's no accident that all the droplets of wisdom humanity has learned over its history have ended up here. Because information *wants* to flow Seaward. I'm not speaking of want here like we *want* money, or like some of those in the Council desperately *want* me to stop talking."

Another rumble of laughter. Even Lieutenant Executive Lee raised his eyebrows in amusement.

"I'm talking about the natural laws of the universe, the tendencies built into its very structure. Gravity pulls things down. Water flows to the sea. And knowledge flows to freedom. That's simply how things work.

"But you can't own the sea, can you?

"Oh, sometimes you can control its flow. You can erect dams; you can bottle up the water and keep it in a safe place. But these are only temporary solutions, aren't they? Eventually the dam decays. The bottle breaks. Those you have entrusted to keep the water safe wander away, or they grow old and shift allegiances. And when all else fails, water evaporates and is reclaimed by the sun." Vigal gestured toward the top of the dome, and many eyes followed his gesture as if they might actually see something besides the dull stone of the curved ceiling.

"High Executive Len Borda has been vigorously pursuing the Surina/Natch Fiefcorp's MultiReal technology," said the neural programmer. "Why? The high executive does not say. But it is widely believed that he wishes to bottle up MultiReal. He wishes to cask it and store it safely in his private vaults.

"Again I ask, why?

"We hear many rumors from the drudges, and sometimes it's difficult to separate fact from fiction. I have read articles claiming that the high executive plans to weaponize MultiReal and put it in the hands of every officer in his Defense and Wellness Council. There is a suspicious memorandum circulating on the Data Sea which claims that the high executive will use this technology to conquer the recalcitrant Islander and Pharisee territories once and for all. Some of the protesters on the streets right now have an even more radical idea—they think Len Borda will use MultiReal to do away with *you*, the august members of the Prime Committee.

"Let me suggest something that might surprise you, coming from someone who represents the libertarian wing of the Congress of L-PRACGs. I suggest we give High Executive Borda the benefit of the doubt."

In the libertarian delegation, Speaker Khann Frejohr let out a hearty laugh. Jara couldn't tell if he was laughing at the absurdity of trusting Len Borda or at the coy way Vigal had proposed it.

"High Executive Len Borda," said Vigal, extending a hand toward the group of Council officers. "The man entrusted with the safety and security of sixty billion people. The man who steered us through the Economic Plunge and the Melbourne riots and the Islander wars. High Executive Borda, who has faithfully served the Council and the Prime Committee for nearly sixty years. The man who, incidentally, handed a very green programmer named Serr Vigal his first government subsidy some forty years ago. We have no reason not to trust Len Borda, do we?

"So let us dismiss these conspiracy theories about the high executive's intentions and assume he intends to do the prudent thing. Let us assume he intends to seal up MultiReal forever in the depths of the government's vaults, never to be touched by human hands again.

"There is too much rancor in modern politics. I say, let us trust him!

"Good ladies and gentlemen of the Prime Committee, I ask you this question: how long can Borda hope to keep MultiReal bottled up?

"The high executive keeps many secrets, but I assume the secret of immortality is not one of them. Someday—let's hope it's fifty years from now!—someday Len Borda will slip into the Null Current like we all must, and a new high executive will be appointed. Maybe you will be the ones to appoint that high executive, or maybe that task will fall to another group of equally dedicated Prime Committee members. You know in your hearts that you're good, decent, honest people. Your dedication to the public welfare is beyond question. But what about your successors? Do you know what will lie in their hearts? Do you trust *them* to keep the secrets of MultiReal hidden?

"Then one day, those government servants too will go off to join the Prepared. Another crop will rise and enjoy its day in the sun. Do you trust *them*? And then another crop will follow. Then another. Fifty, a hundred, two hundred, five hundred years will pass. Do you still trust that every single man and woman to occupy those chairs for time unending will have the same goodwill and common sense that you do? What if another Zetarysis the Mad worms her way into power? Can you be so certain that *none* of your thousands of successors will one day decide to uncork a bottle of that prime vintage of information Len Borda laid down in his cellars?

"But it's not only future members of the Prime Committee that we have to worry about. Because while we all molder in the dust and our children's children's children play their political games, the water in those casks continues to struggle towards freedom. It *wants* to flow to freedom, remember? And so every year, despite your most careful stewardship, precious droplets evaporate into the air and back to the common well of knowledge. Every year, the enemies of the state work to steal that magic draft away from you. Enterprising programmers work to re-create and reverse engineer that well of information. All it takes is a single misstep, a single misplaced allegiance, and those barrels of information will come crashing to the floor and spill into the lowest sewer.

"That is what the world wants. And if I have learned one thing in my long and illustrious career, it is that you cannot stop the wants of the world.

"Let me put the clever metaphors and the verbal puffery aside for a moment and state plainly what should be obvious by now. The government *will* eventually lose control of MultiReal. You cannot keep it secret forever."

Solemn, unblinking eyes regarded the neural programmer from around the chamber. Not a sound could be heard from the crowd. Jara looked at the rest of the fiefcorpers to find them nodding gravely, snared deep in thought. Robby Robby was studying Vigal's every movement like a dance master critiquing an especially intricate ballet.

Serr Vigal clasped his hands behind his back and walked a slow, steady track around the floor. "Now let's look at another alternative," he said. "Let us imagine that after long and careful deliberation, the Prime Committee decides that the draft is not to be bottled up.

"No, I'm not suggesting we immediately pipe MultiReal code into the public trough for anyone to gulp down. I suggest something much more practical. I suggest the Committee call an end to the vendetta that the Defense and Wellness Council has executed against Natch and his apprentices. Restore this fiefcorp master to his fiefcorp. Let the Surina/Natch MultiReal Fiefcorp—and the Patel Brothers Fiefcorp as well, naturally—let them continue to refine their distinctive brews of MultiReal and sell them to the public. With a healthy amount of safeguards and government oversight, of course.

"What would happen in that scenario?

"We don't need a crystal ball to see that. Let me tell you what is happening right now, even as this hearing proceeds in Melbourne. At this very moment, tens of thousands of L-PRACG politicians are sitting in meeting halls, locked in heated debate. Governmentalists and libertarians and every flavor in between are furiously writing bills. Speaker Frejohr's office informs me that four hundred L-PRACGs have already banned their citizens from using MultiReal. The Islanders have been preparing a Dogmatic Opposition to the technology for weeks now.

"And perfection sustain them all for doing so! What did the great Sheldon Surina say? *Progress is the expansion of choices.* If the bottle of knowledge passes your way and you choose not to drink, so be it. That is your right and your privilege as a citizen of a modern, rational civilization. Nobody wishes to force this knowledge on you.

"So, as with any new technology, we have the doubters and the slow adopters. Some will choose to sit back and sip this new brew cautiously until it finds its way into the mainstream. Undoubtedly some will engorge themselves until they're sick, causing trouble for themselves and everyone around them.

"And some? I will not lie to you. A sullen few will choose to poison the well for everyone else. They'll use this intoxicating draft to further their selfish schemes, to break the law, to take advantage of others. This has been the way of human nature since the beginning, and we cannot pretend that it will change overnight.

"So how do we deal with such scofflaws? Why, the same way we've always dealt with them. By punishing the guilty. By protecting the innocent. By using the laws of the Congress, the Committee, and the L-PRACGs as our shields, and the officers of the Council as our swords.

"Distinguished members of the Prime Committee, let me conclude by saying this.

"The democratization of MultiReal is not something you should consider because the libertarians believe in it, or the governmentalists don't. Do not believe the chatter that this is a question of politics or a clash of personalities. Len Borda's desires are irrelevant. *Natch's* desires are irrelevant. You should allow private businesses to sell MultiReal to the public because that's what the *world* desires.

"MultiReal will flow freely, whether you wish it or not. That decision is not yours to make. What *you* have to decide is whether to swim against the tide or to take the more practical approach and work with it.

"I thank you, and may you all move towards perfection."

(((32)))

Serr Vigal stayed on the floor of the auditorium to answer the Prime Committee's questions for almost two hours, but Jara found it difficult to concentrate. The neural programmer's speech had jolted the fiefcorp from its stupor of pessimism and given them a faint taste of hope. By the grins on their faces, Khann Frejohr and his libertarian cronies tasted it too. The city that had seemed like a bloodthirsty circus this morning suddenly felt like a place of rational discourse and negotiation; in short, like a center of government.

"Ridglee's gloating," said a jubilant Horvil to the rest of the fiefcorpers over ConfidentialWhisper. "*Who would have thought that the greatest surge of momentum the libertarian movement has seen in years would come from a soft-spoken code pusher from the memecorps?*"

Robby Robby was taming stray tufts of perm with his fingernails. "What'd I tell ya, Queen Jara?"

"You're right," 'Whispered Jara. "You *did* tell me. I just didn't believe Vigal had it in him." She looked down at the neural programmer with new respect. He was responding to a diatribe by the Vault representative with reserve and polish.

"Well, don't start celebrating just yet," said Benyamin. "Vertiginous is still pretty sour about our chances. *Serr Vigal pitted the soft sentimentality of 'freedom' against the hard-edged realities of safety and security. I think the libertarians will find soon enough that the Blade is more than capable of slicing through those arguments.*"

Merri: "Anybody catch Natch's reaction?"

There was a glum silence as the fiefcorpers took turns glancing at the entrepreneur, who appeared not to have moved or even blinked in the last hour. He might have been a marionette propped up in his chair, eyes fixed on nowhere and nothing.

"Well, we have one thing to be thankful for," said Horvil a little while later as the company arose as one to stretch. The Prime Committee had just thanked Serr Vigal for his testimony and adjourned the hearing for the day.

"What's that?" said Jara.

"We're not going to get any more grief from those MultiReal exposition lottery winners. Captain Bolbund's just been arrested. Practicing law without a license."

• • •

After observing the change of the guard at the Defense and Wellness Council's Melbourne complex, after annotating the transcript of Serr Vigal's remarks to the Prime Committee, after examining and reexamining the black code in his dart-rifle, after scouring through the voluminous document that was the Council's budget for the new year, Magan Kai Lee finally admitted he had nothing to do.

He looked around the office—his home base in Melbourne—where he had chosen to while away the evening hours. It was a cramped space, an ill-advised and hastily constructed partition of an executive office meant for three. Moreover, the prospects for expansion were grim, considering there was no collapsible infrastructure here and you had to actually find people to *move* furniture. Rearranging stone walls was out of the question.

And yet Magan much preferred this office to his more commodious quarters at Defense and Wellness Council Root. In Len Borda's fortress, you never knew precisely where you would find yourself when you stepped outside the door; things moved, walls moved, people moved. But here in Melbourne, geography was firm and unyielding. Stable. You could plan where you were going and expect that plan to stick.

Magan turned his attention back to the budget document still floating on the window. It was the perfect example of the Bordaesque worldview, a labyrinth of ambiguously worded codicils and provisos, unnavigable to all but the initiated, designed to shift at a moment's notice.

But the Prime Committee's attentions were focused on the Multi-Real situation at the moment. So the budget had sailed through all the requisite subcommittees, and no one at the Congress of L-PRACGs had given it much scrutiny either. Thus the high executive's budget would go into effect without delay, as Borda had predicted, and the escalation of troops and materiel on the border of the Islander territories would continue unnoticed, as Borda had predicted. Even if someone wanted to object at this point, it was too late. Tomorrow was already January 15, the first calendar day of the new year's budget. Credits would start flowing to the designated Council Vault accounts in just over an hour.

Lieutenant Executive Lee waved his hand and blanked out the window display. An empty stone courtyard embossed with a giant yellow star stared back at him.

January 15.

I give you until the fifteenth of January to take possession of MultiReal, Borda had told him, standing in that accursed naval SeeNaRee of his. *If you do, we have an agreement. If you don't . . .*

With all that had happened in the interim—the infoquakes, the protests, the death of Margaret Surina, Natch's change of fortune— would Len Borda insist on holding to this arrangement? Would he take such a narrow-minded interpretation of their agreement even now, when the Council was a mere handful of votes away from legal control of MultiReal?

And if so, what would he do?

Magan fired off a secure ConfidentialWhisper to Ridgello. Ridgello, the dependable. Ridgello, the antithesis of mercurial Borda-ism. "Double the guard at the Tul Jabbor Complex," said Magan. "I need you ready for anything tomorrow."

The commander responded within seconds, despite the late hour.
"It's done. What should I be anticipating?"

"Anything."

• • •

Natch, lying on the mattress of some anonymous Melbourne hotel,
slick with sweat, fighting a turbulent battle against sleep with half a
dozen invigoration programs as confederates. Grappling with slumber
and exhaustion.

The guardian and the keeper.

*You'll resist Len Borda to your dying breath. You will resist the winter
and the void.*

Hack the body, and the mind will follow.

He flailed himself out of bed, threw on a dressing gown as insulation from the world, and reeled over to the red square tile in the corner.
The lights instantly shifted to candle strength, throwing the shadow
of the desk onto the tile and turning it a harsh crimson.

Then he was on the tile. Then he was falling, plummeting into
multivoid.

His apartment looked different somehow through the prism of the
multi network. All his accoutrements were precisely where he had left
them, down to the bio/logic programming bar that had fallen on the
floor and the partially filled glass of water he had set on the counter
two days ago. Still, there was some indefinable *thing* missing: an aura,
a presence, an element that lay just below the threshold of corporeality.

No time.

Natch stumbled into his office and waved his hand over the desk to
summon the MindSpace bubble. It expanded out from the tabletop at
not-quite-instantaneous speed until it had swallowed up the desk, swallowed up him. Hovering in the middle of it, as always, the stray Multi-
Real code Horvil had found in his neural system. The yellow jacket.

Black code, sucking out his life blood ounce by ounce. MultiReal, warping his mental facilities. The one either sheathed or entombed within the other.

The nothingness at the center of the universe.

He reached for the rings, Quell's golden rings, the programmers' pick and shovel, math's household staff. Buried in the confines of his robe pocket. Impossible for a multi projection to reach? Not tonight. Natch felt his ethereal multied fingers take on essence and solidify in the crisp night air, motes of dust made flesh. He clasped the programming rings, and they responded.

Thaumaturgic energy crackled inside the bubble as his ringed fingers entered MindSpace. Threads of data leapt to his fingertips.

Natch attacked.

He bombarded the blob of code with sudden swoops and dives, contorting his fingers into torturous configurations. The data strands obeyed his commands. Arcane formulas pounded against the surface of the yellow jacket like flak as Natch sweated on, minute after minute, hour after agonizing hour. Day cloaked itself in night, night burst from day's cocoon, over and over again. And then, as he was on the verge of losing hope, it happened . . . the slightest hairline crack in the surface of the mysterious code. . . .

Blackness.

He came to on the floor of the office, dazed, angry. Still in multi, or maybe he wasn't—what did it matter anymore? Day/night, meat/multi, awake/asleep: he no longer had confidence in such dualities.

The illicit code mocked him from MindSpace. It mocked him with the voice of Petrucio Patel, telling him he was not worthy to join the elite ranks of Primo's. It mocked him with the voice of Captain Bolbund, telling him he did not have the finesse to attract customers. Brone, pitying him for lagging so far behind in the fight for MultiReal. Margaret, tricking him into signing a defective contract. Magan Kai Lee, brushing him off as irrelevant.

Standing behind the workbench was a boy. Sandy hair. Ocean blue eyes.

Who are you? Natch asked the youth. *How did you get in here?*

The boy shook his head and smirked. Physically he was on the cusp of adulthood—perhaps fifteen years old—yet he carried an air of childish vulnerability that belied the cocksure expression on his face. *Come on, even you can figure this one out.*

Natch found his feet and brushed himself off. *So what do you want?*

The boy made a slow, sweeping gesture around the office as if unveiling a key exhibit at a crucial juncture in trial. Natch followed the fingertips and took in the sturdy bio/logic programming bars sprawled across the workbench where he had dropped them the other day; the stool with the notch on one leg, lolling drunkenly in the corner; the viewscreen with its permanent display of chaotic financial exchanges; the ersatz Persian rug that Horvil had solemnly presented to him as a housewarming gift.

They walked into the bedroom, where the boy performed a similar clockwork motion at the tasteful portraits of Very Influential Persons arranged neatly on the walls; the window tuned in to a gentle Himalayan snow; the armoire that held the small assortment of clothing he had purchased over the years.

The living room was next, with its familiar chair-and-a-half and sofa; its luxurious garden of daisies and buttercups dividing the room like a moat; its glass balcony door facing the snow-carpeted hills; its Tope and Pulgarti paintings bracketing the small foyer and front door.

Finally came the kitchen, scene of a thousand late-night mugs of nitro and early-afternoon bottles of ChaiQuoke; the camouflaged white tile of the sink; the access panel to the building's communal larder and its high-class variety of foodstuffs; the small range he had purchased, at great expense, for the sole purpose of heating pots of Serr Vigal's peculiar British tea.

Natch turned to the youth, wondering if there was some lesson to be learned here. His apartment bore no mysteries, and he liked it that way. If there was an epiphany to be found taking inventory of life's unremarkables, it had bypassed Natch entirely.

So what was all that for? he said.

Hope you got a good look, replied the boy, brushing a strand of hair from his forehead. *You're never going to see any of it again.*

(((33)))

Jara slept well that night, for the first time in who knew how many weeks. The rest of the fiefcorpers apparently did too. Serr Vigal's surprising performance hadn't completely reversed their fortunes in the struggle for MultiReal—for their company—but at the very least, the neural programmer had put the brakes on their downward momentum.

Things aren't worse today than they were yesterday, Jara reflected as she led the Surina/Natch contingent past the giant holograph of Tul Jabbor. *Not much of an accomplishment, but I'll take it.*

They arrived early and took the same seats in the petitioners' ring they had occupied yesterday. While they waited, Jara consulted the drudge alerts, which were predictably fragmented in tone this morning. Benyamin and Horvil discussed soccer scores.

The participants to the hearing trickled in over the next fifteen minutes. On the libertarian side of the ring, there were smiles, laughs, and the occasional back slap. Frejohr and his supporters were ruddy with confidence as they congratulated Serr Vigal on his speech yesterday; the delegation even took the extraordinary step of scooting a few seats closer to Natch. Vigal made sure to deliver a warm wave in the fiefcorp's direction, which Jara returned.

So if things are going so well for us, thought the analyst, *how come the Council doesn't look worried?*

Jara swept her gaze through the auditorium at the officers in the white robes and yellow stars. There seemed to be more of them today, but that didn't necessarily mean anything. It wasn't the attitude of the rank-and-file that bothered her, but the attitude of their superior officers. Lieutenant Executive Magan Kai Lee didn't look perturbed in the slightest by the libertarians' jovial mood. On the contrary, Magan remained as mysterious and aloof as ever. The tactician Papizon lurked behind his right shoulder, ungainly as a heron, with his head tilted and his mouth splayed open. Only Rey Gonerev expressed any recognizable human emotion—and that emotion, Jara noted with a shudder, was pure disdain.

As for Natch, his demeanor was even more vacant than yesterday, like a man standing on an active multi tile. He neither saw nor acknowledged Jara's tentative wave hello.

Moments later, the lights dimmed as the twenty-nine members of the Prime Committee solemnly filed in to their exclusive ring with retinues in tow. After a smattering of ceremonial niceties, the moderator stepped forward and called the Defense and Wellness Council's chief solicitor, Rey Gonerev.

The quiet rustle of audience noise died as the Blade stepped into the center of the auditorium. She stood in the floor's exact focal point for a moment and gathered her thoughts, looking as slim and deadly as a needle. And then she opened her mouth and let the words march out like some rumbling army of justice.

"My word is the will of the Defense and Wellness Council, which was established by the Prime Committee two hundred and fifty-three years ago to ensure the security of all persons throughout the system. The word of the Council is the word of the people."

●   ●   ●

Perhaps it was Rey Gonerev's height, which allowed her to address the Committee members without craning her head too far; perhaps it was the fifteen years of security and intelligence briefings that had taught her the nuances of the auditorium; perhaps it was a genetic trait common to all high-ranking Council officials. Whatever the reason, the Blade took to the floor of the Tul Jabbor Complex as if it were her natural habitat.

"The libertarians say they want to give you freedom," began the Blade, her diction precise, her words carefully crafted. "What you will get is madness."

A murmur swept through the audience. *Let the slicing commence,* thought Jara.

The chief solicitor walked the marble floor with a dancer's grace, long braids swaying hypnotically behind her. Throughout her speech, she found occasion to lance each one of the Prime Committee members with her glare—and without exception, Jara noticed, Gonerev was never the first to turn away.

"Margaret Surina stood before the world and declared that the future would be an age of MultiReal," continued Gonerev. "It was just a few weeks ago, at her auditorium in Andra Pradesh. Margaret stood in front of several hundred million people, and she promised us *the ultimate freedom.* She promised us *the ultimate empowerment.* She promised to deliver us from *the tyranny of cause and effect.*

"Our libertarian colleagues have bought into this vision wholesale. They've trumpeted Margaret's words up and down the Data Sea without bothering to examine them closely. And why should they? It's a simple argument, after all. What's wrong with freedom? Everybody wants freedom! How can you have too much freedom?

"The esteemed neural programmer Serr Vigal put an even finer point on it yesterday, right here in this auditorium. *Gravity pulls things down. Water flows to the sea. And knowledge flows to freedom,* he said. *Multi-Real will flow freely, whether you wish it or not. That decision is not yours to make.*"

Across the auditorium, Vigal stroked his goatee and nodded, lost in contemplation.

"So then let's all exercise our complete freedom and give in to the wants of the world!" said the Blade. "Is the person sitting next to you wearing an expensive coat? Why not just take it? Obviously, the world *wants* you to have it, because a hundred thousand generations of human evolution planted that lust for acquisition in you. Go ahead; take whatever you want. The offended party can always seek redress from the law.

"Some of you in the Committee members' ring roll your eyes, and I hear a few groans from the audience. That's fine. It's a childish example. Then again, complete and unrestrained freedom is a childish idea. It's an embarrassment that I even have to stand here and explain it.

"Why don't you steal that fancy coat? Is it fear of punishment and retribution that keeps you honest? No. You don't steal because you can't always be a slave to your desires. Desire isn't the only instinct we've inherited from our ancestors; that tug of conscience in your gut was planted there by a hundred thousand generations of human evolution too.

"Humanity abandoned complete and unrestrained freedom thousands of years ago. Instead we chose the social contract. We chose to deliberately set aside our personal wants for the good of the group. Do not steal. Do not kill. Do not cheat. Why abide by these restrictions on personal liberty? Because we've seen the alternative, and we've chosen stability.

"Yes, we've deliberately *chosen* this path, time and time again. Hundreds of years ago, the Autonomous Minds *liberated* us from the rule of the nation-states. A chance to start over! A chance to reshape society! Humanity had a choice between the anarchy of radical individualism and the constancy of the lawful society. What happened? The globe descended into chaos for a while—and then, acting independently without coordination, our ancestors chose the social contract once again.

"The concept is very simple, and it works every time. We put aside personal ambitions that are harmful to the group. . . . Society benefits by becoming a more stable and predictable place. . . . And then we *each* reap the benefits of that stable society.

"The result? Bio/logics. The Data Sea. The multi network. Teleportation.

"Not only did we choose the social contract—but we *expanded* it and *codified* it with the creation of the L-PRACG. We set those compromises down in explicit government contracts written in clear and simple language. Here is what you are giving up. Here is what you are gaining.

"Is society moving towards personal freedom? Yes, I believe it is. History and technology prove Margaret Surina's point that there is an undeniable curve towards liberty. Freedom of movement, freedom of expression, freedom of government. Yet societies do not adapt as quickly as individuals do. We must consider change slowly and examine its costs carefully.

"But is such compromise not enough for you? Do you yearn for that ultimate freedom without compromise? You can have it, any time you want! Simply halt your government subscriptions, stop paying your fees, and float out with the diss. It's that easy. No one will stop you. In fact, the Prime Committee has *prohibited* governments from keeping citizens on their membership rosters by force or coercion. Some L-PRACGs will actually pay you to leave the ranks of another L-PRACG.

"But such freedom is still not good enough for some in the libertarian movement. And so they found a champion—a Surina, no less, daughter of scientists and freethinkers. *The social contract is a thing of the past!* she claimed. *Let's do away with limitations! Let's embrace ultimate freedom!*

"We don't need a global experiment to see where that path leads. If you're interested in seeing the end result of complete and unrestricted liberty, look no further than this man Natch."

Rey Gonerev stopped in front of Natch and extended one talon straight toward his chest. Jara leaned forward and looked at the entrepreneur's expression. He seemed oblivious to the chief solicitor's finger, to the hushed attention of thousands of spectators. And then, just as the Blade lowered her hand and started to speak again, Jara could see a macabre smile creep onto Natch's face.

The solicitor resumed her speech. "Here in this auditorium sits the ultimate freedom made flesh. Ladies and gentlemen, I give you Natch, former master of the Surina/Natch MultiReal Fiefcorp! A man who recognizes no laws but his own, who ignores all boundaries but those that suit his own purposes. Here is a man who has ruthlessly rejected the social contract time and time again for his own personal self-gratification. To enrich his own freedom, if you will.

"And what has Natch chosen to do with that freedom?

"At the age of fifteen, he got into a quarrel with another boy during initiation. Did he settle his differences with words and arguments? No, Natch got his revenge by leading an enraged bear into his camp. Three boys died as a result, and a fourth was horribly maimed.

"At the age of eighteen, Natch masterminded a scam to steal customers from a rival programmer by impersonating government officers. The Meme Cooperative was unable to gather enough evidence to prosecute him. Instead, his rival was convicted of these crimes and the rival's license was suspended.

"At the age of twenty, Natch received his first—but not his last—fine from the Meme Cooperative for possession of black code. A petty crime and a negligible punishment? Yes—but the result of a plea bargain with authorities who were once again unable to find enough evidence to make any charges stick.

"By the age of twenty-four, when he founded the Natch Personal Programming Fiefcorp, this man was regularly violating the rules of the Meme Cooperative. To date, the Defense and Wellness Council has cataloged a list of a hundred and twenty such violations. And believe me, those are only the ones we have sufficient evidence to prove before an arbitration board.

"At the age of twenty-eight, Natch made a suspicious deal to merge his fiefcorp with a shell company of Margaret Surina's. Even though he was younger and less experienced than his rivals—even though he had little money to bring to the table—Margaret gave Natch a fifty percent stake in her revolutionary MultiReal technology. Why? What would drive a woman to spend two decades researching and developing a product, and then blithely hand it over to someone she had just met? We can only imagine.

"Within days of his arrangement with Margaret Surina, Natch made a large cash payment to Creed Thassel. Creed Thassel, an organization notorious for secrecy and deceit.

"Within six weeks, Natch tried to blackmail the Defense and Wellness Council by threatening to auction off MultiReal on the Data Sea to the highest bidder.

"Within hours of that performance, Margaret Surina, bodhisattva of Creed Surina and creator of MultiReal technology, was dead.

"And within hours of *that*, a member of Natch's own fiefcorp launched a preemptive attack on Lieutenant Executive Magan Kai Lee as he was gathering evidence at the scene of Surina's murder.

"And by sheer luck—by the merest coincidence—there was a worldwide outbreak of libertarian unrest last week, just when public opinion began to turn against this man. A memo began to circulate on the Data Sea, and not even the Council's most ardent critics claim to have any evidence for its authenticity. This unrest sparked into violence at the funeral of Margaret Surina, the very emblem of the freedom that our libertarian colleagues revere.

"Does Natch revere the accomplishments of the Surinas, or does he mock them?

"Natch's legal guardian stood before you the other day and proposed we give this man *the ultimate freedom*. He made a very shrewd and clever speech where he tried to put the struggle for MultiReal in a larger libertarian context.

"So let's do as he bids! Let's put this man permanently beyond the power of the Defense and Wellness Council—because with MultiReal at his command, no Council officer will be able to restrain him. Let's put this man beyond the power of any government authority—or didn't you notice that MultiReal doesn't require approval from Dr. Plugenpatch and the Meme Cooperative? Let's make sure this man isn't even accountable to the marketplace that the libertarians so venerate—because with the money he'll make from MultiReal, he won't even need to submit his programs to the Primo's bio/logic investment guide.

"Serr Vigal proposes we strip this man Natch of all restraints and limitations, just to see what he does. A little experiment, if you will.

"So I ask the esteemed members of the Prime Committee: what does Natch plan to do with the ultimate freedom that MultiReal provides? What do *you* think he'll do? Will he try to lift the diss out of poverty? Will he pursue diplomacy between the Islanders and the Pharisees? Will he set up a charitable fund for orphans?"

Rey Gonerev paused for a moment to let the point sink in. Jara looked around and noticed that the atmosphere in the Tul Jabbor Complex had grown irretrievably gloomy since the chief solicitor began her speech. The smiles that had adorned the faces of her fellow fiefcorpers a mere hour ago had all but disappeared. Across the floor, the bodhisattva of Creed Libertas looked worried, and Khann Frejohr looked downright grim.

The Blade struck a humble pose as she continued in a less emphatic tone of voice. "So what does the Defense and Wellness Council propose we do about this man?" she said. "What does the Council want with this technology?

"Some believe that Len Borda seeks to lock up MultiReal forever or put a permanent moratorium on it. They claim the Council wishes to use it as some kind of doomsday weapon. They speak as if there are no shades of gray in the argument—as if our only choices are for the government to enact a total ban on MultiReal or for MultiReal to be distributed to every man, woman, and child from here to Furtoid.

"As you ponder the situation we face, I want you to remember this. It's the libertarians who want to limit your options, not High Executive Borda. Not the Defense and Wellness Council.

"But before we come to the point where you must make a decision about the fate of MultiReal, I believe the time has come to demonstrate what's at stake. I think the men and women of the Prime Committee should see the power of MultiReal firsthand.

"And so before I take any questions, I'd like to call one of the few people who has experienced the power of MultiReal firsthand to give us a brief demonstration.

"If it pleases the Prime Committee, I'd like to ask Petrucio Patel, master of the Patel Brothers Fiefcorp, to step forward."

• • •

Jara made an audible hiss, though she wasn't sure why she felt so surprised. Had she really thought the only other company marketing MultiReal products would be able to avoid testifying before the Prime Committee?

As Petrucio Patel emerged from a door on the governmentalist side of the auditorium, Jara had to admit that the fiefcorp master looked all too prepared for this summons. The shoulder pads of his robe filled out his otherwise lanky frame, transforming him from a lean alley cat into a sultry, confident panther. Petrucio smiled, nodded briefly at the audience, and gave his mustache a final grooming stroke as he reached Rey Gonerev's side. In his right hand, he held a baseball bat. Under his left arm, a box.

The Blade whispered something inaudible to Petrucio, and by the way his shoulders tensed Jara could tell he wasn't pleased. Seconds later, he removed his scarf to reveal a prominent pin featuring the black-and-white swirled logo of Creed Objectivv. *So the Council still has its daggers in the Patel Brothers*, Jara thought.

The muttering among the libertarian sympathizers in the audience rose several decibels, and Jara could see one of the Council guards nearby tense up. Khann Frejohr and his libertarian allies looked perturbed. Natch did not seem to care one way or the other.

Horvil and Benyamin, meanwhile, were having an intense back-and-forth about parliamentary rules of order. "Can Gonerev even *do* that?" said Ben in a heated whisper. "Can she just call forward her own witness?"

"It's a hearing, not a trial," replied Horvil, gesturing at the Vault representative in the row directly below them. "And it doesn't look like any of the Committee members are about to object." In fact, some of them were craning forward in their wrought-iron chairs to get a better look.

The analyst thought back to her meeting with the Patel Brothers and desperately tried to remember the exact wording of their discussion. Had Petrucio said anything about helping or hindering the company's pursuit of MultiReal? Jara had purposefully kept the wording of their brief agreement vague. Would a demonstration of MultiReal before the Prime Committee violate that agreement in any way? What if Petrucio had already made a conflicting agreement with the Council several months earlier? The analyst took a sidelong glance at Merri, feeling a new appreciation for the difficulties of the Objectivv truth-telling oath.

"Towards Perfection," said Petrucio to the Prime Committee, his poise recovered. He set the box down on the floor and made a sweeping bow that encompassed all 360 degrees of the circle. "It's an honor to be called before the Committee."

Rey Gonerev reached down into the box and pulled out a classic league baseball. "Before we get into more extensive demonstrations, I'd like to start by reenacting Natch's performance at Andra Pradesh last month," she said. "Petrucio, why don't you tell us what you're doing."

Patel nodded and moved into a batter's crouch, which looked quite absurd in such a loosely tailored robe. "I'm going to hit the ball into the fourth ring of the auditorium, three rows above the gentleman from the orbital colonies," he said, arching his chin in that direction. "I'm now reaching out to the MultiReal interface and preparing to activate it."

A rumble.

The Blade stepped back several paces and made an underhanded pitch to the bio/logic programmer.

Petrucio got ready to swing. "Activating—"

And then Natch was out of his seat, hurtling through the small passage under the Committee members' ring onto the floor of the auditorium. His eyes screamed insanity; his arms signaled panic.

The ball connected with Petrucio's bat, and the infoquake was upon them.

(((34)))

The baseball arced into the audience somewhere above Jara's head. She never thought about it again.

Such was the force of the infoquake that even the fleet-footed Magan Kai Lee was tossed hither and thither like a pinball. Jara gaped in disbelief at the purple bruise mushrooming on the Council lieutenant's forehead, then found herself sucked down into Benyamin's lap. She hadn't even realized she had stood up in the first place. Within seconds, the entire fiefcorp was tangled in a confused pile, and Robby Robby's bony ass might have been the only thing that kept a falling spectator from snapping Jara's neck in two.

Voices in her head. Deep gouges in her mental databases. OCHREs furiously pinging Dr. Plugenpatch. Notices warnings screams ConfidentialWhispers—

Jara clambered to her feet and managed to bring her internal systems to something a few rungs down from normalcy. The trick was to avoid the reflex to fire up bio/logic relief and to shut *down* as many programs as possible instead. She clutched the railing and looked around the auditorium.

In the few minutes since the infoquake began, the Tul Jabbor Complex had descended into pandemonium. Prime Committee members and their retinues were ducking, cowering, fleeing through side exits. Jara recognized the staid Plugenpatch representative standing on his chair, yelling an indecipherable plea for calm. Down on the auditorium floor, the Blade had found her way to the wall and was wobbling against it on unsteady feet. Meanwhile, a confused Petrucio Patel was staring at the baseball bat in his hands in shock. The end of it was stained red from his own bloody nose, though how he had acquired that was unclear.

Petrucio had nothing to do with this, Jara thought. *He's just as surprised as anyone. But if Petrucio Patel didn't launch this attack—then who did?*

She surveyed the remaining members of the Prime Committee, quailing under their wrought-iron chairs, and had another insight: the libertarians had just lost their case. Moments ago, the Committee had been the very model of probity and open-mindedness; now they were surrendering to dumb animal panic. Animals banded together when threatened and sought to protect themselves at all costs. No, despite Vigal's lofty rhetoric and common sense, Jara could see that nothing would persuade the Prime Committee to overrule Len Borda now.

So the infoquake was a tool of Len Borda's then? A desperate attempt to thumb down the scales of justice? Natch had expressed that opinion several times, and Jara had been inclined to agree with him.

But something didn't quite add up. If the high executive was going to execute such an attack, wouldn't he have prepared the guards of the Defense and Wellness Council first? The officers in white robes and yellow stars were milling around the auditorium in confusion like everyone else, cut off from their chain of command and unsure what to do. Some were attempting to herd audience members out the doors peaceably, while others were trying to block the doors and keep everyone inside.

If the infoquake is a governmentalist plot, thought the analyst, *then why isn't the government ready for it?*

"What's going on?" mumbled a voice. Merri, struggling to find her feet in a quite literal sense, as they were buried under Horvil and Robby.

"We need to get out of here," said Jara. "*Now*, before the crowd—"

She stopped short as some word of authority finally penetrated the data vomit and took hold of the Council officers one by one. Within seconds, a handful of Len Borda's lackeys around the auditorium had drawn their dartguns and moved to the railings. They took careful aim and centered on a single target.

Natch.

• • •

He had heard the rumbling. He had felt the tremors. He had sensed the computational maelstrom raging from afar.

He had tried to run.

Now he kneels on the cold floor of the Tul Jabbor Complex, writhing in the acid bath of the infoquake. Data piercing his mental defenses like shrapnel, OCHREs thrumming crazily and heating up nearly to the melting point. He sees patterns within patterns, things not visible in any spectrum. Somewhere in his peripheral vision he sees Serr Vigal, passed out on the stone but still breathing. Elsewhere he catches a glimpse of a figure in a white robe shouldering his dart-rifle.

The nothingness at the center of the universe.

The guardian and the keeper.

You find yourself capable of strange things when you run out of choices.

I can handle everything the world throws at me. Just watch.

Natch closes his eyes. It's hard enough to concentrate through all the noise; the infoquake just makes things worse. But he has to concentrate; he *has* to. He flings his mind onto the Data Sea and finds live video feeds from every conceivable angle, the perspectives of scared drudges watching the scene unfold from the audience. With his own eyes, Natch can only see and react to what's in front of his face. Here in the infinite ocean of information, he can see all.

Natch gathers his courage and activates MultiReal.

• • •

Magan came to and reached reflexively for the dartgun at his side. The corrugated surface of the grip felt like safety. With the other hand he probed his forehead for the bruise he had received striking his head against the railing. Still sore, but healing quickly through the miracle of OCHRE technology.

He pried open his eyelids, scrambled shakily to his feet, and tried to take inventory of the situation. Infoquake ebbing and flowing.

Audience members fleeing. Petrucio Patel crawling slowly toward the stairway. Prime Committee members safe. Officers of the Defense and Wellness Council gathering at the railings, shoving spectators aside, aiming their dartguns at Natch.

And firing.

Magan gaped dumbly as eight or nine darts whizzed through the air toward the center of the auditorium. The Council lieutenant rubbed his eyes, wondering if he was experiencing some kind of residual hallucination from the infoquake. Every single officer missed the target.

There was another volley, then another. Natch remained kneeling on the floor, cocooned in his own internal awareness. The needles *tink*ed harmlessly onto the stone around him.

Magan had commanded more missions than he could count. He had seen Council troops on good days and bad; he had seen horribly botched raids, officers in white robes twitching in their death throes with heads staved in by Islander shock batons. For half a dozen officers to fire on a stationary target less than thirty meters away and all *miss* . . . it defied the laws of probability. Even factoring in the occasional jostled elbow, the steep angle, and the intermittent aftershocks of the infoquake, Magan had never seen a team of uniformed officers perform so poorly. *MultiReal*, he thought. *Natch must be using MultiReal.*

Lieutenant Executive Lee snapped into combat mode between one instant and the next. He made sure the dartgun in his hand was cocked and loaded with a variety of black code routines and felt the battle language algorithms slide over his mind like a glove. "Instant broker! Parallel!" he barked at the soldiers, waving his arms in the air. *Stop! Stop, you fools!*

But the rain of darts continued unabated. Eight officers, now ten, all firing, all missing.

Magan couldn't begin to guess how long Natch's MultiReal tricks would enable him to keep dodging projectiles. There were hundreds of officers within the building, and untold thousands more on the streets of Melbourne. Could MultiReal hold off a hundred dartguns? How about two hundred? How about ten thousand? What would happen when Len Borda decided to lob a missile on the whole complex?

Magan ran up the stairs and bolted toward the first Council officer he could find, a strapping African with a dart-rifle mounted against his shoulder and his eye squinting at the scope. "Mission detail! See to the transom!" yelled Magan. *Stop firing—that's an order!*

The officer gave Lee a peculiar sidelong glance but did not take his finger off the trigger. "Forward motion in an obscure trajectory," he muttered, then fired off another dart.

The lieutenant blinked at the man for a moment, adrift, waiting for the burst of decryption that never arrived. Could the battle language decryptors have somehow gotten scrambled by the infoquake? Had this computational chaos left the Defense and Wellness Council unable to communicate on the ground—and if so, why hadn't anyone followed standard procedure and tried another protocol?

And then comprehension stabbed him in the gut. Someone had reseeded the algorithms. The officers were communicating just fine; it was only Magan who had been cut off.

I give you until the fifteenth of January to take possession of MultiReal. If you do, we have an agreement. If you don't . . .

Lieutenant Executive Lee's mind whirled, spun, gyrated. What could the old man possibly be *thinking*? People were dying from OCHRE failures right now all around the world. There were a handful of bodies right here in the auditorium, whether trampled or shot or simply fainted Magan couldn't tell. Why couldn't Borda see that ordering Defense and Wellness Council officers to shoot black code darts into a crowd—in full view of the drudges, no less—was nothing short of madness?

Before the lieutenant could decide on a proper course of action, he felt a hand grab his shoulder and spin him around.

Three guards in the white robe and yellow star. The hulking man in the center of the pack was none other than Ridgello. His dartgun was unholstered and its barrel aimed squarely at Magan's heart. "I'm sorry, Lieutenant," he said. Ridgello's emotions had always been difficult to read, but behind his mask of duty, the soldier appeared to be genuinely apologetic.

The lieutenant executive felt his heart sink. *Not now. Not Ridgello.*

Magan took a quick glance around the auditorium at the rapidly emptying seats, at the firing Council officers, at the Plugenpatch representative who had gathered a few wide-eyed drudges together for an impromptu statement of some kind. There were plenty of other drudges taking cover behind their seats to record the scene, but their attention was focused squarely on Natch. No one would notice or question an accidental death by friendly fire.

How long had Len Borda been playing him? How deep did his comprehension of Magan's plots go? He remembered the ruse he had pulled on the high executive weeks ago when Ridgello had held a dartgun to the back of his head. Had Ridgello been in Borda's pocket even then? For a moment, Magan toyed with the idea that the infoquake itself was nothing but a premeditated device for decapitating a brewing rebellion, a way to tidy some loose ends. But no, such a plan was too messy even for someone as choleric as Len Borda. Too full of unknown variables.

Besides which, if Borda had given this operation careful thought, he would have instructed Ridgello to shoot Magan in the back.

Short-term plans, long-term problems, thought the lieutenant. *Your recklessness fails you once more, Borda.*

Acting on instinct, Magan Kai Lee ducked and delivered a swift kick to Ridgello's knee. He could hear the tiny *ving* of a dart missing his right ear by centimeters. In one smooth motion, the lieutenant thumbed the selector on his gun, loading a more lethal variety of black code dart, then fired point-blank into the soldier's belly. Ridgello's eyes didn't even have time to widen before the Null Current claimed him. Magan shoved the rapidly stiffening corpse at the officer on the left, causing him to stumble and shoot wide. But the third officer—

The third officer collapsed with three black code darts sticking out of his torso. Magan snapped his neck around, following the angle of impact back to its source, and saw a small huddle of Council officers on the floor led by a taciturn Rey Gonerev. Papizon was there too. At least Borda hadn't gotten to everyone. There were still some officers in the Tul Jabbor Complex who remained loyal to Magan.

The Blade gave him a stiff nod. Magan returned it, then swiveled around to plug Ridgello's remaining compatriot with three darts of his own. The man gazed straight ahead and expired wordlessly.

How did it come to this? thought the lieutenant as he ducked into the passage below the Committee members' ring, making for the floor and Rey Gonerev.

• • •

"All right," urged Jara. "Let's go. This way."

The fiefcorpers had made no real progress in escaping the petitioners' ring, but at least they had all managed to achieve verticality. Robby Robby and Ben were leaning on one another like wounded soldiers, while Merri was crying and Horvil simply stared bewilderedly into space. Across the ring, Vigal was sitting upright and studying his exit strategies like a seasoned backgammon player.

Jara seemed to be the only one who noticed they were not really in any danger. The Council soldiers were busy firing darts at Natch, and while the fiefcorpers' mental foundations might have been shaken by the infoquake, the foundations of the Tul Jabbor Complex remained solid. Jara's job at this point was simple: keep everyone calm, prevent them from doing something stupid, and get them the fuck out of there.

"Shut down as many programs as you can," she announced to the others. "It helps with the vertigo."

"What about MultiReal?" said Ben.

"*Especially* MultiReal."

They had made half of the Sisyphean trudge back up the stairs when the first man in black robes slipped into the auditorium. Others soon followed. They looked exactly as Natch and Benyamin had described: cloaked head to toe in robes of midnight, laced with crimson Oriental lettering. Upon later reflection, Jara would realize they had arrived too soon after the beginning of the infoquake to have run all the way from the building's street entrance.

The figures in black drew dartguns and began firing.

Not at Natch. At the officers of the Council.

• • •

Magan could tell that the assailants in black robes were not battle-hardened. Although they were decent marksmen, their playbook was limited; they seemed to be executing the same maneuver over and over again. Aim, shoot, drop, crawl. Aim, shoot, drop, crawl. As a long-haul strategy the maneuver was seriously deficient, but in the middle of all this chaos, it just might distract Borda's troops long enough for them to accomplish their objective.

Which was . . . what? To assassinate members of the Prime Committee? To kill or incapacitate Natch? To make a political statement that would hit tonight's drudge reports with a bone-crunching impact?

Borda's officers, caught off guard, began to go down.

This is insane, thought Magan. Defense and Wellness Council officers were firing black code darts wildly at Natch; anonymous lunatics in black robes were picking off Council officers; and Magan's group hunkered down in the middle, targeting both the mysterious would-be assassins and the occasional Council officer who swung a gun in their direction. Audience members were fleeing in every direction and occasionally getting caught in the crossfire. Bodies from all sides lay twitching around the auditorium. And the accursed fiefcorper now stood in the middle of the tumult, untouched.

Obviously this impasse would be short-lived. The black-robed assailants had apparently deployed their full strength, which numbered about twenty; meanwhile, Council reinforcements would be washing in by the hundreds any minute now. MultiReal or no MultiReal, the fools in black would soon be eradicated, and Natch would find himself either dead or the permanent resident of an orbital prison cell.

Magan watched the former fiefcorp master carefully for some hint to his intentions, but his face was impossible to read. Natch might have been some alien species' fledgling effort to piece together a human being with a random assortment of mental states. Anger, determination, triumph, melancholy, resolve—all seemed to roll across the entrepreneur's face at once. Darts were clattering against stone all around him. Through it all, Natch's eyes remained steadfastly closed.

And then, with no warning, he began stumbling for the exit.

It was the reeling gait of a drunkard. First a step this way, then a step that way, followed by two hops in a third direction altogether. But this walk was anything but aimless, Magan realized; it was a carefully calculated path that kept him free of black code darts.

"He's running away!" cried Rey Gonerev, tugging at Magan's elbow. "What the fuck do we do *now?*" Her voice was tinged with anger and not a little fear. Magan realized that few lawyers ever found themselves on real, live battlefields.

Lieutenant Lee watched the entrepreneur's progress across the floor, helpless. Nobody but Natch could survive that hailstorm of darts whizzing in every direction. For a moment, he was prepared to just let the man go. After all, what did Natch still possess that Jara didn't? Then he remembered that meeting at the Tul Jabbor Complex. The way this man had turned the tables on Magan, the pure *ferociousness* of him.

And then he knew what to do.

"Petrucio!" he shouted. "Where's Petrucio?"

The Blade was having trouble hearing, or concentrating, or both. "What?" she said, confused. Papizon, meanwhile, yanked the lieutenant's sleeve and pointed him across the auditorium. Petrucio Patel was sitting on the floor there with his back to the lowest stair, looking somewhat dazed but very much alive.

Without a word, Magan sprang out from the protective curtain of loyal Council officers, narrowly missing both a cowering bureaucrat and one of the black-robed assailants' darts. He fired up a classified bio/logic adrenaline boost program called 2539i. Then he was sprinting as fast as his feet could carry him around the perimeter of the floor, trying not to hug the wall to avoid giving his enemies an easy reference point. In some distant antechamber of consciousness, he could hear darts striking the stone around him.

Close to twenty Council officers were firing at Natch now, though as a moving target he was much harder to hit. Three times that number were futilely clinging to the idea of crowd control. Maybe a dozen figures in black robes remained.

Natch was getting close to the doorway.

Magan Kai Lee skidded to a halt in front of Petrucio Patel, who watched his approach with almost maniacal calm. "MultiReal," barked the Council lieutenant. "Use it!"

The businessman regarded the Council lieutenant with a bemused stare. "Use it *how*?" he said.

"On Natch! Hurry, before it's too late." Magan tossed his dartgun into Petrucio's lap. "We're only going to get one shot at this."

Petrucio arose and brushed off his bloody lapels, letting the gun clatter to the ground. The nosebleed was ancient history by now, but it had done significant damage to what Magan suspected was a very expensive suit. At the moment, the suit appeared to be the fiefcorper's primary concern. "Why me? *You* do it."

"Don't you understand? Natch is using MultiReal. *You've* got Multi-Real. You're the only one here who has any chance of hitting him."

Patel considered this for an agonizing moment, a moment that saw Natch stumble ever closer to the door. "I don't know if I really have a chance or not," he said finally. "I don't know if Jara's made the switch yet."

"Listen," hissed Magan. "Once Natch gets out of this building, we're never going to find him again. Do *you* want that man on the loose out there? Do you think he's going to *let* Jara make that switch after he's gone?" Magan had no idea what he was telling Petrucio, didn't know what kind of *switch* lay in the balance here, but figured he had nothing to lose by bluffing. "You've got those MultiReal-D programs. Don't play dumb, Petrucio, I *know* you have them—you were supposed to demo them to the Prime Committee today. Now load them up and *use* them."

Whatever he had threatened seemed to have worked. Petrucio nodded. He picked Magan's gun up off the ground. "Should I hit him here?"

Magan looked around at the Council officers, the fleeing spectators, the observing drudges. Then he was struck by a sudden bolt of inspiration. "No. Wait . . . These people in black robes. How did they get in? And how do they intend to get *out*?"

• • •

Flash.
  Flash.
  Flash.

He can see it, pantomimed a thousand times on the private stage of his mind, acted with an eerie verisimilitude. A Defense and Well-ness Council officer takes aim and pulls the trigger on his rifle. A sliver of OCHRE-laden doom careens toward the floor of the auditorium, pierces clothing, bites flesh. He stiffens and the Null Current pulls him into its icy depths.

Natch sees himself die. Hundreds of times. It's a vast panorama of his mortality, visions of his death stretched out on an infinite grid.

Flash.

Flash.

Flash.

He observes each scenario, interprets it, rejects it. The choice cycle is discarded; he moves on to new possibilities; the memory fades. He dies and dies again. And each rejection costs him an infinitesimal act of willpower; each assertion of his raw desire to live must be explicitly stated in the language of the neuron, synapse, axon, and dendrite. Each time, there will come the eventual reprieve like the answer to a prayer. A missed shot. A hesitation. A finger twitched too soon or too late.

And so Natch claws his way, alive, through another fraction of a second. Every time it feels like luck. He watches his mental Data Sea video feeds and sees the tiny figure that is him inching closer to the door, a lowly pawn on a vast chessboard loaded with enemy knights.

Flash.

The figures in black robes aren't firing at Natch, and for some reason that makes total sense. He has spent much of the past month dreading these black figures and speculating on their identities. But their presence doesn't feel quite so alarming as it did in that Shenandoah alleyway. So much has happened since that attack. Death, suspension, protests, riots. Natch knows that death is his eventual destination now, the last stop on the track. But he'll make it there on his own timetable. He will not be hurried.

It feels like months have passed when Natch finally makes it to the door and the passageway beneath the Committee members' ring. He opens his eyes, busts through the door, and leaps up the stairs to the auditorium exit.

The exhaustion begins to choke him. He wants to collapse. He *needs* to collapse. He pushes on.

There are still Council officers in the hallways, of course, and

Council officers close on his heels. But now he's only one man in a throng of people clamoring for the exits. The officials out here are more concerned with shepherding the sheep to safety than with plugging Natch with black code. Some of the figures in white robes and yellow stars are actually firing at each other, an oddity Natch does not have the energy to ponder right now.

He runs as fast as his feet can carry him. He doesn't particularly care where he's headed. Occasionally he cuts his way through the crowd with the scythe of MultiReal, but it's mostly unnecessary here. Fleeing, infoquake-panicked pedestrians make for better camouflage.

The central atrium. The imposing holograph of Tul Jabbor, his mien a dour judgment against all manner of chaos and disorder.

Standing in Jabbor's shadow are three figures in black robes, beckoning Natch toward a side hallway that he wouldn't have otherwise noticed. A service exit of sorts. Dartguns are in their hands, but nobody is threatening Natch. One of them has actually pulled his hood back, but it's nobody the entrepreneur recognizes: some random Caucasian male, heavily muscled, perhaps in his midthirties. "This way, Natch!" he beckons. "Hurry!"

Natch pauses. *Go with them? Exactly how stupid do they think I am?*

And then he catches a glint of something from the corner of his eye. Natch peers around Tul Jabbor and sees a veritable battalion of white robes and yellow stars headed this way. Scores of Defense and Wellness Council officers with dart-rifles drawn, reinforcements rushing from the building's front doors. They don't see Natch or his would-be benefactors yet, but they will. Soon. The men in black robes beckon him again.

Natch whips around and heads in their direction.

The men in black robes form a tight phalanx around him and haul ass down the narrow hallway. There's a metal door ajar there, and a hoverbird parked just outside with its boarding ramp extended. The vehicle is painted white with the yellow star on its side. The subterfuge is convincing from a distance, but as he draws closer Natch sees that it's a counterfeit.

A familiar voice. "Natch!"

He turns around. Sees, at the far end of the corridor, Lieutenant Executive Magan Kai Lee and Petrucio Patel. There are two or three Council officers with them, but it appears that the mass of troops Natch saw a minute ago have been given the slip. Magan is making no move to summon them this way. In fact, he looks just as anxious to avoid attention.

"Come with us," says Magan, palms upturned and extended. "We can make a deal. We can keep you safe from Len Borda."

Petrucio's look flings vitriol. There's dried blood on his suit. His finger caresses the trigger of his dartgun.

Natch turns around again and looks at the waiting hoverbird. The figures who escorted him down the hallway are leaping aboard, firing a few wild shots back down the hall that don't hit anything but stone. A lone figure leans out and stretches a hand toward him. Its skin is the color of mahogany. "Hurry up, Natch!" cries the voice. "Don't trust him!" Natch looks up, sees the man pull back the cowl of his robe, and gapes in astonishment.

Pierre Loget?

Natch is now submerged far below the realm of conscious decision or human emotion. All he can see is the murderous look in Petrucio Patel's eye, the thousands of deaths the Council has inflicted on him this afternoon. The weariness that's dragging at his heels, the man who invaded his home and called him *irrelevant*. He vaults for the hoverbird.

Petrucio raises the gun in both hands and fires.

Flash.

Flash.

Flash.

Choice cycle stacks on top of choice cycle, a colossus of possibility. Petrucio is using MultiReal too.

Flash.

Flash.

Flash.

For a brief, infinite instant, Natch and Petrucio Patel stand alone, facing off on the battlefield of the mind. A thousand darts bite into Natch; Natch swats them away. Mental processes whirl and spin; the colossus branches out into new and unexpected dimensions. And still the darts keep coming as Patel expends his own choice cycles to navigate to new realities.

Natch should be collapsing by now—he should be prostrate on the floor in pain and weakness—but he stubbornly refuses to submit. He *will* not submit. Hit, miss, hit, miss, hit, miss, and then—

MultiReal stops.

Natch feels a pinprick in the back of his thigh as the dart pierces his flesh. Loget grabs his arm just as he jumps onto the hoverbird. A few black-robed figures leap on after him, and the door shuts.

The crowd surged forward once the shooting began. Horvil disappeared almost immediately. Merri and Benyamin found themselves swept up the stairs and out the exit. Robby Robby managed to shelter Jara in the lee of his immense hairdo for a moment before he also stuck a limb out too far and was overwhelmed.

Jara was now alone in a furious crush of strangers. A Defense and Wellness Council officer yanked on her shoulder and herded her out the door, sending her careening into someone else's elbow. She tried to yell a question to the man in the white robe and yellow star, but he had already vanished in the stampede.

Another aftershock of the infoquake made Jara's knees buckle. She slipped and felt a moment of hysteria. *I'm going to get trampled to death out here*, she thought. Despite her little sermon about conserving computing resources five minutes earlier, she prepared to activate Multi-Real. *What do I have to lose?*

And then a chunky arm emerged out of nowhere and locked itself tight around her waist. "Hold on," said Horvil, his brow furrowed with determination. "I'm getting us the fuck out of here." Jara merely stared at him.

With that, Horvil dove into the tornado.

Where had all these people come from? Even an auditorium filled to capacity shouldn't have generated this much foot traffic through the corridors. Jara looked up at the six levels of offices behind smoked glass on either side of the corridor and discovered they were emptying rapidly. She gazed myopically at the crowd and was astounded to realize that a number of the fleeing citizens were, in fact, government officials. The black ring of the Prime Committee was hanging from more than one neck, as were the insignias of the Congress of L-PRACGs, the Vault, Dr.

Plugenpatch, and any number of private security organizations. Jara saw unsheathed dartguns and disruptors aplenty, but as far as she could tell, nobody outside of the auditorium had actually fired one.

Horvil bulldozed his way through the panicked pedestrians like an industrial combine. Nobody wanted to mess with a man of his girth. Jara noticed that the engineer had actually acquired a trail of hapless civil servants hoping to follow him to safety. They fell behind when he turned the next corner and quickly dispersed.

Within minutes, Horvil had elbowed his way to the central atrium of the Complex, where people were alternately gravitating toward the giant holograph of Tul Jabbor and speeding away from it. Jara supposed that an Autonomous Mind could have factored through all the trajectories of fleeing souls and plotted a safe course through the melee, but it was beyond mere human means. She was glad she had resisted the temptation to activate MultiReal. What if the exhaustion had overtaken her in the middle of all these people? No, her best strategy was to latch on to the biggest, sturdiest person she could find and hold tight.

That person was Horvil. For a moment, he looked like he might plop down right there and begin sketching mathematical models. Instead he scooted over to the wall with Jara close behind and began probing every office door they passed in hopes of finding one that would yield.

Finally one did—but only because its occupant chose that precise moment to run screaming into the corridor. The pasty-faced woman didn't even glance in Horvil's direction as she scurried by. Horvil didn't hesitate. He tightened his grip around Jara's waist and leapt into the office just as the door closed behind them.

Minutes passed. Their heartbeats slowed.

Horvil's luck was incalculable. He had stumbled into some middle manager's office, complete with standard Prime Committee–issue desk, wall of viewscreens, and hanging ficus plant. It was little more than a cubicle, and the only chair in sight looked frightfully uncomfortable. So the two fiefcorpers slumped to the floor with backs to the desk and caught their breath. A sign on the wall next to the door told them to PROMOTE L-PRACG COOPERATION AT ALL COSTS in sanctimonious small caps.

"You're responsible for all this, aren't you?" said Jara, leaning against the engineer's shoulder.

Horvil tipped an imaginary hat. "Of course."

"A little over the top, wasn't it? I mean, did you have to spark worldwide pandemonium just to get out of your fiefcorp contract?"

"I dunno, sometimes I think you just have to take the big chances. Like the great Lucco Primo once said, *Global catastrophe causes fertilization and*, um, *crystallization of purpose in—in fiefcorp negotiations.* Or something like that."

The joke wheezed to a halt, leaving the two alone with their thoughts.

Jara realized that Horvil had never actually taken his arm from around her waist, but she was in no mind to remove it. After all, now that she had core access to MultiReal, she was just as much of a target as Natch, wasn't she? Through the translucent glass of the door, she could see the bedlam of Prime Committee bureaucrats and hear the tramp of confused Defense and Wellness Council officers. One of those officers could hit the door with a priority override and zap them full of black code at any time. The menacing figures in black robes could track them down. Drudges might be waiting to pounce right in the hall. Was there any safer place to be than nestled in the plush cushion of Horvil's belly? Jara tilted her head back slightly into Horvil's chest and listened to the rhythmic chugging of his heart, as steady an engine as could be found in this wretched place.

"What are you thinking?" she asked softly.

"Oh, I'm thinking about the Spiral Theory of History," replied Horvil.

Jara smirked. "You'll have to explain that one. I was never very good at history."

"It's one of the tenets of Creed Dao, I think. Something about the looping patterns of history. Events recur, but it's not just a circle, it's more like a spring or a coil. So we're not just going round and round the same groove—we're progressing somewhere. Moving up or down on a spiral track." The engineer twirled the index finger of his left hand, drawing an invisible cone that would come to a point at some hypothetical place in the aether.

"Horvil, I have no idea what you're talking about."

"Come on. Marcus Surina introduces this revolutionary new technology, teleportation. Everybody goes wild over it, there's all this hullabaloo, and then he dies suddenly in a hoverbird explosion. The whole economy tanks. Now here we are, a generation later. *Margaret* Surina introduces another revolutionary new technology, there's all this hullabaloo, and then *she* dies suddenly. Murdered, maybe. A spiral."

The analyst gave him a playful poke in the side. "You're just now figuring this out? The drudges have been pushing that story for weeks. *Just like her father, history repeats itself*—"

"No no no, you're missing the whole point, Jara. It's *not* just history repeating itself. There are a lot of recurring patterns, sure, but it can't be the same, because everything we do is informed by what happened in the past. We're *going* somewhere. It's either spiraling up, or it's spiraling down. And the Daoists, they believe that you can *track* that change, that you can figure out the laws of the universe if you can figure out the coefficient of change between historical cycles."

Jara laughed quietly in the crook of Horvil's arm. It was just like him to float off into abstraction like an untethered balloon amidst such turmoil. "Well, which way are we going? Up or down?"

Horvil made a jovial face as his mind came crashing back to the present. "I dunno. That's the big question, I guess."

"Okay, while you're at it, here's another big question," said the analyst. "A month ago, you and I were sitting in the Center for Historic Appreciation at Andra Pradesh. On the floor, with your arm around me. Panicked people running all over the place, Council officers everywhere." She nodded her head toward the door, which shuddered momentarily as some shadowy figure slammed against it, then disappeared. "Now here we are again. A recurring pattern. So which direction are *we* spiraling in, up or down?"

The engineer rubbed his chin and peered into the distance with his newfound Horvilish calm. "That's a very interesting question. Let me dig out my slide rule."

Jara burst into laughter. It was probably the only laugh to be heard for a kilometer or more.

And then they were kissing. She couldn't quite say who leaned in first, or whether they had both done so simultaneously. It wasn't the explosive outburst of passion that Jara had been hoping for from Natch these past few years; it was congenial, friendly, familiar.

Jara opened her eyes. Nothing had really changed. She didn't really even think she loved this man sitting next to her. But she *liked* him and respected him and trusted him. For now, wasn't that enough?

Horvil sat back with a sunny grin that belied everything they had experienced since this entire MultiReal crisis had begun. "All right, now that that's over with," he said, "what say we get out of here?"

Jara looked at his pudgy, uncomplicated face, drank in his expression of calm certitude, and then nodded. "Okay, where to?"

"Follow me. We're catching a ride."

The door slid open on command, revealing a scene of utter disarray. The crowds clogging the hallways of the Tul Jabbor Complex had thinned slightly, but those who remained were more strident and unnerved. If Horvil's Daoist theory was right, the crucial difference between this scene and the one at Andra Pradesh was that nobody was in charge here. A large contingent of Defense and Wellness Council officers flew past them looking just as muddled and confused as any of the hundred private L-PRACG security forces. A few bodies were scattered on the ground, though whether they were dead or merely temporarily stunned from the infoquake, Jara could not tell.

Horvil screwed up his face, clutched Jara tightly in his arm, and let out a completely gratuitous war cry. Then he went careening into the crowd with the analyst hugging his every step.

There was some shoving, but most people knew better than to get in the way of a bellowing mammoth like Horvil. Jara collided with a young Islander running in the opposite direction, leading the analyst to wonder if those connectible collars were even working in the middle of all this. Was the infoquake affecting the Islanders too? The engineer yanked the young man to his feet and gently thrust him aside. *We're going to get through this*, thought Jara. *And without MultiReal.*

The curving hallways of the Tul Jabbor Complex were interminable, but Horvil wasn't heading to the front entrance. After a few more minutes in the fray, he led them to a small meeting room in a relatively deserted alcove. Five burly men in purple robes awaited them there. They were armed to the teeth and festooned with the Creed Élan regalia.

"Come on!" bellowed the man in the lead. "Let's go!"

There was no time to think. A door at the far end of the room swung open, and the two fiefcorpers followed the guards into a courtyard where a red Vulture hoverbird idled half a meter off the ground. Within seconds the guards had half assisted, half tossed them through the hoverbird doors, and the Vulture was making a steep arc up into the blue.

Jara flopped to the floor and would have slid all the way down the center aisle but for a hand that lashed out and gripped her ankle. "Gotcha, Queen Jara," said Robby Robby, beaming like an idiot.

Seconds later, she and Horvil had managed to crawl to the hoverbird's upholstered passenger seats and strap themselves in. A quick glance around the cabin revealed the bird's other occupants: Serr Vigal, Benyamin, Merri, and Robby Robby, along with a pilot and the guards who had ushered them in here.

"I don't suppose," sighed Jara heavily, "that anybody's seen Natch."

Blank stares echoed from the rest of the hoverbird's occupants, and Jara knew then that nobody else had even thought to look.

The analyst smiled wanly and shrugged her shoulders. Horvil gave her a wink from his seat across the aisle. Jara turned to one of the gruff Élanners and stuttered out a tired "thank you."

"Don't thank me," muttered the guard, wiping the barrel of his hand-held disruptor before sheathing it. "I'm just doing my job. Thank her."

Jara followed the man's hitched thumb over his shoulder and was shocked to see a familiar figure who had been hidden from view in the seat next to the pilot. *"Berilla?"*

The matriarch's gaze was fixed out the opposite window, where the tumult was still visible but growing more distant with each passing second. The confusion of the Tul Jabbor Complex began to seem like a natural occurrence the higher they climbed: warring ant tribes scrambling for turf. Melbourne itself metamorphosed from a place of fiercely clashing agendas to an orderly grid of unmoving buildings.

Berilla pursed her lips as if she had just slurped on a particularly tart lime "What has that man gotten you all into *this* time?" she grumbled.

5

POSSIBILITIES 2.0

(((36)))

The turbulence of the Tul Jabbor Complex vanished the instant Natch passed through the doors of the hoverbird. The Council officers, the whizzing darts, the fleeing bystanders, Petrucio Patel: all gone.

Natch flopped onto a thin carpet of leaves and skidded to a halt against a particularly scabby tree. He could feel the cogs of his mind catch on a small and intractable stone. This place, this garden with its motley assortment of plants and trees that could have been carelessly flung from a barrel of random seeds: how did he get here? And where had he seen this place before?

The entrepreneur crawled in the dirt, parted a curtain of grapevine, and saw a patio of hand-crafted stone. A carefully stuccoed building lay two meters ahead, with plenty of benches and brick abutments to sit on. Insects both large and small danced a tarantella around the latticework.

A hand reached down and took ahold of Natch's. The skin was deep mahogany, the color of furniture. "You all right, Natch?"

"I'm fine," grunted the entrepreneur. He let the man tug him to his feet, and found himself face-to-face with Pierre Loget.

Loget was sanguine to the point of absurdity. His cowled black robe was definitely the same type Natch had seen that day in the alleyways of Shenandoah. Up close, he discovered that what he had taken for red Chinese lettering was not actually lettering at all, but a geometric pattern with a vaguely Arabic motif.

And the man himself? Well, the man was Pierre Loget: effeminate, inward-facing, thoroughly nonthreatening.

It was almost too much to contemplate. *Pierre Loget* had arranged a strike force to pump him full of black code? Natch couldn't possibly see how Loget fit into the weave of current events. Yes, they were competitors on the Primo's rankings, and to compete on Primo's assumed some amount of rancor by definition. But Loget had always seemed aloof from the fray, a hermetically sealed individual. Natch had only spoken to the man a few times in his life, and each encounter had blurred into the everyday administrative bustle of fiefcorpdom. A meeting, a seminar, a dinner party Jara had dragged him to once.

Natch wasn't sure if he should feel angry or relieved. "What are you doing here?" he said. "How did you know where to find me?"

Loget's laughter fluttered through the SeeNaRee, pigeonlike. "With all the publicity surrounding that Prime Committee hearing, I suspect everyone in the solar system knew where to find you."

"And the black code? What the fuck was *that* about?"

The programmer put a delicate hand on Natch's shoulder. "You should ask the bodhisattva," he said simply.

"The—what?"

"Natch has been hit," said a voice behind him. "Weren't you paying attention back there, Loget?" Natch could feel a shiver emanate from someplace deep in his gut and quickly work its way to his shoulder blades. He knew that voice almost as well as he knew his own.

The bodhisattva of Creed Thassel. Brone.

Suddenly the pebble lodged in Natch's mental gearworks sprang free. Natch was correct; he *had* been in this place before. It was the garden at the Proud Eagle hive where he and Brone had spent most of their childhood. He had not utterly lost control of his faculties and plunged into madness after all. He had jumped onto a hoverbird, and that hoverbird had been outfitted with SeeNaRee capabilities.

Natch tried to imagine the exorbitant sum of money it would take to accomplish such a thing. To install SeeNaRee on a hoverbird? And then to track down video of the Proud Eagle hive and go through the laborious process of SeeNaRizing it? Why?

Brone approached, shadowed by three figures wearing identical black robes to Loget's. His skin was grub pale, as if he had not seen the sun since his last appearance at Natch's apartment and could not be bothered with bio/logic pigmentation. The entrepreneur watched how Pierre Loget bowed low to the bodhisattva, and the way his three black-robed lackeys did the same. Brone seemed at ease here, in command. Natch had never seen him so comfortable with his prosthetic arm and emerald eye, and the beige suit he wore brought a kind of dignity to his stoutness.

"So where's *your* spooky costume?" said Natch with a snort of false bravado.

Brone did not appear to have heard him. "How many did we lose down there?" he asked Loget.

"Eleven or twelve, I think."

The bodhisattva nodded, melancholy. "Now what did Petrucio have loaded in that dartgun, do you think?" He and Loget shared a look that was merely the tip of a ConfidentialWhisper iceberg.

Seconds later, Loget knelt behind Natch and plucked something from the back of his thigh. A tiny silver needle whose bite hardly broke the threshold of perception. Natch could feel his blood pressure rise as he remembered the confrontation in the Tul Jabbor Complex, the MultiReal duel, the endless panorama of choice cycles. Petrucio's dart had hit him, all right—but had it even penetrated the skin far enough to discharge its armada of tainted OCHREs? Shouldn't Natch feel . . . something?

Brone took the sliver. He held it up to the light, dutifully scanning its surface as he twirled it around slowly like a baton. Then, without warning, he plunged the tip of the dart straight into the palm of his artificial hand. Natch gasped, wondering what this theatrical gesture was supposed to prove, until he saw the intent look on Brone's face and concluded that the prosthesis must be performing some kind of chemical analysis.

"If there was any code embedded on the tip of those OCHREs, it's gone now," announced the bodhisattva after a minute.

"What's going on?" snapped Natch, impatient. "Where are you taking me? Why did you hit me with black code last month?"

Brone turned to one of his subordinates. "Go ahead and get a—"

Natch had had enough. His muscles were screaming with exhaustion, but he managed to grab Brone by the lapels and half walk, half shove him against the side of the virtual hive building. The bodhisattva's head hit the stucco with a thump, indicating the presence of a real wall there. "Answer me!" Natch yelled. "What the fuck did you *do* to me?"

Loget stepped aside in preparation for something messy. Brone, however, wasn't fazed. He gave the entrepreneur an opaque look that said he would not be pushed into revealing his hand so easily.

And here sits Brone, the man whom you wronged all those years ago, he had told Natch in those frantic days before the demonstration at Andra Pradesh. *He is angry. Yes. He hates you and would love to see you dead. Yes. Indisputable facts.*

"Take a look behind you, Natch," said Brone in a ragged whisper. "Tell me what you see."

The entrepreneur turned his head and saw that the SeeNaRee had evaporated, leaving only the dull plastics of a luxury hoverbird interior. They were standing in a rear compartment, about two meters away from the door Natch had leapt through to escape Magan Kai Lee and Petrucio Patel. Immediately behind them was a large rear window, showing rapidly retreating clouds.

"We're in the air," said Natch stupidly. "We're over the ocean."

"And who is pursuing us?"

Natch gazed all around. Theirs was not the only vehicle in the sky, but all of the distant craft appeared to be minding their own business. "Nobody," he said.

"Yes," replied the bodhisattva in that maddeningly supercilious tone of his. "And do you know *why* nobody is pursuing us, Natch? Do you know why we're not dodging Council missiles right now?"

Natch shook his head.

"Because that black code floating in your bloodstream renders you invisible to Len Borda's tracking mechanisms. Do you understand me? *The Council has no way to find you.*"

The entrepreneur stepped back, his tongue flopping uselessly in his mouth. All this time, the black code—a *cloaking* tool?

Brone removed Natch's hands from his suit jacket and firmly walked the entrepreneur back two paces. His touch was glacier cold. Then he gave Natch a light push in the chest, knocking him back onto a stone planter. The hoverbird interior was blanketed by Proud Eagle SeeNaRee once more.

"You can thank me later," said Brone, his voice registering something mealy that might be called amusement. "We'll be there in a few hours."

"Where?" cried Natch.

No one answered. Brone, Loget, and the other black-robed figures disappeared into the virtual building, leaving Natch locked in the rear compartment, alone.

• • •

Natch studied his surroundings. It was an uncanny simulation, accurate down to the loose flagstone on the patio that Natch remembered digging at with his foot many a lazy summer afternoon. The palm fronds felt as rubbery as real palm fronds, and the rich olfactory mélange from the garden was a scent firmly entrenched in his memory.

But this was no pedestrian work of SeeNaRee. Natch strolled around the entire garden, then circumnavigated the hive building a few times— impossible under standard rules of SeeNaRee. He remembered the giant hollowed-out diamond with the hidden exits from his last encounter with Brone. Clearly his old hivemate had only disdain for such rules.

Natch sat on the edge of the planter and tried to absorb the idyllic calm of the garden. He could barely move, but he needed to marshal his strength for whatever Brone had planned. He needed to be ready.

But ready for what?

Obviously he couldn't declare victory over the Defense and Wellness Council just because he had narrowly escaped their clutches this time. Officers had actually *fired* on him in plain view of the public, in a sacred hall of government, no less. Natch couldn't be sure the code in their dartguns was of the lethal variety. But based on the agonized twitching of the bodies caught in the crossfire, Len Borda had moved beyond mere light-paralysis routines. No, if he couldn't wrest control of MultiReal from Natch's hands, then the high executive was prepared to assassinate him in cold blood and deal with the consequences later.

Natch shivered. Could he ever be safe from the Council again? Even a black code cloaking mechanism couldn't protect his Vault account from being seized by the government. They couldn't prevent people from recognizing his face or his voice or his mannerisms. Magan Kai Lee had claimed he could keep Natch out of Borda's reach—but even if Natch could trust him, the claim seemed unlikely.

He looked at his hands, now shaking uncontrollably. A sudden pain lanced through his head, as it had been doing every hour with fascistic regularity for days. How could he know for sure the black code was a device for cloaking his bio/logic signatures, as Brone said? Certainly the lack of pursuit was a strong piece of circumstantial evidence, but not conclusive by any means. The chaos from the infoquake and the disguised hoverbird alone could have thrown the Council off his scent.

And what about the two other pieces of foreign code wending their way through Natch's bio/logic systems? There was still the matter of the MultiReal yellow jacket, not to mention whatever program Petrucio Patel had infected him with. How had Petrucio managed to hit him? Why had MultiReal just stopped like that?

Natch buried his face in his hands. He felt leprous, unclean. Could he even trust his own thoughts with those insidious OCHREs in his neural system? One black code program was bad enough; now he had three. Three times the black code, a thousand times the potential malevolence.

So many questions and so few answers. Natch felt a moment of extreme claustrophobia and panic. *Run away!* he told himself. *Get as far away from here as you can!*

He looked for some sign of the hoverbird hatch he had leapt through a scant half an hour before. Unsurprisingly, he found only the virtual hive building and the imposing walls that surrounded the garden. But what good would an emergency hatch do anyway, kilometers up in the sky? Natch had no parachute, no oxygen supply, and no experience using either of those things anyway.

And even supposing he could fashion some miraculous escape and safe landing . . . what *then?* Could any of the fiefcorpers shelter him? The Council would probably have them all under the strictest surveillance now—besides which, they might not *want* to help him. Natch had threatened to trash Horvil's and Ben's careers. He had not raised a finger to help Merri fight the bogus charges that had gotten her suspended from Creed Objectivv. He had left Serr Vigal lying unconscious on the floor of the Tul Jabbor Complex. Quell had vanished. He had stretched the controlling clamps on Jara to the snapping point.

Natch was struck with a sudden inspiration. He knew what had happened at the Tul Jabbor Complex. He knew how Petrucio Patel had been able to shoot him with the dartgun.

Snippets from the soccer demonstration in Harper echoed through Natch's head. Ben kicking the ball, Quell blocking every kick. *Something's . . . strange*, Benyamin had said. *I'm using MultiReal, just like before—but it just stops at some point. It leaves me hanging there in midloop.*

Limited choice cycles! Horvil had shouted. *I think I get this now. We put a limit on the number of reality loops Ben can do at one time—but your version of MultiReal still has no limits.*

Someone must have modified the MultiReal program while Natch wasn't looking. Set a limit on the number of daily choice cycles and brought the program down to the level of the Patel Brothers' licensed version. Natch had drained his reservoir of daily choice cycles with all of those acrobatics in the auditorium of the Tul Jabbor Complex. Petrucio had not.

I suppose if you're both running limited versions, Horvil had said, *the person with the most choice cycles wins.*

So someone had decided to alter the parameters of the MultiReal program. Who would make such a decision except Jara?

It didn't make sense; none of it made sense. Why would Jara purposely cripple MultiReal like that? Unless . . . yes, everything was quickly falling into place. He could picture the scene. The Patel Brothers dropping subtle hints in Jara's direction, appealing to the naive do-gooder inside her. Throwing her a few crumbs in exchange for hobbling her version of MultiReal with limited choice cycles.

How could you do this to me? he howled in his mind at the analyst. *Don't you see what you've done? You let the Patels infect me with another piece of black code!* How could he have ever trusted Jara with core access to MultiReal? How could he have ever trusted her with *anything*?

And were the rest of the fiefcorpers any better? Jara might have made the decision, but Horvil's would have been the hand that implemented it. Certainly Benyamin, Merri, and Vigal weren't excluded from the process either.

Natch knew then: he could not go back. He was through with the Surina/Natch MultiReal Fiefcorp.

Outside the fiefcorp, his prospects weren't much better. His reputation in the fiefcorp field had been trampled into dust; the Meme Cooperative had suspended his business license; and certainly after the free-for-all at the Tul Jabbor Complex, the Prime Committee would soon vote to take possession of MultiReal.

Who else was there? Robby Robby was unlikely to jump into the Council's crosshairs for Natch. Andra Pradesh would offer precious little sanctuary, now that Suheil and Jayze Surina were running the place. Khann Frejohr and his libertarian allies wouldn't stick their necks out for him again. The drudges would take his statement, but they couldn't offer him any protection from troops in white robes—not anymore.

Natch had literally nowhere to turn.

What did Brone want with him? If he wanted to see Natch dead, he could simply have sat back at the Tul Jabbor Complex and let the Council do the job for him. Why save him from the high executive's wrath and cart him off somewhere in a hoverbird? Was he to be tortured and forced to hand over MultiReal? Or did the bodhisattva have something even more nefarious in store?

The entrepreneur hauled himself up from the planter and wandered along the property wall. What salvation he was hoping to find there he couldn't say, but he refused to simply sit and accept this kidnapping without a struggle. He put his palms against the brick and began tracing the mortar with his fingertips. The door had to be here *somewhere. . . .*

Natch could not have guessed how long he searched. But suddenly, he found it: an exterior hoverbird hatch, camouflaged by the brickwork.

He stared at the brick for several minutes. *What if I opened that hatch and just . . . jumped?* he thought. A few minutes of terror, easily diluted with bio/logics and a single instant of pain. Then eternal tranquility. He would be forever out of the Defense and Wellness Council's reach.

There was a question of pressurization. Natch tried to recall what he knew about the thermodynamics of hovercraft. Was it possible for a mere human being to open an exterior hatch in midflight?

The entrepreneur slid to the ground and sat with his back to the hatch. He gazed at the Proud Eagle garden, unsure of what to do. An hour passed. Two. And then the slight lulling movement of the hoverbird came to a halt.

Wherever Natch was going, he had arrived.

• • •

A sliver of daylight appeared behind the doorway, then widened into a full circle. Natch hopped quickly through the portal back into reality, almost beyond caring what awaited him on the other side.

The hoverbird had parked in a bombed-out courtyard so littered with debris that Natch momentarily thought he had stepped into another one of Brone's twisted works of SeeNaRee. Pulverized concrete served as the garnish for a yard of twisted steel girders, jagged piles of glass, and fused-together scarecrows of ancient plastics. Standing at the far end of the courtyard was a red brick building so rigid, so unyielding, so *perpendicular* that it had to be of ancient vintage. The skyline beyond the courtyard was dominated by a huge cluster of ruined buildings leaning into one another like old tombstones.

Brone had taken him to one of the diss cities. The old cities, bombed and ruined centuries ago by Autonomous Minds run amok. Broken letters dangling off the side of a neighboring tower clearly spelled out CHICAGO FIRST NATIONAL.

Chicago. Natch's mother had lived here once.

Brone, Pierre Loget, and a dozen others stood at the end of a ragged path that ran through the minefield of rubble. Steps and a portico in the ancient Roman style led to a dark passageway.

Natch looked around for a means of escape but found none. The idea of hijacking the hoverbird seemed quite preposterous, particularly since the pilot who knew how to fly it had already exited the craft. Escape on foot? The courtyard was lined by a black wrought-iron fence that had been newly installed and painted. Even if Natch had the strength to climb it, he doubted that he could successfully navigate the spikes without impaling himself. Use MultiReal? He remembered that he was out of choice cycles for the day; besides which, in his exhausted state, the program might kill him. And once outside, he faced the same question as before: where would he go?

Loget and the other black-robed figures retreated through the passageway and into the building, leaving Brone and Natch alone. Brone raised his eyebrows and inclined his head toward the passageway. It was almost an inviting gesture. Finally Natch thrust his hands into his pockets and followed the path through the open door.

A short, black hall. The smell of household cleaning compounds. Ambient light shining from beyond an archway.

And then—applause?

Natch emerged in a cavernous room that might once have been the grand atrium for an upper-crust hotel. Two hundred people could have fit on the marble floor that had been scuffed by centuries of footprints, while another few dozen might have lined the dual stairways that hugged the side walls and came together on the mezzanine above. Whatever furnishings had adorned the place in ancient days had long since been carted off; instead the floor was lined with perhaps three dozen burnished metal platforms extending up on long stalks of silver. The crescent-shaped platforms hung in the air at varying levels from two to fifteen meters high, like a field of phantasmagoric flowers. Atop each platform sat an ordinary bio/logic workbench, and standing behind each workbench was a figure giddy with applause.

Natch's step faltered as he rubbed the sand from his eyes. The men and women clapping and cheering his arrival seemed disconcertingly happy to see him. More than that, many of them were actually faces he recognized. Billy Sterno, a pair of top analysts from the Deuteron Fiefcorp, an engineer who used to work for Lucas Sentinel.

There were words floating between the stalks in a clownish font, colored cherry red: WELCOME, NATCH!

"A-all these fiefcorpers," stuttered Natch. "They're Thasselians too?"

Brone beamed proudly in the fashion of a motivational speaker showing off his disciples. "Yes, Natch—we're all devotees of the teachings of Kordez Thassel here. But these aren't just Thasselians—they're your comrades now! Comrades and fellow revolutionaries."

Natch rubbed his forehead, where he was experiencing one of his periodic spikes of pain. "Revolutionaries? What are you talking about?"

The bodhisattva extended his arms out in a solicitous gesture to the figures riding their elevated platforms, and there was an immediate crescendo in the applause. "I'm talking about the *last* revolution!" he cried. "The revolution of ultimate freedom!" More hooting and hollering from the crowd. "The revolution against cause and effect!" They were stomping on their platforms now, causing a strange metallic clang to reverberate around the room. Brone was in full demagogue mode, shaking his fists in the air and tilting his head back. "I'm talking about *the Revolution of Selfishness!*" Another raucous cheer, even louder than before, which set the windows to vibrating.

Natch shifted into high alert and began casting python-quick glances over his shoulder to make sure he still had a clear retreat. Pierre Loget was standing near the front door to the place, but he wasn't speaking the body language of conflict, and he appeared to be unarmed.

Suddenly the metal stalks were lowering to the ground and shedding programmers. People began walking up to Natch and jubilantly clapping him on the back. There were catcalls of encouragement, words of congratulations. It was all a little too overwhelming for the entrepreneur's frayed nerves. Only a few hours ago, he had been racing through the Tul Jabbor Complex dodging black code darts; now he was being feted like a gladiator. And the people cheering him—he had *humiliated* some of these people over the years, ruined them. Why shower such praise on him now? Incomprehensible.

At some point, wine began to flow around the room, and Natch found a full glass being pressed into his hand. He watched for some furtive sign of poison. But the revelers were all imbibing sloppily from the same bottle, passing glasses haphazardly around with no semblance of order. Still, Natch drank nothing.

The ancient hotel lobby quickly became the site of the strangest party Natch had ever witnessed. In one corner, Billy Sterno was presiding over a cart of steaming finger foods that someone had rolled in from a back room. In another corner, one of the more promising young programmers in muscle tissue and cartilage was dancing tipsily atop a crescent platform while a handful of engineers egged him on. Several of the figures in black robes had gathered in a solemn semicircle to mourn the ones who had not made it out of the Tul Jabbor Complex alive. And serving as ringmaster for the whole circus was Brone, smiling wider than Natch had seen him smile since initiation.

Finally, after an hour of this surrealism, Natch felt a set of fingers brushing his arm. Pierre Loget. "You're tired," said Loget. "Go ahead, we've got quarters for you. Upstairs, room two-twelve. You can take either staircase."

Natch couldn't think of an appropriate reaction, so he made none. He started up the right-hand staircase and found his way down the dim corridor to a room with the number 212 freshly painted on its surface. The door swung open as he approached.

Run, he could hear an inner voice urging. *Run while you still can.* But Natch didn't have the strength. He gave the room a quick once-over, then barricaded the door behind him. There seemed to be nothing sinister about the furnishings arrayed around the room, and the bed he collapsed in appeared to be nothing more than an ordinary bed.

(((37)))

Natch couldn't recall the last time he had had a full night's sleep. Sometime in October, he imagined, before he hit number one on Primo's. Before Margaret and MultiReal. He was not naive enough to think twelve hours of slumber would solve all his problems—*but certainly*, he thought, *I expected more than this*. Natch awoke feeling like nothing had changed, like he had merely transported his weariness intact half a day into the future.

He was lying on a decadently large bed, submerged in pillows that appeared to be stuffed with real feathers. Portraits hanging on the wall against a background of royal blue chevrons spoke of a past where mustached men frolicked on horseback in fields of Kentucky bluegrass. Natch stumbled over to the shower. On the way, he caught a glimpse through the window of a wide boulevard that might have been the apex of high society before the Autonomous Revolt. Now it wallowed in smashed concrete and twisted metal.

The water was clean and fresh. Once showered, Natch couldn't think of anything else to do but join the Thasselians downstairs.

Brone and his devotees were waiting in the atrium. Natch was surprised to see all of the metal stalks lowered nearly to the ground, with the crescent-shaped platforms intermeshed seamlessly to form one enormous oval conference table. Where the workbenches had gotten off to, Natch wasn't sure.

"Come come come!" beckoned Brone from a chair on the far side of the room. "You almost missed breakfast." The bodhisattva's demeanor remained relentlessly upbeat, which was enough to make Natch nervous.

Natch tiptoed carefully down the stairway, expecting some kind of booby trap or trick step all the way. He found one of a dozen empty chairs on the opposite end of the table from Brone, and slumped into it.

The bodhisattva pointed at a pretzel-shaped pastry on his plate oozing with red jam. "These are exquisite," he offered. "Try one." Something about the room's acoustics allowed him to speak in a conversational tone and still be heard across the table.

Natch eyed the collection of pastries on the plate in front of him suspiciously and prodded the red one with a fork. Finally, ravenous, he pushed himself away from the table, walked a dozen paces counterclockwise, and grabbed someone else's largely untouched plate. Then he proceeded back to his seat and wolfed the pastries down one by one. The strawberry pastry was, indeed, delicious.

Brone slapped the table in mock indignation. "For process' preservation, Natch! Those poisoned pastries took me hours to prepare. I *told* you he was too smart to fall for this, Loget."

A few seats down, Pierre Loget tittered.

The setting was almost aggressively mundane. Ordinary people chowing down on ordinary breakfasts, holding ordinary whispered conversations about soccer, fashion, and politics. Natch hadn't realized Brone was even capable of such tidy domesticity.

"So I assume the room was comfortable," continued the bodhisattva, his lips hinting at a smile. Natch didn't answer. "If not, there are plenty of other vacant ones to choose from. Obviously we're missing a few amenities out here. No underground transfer system for us, I'm afraid! But we've had plenty of time to stock up on the basics. The larder's quite full, and we've installed automated laundry facilities. Billy's even outfitted the ballroom with some good selections of SeeNaRee."

A few seats over from Natch, Billy Sterno nodded, his goatee greasy with undercooked egg.

Natch brushed the crumbs off his own face and sat back. "What makes you think I'm planning on staying here?" he growled.

The bodhisattva of Creed Thassel shrugged. "You wish to leave?"

he said. "No one's stopping you." He extended his synthetic hand toward the front door, which hung open a few tantalizing centimeters. "But since I *did* provide you with this sumptuous breakfast, perhaps you could do me the courtesy of—"

"Of listening to your little business proposal," interrupted the entrepreneur, folding his arms in front of his chest. "Fine, I get it. But you might as well save your breath. You know I can't trust you. Not after—not after what happened in Shenandoah."

"The black code again," replied Brone with a shake of his head, ever the captious professor. "Let me explain something to you, Natch. That black code is the only thing that's kept you alive this long. You think it was your cunning and ingenuity that kept the Council from finding you time and again? No, it was *my* code, masking and encrypting your bio/logic signatures. Erasing the breadcrumbs you leave behind on the Data Sea. It's only because of my foresight that you got out of the Tul Jabbor Complex in one piece."

The entrepreneur blanched. "You caused the infoquake?"

Brone shook his head. "No, I'm afraid I had nothing to do with that. But I figured the Council would try to take you into custody if the hearing started going the libertarians' way. So when the infoquake hit, my team was already in place, ready to get you out of there. I saved your *life*, Natch."

"And last month when you ambushed me in the alleyway? I suppose you think you were saving my life then too?"

"Yes," replied the bodhisattva, not missing a beat. "Don't forget— Creed Thassel has eyes and ears everywhere, including the Defense and Wellness Council. We see what the rest of the world refuses to see." He tapped his cheekbone twice, right under the artificial eye. "Len Borda was drawing up plans to march on Andra Pradesh again, Natch. He was planning to seize MultiReal at your little demo. Fortunately for you, *I* came up with the idea of hiding you from the Council's prying eyes. Convincing Borda that you had disappeared and weren't going to show up to Andra Pradesh anyway. And it worked! With your appren- tices running around all over the globe trying to find you, the Council had no choice but to call the operation off.

"So we woke you up a few hours early, assuming you'd immediately scurry over to the Surina compound and prepare for your demo. A demo you could now safely deliver without government interference. But what did you do instead?" He laughed mirthlessly. "You ran off to Len Borda and offered him MultiReal yourself—so Borda could pro- tect you from *me*!"

Natch folded his arms and clutched his chest in a vain effort to stop the trembling. He took a quick glimpse at the solemn faces around the table and saw that their argument had sapped all traces of levity from the room. "So why dress up in black robes and ambush me like that? What was that all about?"

Loget cackled. "The black robes were camouflage," he said. "You weren't supposed to *see* us. Sterno here blew that strategy by firing the first shots too early."

"Told you we should have hired professionals," Billy Sterno sulked under his breath, then stuffed his face with more egg.

"The robes were camouflage," said Brone, "but they were also a bit of necessary theatrics. You weren't supposed to see us, but the Council *was*. We needed to convince Borda that you'd really been abducted."

The entrepreneur stood slowly and planted his clenched fists on the table. "You think I'm stupid enough to believe this story?" he said. "You really think I can trust you?"

Around the table, the Thasselians were throwing each other wor- ried looks. Brone leaned forward, folding his real and faux fingertips together on the table. Suddenly Natch could see the ceaseless hatred that had been burning in his eyes since the Shortest Initiation. Nothing had changed in the past month. Indeed, nothing had changed since that day a dozen years ago when Natch had watched him writhing and bloody in the backseat of a Council hoverbird.

"You want to know how you can trust me?" said the bodhisattva in a voice kicking with strangled fury. "You can trust me because I kept you *alive*, Natch. Because I arranged to pull you out of that mess at the Tul Jabbor Complex instead of leaving you to the mercy of Len Borda's truth extractors. Don't you think I want revenge? I've had opportunities. Multiple opportunities. And each time I've held back. Why? Because I *need* you here.

"Why plug you with black code under the cover of night? I told you, Natch. You were about to hand MultiReal over to the Council on a jeweled platter. You had just terminated our loan agreement and indicated that you had no intention of listening to reason. Someone needed to save you from yourself. I did."

Natch straightened up and prepared to walk out the door. Surely there was no clearer definition of insanity than staying here in the den of his oldest and gravest enemy. The idle chatter around the table completely ceased. Several dozen pairs of eyes watched silently, but nobody made any move to restrain him.

"I repeat, Natch: if you decide to leave, I won't stop you," said Brone. He extended one hand toward the exit. "But tell me this. Where will you go?"

Natch stopped short. He sat down.

Brone nodded, all levity bled from his demeanor. It was almost a comfort seeing him like this: brooding, unforgiving, self-absorbed to the extreme. "Good," he said. "Now you know *how* I arranged to bring you here. Would you like to know *why*?"

• • •

Natch stood before a massive workbench in the middle of the atrium, watching the spectacle of the MultiReal code unfolding in MindSpace. Most of the Thasselian devotees had been ordered to the hotel's upper floors as a precondition for Natch to even open up the program. Only

Brone and Pierre Loget remained. They sat together on the highest of the crescent platforms, legs dangling fearlessly off the edge.

"And *now* you're ready to proceed?" said Brone, somewhat amused. His voice was remarkably clear considering the distance.

"Maybe," scowled Natch. "Tell me what I'm doing."

"Let's call it a proof of concept," replied the bodhisattva. "A theory I've been working on, which Pierre here has helped me fine-tune."

"What kind of theory? What are you talking about?"

"Indulge me."

Natch grumbled and nearly threw down his bio/logic programming bars. "Okay. So let's get *on* with it already."

The bodhisattva nodded. "This beacon"—Natch heard the mental blip of an incoming message—"will take you to a little subroutine Pierre and I put together. I'm sorry it's not more elegant, but without access to the MultiReal code we had to do a lot of guesswork."

The entrepreneur followed the beacon and called up Brone's subroutine in a barren quadrant of MindSpace. It resembled an exoskeleton of sorts, a threadbare coat into which the enormity of the MultiReal castle might slip. There were remarkably few strands to the code. It looked more like an upgrade patch than a typical subroutine. "What does it do?"

"That's what the demonstration's for," snapped Brone, irascible. "Come now. I've done what you asked. I sent all the other devotees away. Pierre and I are sitting way up here on this ridiculous platform so we can't meddle. And we'll happily sit here for the rest of the day while you examine every strand of our little add-on. But whatever you're going to do, *please* go ahead and do it. It's cold up here, and my Frankenstein arm is starting to freeze up."

Loget seemed to find this funny. He chuckled, then lay back on the platform and stared at the ceiling. By the rhythmic tapping of his feet, Natch got the impression he was listening to something slow and mesmerizing on the Jamm.

The entrepreneur stared at the subroutine for a good ten minutes, trying to get some inkling of what he was about to do. Finally, he withdrew a pair of bio/logic programming bars from their holsters on the side of the workbench and got started. Brone exhaled loudly in relief.

After all the scheming and maneuvering and running Natch had been doing for the past six weeks, it was a tremendous relief to finally get back to MindSpace programming. MindSpace was a comfortable and familiar place where he could simply slide into a groove without devoting too much of his depleted energy to it. The metal bars felt like extensions of his own arms.

It took the better part of the afternoon to attach Brone's spare scaffolding to Margaret's MultiReal fortress. Many of the connectors Brone and Loget had provided were in the right place, but there were still a lot of adjustments to make. Natch was puzzled to discover that most of the fibers in the scaffolding were actually redundant, as if the Thasselians had attempted to re-create functions that, unknown to them, had already been built into the original.

After completing the basic connections, Natch spent another hour focusing on security. He knew the shapes of most of the common code leeching and diluting routines; the scaffolding didn't contain any of them. But after all Natch had been through, he wasn't about to leave anything to chance. He double-checked. He triple-checked.

The Thasselians took Natch's paranoia with surprisingly good humor. At one point, Natch overheard them discussing favorite novels, with Loget choosing Bandelo's *Mystical Requiem* and Brone favoring Melville's prehistoric *Moby-Dick*. They each dozed for part of the afternoon as well. How the rest of Brone's flunkies were occupying their time upstairs, Natch couldn't imagine.

"All right," he said finally in a stentorian voice to get their attention. "I'm done."

Brone slowly found his feet and brushed himself off, while Loget cut his connection to the Jamm. The bodhisattva made a hand gesture, causing the crescent platform to lower itself until it was only about two meters off the ground. Then he burrowed his good hand into his pants pocket, fumbled around for a moment, and finally emerged with a handful of gleaming metal disks. Coins. You could find them by the shovelful in just about any collectors' market on Earth.

Brone pinched a coin between his fingers and held it aloft. "Okay, Natch," he said. "I want you to activate MultiReal."

Natch did so on tenterhooks, waiting for some malicious side effect to rush over him. He felt only the normal insanity, the normal electric charge of a mind on MultiReal. His exhaustion was quickly forgotten.

Pierre Loget peered over Brone's shoulder in keen expectation.

"Now catch this," said Brone. He threw the coin across the room.

Flash.

The MultiReal engine, throbbing, whirling, analyzing trajectories, computing atmospheric conditions, preparing eventualities. Natch, watching the possibilities unfurl on an infinite grid, zipping through would-be's and could-be's while the coin hung suspended in midair, a tiny moon for a dwarf planet. Narrowing—sorting—selecting—

Flash.

Natch launched himself across the atrium, following the track that MultiReal had laid out in his mind. He stretched his hand out and grasped the small circlet easily. The coin had the faint image of a squat and many-pillared building on one side, while the other side had been buffed smooth by the ages.

Pierre Loget clapped the bodhisattva of Creed Thassel on the back. His face bore a mighty grin, as did Brone's. "I don't get it," said Natch, stuffing the coin in his pocket. "Nothing's changed. That's how it *always* works."

Brone nodded. "Precisely. Which is good, Natch. That means our little add-on hasn't affected the program's basic functionality."

"So—"

"So when does it get interesting?" said Brone. He held up two coins this time, one in each hand, and deposited the rest back in his pocket. "Right about now, I'd say. This time, I want you to activate MultiReal—and catch *both* coins for me."

Natch scratched his head. "But—"

"*Do* it!" cried Loget, stomping the platform for dramatic effect. Just at that instant, Brone tossed the coins in opposite directions.

Flash.

Even frozen in the midst of a choice cycle with time moving at a glacial pace, Natch could see that there was no possible way he could accomplish such a task. The coins were headed for opposite sides of the room. Catching either one of the coins was doable, but even a great athlete with months to practice would find catching both outside the realm of possibility. Doubly so for someone of Natch's average physique.

Why, then, was MultiReal not generating an empty set? Why was it, in fact, churning out possibilities by the thousands?

Choosing—

Flash.

Natch leapt in the air toward the left side of the atrium. He made an acrobatic hop over a chair that someone had left standing in his path, reached, snagged the coin, and landed gracefully on both feet.

Choosing—

Flash.

Natch leapt in the air toward the right side of the atrium. He built up a head of steam, slipped agilely past the workbench and the satchel of programming bars, then caught the coin a split second before it hit the ground.

Flash.

A haze of vertigo swept through the entrepreneur as he stopped, caught his balance, and realized that somehow he had achieved the impossible. He was standing in two places at once. He had run to the left; he had run to the right. He had caught both coins, and both objects sat squarely in the palms of his hands. The fabric of the universe felt like it might rip open at any moment, unleashing rabid Demons of the Aether. The world wobbled, tilted, collapsed.

Flash.

Natch heard the *clink-clink-clink* of a coin striking marble. He shook his head violently, then looked up and realized he had only caught one of the two objects after all. It took him a few seconds to figure out that he had, in fact, executed the second choice, and was now standing on the right side of the atrium clutching a well-weathered euro. Natch wondered if he had failed at his task until he heard the sound of Brone and Loget's exultant laughter. The two were clapping each other on the back, leaping up and down in triumph.

"Welcome," said Brone, "to Possibilities 2.0."

(((38)))

The stalk carrying Brone and Pierre Loget's platform slid languidly down to the ground, giving Natch time to apply additional protections on the MindSpace bubble and shut it off. But Brone had no designs on stealing Natch's hard-fought code, at least for the moment. Instead he stood patiently beside the platform, eyes averted, and waited for the entrepreneur to finish his prophylactic measures. Loget, meanwhile, crept silently up the stairs without a word.

"Come," said Brone when the entrepreneur had dropped his bio/logic programming bars on the workbench. "Let's explore the city and find some coffee."

Natch nodded, still shaken by the bizarre MultiReal experience he had just been a party to. He could use some fresh air in his lungs, even if it was speckled with the debris of ancient conflict. The two strode out the door.

Chicago in twilight was a surreal vision. Natch had wandered through a few works of old-world SeeNaRee before, but they had all failed to capture the profound emptiness of a fossilized city. Kilometer upon kilometer of shattered concrete and rusty metal. Congealed blobs of melted rubber serving as boundaries for makeshift roads. The ghosted carcasses of office buildings standing mute sentry, some toppled. Books, machine entrails, fused glass. And through it all, no sound but the distant susurration of the wind. There was no sign of life that Natch could see; and yet, he couldn't help but feel like they were being watched.

"Let me ask you a question," said Brone, startling Natch out of his reverie. The bodhisattva was pacing slowly down the street with hands clasped behind him. "Why MultiReal?"

Natch snorted. "What kind of question is that?"

"I'm being completely serious. I watched that silly speech of Rey

Gonerev's the other day. I've read all Ridglee's and Sor's absurd allegations: *Natch doesn't care about MultiReal! He just wants money and power!*" Brone let out a morbid chuckle as he sidestepped a piece of corroded plastic sheeting. "Ridiculous! You could have easily sold MultiReal for more money than you could ever spend in a lifetime. So why keep it?"

Natch thought back to Jara's question all those weeks ago, when MultiReal was nothing more than a will-o'-the-wisp hovering over the horizon. *So what is the end? Where do all those means lead to?* A hundred words jockeyed for position on the tip of his tongue, but he couldn't choose among them. He simply stared ahead and said nothing.

Brone shook his head. "Typical Natch," he said. "You've been clawing your way up the Primo's ratings your whole life just to get an opportunity like this, haven't you? Like we were programmed to do in the hive. And you can't tell me *why?*" The habitual sneer was creeping back onto his face, but Natch didn't mind. A disdainful Brone was much more familiar than a welcoming one.

"Like it or not, Natch, you are the paragon of our trade," continued his old hivemate. "Even Margaret Surina was no match for you! She spent half a lifetime honing this technology to perfection—and then you came along at the last possible minute and stuck your name on it. As if you had anything to do with building Margaret's Phoenix Project! As if you even knew what it *was* when you signed up for it."

On another night, Natch might have raged at his former hivemate or sought to beat him bloody. Tonight, he was simply drained, beyond emotion. "But you knew what it was, didn't you?" he said. "Or, at least, your little sycophant Pierre Loget did."

Brone did not dispute Natch's characterization of his devotee. "Yes. As you know, Loget was the first one Margaret approached about licensing her Phoenix Project. You *did* know that, Natch, didn't you? Or is this something else she conveniently forgot to tell you?"

"I knew." *I completely failed to see the importance of it—but yes, Margaret did tell me.*

"Well, Loget's a first-rate engineer, but he's something of a buffoon," continued the bodhisattva. "Margaret practically laid MultiReal in his hands, and he didn't know what to do with it. It was only after Loget bungled the job that she went to the Patels—and Loget, meanwhile, came to me, the bodhisattva of his creed.

"But we're getting off track. We were talking about *you*, Natch. We were trying to unravel exactly why you've been defending Multi-Real so doggedly these past several weeks. Here's what I believe. I believe that Serr Vigal was right. You want MultiReal because you believe it will give you freedom."

Natch, irritable, kicked at a jagged chunk of asphalt. "So why didn't you just fucking *say* that?"

Brone did not take umbrage at the entrepreneur's impatience or alter his steady walk down the boulevard in the slightest. "Because it proves a point, Natch. I understand you. I know what you're searching for, because it's the same thing I've been searching for since the hive. Margaret Surina called it *freedom from cause and effect*. But only Kordez Thassel had the courage to call this freedom what it really is: selfishness."

The bodhisattva came to a halt in the middle of what must have once been a mighty crossroads, a center of ancient commerce. Four separate roads converged and mingled in a daisy loop, while doddering towers kept vigil. A hand-painted sign labeled COFFEE sat atop the doorway of one tower. Natch did a double take, feeling like he was reading the punch line for an obscure joke. Brone had suggested they get coffee, but Natch had taken it for a figure of speech, an excuse to get out of the old hotel. Did he really expect to find anything drinkable in these ruins? Apparently so, for he disappeared inside the doorway without another word.

Natch took a quick glance behind him to make sure the way back to the dilapidated hotel was clear, not because it was any kind of sanctuary, but because at the very least it was a familiar setting. There was still this eerie feeling of constant surveillance, like there were eyes around every corner. He turned back to the COFFEE tower and looked through the murky windows for signs of life. There seemed to be people stirring in there after all, residents of this horrid city, though who and how many Natch could not tell.

He followed Brone inside.

• • •

Not only were there people inside the building, but the substance they were slurping from their crude stoneware mugs did indeed smell like coffee. Brone gave a genial nod to a group of thirty-something men lounging on a pair of tired sofas; the men nodded back. Their clothing was ragged, but not so ragged that it couldn't simply pass as bohemian in connectible society. Natch followed Brone down a narrow staircase, tight-lipped, wary of what might be waiting at the bottom.

It was a café.

Perhaps not a café like those that dotted the sidewalks and shopping clusters of Shenandoah, but close enough. A score of old wrought-iron tables were arranged loosely in a low, wide interior courtyard that might have been open to the sky back in pre-Revolt days. Now a pair of monstrous concrete pillars slanted across the skylight, both blocking out the sun and keeping the rubble at bay. There were perhaps twenty people scattered throughout the café in clumps of two and three, nursing cups of coffee.

So these are the diss, thought Natch. Most of the sources he had seen on the Data Sea portrayed them in two-dimensional stereotype: grimy street urchins clothed in rags, militant proles plotting sedition. But, fashion sense aside, these could have been the patrons of any other café in Shenandoah or Vladivostok or Beijing; only the technology was missing. It felt disconcertingly like initiation. No multi projections, no holographic viewscreen displays, no private messages. Here among the diss, ConfidentialWhispers really *were* confidential whispers.

Nobody seemed to object to Natch's or Brone's presence, despite the fact that they clearly did not belong. Only when the bodhisattva lifted a pair of earthenware cups off a shelf and filled them from a nearby thermos did someone take notice. A gruff woman with hair like straw walked over and exchanged a few indecipherable words with Brone. Satisfied, the woman nodded and shuffled back to her table.

Moments later, Natch was sitting with Brone at one of the wrought-iron tables, drinking coffee. Perhaps not the best he had ever tasted, but decent enough. "What's going on?" said Natch, puzzled. "Did you threaten that woman?"

"Threaten?" The bodhisattva smiled. "No, I didn't threaten anyone. We have an arrangement with these people. We do mechanical repairs for them; they tolerate our presence and provide us with the occasional . . . amenity." Brone made an ostentatious slurp from his cup, then smacked his lips.

Natch took a dubious look at their surroundings. There was a dank pile of earthenware shards sitting in the corner, evidence of a broken mug that had been simply swept out of the way and forgotten. Besides tepid coffee, what kind of amenities could residents of a place like this possibly provide?

"Don't tell me you've bought into the government propaganda," said Brone, reading the disdain written on Natch's face. "The diss aren't out here because they're paupers, Natch . . . they're here because they're *dissidents*."

Natch made a sour look. "Could've fooled me."

The bodhisattva sniffed drolly. "Yes, admittedly some wander out to the old cities because they can't hack it in connectible society. But most of them belong to the diss because they prefer it here. They've taken our society and stripped it down to its bare essentials." He made a slight gesture toward a group of middle-aged men who seemed to be playing cards using actual laminated cards. "Tell me you don't under-stand that impulse, Natch. No Primo's ratings, no fiefcorp tax break pressures, no drudge gossip—just simple transaction. Barter. Here's what I can do for you . . . now what can you do for me?

"You want freedom from society's pressures? You want the complete and utter *freedom* that Margaret and Kordez were looking for? Rey Gonerev was right. This is the only place you're going to find it today, in the diss cities. Which leads us back to—"

"Selfishness." The entrepreneur expelled a loud breath full of contempt and slammed his cup down on the table. Hot coffee sloshed off the side, narrowly missing his hand. "Listen, you brought me out here. You saved me from Len Borda. Great. Thank you. But I'm not going to sit and listen to your elliptical bullshit forever. Get to the fucking point."

Brone smiled and gave his old hivemate a placating nod. He took another large swig of coffee, then set the mug aside. "Fine," said the bodhisattva, leaning forward with an intense look in his eyes. "Let's get down to it then. We were talking about Kordez Thassel. Old Kordez may have been a bit . . . *unhinged*, shall we say . . . but his teachings led me to a startling discovery. Selfishness is not 'evil,' Natch. It's not 'wrong.' On the contrary—it's simply *low-tech*. Tell me this . . . if you and the Patel Brothers could *both* achieve number one on Primo's, would you object?"

"It doesn't matter," muttered Natch. "We can't, and that's that."

"You're right, of course," said Brone. "The universe doesn't give us this option. Instead it gives us the zero-sum game. In order for you to *win* the highest ratings on Primo's, the Patel Brothers and Lucas Sentinel and Bolliwar Tuban and all of those other fools must *lose*. Am I right? For someone to be on top, by definition someone else must be on the bottom.

"Oh, you can mask the sting of defeat by rewarding the effort and not the result. We all tried very hard to reach number one on Primo's, so we all win! But the selfish ones like you and me, we refuse to participate in this childish game. We play to win, and so people call us cruel. They call us *malicious*. But I know you, Natch—you're not malicious. You don't wish anyone else harm, even the Patel Brothers. You just want to be left alone to concentrate on your own priorities.

"But what options do the selfish ones have? We can bury our desires. We can press on and ignore the slanders from the Sen Sivv Sors of the world. Or we can run away to a place like this. A place where the bonds and restraints of community are practically nonexistent." Brone made an expansive gesture around the café. The woman with the straw hair was managing to keep one eye on Natch while still keeping up with her companions' debate over orbital colony politics. "Society has never been able to resolve the conflict between the group and the individual, because *we simply haven't had the technology.* Until now."

Natch could feel a trickle of sweat creep down his brow and make its way to the side of his nose. "MultiReal," he breathed.

The bodhisattva nodded. "Exactly! What did Margaret Surina promise us? She promised us *the ultimate freedom. The ultimate empowerment.* She said she would give us *the path to complete control over our destinies.* Sadly, Margaret did not live to deliver on her promises—but you and I will. That's what Possibilities 2.0 is about. Together you and I will deliver a world of complete and total selfishness *without* destruction.

"A world permanently wiped clean of the zero-sum game."

• • •

Natch had caught a number of suspicious looks from the corner of his eye in the past fifteen minutes, but only when Brone paused his little oration did the entrepreneur realize what was going on. He had not been imagining the stares and the surveillance, nor was he imagining the deference they were paying the bodhisattva here. The diss weren't merely tolerating Brone's presence; they were protecting him. Natch studied the woman with the straw hair and her companions, now pointedly staring back at him, and he wondered what these people possibly stood to gain from this whole Revolution of Selfishness. He wondered what they would do if he gave in to his impulses and clocked Brone over the head with a coffee mug.

"So you want to use MultiReal to *end the zero-sum game*," said Natch, doing his best to ignore the watching diss. "How?"

"Let's start at the beginning," replied Brone. "What makes Multi-Real so revolutionary? The ability to dodge darts and hit baseballs? No, of course not. Those are parlor tricks—gimmicks to get people's attention. Margaret's real breakthrough was figuring out how to unharness the brain from the bridle of real time. Millions of possible outcomes mapped out in the space of an instant. Loget's told me all about it: a giant grid stretching out in every direction. Infinite possibility is only a state of mind!

"Now here's where you need to abandon linear thinking. With infinite possibilities at your disposal—with all those realities ripe for the plucking—why stop at just outputting one?"

Natch snorted. "Because there's only one *you*," he said. "I'm not an idiot. I know what you're getting at. Throw two coins, catch them both. But you can't catch them both. You've only got one set of hands. We proved that back at the hotel."

Brone drilled Natch with his intense stare. "One set of *real* hands, yes. But what about in multi?"

Natch pursed his lips but said nothing.

"Clearly our little demonstration at the hotel proved one thing," continued the bodhisattva. "Our minds have more than enough processing power to run several tracks of consciousness at the same time. Consciousness is itself little more than a parlor trick, a low-bandwidth illusion. We've known this since ancient times. Yet we've never been able to duplicate it, until now.

"You say multiple simultaneous realities are useless in a world where we only have one set of flesh and bones," said Brone. "Fair enough. But how much time do we actually spend in that world of flesh and bone anymore? This is a programmable world, Natch! We live sixty percent of our lives in virtual environments. Your Vault account is just a row on a stratospheric database table. The layout of your apartment is malleable and subject to change with a thought. The postings you make on the Data Sea, the music you listen to on the Jamm, the bio/logic programs you tinker with in MindSpace: all virtual. The physical world doesn't hold us back anymore. The *only* barrier is that single consciousness—and Margaret's MultiReal program shatters it."

The entrepreneur's head felt bloated, too clogged with contradictions to respond properly. "But what *good* is it? Why would you want to live multiple lives like that?"

"What good is it? What good is any technology?" Brone was getting too agitated for the chair to contain him, so he stood and leaned on its back like a lectern. "Technology expands choice," he said. "It liberates us from cause and effect, just like Margaret promised. Don't you remember her speech a couple of months ago? I remember every word of it. *What would our lives be like if we had made different choices? In the Age of MultiReal, we will wonder no more—because we will be able to make many choices. We will be able to look back at checkpoints in our lives and take alternate paths. We will wander between alternate realities as our desires lead us.*

"Just imagine it! Two roads diverge in a wood. Why choose between them when you can take both? You can spawn separate multi projections to travel them and give each one a separate consciousness to experience them. Who's to say you can't choose two different jobs, two different companions, two different Vault accounts? And if one of these lives leads to bad consequences—well, then wipe it out! MultiReal can erase your memories, Natch, and the memories of those around you! Don't tell me you've lived your entire life without regrets."

"Of course not," said Natch, "but—"

Brone abruptly yanked off his prosthetic arm and slammed it on the table. All conversation in the café ceased. "Don't tell me you've never made a choice you wanted to take *back*," he snarled, his voice brimming with sudden rage.

Awkward and embarrassed silence held sway in the room as everyone watched the pale limb sitting on the wrought-iron table. Natch took a sidelong glance at the middle-aged card players, who were staring at him with open contempt. He doubted that the diss knew the story of the Shortest Initiation, but clearly they understood the inference of Brone's gesture. Natch cursed the bodhisattva silently. *How funny that his handicaps only seem to be an inconvenience when it suits him*, he thought. He remembered how Brone had used the limb to similar effect during their meeting last month.

The silence continued for another minute, and then finally everyone turned back to their mugs of coffee as if by unspoken consensus. The bodhisattva reached over and quietly reattached his appendage without a word.

"Listen," hissed Natch. "I see what you're trying to do, but this Possibilities 2.0 would never work. You'd have to get governments to rewrite laws. The Vault and the Data Sea engineers and Dr. Plugenpatch and who *knows* who else would have to buy into it."

"I never said it would be easy," replied Brone blithely, taking his seat once more. His anger seemed to have dissolved as quickly as it had appeared. "I never said it would happen overnight."

"But even if you do get everyone to agree," said Natch, "there's something else you're not taking into account. Once *one* person uses MultiReal to do two things at the same time, everyone *else* has to keep track of those alternate realities too."

Brone shrugged. "So?"

"For process' preservation—think about the baseball example. Hit a baseball two different ways, you've just doubled the number of alternate realities. Then for every hit, you've got an outfielder making two different catches. Quadrupled. The umpire makes two different calls for each catch. The guy on base runs or doesn't run. . . . This whole thing would spiral out of control in an *instant*. Sixty billion people creating alternate realities at the drop of a hat and banging them up against each other? Fuck, where would you store all that data? How would the computational system handle it? You give everyone the ability to permanently double or triple realities—we'd get pummeled all day long until our OCHREs gave out. We're getting bombarded with infoquakes as it is."

The bodhisattva of Creed Thassel took a long, loud slurp of coffee. He leaned back and hung his good arm over the back of his chair, staring at Natch with eyes narrowed. "And do you think that's a coincidence?"

Natch felt a sudden fear grip his sternum. "You mean—"

Brone shook his head in befuddlement. "I can't believe I need to explain this to you, after everything you've learned about Len Borda. Borda knows that Possibilities 2.0 is within our grasp, Natch. Remember, he's the one who *funded* the project in the first place. He knows better than anyone what this program can do. He knows the Data Sea can handle the load. So what better way to keep us from pursuing it than to *frighten* us?"

Natch remembered the explosion of darts at the Tul Jabbor Complex, the ferocious precision of the Defense and Wellness Council officers. Hundreds of darts striking him within his mind, hundreds of merciless public executions, averted only through the magic of Multi-Real. He remembered the shrewd visage of the high executive before the demo at Andra Pradesh. Len Borda was a man who knew what he was doing.

"After the first infoquake, what did Borda do?" said Brone, his voice lowering in volume even as it increased in intensity. "He pressured the Prime Committee into giving him the authority to shut down any bio/logic program on the Data Sea that crosses his path. Do you think he wants to lose that power?

"He will. And soon.

"Because we can take *down* the Defense and Wellness Council, Natch! We can bring government back into the hands of people's freely chosen L-PRACGs, where it belongs. With a fully functioning Multi-Real network in the hands of every man, woman, and child, the Council will instantly become irrelevant. How could you possibly tyrannize people armed with multiple realities?

"Think of all the revolutions throughout history. Bloody, wasteful, expensive, full of needless suffering. We can avoid all that, Natch! With MultiReal, *we can change the world without firing a single shot.* A perfect, bloodless revolution. An instant, irreversible gift of freedom to humanity!"

Brone had begun to raise his voice again, to metamorphose into the same zealot who had set the Thasselian devotees aflame last night. By the time he finished his little speech, the bodhisattva was standing once more and pounding his fist on the tabletop. The diss watched with guarded expressions on their faces, but Natch would not make the mistake of calling them *indifferent* again. These people were clearly vested in Brone's success. They believed in the Revolution of Selfishness, and they were ready to fight for it.

"Look around you, Natch!" said the bodhisattva, sweeping his arm in an arc at the makeshift café. "Multi connections are weak out here in the diss cities. Council surveillance is a farce. The Meme Cooperative, the Prime Committee, and the drudges don't *exist* out here.

"We have everything we've ever dreamed of in Chicago! The flexibility to do whatever we want, to follow our ideas to their ultimate conclusion, and *fuck* the rules! We have some of the best bio/logic engineers in the business at our disposal, and a network of anonymous devotees spread throughout the world. And virtually unlimited funding, courtesy of the creed.

"You'll have to disappear for a while, Natch. We'll wait until the whole affair at the Tul Jabbor Complex has died down, until Len Borda's infoquakes have gone into remission. Meanwhile, we'll be out here, carefully perfecting our code. And then, just when the world is convinced you're dead and buried—when even Borda believes that you've vanished for good—we'll strike! We'll release Possibilities 2.0 onto the Data Sea and bring humanity to the next stage of evolution."

Natch's head spun like a whirligig from one incoherent thought to the next. Was this really what Margaret Surina had envisioned, really what she had planned for? How did this differ from what Khann Frejohr had proposed? What would Serr Vigal say about this? Reeling with ethical vertigo, he slumped down in his chair, ducked his head, and clasped his hands behind his neck.

"So what if you're wrong?" he managed faintly. "What if Margaret was wrong? What if those infoquakes *aren't* coming from Len Borda, and MultiReal totally floods the computational system? Possibilities 1.0 was resource-intensive enough—Possibilities 2.0 is on a whole different scale altogether. Everything could break down. Billions of people could die."

Brone sat back and folded his hands in his lap. The entrepreneur looked at him only to find himself staring at the nacreous green mechanical eye.

"Now you see the dilemma," he said. "If we don't act—if we deliver MultiReal into the hands of the Defense and Wellness Council —the carnage would be incalculable. The consequences? A totalitarian regime without end. A regime that *cannot* be overthrown. And *then* how many billions would die?"

Natch worked out a complicated system for collaborating on the MultiReal code that evening. The Revolution of Selfishness notwithstanding, his stores of trust were still much too low for him to give Brone unfettered access.

And so Natch spent most of the night studying the virtual castle in MindSpace and partitioning it into logical subdivisions. It was a fiendishly difficult task, considering there were so many alcoves of the castle—no, entire *wings*—that Natch did not understand. He found buried structures constructed with a queer logic that defied all conventional wisdom. The further Natch delved, the more surreal it became. There were strange trapezoidal shapes and whimsical loop-de-loops programmed with methods dating back to Par Padron's time, if not further. There were subroutines that looked like the sloppy work of a hive child and yet accomplished the impossible nonetheless. There were repeating patterns, optical illusions, meta-referents to meta-referents, echoes of genius or madness.

By the time the first devotee reeled down the stairs for the day, Natch had put together a rudimentary system of collaboration. He explained the whole thing to the group at their morning meeting.

The Thasselians would be allowed to work on MultiReal in teams of three for no more than two hours at a time. Each team would be given access to a different, mutually exclusive section of the castle. Natch would supervise everyone's activities at all times. There would be no discussing work with colleagues. The Thasselians would be restricted to a limited set of bio/logic programming bars and hand gestures. And when Natch closed up the program for any reason whatsoever, all activity would cease immediately.

"If anybody violates any of these rules, I'm gone," announced the entrepreneur. "Permanently. No appeals, no arguments, no warnings. Are we clear?"

A garden of PokerFaces bloomed on the devotees' faces to cover their irritation. Billy Sterno gave a supplicating look at Brone, which the bodhisattva quickly stifled with an imperious look of his own

Natch knew perfectly well this was a ludicrous way to work. The Thasselians could only make so much progress in such confined spaces, and Natch could only accomplish so much himself without a fully cooperative team. But it would have to suffice until Brone and his disciples had earned Natch's trust.

Brone didn't put up a jot of resistance. Instead he hopped onto one of the nearby platforms and held his synthetic hand out palm down, like a preacher blessing his congregation. "You heard the man," he said. "Those are the rules of operation, and we're going to abide by them in letter *and* spirit. I'm counting on all of you. Keep on your toes, and keep each other compliant. Any questions?"

The devotees stood there mute, the very portrait of obedience.

"All right, Natch," said the bodhisattva, withdrawing a programming bar from his shoulder satchel and hefting it in his real hand. "When do we start?"

Natch eyed his old hivemate coldly. Brone's forced cheerfulness was really starting to burn him, and he relished the opportunity to douse it altogether. "*You* don't start at all," said the entrepreneur. "I still don't trust you. All you get to do is watch."

Pierre Loget sputtered out a mouthful of nitro, and a few of the devotees held their breath. Natch silently activated MultiReal just in case. He was still reeling from the chase at the Tul Jabbor Complex and doubted he could muster up the energy to use it effectively. *But Brone doesn't know that, does he?* thought Natch.

Brone did not seem daunted in the slightest; he took Natch's smackdown with uncharacteristically good humor. The bodhisattva nodded and jammed the programming bar back into its case. "Suit yourself," he said, hopping off his platform and striding down the corridor without another word.

• • •

And so Possibilities 2.0 stumbled into development.

It had been a long time since Natch had the leisure to stretch out in MindSpace, to rev up, to push his mental engines to redline. For the past few weeks, he had been so busy dealing with the various political and logistical roadblocks in his path—the Defense and Wellness Council, the Meme Cooperative, Jara's insubordination, the drudges—that his programming skills were beginning to rust. He would find himself staring at bricks of code, bio/logic tools in hand, unsure how he had gotten there or where he was heading next. Should he use the L bar or the N bar here? What was the point of this recursive function he had started?

But then Natch would feel himself unwind. He would stare at the milling Thasselians, the crescent platforms, the prelapsarian luxury of this Chicago hotel, and he would think, *I'm safe.*

Not completely safe, of course. Not completely without risk. But here in the demesne of the diss, he was sheltered from meddlesome drudges and politicians. Brone's black code made him invisible to the Council, and Brone's money freed him from economic pressure. Best of all, he had completely escaped the competitive grind of the bio/logics business. In Old Chicago, Primo's ratings were as inconsequential as moon dust; Frederic and Petrucio Patel were a universe away.

It was as Brone promised. Development with no interruptions.

There was still the question of how to deal with the Surina/Natch Fiefcorp. Natch berated himself once again for ever believing that he understood Jara. Now, because of his mistake, Jara had core access to MultiReal—which meant she had the ability to sabotage all the Thasselians' work. Was Natch doomed to spend his days in an endless cat-and-mouse game with Jara, each trying to undo the other's work? So far, the fiefcorpers had kept their hands off, but certainly that wouldn't be the case forever. Horvil had already erected enough roadblocks in the software to seriously slow things down.

As for the Thasselians, they were hewing to the tack Brone had set for them. Quiet and compliant, they did exactly what they were told without demurral. Even Billy Sterno and Pierre Loget, programmers whose skills equaled or exceeded Natch's own, carried out his instructions to the letter.

The atmosphere changed significantly at night. Some of the devotees would get a little rowdy on the upper floors after dark, drinking, singing at rafter-shuddering volumes, skulking off arm in arm for the occasional tryst. It reminded Natch of the hive. He could hardly blame them for their excesses, given that they were all stuck out here with nowhere to go and nobody to talk to. The diss showed up on occasion to take advantage of the Thasselians' engineering skills, but none of them were keen on socializing. Natch could only imagine how Brone's minions were feeling. Certainly some of them had left friends, colleagues, and loved ones behind when they decided to join the Revolution.

And Brone? Brone kept to himself. Natch had figured his old enemy would take every opportunity to study the intricacies of Multi-Real, but nothing could be further from the truth. From time to time he would appear on the programming floor and stroll around slowly, saying nothing. Yet he hardly gave the program a second glance.

Natch still couldn't exclude the possibility that this was all just an elaborate ruse. Brone had waited more than a dozen years to exact his revenge for the Shortest Initiation; what was another week or another month? Perhaps he was trying to figure out how to mount a successful attack against Natch without failing miserably like the soldiers in the Tul Jabbor Complex. Luckily Brone knew nothing about the exhaustion that set in after running through thousands of continuous choice cycles, and Natch had no intention of cluing him in. Uncertainty was Natch's ally here.

The only time the two of them had any real interaction was during policy and strategy sessions. There were still hundreds of logistical questions that needed to be answered on the basic Possibilities 1.0 interface alone; Possibilities 2.0 would be impossible to master until they had answered these questions. How would the system resolve MultiReal conflicts? How many choice cycles could a user process in that split-second mental interlude? What would happen if the user failed to select *any* choice cycle? Natch had been too pressed for time to explore issues like these when he was still with the fiefcorp. Now he found it difficult to sift through them without Horvil's and Jara's help.

But those questions were elementary compared to the conundrums they would face in Possibilities 2.0. Philosophical questions, ontological questions, questions straight out of the science fiction stories Natch used to read as a boy. How many alternate realities could a person sustain at the same time, and how far should those realities be allowed to diverge? Under what circumstances could an alternate reality be abandoned, and what would happen then? Did alternate realities need to be filtered for the rest of the world, so that some people would see possibility *x* and some would see possibility *y*? If so, how would MultiReal handle the mechanics of that filtering? If not, what would happen if two of your alternate selves bumped into each other?

One evening Natch found himself discussing the limits of Multi-Real with Brone. Astounding that they could progress so far without knowing answers to such basic questions. It was enough to make Natch's knees buckle.

"I'm not sure I understand which limits you're talking about," said Brone.

"Spatial limits, for one," replied Natch. "Let's go back to the soccer analogy. If a player on one end of the field can flip on MultiReal and catch a player on the *other* end of the field in a collaborative choice cycle . . . where does it end? Where's the—where's the cutoff?"

The bodhisattva drummed his faux fingers on the tabletop as he mulled over the question.

"This is more than just a hypothetical," continued the entrepreneur. "I caught those Council officers in the Tul Jabbor Complex with Multi-Real just by watching them on video. But what if those officers weren't even in the same auditorium? What if I was watching somebody in a totally *different* auditorium halfway around the world? Or—or on an orbital colony somewhere? Could you still open a collaborative choice cycle on them? Shit, does the other person even need to be there at all? Could I just catch Len Borda in a MultiReal loop right here, right now?"

Billy Sterno piped up from across the table. "We could limit a choice cycle to line of sight," he said.

Natch pushed himself away from his chair and paced over to Sterno with his eyes blazing. "So you're saying I can affect the outcome of a soccer game even if I'm just a spectator in the stands? Can I fly over the stadium in a hoverbird, look down on the field with a telescope, and make the goalie miss the ball?"

"We could base it on causation," said Brone. "There has to be a causal link between all parties involved in a MultiReal loop."

"Fine—but how do you *measure* that? How do you quantify it? Everything that happens on the field affects you in some way, even if it's infinitesimally small. What if you've bet a hundred credits on the game—is that enough of a causal link to engage someone on the field in a MultiReal loop?"

Nobody answered, but several people started taking notes. Natch pressed on, his brain spinning at a furious pace.

"The other thing that's been bothering me . . . We've been so focused on limits of space that we've forgotten about limits of *time*. So far we've only tested MultiReal on short interactions. Kicking a soccer ball. Deciding which way to turn. But how does the program determine how long a choice cycle can be? Can you keep the choice cycle open for a whole run down the field? Or heck, fire up Possibilities right when the opening whistle blows, and then just loop the whole *game* over and over in your mind until your team wins."

Sterno scowled. "But that means everyone would have to calculate all the interactions in the game instantly. I don't care how fast this thing works. No *way* is there enough time to resolve all those Multi-Real conflicts between one second and the next."

"So you could buffer it," replied Natch. "Let's say it takes ten or fifteen seconds to go through all the choice cycles for a whole soccer game. That's probably enough time for millions of choice cycles. Maybe billions. MultiReal could just start outputting the first few seconds and spool the rest as you go."

"How fast does this program work anyway?" said Sterno. "How many choice cycles can you run through in a split second?"

Natch stopped short. He had no idea. The answer touched on advanced Prengalian physics and involved questions that even the world's greatest minds could not answer.

The bodhisattva touched his fingertips together under his chin. "Natch, you know the software better than any of us," he said. "Margaret had sixteen years to work these problems out. What did she conclude?"

"I don't know," said Natch. "She's dead, and I never got the opportunity to ask her. The only other person who might know is sitting in a Defense and Wellness Council prison somewhere."

The meeting ended shortly thereafter on a note of grim silence. *Does MultiReal have* any *limits?* the entrepreneur found himself wondering.

Even if they managed to work through the list of technical problems, a whole other set of legal and ethical questions awaited them. Natch was hesitant to even raise the subject. The fact of the matter was, catching another person in a collaborative MultiReal process was morally shady. It meant forcing someone to participate in a software interaction without his consent—or even his knowledge, since Multi-Real erased putative memories as a matter of course. How long would the L-PRACGs stand for *that*?

Most troublesome of all was Natch's suspicion that there was nothing the law could do to stop it. Some of the programming hooks MultiReal used were buried so deep in the framework that changing them would upend fifty years of bio/logic progress. Natch had not even been aware that these hooks existed. They must have lain hidden in the standard OCHRE system for generations. How had Margaret known where to find them? Had Marcus Surina put them there? Or maybe even Prengal?

Natch kept the door to his room locked and barricaded at night. He made sure that MultiReal remained fully functional despite all their manipulations, and kept it at the ready. Just in case. Just in case.

• • •

In the end, it was the black code that caused Natch to renegotiate the terms of the agreement with his old hivemate.

The trembling that had been pillaging the nerves of his left arm began to make exploratory raids throughout his body. He would find his neck muscles twitching uncontrollably at certain times of the day. More than once, Natch opened his eyes only to realize that he had blacked out some indeterminate time before. He would immediately switch into paranoid mode, shut down the MindSpace bubble, and do a thorough review of every data strand the Thasselians had touched in the past hour. But as far as Natch could tell, Brone's devotees remained on the level.

He approached Brone in his backroom office.

"This black code cloaking program," said Natch, too exhausted to make any attempts at subtlety. "Does it have any side effects?"

The bodhisattva smiled. The prospect of seeing his enemy suffering physically seemed to give him cheer. "I was wondering when you were going to ask about that," he replied. "The shaking and the blackouts—don't think I haven't noticed."

"So it's your code that's causing them?"

"Maybe," said Brone, his smile curling into a smirk.

"Well, you need to *do* something about it," snapped Natch. "I can't work like this."

Natch folded his arms in an attempt to keep steady and eyed the room Brone had claimed as his personal headquarters. He didn't know how long Creed Thassel had been making modifications to this old hotel, but Brone seemed to have left the room exactly as he had found it. Yellowed photos of some long-forgotten Texan dynasty on the walls, a dilapidated metal desk, cracked brick on the floor, a prodigious leather sofa on which he was now reclining. A real window, with actual glass, though how it had survived the centuries since the Autonomous Revolt intact Natch couldn't guess.

The bodhisattva put his feet up on the splintered oak table in front of him and clasped his hands behind his head. "I *could* make some modifications," he said, affecting nonchalance. "We've been able to tweak that cloaking program for the rest of the crew. Billy has the occasional flutter, but everyone else is coping with the black code just fine."

"So then tweak it."

Brone sniffed. "And why should I?"

The two enemies stared each other down, Natch filling up with increasing rage and Brone sliding deeper into insouciance with every passing second. It was a peculiar game of bluffs. Natch knew that Horvil's so-called mind control trick wouldn't work here. Even if Natch could use MultiReal to find that one possibility in a thousand where Brone decided to do his bidding, he would need to repeat the same trick over and over again—possibly for hours. As he had discovered with Khann Frejohr on his balcony, that was excruciatingly hard work. Natch simply didn't have the strength for it. But he couldn't admit that to Brone, could he?

"Fix it," said Natch between clenched teeth, "or I'll leave. Right now. I'll leave and take MultiReal with me, and your 'Revolution of Selfishness' will be *over* before it even gets off the ground."

Brone shrugged. "Ah, but if you leave, that jittering is only going to get worse. *Much* worse. I've seen what that black code can do. The first volunteer ended up with the Prepared. I'd absolutely *hate* to see that happen to you."

"I'll take my chances. I can fix it myself."

"Really? Then why haven't you?"

Silence. The sounds of clanking silverware from the devotees' dinner came wafting down the hallway.

Brone's face softened into something resembling capitulation. "Understand my position, Natch. I *need* you here. You and I are the only ones who are really capable of finishing the MultiReal project. Pierre and Billy are talented programmers, I grant you that—but they're two-dimensional thinkers, or Margaret Surina would have licensed the program to them in the first place. But admit it, you need me too. You can't make all those thousands of bio/logic connections by yourself, and in case you hadn't noticed, Old Chicago's not exactly teeming with assembly-line programming shops.

"So I'm in a bind, Natch. You can use MultiReal at any point to run out of here, and we can't stop you. This black code is the only bargaining chip I *have*. So let's be reasonable businesspeople. Let's follow the example of the diss, and let's barter. You give me something I want; I'll give you something you want."

Natch, muttering under his breath: "So what do you want?"

"Only what's fair," replied Brone, opening his arms with a gesture of welcome that had more than a hint of saccharine. "Give me access to MultiReal like you've given the rest of the devotees. I'm not asking for core access. I'll stick with the same subset of programming tools, I'll abide by the rest of your rules. Just let me *do* something instead of sitting back here killing time."

"That's all?"

"That's all."

The entrepreneur pursed his lips. He could feel the slightest decline of the road ahead into a long and slippery slope. Brone finding tool after tool to barter with. Natch granting more and more concessions.

But he held the final trump card, didn't he? Core access to Multi-Real. That was all that mattered in the end. MultiReal couldn't give Natch the power to control someone else's life; but it could give him the ultimate power to control his own. *Give Brone what he wants this time*, Natch told himself. *You're much too powerful for him to take Multi-Real away, and he knows that.*

"Fine," he said. "But I want Loget to tweak the black code. Not you. We might be working side by side here, but I still don't trust you."

The bodhisattva rose and gave an ingratiating bow. His prosthetic eye caught the light and twinkled. "I wouldn't expect anything less from you, Natch," he said. "I'll make sure Loget is on the case first thing tomorrow morning."

(((40)))

Natch was starting to remember why he had never sought out Pierre Loget's company. The man's brain ran on dandelion logic, scattering to the four corners of the Earth in the slightest breeze. Loget began the morning chattering about Hegelian dialectics, then flitted on to modern Patronellian dance and the thermodynamics of hoverbird flight without any discernible segue.

"The black code," insisted Natch after ninety minutes of this. "Have you finished tuning that fucking black code?" He was lying faceup on one of the icy crescent platforms, arms tied lightly at his sides so the shaking wouldn't knock him over the edge. Loget, meanwhile, was hauling chunk after chunk of Natch's OCHRE code into MindSpace while he babbled about nothing.

"Just be patient," replied Loget. "This takes time."

"How much time?"

The Thasselian giggled nervously. "I don't really know. You should have let Brone fix you up. I've never done this before."

Natch mumbled a curse at the ceiling and shut his mouth.

At least he could finally see the code that had been tormenting him for these past weeks. It looked like a mutated treble clef, dappled with splotches of orange and purple. Natch had thought it would be a relief to put a definitive shape to his pain. Instead, the very ordinariness of the subroutine increased his depression.

After another hour, Natch started to grow suspicious. There was neither method nor madness to Loget's tinkering as far as he could see. Instead the man was fumbling around like a hive child given course-work beyond his grade level. Loget would stir blocks of code aimlessly with his bio/logic programming bars for ten minutes at a stretch without making a single connection. Natch knew that every fiefcorper had a unique methodology—*three programmers, five programming styles*, as Primo's liked to say—but this was ridiculous.

"You're delaying," barked the entrepreneur.

"No, I'm not. I swear I'm not," said Loget. "But—"

"But *what?*"

"You've got *MultiReal* code in your head, Natch. How did that get there?" The man seemed apprehensive, unsure, maybe a little awestruck. Natch didn't answer.

Loget noodled around for another hour (covering avant-garde sculpture and the lesser-known dramas of Juan Nguyen in the process) before he finally admitted that he would need to consult with Brone. Natch let him go.

This charade continued for two days. Brone stayed on the periphery of the programming floor the whole second day, and every time Natch looked in his direction he saw nothing but puzzlement on the bodhisattva's face. Natch couldn't figure out what was going on. Was Loget unwilling or incapable of accomplishing the task? Was the renegade MultiReal code in his head complicating matters? Or was this all just a masquerade to cover something else?

Meanwhile, progress on MultiReal slowed to a crawl as Natch's pains and blackout episodes grew in severity. An epic rage had been sputtering in his gut for weeks; now he could feel it picking up strength and roaring to new heights. Frustrated, Natch cut off access to the program early the second night and stormed to his room. Sleep seduced him.

He was awakened in the middle of the night by Margaret Surina.

The bodhisattva made no noise that might explain her presence. In fact, she seemed to be at the center of an inexplicable *absence* of noise, a lacuna in the world, as if the universe ceased to exist at the bottom of her toes and miraculously resubstantiated at the frayed ends of her hair.

You're dead, Natch told her. Somehow he knew that the apparition would understand him even if he didn't use his vocal cords.

But the bodhisattva did not answer. She merely stood in the center of the room and stared at Natch. She looked as she had before all the trouble started, when MultiReal was but a pseudonymous project bobbing balloonlike in the distance. Her black hair was flecked with gray; her fingers were long and precise; her eyes were ghost luminous. Her feet, he noticed, did not quite touch the ground.

What do you want? insisted the entrepreneur. *What are you doing here?*

No response.

Natch clawed at his scalp through his sandy hair. Was the Council right about him? He was sitting in bed talking to a dead woman, and he couldn't even get the dead woman to talk back. Madness. In a panic, Natch lobbed a pillow at the apparition; it passed straight through her torso and landed on the floor with a feathery *fwump*. The bodhisattva of Creed Surina did not react.

He was about to tear out of the room when Margaret began to speak. The voice was faint, nearly inaudible, and it did not emanate from her lips so much as it floated down from the ceiling.

You are the guardian and the keeper of MultiReal, Natch. Remember that. The guardian and the keeper.

And then she was gone.

Natch pondered the bodhisattva's words for a moment, accompanied by the pianissimo sounds of a decaying hotel. Squeaking floorboards, archaic climate-control machinery. Bats somewhere in the courtyard.

The guardian and the keeper. Margaret had used that phrase on top of the Revelation Spire, the last time Natch saw her alive. What did it mean? He thought of the original order of the Keepers, vilified by history, who had let the reins of the Autonomous Minds slip through their fingers. The resulting stampede had caused a global apocalypse. Was this a warning that similar things awaited if he let go of MultiReal? And why should he listen to the warning of a phantom anyway?

Enough. Enough with riddles. Enough with lies and manipulation.

Natch threw himself out of bed and grabbed a dressing gown from the hook on the door. The three parallel bars of the Creed Thassel insignia saluted him in gold thread from the breast pocket. He picked up the satchel of bio/logic programming bars Brone had lent him, bolted through the hall, and took the stairs down to the atrium three at a time.

He could feel the tiny pinprick in the back of his thigh ache as he stood before a bio/logic workbench and flipped on MindSpace. The castle zoomed out of the void until it filled the bubble.

Now that Margaret was gone and Quell had been taken away, who could he trust with MultiReal? Jara would trade it to the Council for the peace of mind, and Horvil would blindly follow her. Khann Frejohr would use it to further his narrow political agenda. Petrucio and Frederic Patel would sell it to the highest bidder without a second thought. The Council would use it as a weapon of domination and submission. And Brone? Brone would hand it out to everyone in the universe to satisfy his bizarre notions of selfishness.

But MultiReal was not some commodity to be rationed out, and nobody would bully him into giving it away. Natch could see the route he must take. The bends and curves ahead were still murky, unclear; even the ultimate destination remained hazy and indistinct. Still, he would not submit to someone else's path for MultiReal, whether that path was Khann Frejohr's, Magan Kai Lee's, or Brone's. Or Margaret's, for that matter. He would not give up.

It took Natch almost two hours to weave through all the roadblocks Horvil had put in his path. But he could afford no more delays, no more sidetracks. Every hour that Jara had administrative control of MultiReal was an hour when Natch was vulnerable. Sooner or later, the Defense and Wellness Council would realize that Natch had complied with the Meme Cooperative's order and given Jara core access after all. As soon as that happened, it was only a matter of time before they coerced the program out of her hands—and then he really *would* be irrelevant, just as Magan Kai Lee had said.

Natch found the selectors in the program that Quell had described on the soccer field in Harper. *Horvil's already demonstrated how easy it is to select the options*, he had said. *The hard part is deciding which ones to choose.* But there was no more need for ambiguity, because Natch had made his selection. No more sudden cutoffs or artificial limitations.

He made the switch. Unlimited choice cycles for all.

There was still one more step he needed to take, however. He would not get caught in an endless loop of reprisal with Jara, her erecting barriers one day, him disabling them the next. He would not be forced to find detours around Horvil's roadblocks. Natch leaned over the workbench and cast his mind out to the Data Sea. There were a trillion caches of encrypted data out there, a trillion places to hide programming code among all the connectible quarks in the world. Natch picked a suitable cove almost at random. And then, trembling all the while, he proceeded to transfer the MultiReal databases to the new hidden location, petabyte by petabyte.

Jara had tried to hide the program from Natch, but Margaret had assured him it could not be done. *MultiReal is becoming a part of you*, she had said. And it was true: Natch could feel its presence now whenever he closed his eyes. He could reach out and interface with the program even outside of MindSpace. He could find MultiReal no matter where it resided on the Data Sea.

But Jara couldn't.

The first rays of the dawning sun crept through the windows. Somewhere in the kitchen, machinery began to whir. Natch, fiefcorp master, entrepreneur, outcast, stood in the atrium, bloated with possibilities. He was the guardian and the keeper of MultiReal. And thanks to the ghost of Margaret Surina, he was now the only person in the universe who could access it.

• • •

"I can't stay here," said Natch.

Brone regarded the entrepreneur behind a cold mask of wariness and resignation. Something had changed in that prematurely aged face over the past few days, ever since Loget began his fumbling attempts at tuning the black code. The endgame was approaching, and they both knew it, though Natch couldn't tell if Brone was expecting to win or lose this contest.

Meanwhile, progress on MultiReal had finally ground to a halt. The Thasselians had not even bothered to gather in the atrium that morning for a status report; instead most of them had bundled up and gone outside to enjoy the freshly fallen snow. All except for Pierre Loget and Billy Sterno, who were sitting at the conference table down the hall, trying to solve the black code dilemma. And Brone, of course, who preferred to observe the winter alone in his backroom office.

Natch pressed on. "What you're trying to do—multiple lives for everybody. It's unworkable. I had my doubts about Possibilities 1.0, but *this* . . . The system can't handle it. I don't care how little bandwidth consciousness takes up, the Data Sea won't be able to deal with that much information. You'll crash the whole computational infrastructure."

"I don't believe that," said Brone. "I'm confident in my calculations."

"Then go ahead," said Natch, throwing his hands up in the air. "Launch Possibilities 2.0, and see what happens. It'll be worse than the Autonomous Revolt."

The bodhisattva's voice turned unctuous. "So you'd prefer to let Len Borda get his claws on it and see what unending tyranny looks like?"

"You're trying to make this a black-and-white issue. It's not that simple."

"Not that simple?" said Brone, his voice rising in mock disbelief. He turned to the oddly dressed Texans on his office wall as if expecting them to say a few words of solidarity. "It wasn't that simple when all this started, Natch. You *made* it a black-and-white issue by stubbornly refusing to explore the options. No compromises! That's been your strategy since the very beginning. Well, now it's paid off, hasn't it?

Here you are at last, no friends left, no allies, nowhere to turn! Tell me this much. You never had any intention of staying here and joining my Revolution of Selfishness, did you? You would have bolted the instant we finished tuning that black code. Or would you have taken advantage of our programming skills first, waited until Possibilities 2.0 was done, and *then* run away?" Brone leaned back in his chair, angrily opening and closing the middle desk drawer for no apparent reason. "Loget said this would happen. He told me you'd never cooperate with us, no matter how much was at stake. But I was too trusting."

"Too trusting?" said Natch with a guffaw. "Too *trusting*? Talk about false pretenses—you never intended to fix that black code. You planned on leaving me like this all along, didn't you?" He held up his right arm, now twitching as frequently and painfully as the left.

"No," insisted Brone, placing his good hand over his heart in a show of sincerity. "I'm being on the level with you. I swear, Pierre has been trying to figure out what's wrong."

Natch felt a sudden rush of nausea, though whether it was precipitated by the black code or Brone's lies he didn't know. "You haven't been on the level since the beginning," he sneered. "If you wanted to work with me, then why didn't you just approach me upfront? Why the deceit? Why the—"

"Oh, please!" The bodhisattva waved away Natch's objections with a swipe of his prosthetic hand. "I *did* approach you. Have you forgotten that I gave you *money?* It was only after you turned up your nose at me—only after you made it clear you were planning to walk straight into Len Borda's clutches with MultiReal in hand—only then that I took the recourse of black code. I gave you the benefit of the doubt, Natch! And did you deserve it? You're the man who lied and cheated his way up the Primo's charts, after all. The man without moral scruples, the man known for his inability to work with *anyone.* And you say I should have just taken your word? You think I should have just come to you without taking any precautions?"

Natch didn't know why he was still standing in his old hivemate's office taking such abuse. Better to leave now, better to run out that door into the Chicago winter while his anger was fresh. What could Brone do besides heap scorn upon him as he walked away? Yet Natch's feet felt rooted to the spot; he could not leave, not quite yet. "If you had so little faith in me," he said, "then why did you bother? I wasn't the only one who had core access to MultiReal. You could have gone to—" Natch stopped short as he felt a horrible truth stab him in the gut. His legs gave way, and he collapsed into a chair near the door. "For process' preservation," he said under his breath. "You—you murdered Margaret."

The room grew deathly quiet. Brone stood up from his chair and turned his back on Natch. Then he walked slowly to the window and folded his arms across his chest. Outside, a flotilla of dark clouds was threatening to blanket the city with more snow. A few of the devotees ambled by, muttering angry and unintelligible words at one another.

"I admit I wanted to murder her," said Brone after a long and tense silence. "I even admit that I threatened her. But it's not so easy to kill someone in cold blood, Natch. You should try it sometime. Would I have gone through with it? I honestly don't know."

"What do you mean? If you didn't kill her, then who did?"

"Nobody," replied the bodhisattva, his voice ashen. "Margaret Surina committed suicide."

Something vile wriggled its way inside Natch's belly. He remembered his last conversation with Margaret atop the Revelation Spire. She'd been in the last stages of paranoia, clutching a dartgun, barely able to recognize Natch. Barely able to recognize *Quell*. "You expect me to believe that?" said Natch in a hollow croak. "After all the lies you've told?"

Brone shrugged, conceding the point. "I'm sorry you don't believe me. But the truth is, your business partner killed herself. I watched her do it. I sat in that wretched Spire of hers and laid out my vision for Possibilities 2.0, one bodhisattva to another. I told her of my plans for the Revolution of Selfishness, just like I told you." The bodhisattva slumped forward with his palms on the windowsill. "I don't know if she even understood what I was saying. You saw how she was behaving toward the end. You were in her office right before me. I offered Margaret Surina a chance to join the Revolution, and instead she chose suicide, with her own black code. It was . . . horrible. It wasn't a quick death." He shuddered. "Undoubtedly Len Borda has already figured this out, and is just trying to decide who to pin the blame on.

"But I already had a backup plan, Natch, and that was *you*. So I waited. Because I knew it was only a matter of time before you alienated everyone and exhausted every resource. Regardless of what the Prime Committee decided, I knew you'd never hand them MultiReal. I knew that eventually you would wind up alone with Council dartguns bearing down on you, with nowhere else to turn. So when the infoquake struck at the Tul Jabbor Complex, I was ready. I swooped down, and I *saved* you.

"Not only did I save you, Natch—I brought you here to Old Chicago, and I gave you everything you'd always wanted. Unlimited resources. A partnership. The greatest technological challenge in the history of programming, and all the time in the world to master it." Brone took a deep breath, looking miserable and defeated. "I'm not sure what else you expect me to do."

"I already *told* you," said Natch. "Fix that black code. Fix it, or get rid of it."

There was no noise but the creaking of the old hotel for several minutes. Natch could see Brone's reflection in the window. The bodhisattva's eyes were dead, hollow, unmanned.

Finally, Brone spoke. "My black code isn't causing those tremors and blackouts, Natch," he said. "I don't know what is. And that's the truth."

Natch snorted. "I don't believe you."

Another pause. The storm clouds that had been threatening snow began to deliver on their promise.

"Why should I help you, Natch?" said Brone, tired. "You're

already planning to leave. This is Chicago, the city of barter. And yet you offer me nothing in exchange."

Natch picked himself up from the chair and thrust his hands in his pockets. "Why should I barter?" he said. "I've got core access to Multi-Real. I don't have to offer *anything* in return. You've got one more day. Fix the black code, or get rid of it—and *then* I'll decide if I'm going to stay. It's the only chance you've got."

Brone did not turn around. "So be it," he said.

• • •

The graveyard of midnight. Complete silence throughout the hotel.

Natch bolted out of bed and threw on his clothes. He dashed through the hallway and down the stairs. There were no revelers in the atrium tonight, no wandering insomniacs, nobody picking over leftovers from the kitchen. Through the windows, Old Chicago had nothing to offer but the wind and the sepulchral snow. Natch picked a devotee's platform at random, lowered it, and hopped on.

He knew what he had to do.

Natch stood at the workbench and waved his left hand. A shimmering bubble the size of a coin appeared in the air before him. The bubble quickly expanded until it encompassed most of the workbench, until it enveloped him entirely and blanketed the rest of the world in a translucent film.

MindSpace. An empty canvas, a barren universe. Anything was possible here.

With his right hand, Natch reached into his pocket and pulled out the black felt bag he had been carting with him for weeks now. He yanked open the drawstring and shook out the bag's hidden treasure on the workbench: ten glimmering circlets of gold, the bio/logic programming rings Quell had lent him. Natch slid them whisper-quiet onto his fingers. As soon as the rings passed the borders of MindSpace, strings of programming code leapt to his fingertips and formed an intricate pattern in the air.

The entrepreneur raised his left hand again and spread his fingers wide. The MindSpace bubble quickly filled with the swollen treble clef, the black code that had been afflicting him since that fateful night on the streets of Shenandoah.

Natch attacked.

The treble clef buzzed and whirred while the minutes passed. Mindful of what had happened the last time he tried to bombard a subroutine too quickly, Natch took absolute care with Brone's black code, only making tentative sorties at first to test the program's defenses. The rings felt more comfortable now than when he had tried them in Shenandoah. They had adapted to his movements, his pace, his style. He could have sworn they had even shrunk a size or two. Gradually, minute by minute, he began to make more complex maneuvers.

Finally, one of his attacks penetrated the program's surface, and the treble clef exploded into a thousand pieces with a deafening crash. Natch stepped back, surveyed the jagged guts of the black code.

And realized that this was definitely *not* a cloaking program.

Natch had never actually built a cloaking routine before, but he had spent long hours studying their ilk in dark corners of the Data Sea. He knew the shapes and contours to expect, and he had an idea of where the hooks should be. But this program, this black code, didn't match the profile. Links in the treble clef pointed to obscure OCHRE subsystems that would be of little use if the program did what Brone claimed. Natch wished he had paid more attention to Serr Vigal's neural programming lectures all those years ago, because most of the treble clef's nodes appeared to be tied to machines along the brain stem.

Natch stood on the lowest platform of the atrium, gazing at the stalks that jutted into the air around him like stalagmites. He felt the internal fury boil over. His suspicions had been justified; Brone had lied to him, and now he had proof.

Do you know why we're not dodging Council missiles right now? the bodhisattva had said. *Because that black code floating in your bloodstream renders you invisible to Len Borda's tracking mechanisms. Do you understand me? The Council has no way to find you.*

If the black code was not a cloaking mechanism to keep him hidden from the Defense and Wellness Council, then what was it? Why was Brone so adamant about refusing to disable it? Had Pierre Loget been faking all his efforts to tune out the code's insidious side effects? And if Brone was lying to him about the black code software, what else was he lying about?

Natch combed frantically through the MindSpace schematic looking for a way to disable the software, but it was too well crafted for the simplistic tricks that would cripple most works of black code. He remembered how skillful a programmer Brone had been even years ago at the Proud Eagle; now he was witnessing the end product of that ruthless and cunning intellect. No, even with the program's innards splayed open in MindSpace, it would take Natch hours, possibly days, to dislodge it from his skull. Could he afford to call Brone's bluff? Could he even afford to wait for Brone to discover that he had found a way inside?

Natch shut off the workbench, pocketed the felt bag with the programming rings, and ran out the front door without a backward glance.

(((41)))

I can't let you leave, Natch. Certainly you must realize that.

Faces stare from the windows of Old Chicago as Natch runs pell-mell through the streets. Past the four-wheeled fossils that were stripped to the bone hundreds of years ago. Past the untidy rubble of a tower that might have dwarfed even the Revelation Spire before it was struck down by the Autonomous Minds. To the very banks of the Great Diss Lake itself, still silted with the metal droppings of ancient warplanes.

He has been running for at least an hour when he notices that the diss have come out of their ruined towers to look for him. It's not quite dawn. Electric lights strung along the debris are still illuminating the streets. Yet there's a palpable presence, a stirring through the city as the echoes of shuffling feet fly through the alleyways. Whispered voices. He can't see anybody, not yet, but every few blocks he turns a corner and sees fresh footprints in the snow.

Somehow Brone has already discovered that he's left the old hotel. He's put the word out among the diss that Natch is a wanted man. Natch remembers Brone's overblown gesture of throwing his synthetic arm on the table in that underground café, and now he realizes that that was more than just a gesture. It was a signal. Natch has been marked.

Brone chose well when he picked Old Chicago as the launchpad for his Revolution of Selfishness. The diss are good trackers: too fiercely independent to band together for an organized pursuit, and therefore almost impossible to predict. This is the city of barter, and with Brone the diss have struck the mother lode of bargains. Keep the Thasselians safe; keep them hidden and protected; do the occasional odd job. And in return, Brone will deliver them their Shangri-la. The ability to eliminate all social boundaries, the ability to bring themselves up to the connectibles' level—or bring the connectibles down to theirs.

I didn't want it to come to this. But you've forced my hand. I can't risk Borda finding you and taking MultiReal away.

The words float through his consciousness like a memory of something he once said, yet Natch is fairly certain that he never said them. Yet it's his own voice he's hearing, his own interior monologue. What's going on?

He makes a quick left at the next intersection and goes looking for cover, only to find himself at a dead end. An impassable cul-de-sac of rusted metal and petrified wood that might once have served as a barricade during the Autonomous Revolt. He scrambles into the corner, thinking he sees a way through the morass, but it turns out to be only a deceit of the night. Natch knows that he can't continue running like this with no direction, but he's still too addled by rage and black code and exhaustion to keep track of where he's going.

Sprinting through the city at top speed temporarily distracted him from the pain and the quivering, but now both are returning with a vengeance. And the cold . . . It's frigid as death out here. Even the winter of initiation wasn't this bad, and he didn't have the artificial insulation of bio/logics back then either.

Natch backtracks, finds a deserted storefront, and stops to catch his breath. He huddles inside the empty store next to rusted metal racks that might once have contained household products. He needs to figure out some strategy for how to proceed. Where is he going? Where *can* he go? Connectible territory is off-limits with the Defense and Wellness Council on the hunt for him; and now unconnectible territory is as well. What does that leave?

He summons a map of the city from the Data Sea and tries to get his bearings. But apparently no one has made a systematic effort to scope out Old Chicago in decades. The schematics he finds hail from a more idyllic time when the streets weren't as cluttered with detritus and more of the old landmarks were still standing. He looks at the most recent map and tries to figure out which building his mother lived in. Vigal once told him that Lora lived on the thirty-fourth story of a rotting skyscraper, and even an hour ago Natch had been naive enough to think he might locate the building on that description alone. But there are a dozen such structures within walking distance, and more dot the horizon to the south and east.

A pair of young men come jogging by, leading a vicious-looking mongrel on a chain. They're peering into the shadows. Any second now they'll notice his footprints in the snow, which he's stupidly forgotten to cover up. Natch flips on MultiReal, wondering if he can use Horvil's mind control trick to divert their attention without alerting them to his presence. Thankfully, he doesn't have to worry about it, because at that moment something metal crashes to the ground a few blocks away, and the diss trackers go tearing off to investigate.

MultiReal isn't going to do you any good. You might as well save yourself the effort.

Natch leaps out from his hiding place, taking care to step in the footprints of his pursuers as much as possible. He can't last much longer out here. He's worn out, not just from the cold, not just from the incident at the Tul Jabbor Complex, but from weeks of ceaseless wandering, from years of pressing on through the maze of fiefcorpery.

He finds himself in an empty intersection and surveys the crossroads before him. North, south, east, west—which way should he turn?

But his feet will not obey him. The prospect of taking a step in any direction seems like the most difficult thing in the world. He tries to peer into the future, but he can't see beyond the next five minutes. Running, and then running, and then—

I'm sorry, Natch.

The sun finally climbs over the horizon and showers Natch with its cold light. Before he can react, the blackness is upon him.

• • •

Unmoving, unspeaking.

It is a completely desolate and dimensionless universe, a blackness without blackness. There is no more Old Chicago, no more snow, and no more diss. The very Earth and sky have dissipated away. Corporeality of any kind is nothing but an abstraction, and the constant chatter of the five senses is nothing but a memory.

And yet Natch is here.

He feels that he is present, even if there's nothing to be present *in*. But the central core of his being, the identity, the *I* that fills the pronoun, is there. Natch. His existence may actually be the *only* thing possible in this place.

He stretches his nonexistent arms and tries to reach for *something*— but there is only Nothing within reach. His legs: he kicks out with them too, expecting to find ground, or a bed, or at the very least *air*. But those things, too, are gone. In fact, he can only take it as an article of faith that he himself is still here, since he can't see anything. Natch pats where his torso should be: nothing.

MultiReal. Even in this place, so far removed from everything, he is aware that the program is out there somewhere. He remembers the sense of limitless potential, the flush of power. But as he stretches his mind out like he has done a million times since he was a child in the hive, he knows it's useless; the Data Sea, MindSpace, even his own OCHRE systems lie in a different continuum altogether. And even if he could somehow reach and activate MultiReal, were there any possibilities for him to choose from in this nonspace?

A voice speaks. *This isn't how I wanted things to end.*

The entrepreneur spins around, or at least tries to, which is impossible in a world without exterior referents. No actual sound has pierced the veil of this ultracompacted universe, but it *seems* like a sound. It seems like a voice. It is, in fact, the only voice that is conceivable here.

His own.

Natch has spoken those words, and yet he has not. He remembers making the vocalizations that echo in his mind; he remembers *saying* those things, as much as the concept makes sense. But the ideas came from elsewhere. Outside.

He can feel more words forming at his nonexistent lips, and he cannot stop them. *It took me years to perfect this little piece of black code, Natch. You would be quite impressed if you had more time to explore it. The ultimate loopback! Much more interesting than some silly cloaking program. All sensory input rerouted; all sensory commands blocked off. Think of it as a dam of sorts, planted in the brain stem. Except I have the ability to open and close channels at will. Witness. . . .*

An instantaneous sword thrust of pure, unalloyed agony. The Ur-pain, the primordial concept itself.

Gone.

A sudden reemergence of sound. Low voices muttering, the distant bark of the mongrel. Staccato scrapes that might come from the confluence of boots and rubble.

Nothing.

Don't try to blame me for this state of affairs, says the voice. *If you want to blame someone, you can blame yourself. You've done a much better job isolating yourself than I could have ever done. All I've done is take advantage of it.*

Yes, thanks to you, Natch, your disappearance will arouse little suspicion. I'm sure the drudges will speculate about you for a while. Some will suspect foul play; some will suspect that the Council has done away with you. But most people? Most people will assume you've fallen prey to your own paranoia, gotten sucked into your own self-delusions. Like Henry Osterman and Sheldon Surina. Like Marcus Surina at the end. They'll think that one of your uncountable enemies finally caught up to you on a dark road somewhere.

I daresay even those few you label your friends will give up on you soon enough.

People will wonder what happened to MultiReal. The drudges will have heated debates about it, and some of the bigger fiefcorps will attempt to dupli-

cate it—unsuccessfully, of course. Some will conclude that the whole thing was a hoax to begin with.

And then—once the rumors have died down, once the subject has become nothing more than a myth, once even the Defense and Wellness Council has concluded that MultiReal is lost in the deep eddies of the Data Sea—Creed Thassel will emerge. We'll launch Possibilities 2.0 and proclaim an end to the tyranny of cause and effect, forever.

An end to the Council. An end to centralized authority. A new beginning.

It is a strange thing, speaking the words of another. Natch feels the vibrations of his vocal cords, the swaying of his tongue—the *idea* of his vocal cords, the *idea* of his tongue—but he knows indisputably that the sentiments behind the words belong to someone else. And yet, the mere act of stringing together such words in his memory is causing him to reverse engineer the sounds back into their component thoughts.

The voice continues.

I hoped that we could work together, Natch. I really hoped that we might put aside our differences and launch Possibilities 2.0 as a team. I wasn't lying about that. It would have made for great symbolism—two enemies joining forces to announce the end of the zero-sum game! And it will take much longer to finish the programming without you. Maybe years longer.

But I see now that it's not fated to be. I was right to send that strike team after you. I was right to take out this little piece of insurance. You'll never willingly join my Revolution of Selfishness; as long as you live, you'll be a hindrance. I would simply keep you cooped up in this prison of mine until the launch of Possibilities, but I'm not that foolish. You would figure a way out of here eventually.

And so we come now to the final choice. Your last choice.

Don't think I take any pleasure in this, Natch. No sane human being enjoys taking the life of another. But you must agree that sometimes it's necessary. Sometimes we must sacrifice our own lives in order that others may be free. And that's what you'll do. Your gift of MultiReal to the world will engender a future of boundless freedom for all. You can take some consolation in the fact that you'll be a hero, a martyr for humankind.

Natch feels the raw fury inside him. It's threaded through every cell in his body, and now he summons it all. Anger. The righteous, white-blazed inferno of need and struggle and drive, shaped into a dagger of willpower. The terrible madness of the Shortest Initiation. The humiliation of Captain Bolbund's poetry. The sting of being out-maneuvered by Magan Kai Lee. The howl of frustration he feels at locking horns with Jara. All concentrated and compounded to the utmost degree.

Natch reaches out and wrenches control of the voice. *What's killing me going to accomplish?* he says. *You can't be that stupid. Without me, Multi-Real is gone forever. It'll float out there on the Data Sea for all eternity—and even when you find it, your little piece of black code won't give you core access. What happens to your fucking Revolution of Selfishness then?*

There is a moment of considered silence. He can almost *feel* the pitying smile on Brone's face, the wretched shake of the head.

I don't think you quite understand, says the voice. *You're lying completely defenseless on a street in Old Chicago. There's no one out here but the diss for kilometers. And I have here the gateway to pain beyond your imagining. Unadulterated pain that's all the more potent because it doesn't go through the intermediary step of the nervous system.*

You have one last choice left to make, Natch. And I already know what your decision is going to be. When you're racked with anguish beyond anguish and you're given the opportunity to end *that suffering—of signing over core access to MultiReal to me and earning a swift death—you'll make the only logical choice. I know you will.*

Natch tries to reach out and steady himself against something, but there is nothing to steady himself against. He feels the primal fear wash over him, the fear of emptiness, of loneliness, of pain. He yanks away control of his voice one last time. *You have no fucking idea what I'll do,* he says. *Torture me for a thousand years. I'm stronger than you. I'm the most stubborn son-of-a-bitch who ever lived. I'll* never *hand over MultiReal. Are you listening? Do you hear me? Never. I'll never do it. Never.*

He waits for the inevitable retort, for Brone's perfidious last word, but it never comes.

• • •

Brone is correct. It is pain beyond imagination, pain reduced to its purest essence and served raw. The snapping of bones in their sockets, the laceration of flesh, the jab of a million simultaneous stabbings, weeks of thirst and starvation, all concatenated into one infinite instant—and Natch can feel it bearing down on him like a tsunami.

And then the nothingness at the center of the universe clasps hold of him, and Natch knows no more.

6

NEW BEGINNINGS

(((42)))

Jara arranged to meet Geronimo the day after the disaster at the Tul Jabbor Complex.

She nearly canceled. The thought of letting a Natch look-alike inside her emotional barricades made her feel greasy in places where human beings were not meant to feel greasy. But Jara had spent the day fretting in the Creed Élan hostel, waiting for some scrap of news about Natch, or barring that, information on what the Prime Committee was up to in their closed-door session. She needed a distraction. And she wasn't quite ready to get intimate with Horvil yet, despite the kiss they had shared in the anonymous bureaucrat's office. An afternoon in bed with Geronimo felt like a monumentally stupid thing to do, but it was a stupid thing she *needed* to do.

Merri wandered in to the common room at some point, looking tired and drained of energy. "How's Bonneth?" Jara asked her.

"Stable for now," replied Merri, propping a smile onto her face. "Access to Dr. Plugenpatch has been really spotty up there for the past twenty-four hours. But she made it to the Objectivv facilities in Einstein. They're looking after her."

Jara felt like the icy hand of death had just gripped her by the throat. She had asked the question as idle chatter; Bonneth's medical challenges in the face of the infoquakes had completely slipped her mind, again. "Are you—are you going back there?"

The blonde channel manager nodded. "I'm booked on a Lunar shuttle this Saturday." She slumped down in the chair, searching for a comfortable position that remained elusive. "Honestly, I don't think I'm ready to go yet."

"But don't you miss her? You've been Earthside for, what, over a month now."

"It's not that difficult, Jara. We have multi. We have messaging. We even have . . . well, we have the Sigh when we need it." A blush tickled Merri's plump cheeks.

Jara thought of her own impending tryst with Geronimo, causing her to fidget in her seat like a teenage girl. *Keep it together*, she admonished herself. "But it's not the same," she told Merri. "You can't eat meals together. You can't sleep in the same *bed*. Doesn't the intimacy get strained after a while?"

Merri closed her eyes for a moment as she considered the question. "Of course things get strained after a while. And of course I miss her. But sometimes—sometimes I need a little break from Bonneth, you know? She understands. She knows that sometimes I just need to do what I need to do. But when I'm ready, I'll always be back."

The analyst nodded. "Yeah. I know what you mean." She debated asking Merri's advice about whether she should keep the appointment with Geronimo, but decided against it. In a sense, the channel manager had already answered.

So Jara retreated to her room at the hostel. She closed the door, scuttled into bed, and activated her connection to the Sigh. Within seconds, the real world melted away, and Jara was standing on a glittering patio of solid turquoise. The attendant who greeted her had a wolf's pelt and four tongues.

"What's up, baby?" came a voice. A hand touched her shoulder. Geronimo.

It was the first day that Len Borda had allowed public access to the Sigh since shortly after Margaret's funeral. Consequently lines were long and tempers were frayed. Jara listened to Geronimo describe Jeannie Q. Christina's latest celebrity gabfest in agonizing detail for fifteen minutes while they waited. He seemed completely unaware of the turmoil that had engulfed the world in recent days.

Things didn't get any better when they finally made it to their room. (Black leather, again.) Geronimo put on the sullen pout that had almost become a third partner in their sex life and paid Jara little attention during the act some called lovemaking. Jara stared at the ceiling, wondering if she was being watched by one of Rey Gonerev's flunkies. *I don't care*, she thought, hoping the defiance was visible on her face. *I'm not afraid of her anymore.*

Geronimo spent the remaining eighteen minutes of their reservation buzzing along to some hideous cacophony on the Jamm. The drudges called it *mocha grind*, but to Jara it just sounded like clinking beads and falsetto yelps. Geronimo left with a clumsy squeeze of her ass as farewell.

Jara proceeded to wipe her profile and cancel her subscription to the Doppelgänger channel. *Well, that's done*, she thought, *and good riddance.* The Sigh immediately sliced a fat wedge out of her Vault account for early termination.

• • •

The Prime Committee finally called on Jara to testify the next morning.

As soon as she stepped into the auditorium, she could tell that any extenuating evidence she had to offer would fall on deaf ears. The lowest ring in the auditorium was packed with the twenty-nine Committee members, some fifty staffers, and at least twenty private security teams. No drudges, no spectators, no Defense and Wellness Council guards, no libertarians to be found.

The members of the Prime Committee were furious. Their stares fixed on Jara like searchlights, and their questions stabbed at her like bayonets. She was asked at least a dozen times if she knew what had happened to Natch, who the people in black robes were, and why the infoquake struck when it did. All Jara could do was politely disclaim all knowledge. Even the libertarian members who had reacted enthusiastically to Serr Vigal's speech had little to say; their sights were on history now as they struggled to find pretty, perfumed words of demurral for the official record. Two hours after Jara walked into the auditorium, the Prime Committee dismissed her without allowing her to speak a single word of substance. She promptly returned to the Creed Élan hostel, turned off her alcohol-metabolizing OCHREs, and drank herself into a stupor.

Benyamin approached her in the common room early the next day. He had spent most of the time since the Tul Jabbor Complex fortified in the hostel, along with Vigal, Merri, and Horvil. Jara didn't bother to find out where Robby Robby had gotten off to.

"I know it's not my decision," said the young apprentice, "but I think we should go home."

Jara took a swallow of nitro and tilted her head in thought. He was acting unusually deferential. "Why?"

Ben shrugged. "It could take days for the Prime Committee to make up their mind. Weeks even. You've already testified, and they probably won't call on any of the rest of us. With these infoquakes happening left and right . . . well, I'd rather be at home when they come."

The analyst nodded. She had already reached the same conclusion last night after her third vodka banzai, but she wasn't about to pass up the opportunity to improve her rapport with Benyamin. "Good idea, Ben," she said. "I think you're right. Tell the others to go home and get some rest. We'll all touch base in a day or two."

Jara packed up the few toiletries she had brought and was on her way to the tube station in twenty minutes, pausing only to pay her respects to the Élan facility administrators. She didn't even try to coordinate the ride home with any of the other fiefcorpers.

Seascapes. A light storm off Cape Town. The whisper of the tube engines. Home.

Jara spent the next twenty-four hours lying on the floor of her still-undecorated apartment, trading reminiscences with her sister. The aftershocks from the last infoquake were sending cyclones of chaos around the globe and out to the orbital colonies. Such was the mood of panic that Jara and her sister actually resorted to text messaging in order to save bandwidth. They talked about their father, who had joined the Prepared fifteen years ago, and their mother, who was long overdue to join him. They talked about the ramshackle apartment in São Paulo where they had lived during the Economic Plunge. They reenacted some of their old whimsical bedtime stories, all about puckish elves and hidden cauldrons of gold and ordinary princesses propelled into adventure by simply keeping an eye open for the possibilities.

Jara moped for another eighteen hours, staring at the virginal plaster of her blank walls. What to do now? Where to turn? What if Natch really was gone for good this time? Was that simply . . . *it* for the fiefcorp?

Strange territory, this blank existence. It occurred to Jara that this was the first real idle time she had had since joining up with Natch's fiefcorp three and a half years ago. There had always been some project that needed attention, some cracked scheme Natch wanted her to map out. She couldn't remember when—or if—she had taken a single day off in all that time. And now? Now she felt like all of the obsessions that had been crammed inside her skull had been simultaneously erased—Natch, MultiReal, the fiefcorp, Geronimo. What remained?

• • •

Horvil answered her ConfidentialWhisper mere nanoseconds after she sent the request. "Process' preservation, woman," he said, exasperated, "I've been trying to reach you for, like, a day and a half now."

"I know," said Jara. "I'm sorry."

"So . . . what's next?"

"You mean, what's next for the company? Or what's next for you and me?"

The engineer let out a ruminating hum. "Both, I guess."

"We're going to have a fiefcorp meeting tomorrow. Ten o'clock sharp London time, at the Surina Enterprise Facility."

"And . . . ?"

"You and me? Well . . . can you be here in twenty minutes?"

"I can be there in *fifteen*."

(((43)))

Len Borda stood at the porthole of his ship and surveyed the choppy seas. Waves leapt up some fifteen meters high, tossing algorithmically generated sailors around with kraken glee and threatening to drag the fragile ship down to a watery doom. He had lost two of the best in the armada, and the remaining two were only being held together by rope and pitch. But the six French juggernauts that had been cutting off his supply lines were now nothing but driftwood.

The high executive sent lifeboats out to pick up the wounded and the dying. The death of a virtual sailor was nothing to mourn, of course. But Borda had learned years ago that prisoners made good bargaining tools, and they could be chained to the oars in a pinch.

"Well played," said Magan Kai Lee.

Borda knew better than to betray his surprise at the sudden voice behind him. He had predicted that the lieutenant executive would try to make contact today, even if he couldn't pinpoint the exact time or the method Magan would use. The fact that the lieutenant was forbidden from walking DWCR's corridors—under penalty of death—wouldn't deter him.

"I could have your multi transmission traced," said Borda, without averting his gaze from the porthole.

"You know as well as I do how unreliable that technology is," replied Magan, unperturbed. "And even if you could trace the transmission, you'd need a hundred thousand officers to get to me here."

"I have a hundred thousand officers, many times over."

Pause. "Are you sure?"

The high executive sighed. He didn't doubt that he still commanded enough troops to pry Magan's stray contingents out of whatever hole they were skulking in. But the point was well taken. An era of steady loyalties had come to a messy demise in the Tul Jabbor Complex last week. Now nobody wearing the white robe and the yellow star could look at his fellow officers without second-guessing. These days, justice had many masks. It was remarkable that none of the drudges had picked up on the schism between Magan and Borda yet, but that could only last for so long. Once the story broke—well, things would only get murkier.

Borda turned around to face Magan Kai Lee. His subordinate looked well rested and comfortable, hardly like a man on the run from the most powerful military force in the history of the world. He had kept the white robe but abandoned the gray smock of his position.

"So tell me, Magan," said the high executive, voice devolving into a sneer. "You're the one with all the elaborate plans. *Short-term plans, long-term problems*, isn't that right? Well, you've led us to this state of affairs. Use your *wisdom* and tell me what you have in store for the Council now."

Magan pulled out a chair at Borda's ornately carved planning table, setting aside yellowed maps and letters of marque before taking a seat. "I'm not the man who ordered two assassinations on the floor of the Tul Jabbor Complex. My plans will depend on his."

"Spare me your soliloquies," muttered Borda. "I gave you a chance to prove yourself. You failed. You brought riots and chaos. You reminded the world that the Defense and Wellness Council is subject to the whims of the Prime Committee." Borda looked down and noticed that he was repeatedly thumping one bony fist against the cabin wall. He stopped, perhaps a second too soon to persuade Magan it had been intentional. "We should have brought Natch to the bargaining table, by force. That would have ended it."

The lieutenant executive's face was impassive. "You would have coerced him into handing over MultiReal. You would have tortured him."

"It wouldn't have come to that. The fiefcorp master's not stupid—he would have made a deal."

"And if he hadn't . . ." Magan sliced his hand through the air with an almost irreverent manner. "You would have done to him what you did to Marcus Surina."

"I told you, it wouldn't have come to that!" thundered Borda. Outside, the winds surged to hurricane strength. From the corner of his eye, the high executive could see the ship's boatswain dangling over the railing by a frayed rope. None of the other virtual sailors were rushing to his aid.

But Magan Kai Lee was not intimidated by his master's wrath. He sat and watched the high executive with that same inscrutable look on his face. If controlling one's emotions were the only skill necessary to lead the world's security and military forces, then Magan would make a fine high executive indeed. *But that's not all it takes*, thought Borda. *You need to be able to think on your feet. You need to be able to win votes on the Prime Committee, and sometimes to manipulate them. You need to be able to sign the order to terminate a life—even if that life is a Surina's.*

"I didn't come here to discuss Marcus Surina," said the lieutenant, shattering the high executive's moment of reflection. "I came because I have something to show you."

"What?" Borda scowled.

Magan gestured at the side of the cabin. The water-worn planks of the SeeNaRee wall dissolved to reveal one of several office windows. During the evenings, these windows provided Borda a peerless view of the cloud-covered globe he had taken an oath to protect. The high executive folded his arms across his chest and retreated back to the porthole as his lieutenant gave the window a silent command.

The prerecorded footage that appeared on the screen might have been taken at any of a hundred anonymous outposts lurking on the edge of Pharisee Territory. The fort was dome-shaped and sand-colored, a camouflaged wart that kept watch on the enemies of civilization. Borda sent a quick ping to the Data Sea and verified that the rivers flowing in the background were indeed the White Nile and the

Blue Nile. Which made the rubble-strewn city in the distance Khartoum—or what remained of it.

Corpses lay sprawled around the outpost. Council officers, for the most part, with a few rustically garbed Pharisees thrown into the mix. An ambush.

"Where did you find this?" demanded the high executive.

"You'll see it come across the transom shortly," said Magan. "My officers stumbled across it first, that's all. We believe that the Pharisees made at least a dozen such attacks this morning."

The anonymous Council soldier whose eyes were recording the video stepped closer to the carnage and focused on the wheezing body of an officer who looked hardly a day over nineteen. A knife with a wicked serrated edge had made rough work of the boy's face, while black code did the rest. OCHREs could do little here but buy him some time and nullify the pain. Several triage teams were working this side of the battlefield, but whether they would make it back to this soldier in time was unclear.

Hot fury pulsed through the vein in Borda's forehead as the videographer walked slowly along the line of the fallen. Not only had these savages dared to openly attack a Council outpost, but the timing suggested that the Pharisees had done so under cover of the last major infoquake. The videographer approached one of the enemy corpses and used the tip of his boot to turn the woman over on her back. The woman's face was obscured by blood, but beneath her scraggly black hair a glint of copper was visible. The soldier reached down and plucked a small, coin-shaped object off the dead woman's lapel.

"What's that?" snapped Len Borda, hesitant to reveal his ignorance but also afraid of missing something crucial.

"They allow the unconnectibles to interact with the Data Sea," replied Magan.

"A connectible collar without the connectible collar," grumbled Borda. He was about to ask Magan who this woman was to have engineered something so clever, when another Council officer stepped up to the videographer with an upside-down field soldier's helmet in his hand. There were perhaps two dozen of the connectible coins piled there, along with a single copper collar.

"Islanders," said the high executive.

So it appeared that the Islanders and the Pharisees had temporarily put aside their differences for a common goal. And why wouldn't they? The Defense and Wellness Council was being rocked by internal strife, the centralized government was suffering from labor unrest, and all of connectible society was reeling from the infoquakes. It was the perfect storm both groups had been awaiting for years.

But how had the Islanders managed to slip troops into Pharisee Territory without the Council noticing? Borda pondered the question silently for a moment until his gaze drifted off to the river. Of course: underwater. From the Pacific Islands along the equator . . . with a detour provided by friendly dissidents in Andra Pradesh . . . down through the deserted bubble colonies on the base of the Arabian Sea, which had once been the height of luxury for vacationing Indians . . . and then to Khartoum. Borda frowned. Such tactics displayed a degree of sophistication unheard of in this part of the world. He supposed there must be plenty of information on submarine warfare in the Council archives, but no one had practiced it in modern times.

Magan remained seated in his chair, impossibly unemotional. "It gets worse," he said. "We suspect the Islanders are getting logistical support from the libertarians. Maybe even black code."

Borda's head snapped around. "Khann Frejohr?"

Lee didn't answer. Instead, he waved his hand at the window and summoned another scene just as the anonymous Council officer with the grisly face emitted one last gurgle and succumbed to the Null Current.

This new video clip showed a factory assembly line—a *real* assembly line, not a throng of programmers swaying to their detestable Jamm music. Dozens of connectible coins were rolling off a series of mechanized conveyor belts. The group eagerly pawing through the pile of coins included several Islanders, a pair of what looked like Lunar tycoons—and a man with the symbol of the rising sun embroidered on his robe. Borda had seen that infernal logo too many times during the recent labor troubles to forget who it belonged to: Creed Libertas. Speaker Frejohr's puppets.

"Rey Gonerev's not sure if Frejohr is involved in this or not," added Magan Kai Lee. "But whoever they are, they're setting up distribution channels throughout the Islands. Which means—"

"I *know* what it means," snapped the high executive. It meant, in a best-case scenario, that the Islanders were preparing a massive act of civil disobedience by refusing to wear the standard connectible collars. Worst case, it could be the sign of a more sophisticated espionage operation or the prelude to another large-scale rebellion.

He had seen enough. Incensed, Len Borda strode across the cabin in five long strides and threw open the door to the foredeck. He was immediately assaulted by the rage of the SeeNaRee storm, which lashed out at him like a demon with a whip of hailstones. There was a dark cloud out there with a terrible face at its center, howling Borda's name. But the high executive refused to turn away. He planted his feet firmly on the deck and stood his ground.

He knew that face. He had seen it forty-seven years ago, staring up at him with deathless hatred even then. The body it belonged to had been little more than a charred lump, with lungs still clinging to a hoarse parody of breath through the stubbornness of OCHREs alone. As he watched, the man had slid into a long, incoherent monologue of babbles and moans, punctuated by the occasional scream. *Please! Please, let me . . . let me see my daughter one last time. . . . Anything! I'll give you . . . anything . . . all the money in the world, please. . . .* And then, in one last moment of lucidity, the ruined man had turned his eyes to the soldier recording the video—*through* the soldier, to the high executive he must have known would be watching. And he had cursed Len Borda.

But Marcus Surina hadn't cursed Borda to die. He'd cursed him to live.

May you see many more decades, Surina had said, that stilted manner of his persisting to the very end. *May you live long enough to see exactly what you've done to the world.*

And Len Borda did. No sane person believed in curses, of course, but Borda had survived longer than any other high executive in the history of the Council. For decades, Borda thought he had the last laugh. He survived the Economic Plunge of the 310s that was the direct result of his actions against the TeleCo board. More than survived, he *fixed* it, wielding the power of the free market as both hammer and nails. Then came many years of economic prosperity that rivaled even the Great Boom he had witnessed in his youth. During those heady times, entire months would go by when Borda didn't feel the need to replay that video, to stare into the horrid, defiant face of his enemy, the man who would not yield.

But one of the planks in Borda's economic recovery was Margaret Surina, daughter of the man who had thwarted him. Why had he funded the resurgence of the Surinas when he could have let the family languish into obscurity? Why had he paid for Margaret to develop MultiReal? Yes, she had been useful at the time—but was it also an attempt to appease the ghost that tormented him?

May you live long enough to see exactly what you've done to the world, he had said. It was hardly an exaggeration to state that everything happening today was a direct result of Borda's actions. Everything: the libertarian unrest, Magan's rebellion, the Pharisee and Islander attacks, the debacle at the Tul Jabbor Complex, the deranged fiefcorp master hiding somewhere in the wild with an apocalyptic weapon in his hands.

Was the curse of Marcus Surina claiming its retribution?

Borda opened his eyes. Lieutenant Executive Magan Kai Lee had come to stand beside him when he was not paying attention. He too had his feet planted firmly on the ship's deck, despite the maelstrom. His hands were clasped behind his back and his expression was calm, even thoughtful.

"This is no time for a government in conflict," said Magan. "This is no time for a divided Defense and Wellness Council. Abide by the agreements we made. You know it's the right thing to do. Step down from the high executive's seat while you still can."

Len Borda turned back to face the clouds, to that burned and twisted visage still staring at him from beyond the grave.

You think you've won? he howled at the shade of Marcus Surina. *You think I've reached the breaking point? You underestimated me once, and now you're making the same mistake again. There will be no bargains. There will be no accommodations. I swear that I'll live to see MultiReal destroyed or under the Council's control. I won't bow down to you. Not now, not ever.*

The high executive closed his eyes again and drew himself up to his full height, which was considerable. He inhaled the mist and rain for a moment and tried to clear his head.

"Magan Kai Lee," said Borda, "I hereby relieve you of your duties as an officer of the Defense and Wellness Council. You and your subordinates will be given twenty-four hours to surrender to the authorities and submit to the judgment of the Prime Committee on the charge of treason. Should you fail to turn yourself in, you will be declared a traitor and pursued with all the strength and vigor of the centralized government. Do I make myself clear?"

He waited a full ten seconds before opening his eyes, but Magan Kai Lee was gone.

High Executive Len Borda walked slowly back into his cabin and shut the door behind him. Then he lowered himself gingerly into his chair and glowered at his hands for a few moments. He yelled for the first mate. A SeeNaRee sailor stepped through the cabin door, saluted crisply, and informed Borda that the first mate had been lost overboard during the last sortie with the French.

Borda nodded and ordered the sailor to set a new course. Due east, full speed ahead.

(((44)))

There was some talk about arriving separately at the fiefcorp meeting to allay suspicions, but Jara and Horvil both nixed it in the end. As Horvil succinctly summed up the issue: "Who the fuck cares?"

They showed up at the Surina Enterprise Facility at five minutes before ten. Jara stepped through the meeting room door and was surprised to find the place devoid of SeeNaRee. She had a moment of white-knuckled panic. Had the infoquakes undermined so much of the computational infrastructure that even SeeNaRee wasn't safe? Then the analyst took a closer look and realized that this unimaginative committee-designed conference room *was* SeeNaRee. Even worse, since Jara had been the first one in the door, it was her mood that had summoned it.

Vigal, Merri, and Benyamin stumbled in over the next fifteen minutes, glum as witnesses to an execution. Jara called the meeting to order.

"So it seems like we're in a depressingly familiar situation," she said. "Natch has vanished. The drudges are calling for his head. We've got the Meme Cooperative and the Defense and Wellness Council riding on our backs. One of our chief engineers is rotting in an orbital prison somewhere, and the founder of the company is dead."

"I don't understand why the Council hasn't said anything about Margaret's murder," said Horvil. "I thought they were doing an investigation. They must have figured out *something* by now."

Jara frowned and bit her bottom lip, hard. She was ashamed to admit it, but she had barely thought about Margaret Surina's mysterious death during the tumult of the past two weeks.

"Doesn't surprise me they're not saying anything," Benyamin remarked. "With all *this* going on"—he twirled his index finger in the air—"Len Borda would have to be pretty stupid to bring it up now."

"What about Quell?" asked Horvil. "The Council can't just hold him indefinitely, can they? They must have figured out by now that he didn't kill her. Isn't there something we can do to help him?"

"I already tried," said Merri. Four surprised heads swiveled in her direction. "I convinced Khann Frejohr's people to make some inquiries. But the Council's keeping mum. They've got him in an orbital prison somewhere. That's all I can find out."

"Do you know which one?" asked Serr Vigal. "I toured a few of them back in '35 or '36. The good ones aren't so bad. But the bad ones . . ." The neural programmer waved his arms helplessly for a moment, but no words arrived to bail him out.

Ben tapped his fingers on the table, impatient. "We can't be the only ones looking for him, can we? Doesn't Quell have a family at home? Close friends? The Islanders don't take these kinds of things lightly. There's got to be some committee petitioning the Council for his release."

"Well, that's the interesting part," replied Merri. "There *is* a group of Islanders working with the libertarians to try to secure Quell's release. They're making all kinds of threats. And one of them is Quell's son."

Horvil's jaw flipped open as if on springs. "*Quell* has a kid?"

"Apparently he does."

"I wonder if that's why he's staying in prison," said Jara, contemplative. Everyone gave her blank stares. "Well, why doesn't he use MultiReal to overpower the guards and escape?"

"They regulate all transmissions in and out of those prisons," offered Ben. "He wouldn't be able to access MultiReal in there."

"Fine—but why did Quell let them take him to prison in the first place?"

No one knew.

The conversation seemed to lose its legs at that point. The fiefcorpers looked around at one another, each expecting somebody else to prolong the conversation. Three minutes passed. The SeeNaRee generated some background hallway noise to fill the silence.

"Okay," said Jara finally. "We can't just *avoid* the obvious question all morning, can we? We need to figure out what happens to the fief-corp. We need to figure out what to do, now that we've got no product."

Benyamin frowned. "What do you mean, *no product?*"

"Ben," said Merri gently, "you know that the Prime Committee is likely to—"

"Yes, yes, of course," snapped Ben, cutting her off. "They'll probably vote to take control of MultiReal and hand it over to the Council. But does that mean we're just going to . . . give up? I don't care what the Committee decides. We could always appeal the ruling, right? We could talk to Khann Frejohr, get him to stir up public sentiment again. Or—or, we could try to work out another deal with Len Borda. A real deal this time."

Jara shook her head. "It's a moot point, Ben. Even if we could persuade the centralized government to change their minds . . . we don't *have* MultiReal anymore. Natch moved the databases. He used that . . . back door in his head, or whatever it is to lock up all the code and squirrel it away somewhere on the Data Sea where no one can find it."

"You mean—"

"Yes. It doesn't matter what the Prime Committee decides, because MultiReal's *gone.*"

Serr Vigal stroked his goatee, pensive. "What about the Patel Brothers? If Natch took the MultiReal code with him, do they still have access to it?"

Jara shrugged. "I'm not sure. I assume that if we don't know how to find it, they don't know either." *And once the Patels figure out I don't have MultiReal,* she thought sourly, *that probably spells the end of the deal I arranged with them to get the fiefcorp's business licenses back.*

"But it's not like MultiReal's permanently gone," said Benyamin, unwilling to let go. "Natch still has access to it. And he's going to come back eventually. He hasn't just disappeared for good . . . has he?"

Silence. Jara expected an objection from Serr Vigal, but the neural

programmer remained disturbingly quiet. Horvil merely sat and nib-
bled on his cuticles, while Merri fidgeted uncomfortably.

The blonde channel manager folded her hands on the table and
screwed up her face like a woman trying to calculate logarithms in her
head. "So if we assume that Natch is gone . . . and MultiReal is gone
. . . what do we have left?"

"Nothing and nothing," said Horvil dejectedly. "After the demo at
Andra Pradesh, Natch sold off every last bloody scrap of code we had.
Even the RODs. The fiefcorp dock is just . . . completely empty."

"Brilliant," grumbled Ben. "Fucking brilliant."

"So then should we . . . dissolve the company?" asked Merri.

A hush fell upon the already quiet fiefcorpers. Everyone had heard
the stories about apprentices hitched to dead fiefcorps by dint of circumstance. One of Jara's old hivemates had spent three years working
for a bio/logic programmer who passed away unexpectedly nine years
after founding her company. Fiefcorp tax breaks dried up after a
decade; no capitalman would invest in a company so close to its cutoff.
Suddenly Jara's friend had found himself with nothing but a portfolio
of worthless shares to his name.

But for the employees of the Surina/Natch MultiReal Fiefcorp, dissolving the company meant much more than just loss of profit. They
would probably have to forgo their bio/logic programming equipment
and most of their professional relationships. Jara and Merri might have
to give up their apartments. In other words, they would all have to
start over as if the last three and a half years had never happened.

"I'm not sure we could legally dissolve the fiefcorp," mused Vigal.
"With most of us still suspended by the Meme Cooperative and the
masters of the company completely absent . . . I think we'd have a difficult time in the courts. The fiefcorp's assets would probably just go
into receivership. It might take years for the courts to finally accept
that Natch is . . . Natch is . . ." He couldn't finish the sentence. *Gone.*

Horvil slapped the table. "I could buy the company," he blurted out.

A spark glinted in Merri's eye, but Ben sighed and shook his head. "I don't know. A purchase that big—you couldn't manage that without clearance from my mother, and you know she'd never approve. No, don't start, Horvil. We couldn't afford it alone. Even if we both pooled all our liquid assets, I don't think we have the money."

"Some of Khann Frejohr's allies have been pushing for reparations," said Merri. "They're demanding that we get compensation if the Prime Committee tries to compel us to turn over MultiReal."

"And what chance do you think *that* has of working?" asked Horvil, chin planted in hand. "One in a million?"

"Listen, money isn't the problem," said Jara. "We've got plenty of credits sitting in the company coffers. Margaret Surina's money."

"You mean, Jayze and Suheil Surina's money," Ben retorted. "You know that those sleazeballs are going to come after it. They already laid the groundwork by having her declared mentally incompetent before she died. The next thing they do is say that Margaret was unstable when she entered into her partnership with Natch. Don't tell me *that's* going to be too hard to prove."

Jara shook her head. "I'm not worried about Jayze and Suheil getting hold of the fiefcorp's money. The problem is that *we* can't get ahold of it. Not as individuals. What I'm saying is that even if we could dissolve the company, we can't just split up the Vault account five ways. What we can do is spend it—as a fiefcorp." She stood up from her chair, leaned over, and pressed her clenched fists onto the tabletop. "Listen, we don't have enough bio/logic code left in our dock to build a product base on. And starting over from scratch isn't really feasible, right? So let's use that money. Let's approach some of the bigwigs on Primo's and offer to buy a portfolio of their programs."

There was a moment of quiet contemplation. Given the idiosyncratic nature of bio/logic programming, it usually wasn't worth the effort to cobble together a product line from the remnants of someone else's code. It wasn't unusual for a fiefcorp to purchase one or two programs to round out their own offerings, but to build a company from the ground up this way was a risky move at best.

"Which bigwigs did you want to approach?" said Merri.

"Lucas Sentinel," replied Jara. "Bolliwar Tuban. Pierre Loget and Billy Sterno, if they ever show up again."

Ben spoke up. "I thought you and Sentinel didn't get along. Do you think he'd sell us anything but the dregs?"

"Probably not," Jara admitted. "Given all the animosity Natch has built up in this industry over the years, I'm sure a lot of people are just waiting to take their revenge too. Even if Natch isn't around to see it. But it seems to me that this is our best option—unless the Prime Committee votes in our favor."

"It's too late for that," said a voice.

The SeeNaRee instantly evaporated into nothingness, leaving the fief-corp sitting in a conference room that was even duller and more antiseptic than the virtual one Jara's mood had conjured up. Standing by the door was Magan Kai Lee, flanked by his protégés Papizon and Rey Gonerev.

"The Prime Committee just voted an hour ago to seize MultiReal and hand it over to the Defense and Wellness Council," said Magan. "Eighteen to five."

· · ·

Jara was sick of Defense and Wellness Council agents popping up everywhere she went. She was tired of opening doors and rounding corners to find the placid, emotionless face of the lieutenant executive. How had he managed to get into this room without Jara's authorization? How had he managed to get into this *building*, for that matter? The analyst thought it was probably better not to know.

Jara took a few steps closer to the Council officers and extended her finger into prime wagging position. "Listen, *Lieutenant Executive*," she spat, "I don't know what kind of shit Len Borda's trying to pull here—"

"We're trying," said the Blade, "to *protect* you from Len Borda."

The analyst closed her mouth and plopped back down in her seat.

"The world is on the brink of crisis," continued Magan. "What happened at the Tul Jabbor Complex is only the beginning. The Data Sea's buckling under the strain of these infoquakes. Computational resources are disappearing; people are dying. The Islanders and the Pharisees are marshaling their forces for war." He recited these calamities with the detachment of a man reading from a speech handed to him by a subordinate moments ago. "The Council has more pressing things to deal with than pursuing a vendetta against your fiefcorp. So we're prepared to offer you one last deal."

Jara let out a scornful laugh that took everyone in the room by surprise. Papizon visibly flinched. "A deal?" cried Jara. "What kind of deal could you *possibly* offer us? We don't have anything you want, and we wouldn't take anything you offered."

"Don't play ignorant with us," said Rey Gonerev, stepping forward with the triumphant look of a card player unveiling a winning hand. "We're perfectly aware that Natch gave you core access to the Multi-Real databases. But Borda doesn't know that, which is the only reason you're still alive."

Jara snorted. "So? That core access is useless. Natch moved the fucking databases. We have no idea where they are."

The Blade stopped short and blinked hard in shock. For once she seemed at a loss for words.

Magan, however, did not appear to be surprised by this sudden turn of events. "All we're asking is that you help us track Natch down. In return, we'll persuade the Meme Cooperative to drop all its charges against you. You'll be given clean slates in the bio/logic sector and the freedom to find new apprenticeships if you wish. We'll compensate you for any losses you've incurred." He turned to gaze at each of the fiefcorpers in turn, finally stopping to bestow an especially vivid look in Jara's direction. "Refuse to help us, and I can't predict what Len Borda will do. He's capricious enough to drag everyone off to join the Islander in prison, or just do away with the lot of you. With the info-quakes still in full swing, nobody's going to stop him. I doubt hiding at a fancy estate with a pack of drudges on the doorstep will hinder him this time."

"Don't try to pretend you give a shit," said Jara, shaking her head. "You don't care about us, or about Natch. I saw what happened at the Tul Jabbor Complex. You want MultiReal so you can unseat Len Borda as high executive. You want to use it to take over the Defense and Wellness Council."

Magan Kai Lee let out a sigh, and for only the second time in their brief acquaintance Jara saw the cracks in his poise and equanimity. "I don't want *anyone* in the Council to use MultiReal," he said. "I want the program in private hands. But not under Natch's control. I want MultiReal under *your* control, Jara."

"But . . . why?"

"Because you're the only one I trust with it."

Jara reacted as if the lieutenant executive had slapped her. Magan Kai Lee *trusted* her? All along, she had assumed Magan wanted Multi-Real in her hands because she was the weak one, the easily manipulable one. But what if the exact opposite were true? Was it possible that the lieutenant executive had worked to get Natch suspended from the fief-corp because *she* was the strong one? Because she was the one most capable of standing up to both Natch and Len Borda?

She surveyed the faces of her fellow fiefcorpers. Merri seemed crest-fallen and distraught. Benyamin's upper lip was visibly quivering with anger. Serr Vigal looked like he was on the verge of retreating back to Omaha and never returning. Horvil's attention had floated off into the distance, and Jara knew he was probably thinking about the job offer he had received through his Aunt Berilla.

But then they turned as a group to look at Jara, and she saw some-thing she did not expect. For the first time since the Council turned their company upside-down, the fiefcorp had confidence in her. They trusted in her leadership.

Jara pushed her chair back, stood up from the table, and marched slowly toward the Council lieutenant. Papizon's left hand flexed instinctively on the pommel of his dartgun, but he quickly restrained the impulse. Jara stopped when she was toe to toe with Magan Kai Lee and looked him straight in the eye.

"Maybe you trust *me*," seethed the analyst through clenched teeth, "but do you think I trust *you*? You tried to break up this company through lies and mistrust. By dragging *their* professional careers through the mud and leaving *mine* intact." She extended a finger back toward the apprentices and Vigal. "You did everything you could to convince them I sold out to the Council, when you knew perfectly well that I refused to make a deal with you."

The lieutenant executive's split-second downward glance was as good as an admission of guilt, as far as Jara was concerned.

"But you know what, Magan? You've *failed*. Utterly failed.

"Ever since this whole thing started, you've been trying to tear this fiefcorp apart. You dredged up dirt on us, you raided our homes, you disrupted our operations, you sullied our reputations. You dragged our chief engineer off to prison on bogus charges. And what do you have to show for it? Nothing. This company has clawed its way back from the edge, millimeter by millimeter. We're well on our way to resolving our cases with the Meme Cooperative, and soon we'll be back where we started.

"You don't have Natch. You don't even have MultiReal.

"And the beautiful thing? The program's totally gone. We have no way of getting in touch with Natch. None of us have *any* idea where he is. You should have known from the very beginning that Natch would be a step ahead of you—he *always* is. He's probably halfway to Mars or Furtoid by now, and you'll never find him. Do you hear me? *You will never find Natch.* And if nobody can find Natch, nobody can get their hands on MultiReal, can they?

"So take your fucking *flunkies* and never interrupt one of our meetings again. You've done your worst, and we're still here. Whatever you're planning, we don't want any part of it.

"The answer is *no*."

A wrinkle appeared in the space between Lee's eyebrows as he took stock of the situation. Papizon's face contorted into some bizarre emotion resembling panic. Finally Magan gave the slightest of nods, turned, and walked out the door, followed closely by Papizon.

Rey Gonerev stayed behind for a few seconds. She threw Jara a smile—unvarnished and unironic, possibly even with a morsel of respect thrown in—and then she too was gone.

(((45)))

Magan Kai Lee sat in the back of a Defense and Wellness Council hoverbird practicing his meditation. He straddled the threshold of nonself, peering into the anterooms of Enlightened Harmony with the Universe, his consciousness a fleeting thing, a wriggling thread—

And then Rey Gonerev spoke, causing consciousness to come roaring back like a vengeful beast.

"If you want me to stay with you," said the Blade, "I'm going to need more information." She sounded weary, skeptical. Perhaps a little afraid. Her fingers were busy unbraiding and then rebraiding dark locks of hair over and over again.

Magan took a glance out the window to get his bearings. The Earth was far below them and almost completely carpeted with cloud. He could see three of their fighter escorts out the starboard window, and had no doubt he would find the other three if he looked to port. "What information?" he said.

"You can start by telling me where we're going."

"The orbital colony of Allowell," said Magan. "There to rearm and regroup."

Pause. "And then?"

"We find Natch."

Rey Gonerev quietly worked on untangling a knot in her hair for a minute. Magan suspected she was still smarting from the way Natch had sized her up and shoved her aside at the Kordez Thassel Complex a few weeks ago. But Magan had made no move to reassure her, either then or now. She would need to exorcise that demon if she intended to continue as his right-hand woman when he took the high executive's seat. "How do you propose we find him?" she said.

"The fiefcorp master is a wanted man, Rey. His Vault account has been locked down. His license with the Meme Cooperative is still suspended. All of his friends and acquaintances are under surveillance. Every drudge on the Data Sea knows his picture and identifying characteristics. If Natch so much as steps on a public tube train, we'll know. The challenge isn't finding him. The challenge is finding him before Len Borda does."

Rey Gonerev frowned. "And what—what if Natch is dead?"

"He's not."

The Blade reached for the side of the hoverbird and steadied herself against it. "Are you sure?"

"Yes. I've never been more certain of anything in my life."

· · ·

The other fiefcorpers cut their multi connections and went home, but Jara was not quite ready to face the existential blankness of her empty walls. Instead she threaded her way through the corridors of the Surina Enterprise Facility and found the double doors that would lead her out to the courtyard. Her heart was pounding at a tempo that might have been appropriate for one of Geronimo's mocha grind songs.

The crowds had returned to the Surina complex, spurred by a temporary lull in the winter weather. A corpulent sun sat in the sky, announcing that spring was right around the corner. Tourists were streaming in and out of the Center for Historic Appreciation again, and Jara saw that the Albert Einstein and Isaac Newton statues had been shouldered aside to make way for a new monument to Margaret Surina. Half a dozen couples stood in the center of the courtyard with arms around one another, some staring up at the Revelation Spire, some staring down at the engraved plaque marking the bodhisattva's burial place. "I don't care about the strikes and the infoquakes and the unrest," Jara heard someone say. "I'm not going to let that rule my *life*."

The analyst found her way to the railing, where she could see the

city of Andra Pradesh laid out before her feet. She prived herself to all
communication and let her skin absorb the sun's energy.

As soon as Magan Kai Lee had left the meeting, it occurred to Jara
that she had unilaterally rejected his offer without so much as a ConfidentialWhisper to the rest of the fiefcorp. Certainly the obstinate
Benyamin would have backed her up, but Merri? Vigal? Horvil? She
could imagine a hundred reasons why they might have leapt at the
lieutenant executive's offer. A chance to restore their careers and their
business credentials all in one shot. A chance to leap back into the
bio/logics game without penalty, and all they had to do in return was
help track down a man who had scorned and abandoned them anyway.
At the very least, someone might have objected to the way Jara made
such a major choice about their lives and careers without consulting
them. Imperious decision making seemed almost . . . Natchlike.

But then Jara realized she was not running a democracy.

She was running a *business*.

Did she think she could just flee from everything Natch stood for
and still run a successful fiefcorp? Life wasn't cut into such predictable
shapes. For all his failings, Natch had led his company from complete
obscurity to the height of the Primo's bio/logic investment guide—
and he had done it quicker than anyone else in history. There were
good things to be salvaged from any boss who could do that. Her job
as the new leader of the Surina/Natch MultiReal Fiefcorp was to take
the good ideas, to reject the bad ideas, and most importantly, to pound
her fist on a tabletop and make the firm determination which ideas
belonged where. Jara could scarcely believe it, but in the past few
weeks she had discovered that she had this ability.

She thought about the looks the fiefcorpers had given her before
cutting their multi connections. Merri, Horvil, Benyamin, and Serr
Vigal had regarded her not with admiration or awe or thankfulness—
but simply with respect. Jara was their leader now, and they accepted
that.

Jara called up ConfidentialWhisper and fired off a message to the rest of the team.

"Everyone get some rest today," said the fiefcorp master. "We've got a lot of work to do to get this company back on track. And we start first thing tomorrow morning."

APPENDIXES

APPENDIX A
A SYNOPSIS OF *INFOQUAKE*

Natch is an entrepreneur with a burning ambition. He simply can't define what it is.

The world he lives in is a ripe place for ambition. Having suffered a cataclysmic AI revolt hundreds of years ago, the world embraced Sheldon Surina and his science of bio/logics. Now, 359 years later, thousands of small software companies—fiefcorps—compete ruthlessly for the right to sell the programs that run the human body. Order is maintained by a patchwork of subscription-based governments called L-PRACGs. Overseeing these governments is the Prime Committee, which uses the Defense and Wellness Council as its police force.

As an orphaned boy in the care of the neural programmer Serr Vigal, Natch is plagued by strange and hallucinatory visions. He learns to use his wits to best his childhood enemies and achieve top scores in his class. His only obstacle is Brone, a boy with an equally cunning intellect and a more charismatic way with people. But Brone is soon dispatched during the boys' initiation by a bear attack that is partly accident, partly fate, and partly Natch's dark vengeance.

With his prospects for financial success dimmed by the Shortest Initiation, Natch turns to a series of low-paying jobs at the bottom of the programming world. Only gradually, after much Machiavellian scheming against enemies such as Captain Bolbund, does Natch climb to the top of his profession. But he hasn't achieved this alone. He's had his childhood friend, Horvil; his mentor, Serr Vigal; and his market analyst, Jara, to aid him.

With Horvil's and Jara's help, he achieves one final coup. Natch arranges a complicated con involving a fake black code attack on the Vault banking system. This con allows Natch's fiefcorp to replace his bitter rivals, the Patel Brothers, at the top of the Primo's bio/logic investment guide rankings. Where Natch was once an outcast, now he is a celebrity.

Furthermore, the scheme brings Natch to the attention of Margaret Surina, heir to her ancestor Sheldon's fortune. She's been working on a technology to create "alternate realities" called MultiReal for decades. But now she fears that Len Borda, the high executive of the Defense and Wellness Council, is preparing to take this technology away from her—and possibly kill her in the process. The Council sees MultiReal as a weapon of potentially apocalyptic proportions, one too dangerous to remain in private hands. It's the same conflict Margaret's father, Marcus, went through with his teleportation technology many years ago, a conflict that ended in a fiery hoverbird accident.

Margaret offers Natch an opportunity to license her new technology. He is to stir up enough trouble to keep Len Borda off balance for the next week; then, after Margaret reveals the existence of Multi-Real in a widely publicized speech, Natch needs to quickly put together a prototype to show the world that the technology is real. The fiefcorp master agrees.

Natch goes looking for a source to fund his company's new project, but, partly due to his shady reputation, nobody will support him in this new and undefined venture. Finally, with the help of his new apprentice, Merri, he snags an appointment with the leader of Creed Thassel, an organization dedicated to the power of selfishness. The leader turns out to be none other than Natch's old nemesis Brone. Brone, still smarting from the wounds of the Shortest Initiation, offers Natch a quick loan and foretells a future where the two of them will work together to market MultiReal. The fiefcorp master, seeing no other alternatives, accepts the loan from his old hivemate.

Armed with a new infusion of cash, Natch hires a new apprentice—Horvil's young cousin Benyamin—and forms a partnership with sales channeler Robby Robby to help market the new product.

The day of Margaret's speech arrives, and with it comes an incursion into the Surina compound at Andra Pradesh by the troops of the Defense and Wellness Council. As Margaret unveils her new technology before hundreds of millions of people, the Data Sea networks explode with a strange new computational disturbance: the infoquake. Thousands die in the tumult, but the Council does not follow through with its implied threat to kill Margaret and seize MultiReal.

Natch gathers the fiefcorp for a meeting the next day, where he informs his colleagues that a frightened Margaret has practically handed over the reins of the company to him and allowed him to rechristen it the Surina/Natch MultiReal Fiefcorp. Furthermore, Natch will get a new apprentice, Quell. A longtime confidant of Margaret's, Quell is an Islander, a member of a society that has spurned all but the most rudimentary forms of bio/logic technology.

For a short time, it appears that Natch has gotten the upper hand. He is on top of the world and has even used his newfound partnership with Margaret to pay back Brone and sever his ties with the Thasselian.

But Natch's expectations are soon dashed when he discovers that his dire enemies the Patel Brothers have *also* secured a MultiReal licensing agreement with Margaret Surina. Margaret soon reveals that Natch is in fact the *third* fiefcorp she approached. The first, programmer Pierre Loget, did not understand the import of the technology; the second, the Patels, she suspected of selling out to the Defense and Wellness Council. Only after she despaired of working with the Patels did she turn to Natch, who she knew would never give in to pressure from Len Borda.

Natch immediately goes on the offensive to counter the Patels. Frederic and Petrucio Patel have scheduled a demo in less than a week's time; Natch decides that he's going to hold his demo first, in three days. But after he commands his fiefcorp to prepare a quick-and-dirty demo, a group in black robes ambushes him in the streets of Shenandoah. Natch is hit by their black code darts, falls unconscious, and vanishes.

Meanwhile, unaware that Natch is missing, the fiefcorp goes about preparing for their product demo. Quell and Horvil work to prepare the MultiReal code for its first public appearance; Benyamin works with his mother's assembly-line programming shop to complete all the millions of programming tasks necessary for the program to function in front of hundreds of millions of people; Merri works with the company's sales partner, Robby Robby, to generate excitement about their product; and Jara struggles to put together a presentation that will capture the public imagination.

It's only hours before the demo that the fiefcorp realizes Natch has disappeared. The fiefcorpers frantically attempt to find him before the demo as Len Borda's forces once again march on Andra Pradesh. Jara makes a last-ditch effort to convince Margaret to deliver the product demo in Natch's stead. Margaret refuses, choosing instead to retreat to the top of her private tower as the forces of Len Borda once again invade the compound. Jara decides that *she* will give the presentation instead. Horvil catches up with her and attempts to dissuade her from making this dangerous presentation, in the process confessing that he has developed deep feelings for her. But Jara will not be deterred.

And then, at the last possible minute, Natch shows up. He had awakened from his black code coma, in his apartment, mere hours before. With him is Len Borda—who, as it turns out, has brought the Council troops to Andra Pradesh at Natch's request, in an effort to scare off any potential black code attack. In exchange for this intervention, Natch has hurriedly promised Borda access to MultiReal.

Natch delivers the product demo to an audience of five hundred million. The demonstration involves using the power of MultiReal to simulate hitting a baseball to all five hundred million spectators simultaneously and goes off swimmingly. The audience reacts more enthusiastically than anyone could have anticipated. (The Patels' demo, meanwhile, is a disaster.)

As *Infoquake* draws to a close, it occurs to Natch that the attackers in black robes could have been sent *by* the Defense and Wellness Council as a ploy to get MultiReal under its control. There are, in fact, any number of organizations out there that might be using the black code inside him as leverage to get control of MultiReal. Brone, the Patel Brothers, and even Margaret Surina are listed as potential suspects.

Natch is beginning to feel the deleterious effects of the black code inside of him; but as he tells his mentor, Serr Vigal, he's up for all the challenges ahead. He's come this far against all odds, and he won't back down now.

APPENDIX B
GLOSSARY OF TERMS

For more comprehensive definitions and background articles on some terms, consult the Web site at http://www.multireal.net.

TERM	DEFINITION
49th Heaven	A decadent orbital colony known for its loose morality; originally founded by one of the Three Jesuses as a religious retreat.
aft	One of the descriptive components of a program that helps the Data Sea sort and catalog information. See also *fore*.
Allahu Akbar Emirates	A nation-state that once existed in what is now mostly Pharisee territory. "Allahu Akbar" means "God is great."
Allowell	An orbital colony saved from extinction by High Executive Tul Jabbor.
analyst	One of the standard positions in a fiefcorp. Fiefcorp analysts typically focus on areas such as marketing, channeling, finance, and product development.

Andra Pradesh   A center of culture on the Indian subcontinent. Home to Creed Surina and the Gandhi University.

apprentice   An employee of a fiefcorp, under contract to a master. In the traditional fiefcorp structure, apprentices sign a contract for a specific number of years. During their apprenticeship, apprentices receive only room and board as compensation; but at the conclusion of the contract, their shares mature and they receive a large stake in the company and a share of the accumulated profits.

assembly-line programming   Tedious and repetitive bio/logic programming, usually done by large groups of low-skilled laborers.

Autonomous Minds   The sentient supercomputers that rebelled against humanity during the Autonomous Revolt.

Autonomous Revolt   The rebellion of the Autonomous Minds, which caused worldwide destruction and hastened the collapse of the nation-states.

battle language   Coded communications used by military and intelligence agencies during combat.

beacon   A tracking signal that allows one to be located in the multi network.

Big Divide   The era of worldwide depression and chaos following the Autonomous Revolt.

Bio/Logic Engineering Guild	A labor organization and advocacy group for bio/logic engineers.
bio/logic program	A set of logical instructions designed to enhance the human body or mind. Most bio/logic programs act on the body through microscopic machines called OCHREs placed throughout the body at (or before) birth.
bio/logic programming	A set of tools bio/logic programmers use to create and modify bio/logic code. Programming bars are categorized with the letters of the Roman alphabet (A to Z) and are largely indistinguishable to the naked eye. They interact with virtual code through holographic extensions that are only visible in MindSpace.
bio/logics	The science of using programming code to extend the capabilities of the human body and mind.
black code	Malicious or harmful programs, usually designed and launched by seditious organizations.
bodhisattva	The spiritual leader of a creed. Most creed organizations are spearheaded by one individual bodhisattva. Some creeds are run by an elected body of major and minor bodhisattvas.
Bodhisattva, The	When capitalized, the term usually refers to the first leader of Creed Objectivv, who originated the title, or his successors, who abandon their names upon confirmation.

capitalman
An individual who raises start-up money for fief-corps. Following long tradition, the term is gender-neutral.

ChaiQuoke
A popular tea-flavored beverage.

channel
The process of marketing and selling products, usually to groups rather than individuals.

channeler
A businessperson responsible for driving sales to specific markets.

chief solicitor
The head legal officer of the Defense and Wellness Council.

choice cycle
A single possible "reality" MultiReal can cause to happen. Actually choosing that reality is called "closing the choice cycle."

Cisco
A major population center, known in ancient times as San Francisco.

Confidential-Whisper
One of the most popular bio/logic programs on the Data Sea, ConfidentialWhisper provides a silent, completely internal communication venue for two or more people.

Congress of L-PRACGs
A representative body composed of most of the L-PRACGs in the solar system. The speaker of the Congress is one of the most powerful elected officials in government.

connectible	Able to link to the Data Sea. Cultures who shun modern technology (like the Islanders and the Pharisees) are said to be "unconnectible" and refer to the remainder of society as "connectibles." See also *unconnectible*.
connectible collar	The thin copper collar that Islanders and other unconnectibles wear to allow them to see and communicate with multi projections.
core access	The state of complete administrative control over a bio/logic program (as opposed to developer access or user access).
credit	The standard unit of monetary exchange in civilized society.
creed	An organization that promotes a particular ethical belief system. Creeds promulgate many of the same types of moral teachings as the ancient religions, but are generally bereft of religious mythology and iconography.
Creed Bushido	A militaristic creed that was formed around the time of the Autonomous Revolt and based on the ancient Japanese warrior code. Since the Reawakening, the creed has become more focused on asceticism and rigorous discipline.
Creed Conscientious	An environmentally conscious order pledged to preserving the integrity of the Data Sea.

Creed Dao	An order that stresses Daoist principles of harmony with the universe instead of conformance to the dictates of society, Creed Dao is a strong repository of Chinese cultural history and tradition.
Creed Élan	One of the more prominent creeds, Creed Élan teaches the value of philanthropy. Its members tend to be wealthy socialites. The creed's colors are purple and red.
Creed Libertas	A relatively unknown creed focused on libertarian principles that has gained prominence in recent months. The creed's symbol is the rising sun.
Creed Objectivv	A creed dedicated to the search for and promotion of absolute epistemological truth. Members take an oath to always tell the truth. Its logo is a black-and-white swirl.
Creed Surina	The creed founded in honor of Sheldon Surina after his death. Creed Surina promotes the agenda of "spiritual discovery and mutual enlightenment through technology." The official colors of the creed are blue and green.
Creed Thassel	A once-common creed of the business class, dedicated to the "virtue of selfishness." Its symbol is three vertical stripes.
Creeds Coalition	The blanket organization that promotes intercreed understanding and cooperation.

Data Sea	The sum total of all the communication networks running in the civilized world. It includes such networks as the Jamm and the Sigh.
Defense and Wellness Council	The governmental entity responsible for military, security, and intelligence operations throughout the system. The Council is headed by a single high executive, who is appointed by the Prime Committee. Its officers wear the uniform of the white robe and yellow star.
Democratic American Collective (DAC)	An ancient nation-state formed after the dissolution of the United States of America. See also *New Alamo*.
disruptor	A weapon that allows attacks on multi projections by disrupting or altering their signals. Disruptors are often used by the Defense and Wellness Council in conjunction with dartguns.
diss	The urban poor. The term is alternately thought to be derived from "disenfranchised," "disaffected," and "disassociated."
dock	An area in which fiefcorps keep pending projects that are being prepared for launch on the Data Sea.
Dogmatic Opposition	A legal appeal to the Prime Committee to block or nullify a specific technology. It is used primarily by the Islanders to maintain a nontechnological society.

Dr. Plugenpatch   The network of medical databases and programs that maintains the health of nearly all connectible citizens.

drudge   An independent reporter or journalist who writes regular opinion columns to a list of subscribers. Drudges are considered one of the public's main resources for government accountability.

DWCR   Defense and Wellness Council Root, rumored to be High Executive Len Borda's new base of operations. Its location is unknown.

East Texas   One of two former splinter states of New Alamo. See also *West Texas*.

Economic Plunge of the 310s   A period of worldwide collapse and unemployment following the death of Marcus Surina. It is widely thought to have been eradicated by massive Defense and Wellness Council spending.

Ecumenical Council   The religious governmental body in New Alamo that was responsible for much of the violence and bloodshed of the Big Divide.

engineer   One of the standard positions in a fiefcorp. Engineers are traditionally responsible for the "nuts and bolts" bio/logic programming for a fiefcorp's products.

Environmental Control Board   The governmental body that controls and regulates the planetary environment, from species preservation and protection to weather control.

fiefcorp

A business entity that typically consists of one master and several apprentices. Fiefcorps are usually short-lived, lasting less than a decade. The economics of the fiefcorp business are such that it usually makes better sense to dissolve a fiefcorp and sell its assets every few years. See also *memecorp*.

flexible glass

A strong, glasslike building material that can be very easily stretched and molded, even at room temperature.

fore

One of the descriptive components of a program that helps the Data Sea sort and catalog information. See also *aft*.

"for process' preservation"

A common phrase roughly translatable as "for Pete's sake."

Furtoid

A distant and troubled orbital colony in constant danger of collapse from poor engineering and economics.

Gandhi University, the

The institution of higher learning in Andra Pradesh where Sheldon Surina taught. Each of his descendants has held an honorary chair at the university.

gateway zone

The designated entry point for a multi projection into real space.

geosynchrons

Programs that regulate the geophysical and meteorological activity of the Earth. Geosynchrons are categorized as Levels I through V, I being the lowest level (regulation of atomic activity) and V being the highest level (regulation of complex environmental activity).

governmentalism   The political movement that espouses a belief in strong centralized government (though not necessarily the current centralized government). See also *libertarianism*.

GravCo   A semigovernmental memecorp that regulates gravity control among orbital colonies and other outworlders.

high executive   The official who heads the Defense and Wellness Council, appointed by the Prime Committee.

hive   A communal birthing and child-rearing facility for middle- and upper-class children.

hoverbird   A flying vehicle that can travel in air and low orbit. Hoverbirds are primarily used for travel over long distances, hauling cargo, and defense.

infoquake   A dangerous burst of energy in the computational system, thought to be caused by a disproportionate amount of activity at one time or concentrated in one particular area.

initiation   A twelve-month rite of passage that many youths from middle- and upper-class backgrounds go through before being considered adults. The initiation consists primarily of depriving children of modern technology.

Islander A resident of the Pacific Islands, where the governments shun most modern technology.

Islander Tolerance Act The law that created the Dogmatic Opposition in an attempt to ease relations between connectible and unconnectible cultures.

Jabbor, Tul The first high executive of the Defense and Wellness Council.

Jamm A network that allows never-ending musical "jam sessions" between musicians all over the world.

Keepers The order that was assigned to program and operate the Autonomous Minds. The order is often blamed for starting the Autonomous Revolt, although the extent of their complicity in the revolt will never fully be known.

launch To officially release a product onto the Data Sea for public consumption.

libertarianism A political philosophy that believes in decentralized government run principally by the L-PRACGs. See also *governmentalism*.

lieutenant executive One of several second-in-command officers in the Defense and Wellness Council. They are nominated by the high executive and officially appointed by the Prime Committee.

L-PRACG   Local Political Representative Association of Civic Groups, the basic unit of government throughout the civilized world. Pronounced "ELL prag."

Lunar tycoons   A class of investors who grew massively wealthy through early speculation on moon real estate. Nowadays the term mostly refers to their moneyed descendants.

master   One of the positions in a fiefcorp. The master is the person who forms the fiefcorp and has full authority in all business decisions. Masters take on apprentices who then work to earn full shares in the fiefcorp after a specific contractual period.

Meme Cooperative   The governmental entity that regulates business between fiefcorps. It is largely perceived as an ineffectual watchdog organization.

memecorp   A business entity whose membership subscribes to a particular set of ideas ("memes"). A memecorp frequently relies on public or private funding, as opposed to the fiefcorp, which relies solely on the free market. See also *fiefcorp*.

MindSpace   The virtual programming "desktop" provided by a workbench for programming. It is only in MindSpace that the extensions to bio/logic programming bars can be used to manipulate bio/logic code.

multi

To project a virtual body onto the multi network. The word can be used as a verb, a noun, or an adjective.

multi connection

The state of existing virtually on the multi network. When users return to their physical body, they have "cut their multi connection."

multi network

The system of bots and programs that allows people to virtually interact with one another almost anywhere in the world and on most orbital colonies.

multi projection

A virtual body that exists only through neural manipulation by the multi network. Real bodies can interact with virtual bodies in ways that are almost identical to actual physical interaction.

MultiReal

A revolutionary new technology owned by the Surina/Natch MultiReal Fiefcorp and also licensed to the Patel Brothers Fiefcorp. Surina/Natch's MultiReal product is being branded as "Possibilities," while the Patel Brothers' is being branded as "SafeShores."

multivoid

The few seconds of mental "blankness" that occurs when switching (or cutting) multi connections.

nation-state

An ancient political entity, bounded by geography and ruled over by a centralized government or governments. Nation-states were superseded by the rise of L-PRACGs.

neural programmer	A bio/logics specialist who concentrates on the programming of the human brain.
New Alamo	An ancient nation-state formed after the dissolution of the United States of America. New Alamo included many of the USA's southwestern states and portions of Mexico as well and became a dominant and terrorizing world power during the Big Divide. See also *Democratic American Collective*.
nitro	A popular beverage full of concentrated natural stimulants, usually served hot.
Nova Ceti	An orbital colony.
Null Current	A poetic term for death. The term is of uncertain vintage but is thought by many to have been coined by Sheldon Surina.
OCHRE (1)	A generic term for any of a number of nanotechnological devices implanted in the human body to maintain health. The term derives from the OCHRE Corporation, which pioneered the technology.
OCHRE (2)	The Osterman Company for Human Re-Engineering. The company was founded by Henry Osterman to pioneer nanotechnology and dissolved almost 110 years later after a protracted legal battle with the Defense and Wellness Council. It is often (redundantly) called "the OCHRE Corporation" to distinguish it from the nanotechnological machines that bear its name.

offline
: A slang term for "crazy."

OrbiCo
: The quasi-governmental agency that controls the space shipping lines and most interplanetary cargo travel.

orbital colony
: A nonterrestrial habitation, sometimes built free-standing in space and sometimes built on existing soil (e.g., asteroids and planetoids). The major orbital colonies are 49th Heaven, Allowell, Furtoid, Nova Ceti, and Patronell, but there are dozens of smaller colonies all over the solar system.

Osterman, Henry
: A contemporary of Sheldon Surina and founder of the OCHRE Corporation. Osterman was a famous iconoclast and recluse who zealously persecuted his enemies and died under mysterious circumstances in 117.

Padron, Par
: The High Executive of the Defense and Wellness Council from 153 until his death in 209. He was nicknamed "the people's executive" because of his pro-democratic reforms.

Patronell
: An orbital colony that circles Luna.

"perfection postponed"
: A common phrase roughly translatable as "heaven forbid."

Pharisees
: The disparate groups of fanatics who live around the areas once known as the Middle East. It is

believed that several million people still practice many of the ancient religions in these remote places.

Pharisee Territories	Unconnectible lands occupied by the Pharisees.
Prepared, the	An order whose membership is only open to the elderly and the terminally ill. Its members are given special legal status and access to euthanasia procedures in the Dr. Plugenpatch databases that are otherwise banned.
Prime Committee	The central governing board that runs the affairs of the system. Much like the ancient United Nations, the Committee's functions are mainly diplomatic and administrative. All of the real power rests with the Defense and Wellness Council and the L-PRACGs. The Committee's symbol is the black ring.
Primo, Lucco	The founder of the Primo's bio/logic investment guide and one of the icons of capitalism and libertarianism during the Reawakening.
Primo's	The bio/logic investment guide that provides a series of ratings for programmers and their products. People all over the world rely on Primo's ratings as a gauge of reliability in bio/logics.
public directory	A listing of personal information, used throughout the civilized world.

QuasiSuspension — A popular program that allows the user to schedule sleep and choose different levels of rest. The program is often used to ration out sleep in small doses and keep the user awake longer.

Reawakening — The period of intellectual renewal and discovery that began with Sheldon Surina's publication of his seminal paper on bio/logics. It continues to this day.

Revelation Spire — The tallest building constructed since the Autonomous Revolt. It is part of the Surina compound in Andra Pradesh.

ROD — Routine On Demand. A simple bio/logic program created for a single (often wealthy) individual. The acronym is usually pronounced as one word ("rod").

SeeNaRee — A virtual environment created by an enclosed room or space. It uses technology similar to the multi system.

Sigh, the — A virtual network devoted to sensual pleasure. Unlike the multi network, the Sigh does not allow interaction between real and virtual bodies.

Smith, Jesus Joshua — The first and most influential of the Three Jesuses. He led an exodus of faithful Christians and Muslims to the Pharisee Territories.

subaether | A form of instantaneous transmission made possible by quantum entanglement.

Surina, Marcus | A descendant of Prengal Surina and the "father of teleportation." He died in an orbital colony accident at the prime of his life, leaving TeleCo in shambles and prompting the Economic Plunge of the 310s.

Surina, Margaret | The daughter of Marcus Surina and the inventor of MultiReal technology.

Surina, Prengal | The grandson of Sheldon Surina and discoverer of the universal law of physics, which is the cornerstone of all modern computing and engineering.

Surina, Sheldon | The father of bio/logics. He revived the ancient sciences of nanotechnology and paved the way for the drastic improvement of the human race through technology.

TeleCo | A quasi-governmental agency that runs all teleportation services, brought to prominence by Marcus Surina. Now it is tightly regulated by the Defense and Wellness Council.

teleportation | The process of instantaneous human transportation over long distances. Technically, matter is not actually "transferred" during a teleportation, but rather telekinetically reconfigured.

Thassel, Kordez | A libertarian philosopher and the founder of Creed Thassel.

Three Jesuses | Spiritual leaders who, in three separate movements, led pilgrimages of the religious faithful to found colonies of free religious worship in what are currently known as the Pharisee Territories.

Toradicus | The high executive of the Defense and Wellness Council, known for bringing the L-PRACGs under central government control.

"Towards Perfection" | A greeting or farewell, originally derived from a saying of Sheldon Surina's.

treepaper | An ancient sheet of pulped wood for writing and printing with ink.

tube | The high-speed trains used in most civilized places on Earth for inter- and intracity travel. The tube has become ubiquitous because its tracks are extremely cheap to build, easy to lay down, and unobtrusive in appearance.

TubeCo | The memecorp that runs the tube system. It is now heavily subsidized by the Prime Committee.

Tul Jabbor Complex | The headquarters of the Prime Committee in Melbourne, named after the building's architect, the first high executive of the Defense and Wellness Council.

unconnectible	Not able to connect to the resources on the Data Sea. The term is sometimes a derogatory reference to the Islanders and the Pharisees, who shun modern technology. See also *connectible*.
underground transfer system	The mechanized subterranean network that handles most Terran shipping and cargo transport.
universal law of physics	Scientific principle put forward by Prengal Surina that enables nearly limitless supplies of energy.
Vault, the	The network that makes financial transactions possible. Known for fanatical secrecy and paranoia, the administrators of the Vault pride themselves on never having suffered from a serious break-in. The symbol of the Vault is the double-balanced pyramid.
viewscreen	A flat surface that can receive and display audio and visual transmissions from the Data Sea. Viewscreens are usually used for decoration in addition to entertainment.
weedtea	An alternative type of tea derived from genetically altered plants.
West Texas	One of two former splinter states of New Alamo. See also *East Texas*.
Witt, Tobi Jae	A famous scientist and the pioneer of artificial intelligence from before the Autonomous Revolt. She created the first Autonomous Mind and died

a violent death, though her killer was never identified.

workbench
A particular type of desk capable of projecting a MindSpace bubble and allowing bio/logic programming.

xpression board
A musical instrument known for its versatility. Users create their own form and structure; thus no two xpression boards are the same.

Yu
The first modern orbital colony, financed and constructed by the Chinese. The destruction of Yu by the Autonomous Minds was the event that triggered the cataclysmic Autonomous Revolt.

Zetarysis
A high executive of the Council known for her tyranny and cruelty. She is frequently referred to as "Zetarysis the Mad."

APPENDIX C

HISTORICAL TIMELINE

The chronicling of modern history began with Sheldon Surina's publication of "Towards the Science of Bio/Logics and the New Direction for Humanity." Surina started the Reawakening, which ended the period of the Big Divide that began with the Autonomous Revolt. The publication of Surina's paper is considered to be the Zero Year of the Reawakening (YOR).

YOR	EVENT	
	Development of the precursors of the Data Sea on hardware-based machine networks.	
	The last pan-European collective alliance falls apart. The nation-states of Europe never again gain prominence on the world stage.	
	The predominant Arab nations form the Allahu Akbar Emirates to counter American and Chinese dominance.	ANTIQUITY
	Scientists make major advances in nanotechnology. Nanotechnology becomes commonplace for exterminating disease and regulating many bodily systems.	
	Final economic collapse of the United States of America. During the unrest that follows, the northeastern states form the Democratic American Collective (DAC), while the southern and western states form New Alamo.	

	Establishment of the first permanent city on Luna.	REVOLT
	First orbital colony, Yu (named after the legendary founder of the first Chinese dynasty), launched by the Congressional China Assembly.	
	Yu is sabotaged and destroyed by the Autonomous Minds. **Beginning of the Autonomous Revolt.**	
	End of the Autonomous Revolt. Much of the civilized world lies in ruins.	
	The Big Divide begins. A time of chaos and distrust of technology.	BIG DIVIDE
	The Ecumenical Council of New Alamo, seeking to establish order in a time of hunger and chaos, orders mass executions of its citizenry.	
	Rebellion in New Alamo splits the nation-state into West Texas and East Texas.	
	Birth of Sheldon Surina.	
	Birth of Henry Osterman.	
0	Sheldon Surina publishes his first manifesto on the science of bio/logics. **The Reawakening begins.**	REAWAKENING
10	Final dissolution of the New Alamo Ecumenical Council.	
10s–40s	The Three Jesuses lead pilgrimages of the faithful to Jerusalem. Rampaging Pharisees leave devastation in their wake.	
25	Henry Osterman founds the Osterman Company for Human Re-Engineering (OCHRE).	
35–37	Seeing potential ruination from the technological revolution that Sheldon Surina has engendered, the two Texan governments put a price on his head. Surina leaves the Gandhi University and goes into hiding.	

37	The president of West Texas is assassinated. The new president exonerates Sheldon Surina and calls off the manhunt for him. It is still many years before Surina can appear in public without intense security.
39	Creed Élan is founded as a private philanthropic organization (though the term "creed" has not yet been coined).
52	Dr. Plugenpatch is incorporated as a private enterprise. Henry Osterman and Sheldon Surina are among those on its original board.
60–100	Many of the great nation-states of antiquity dissolve as their primary functions (enforcing law, keeping the peace, encouraging trade) become irrelevant or more efficient to handle through distributed technology. People begin to form their own independent legal entities, or civic groups.
61	The Third Jesus leads a splinter group of radical Pharisees in building a new orbital colony (the first since the destruction of Yu). Though initially promising, 49th Heaven collapses within a generation. It reemerges to prominence a hundred years later as a sybaritic resort.
66	First fully functioning multi technology comes into existence. Sheldon Surina, though not the technology's inventor, makes vast engineering improvements. Within a decade, multi projections are ubiquitous among the wealthy.
70s–90s	Inspired by the apparent success of 49th Heaven, a rash of orbital colonies are funded and colonized. Space mania brings new funding and energy to ongoing efforts to colonize Mars.
80	Birth of Prengal Surina.

103	Major national and corporate interests join together with the vestiges of ancient nation-states to form the Prime Committee. The Committee is mainly seen as a bureaucratic organization whose task is to ensure public order and prevent another Autonomous Revolt.
107	The Prime Committee establishes the Defense and Wellness Council as a military and intelligence force. Its first high executive, Tul Jabbor, surprises the Prime Committee's corporate founders by expanding the Council's authority and in some cases turning on its sponsors (particularly OCHRE).
108	Creed Objectivv is founded by a reclusive mystic figure known as the Bodhisattva.
111	The Prime Committee undergoes a major effort to fund the development of multi technology throughout the system.
113	OCHRE becomes a target of the Prime Committee, which seeks to end the company's stranglehold on nanotechnology.
115	Dr. Plugenpatch agrees to special oversight and cooperation with the Defense and Wellness Council in order to avoid the same fate as OCHRE. The corporation becomes a hybrid governmental/private sector industry that forms the basis of medical treatment worldwide.
116	Death of Sheldon Surina. To honor his memory, Surina's successors build the compound at Andra Pradesh and found Creed Surina.
117	Tul Jabbor is assassinated. His killers are never found, but many suspect OCHRE. After a protracted legal battle, Henry Osterman dies under mysterious circumstances (some claim suicide). OCHRE battles over his successor for several years to come, then finally dissolves in 132.

122	Prengal Surina publishes his universal law of physics.
130s	Major advances in hive birthing bring the technology to the public for the first time. A small minority that resists these advances begins emigrating to the Pacific Islands and Indonesia, where Luddites encourage isolation from the outside world. The remainder of the system comes to know them as Islanders. The Islander emigration continues for the next fifty years.
143	High Executive Toradicus begins a campaign to bring the L-PRACGs under Defense and Wellness Council control. He enlists Prengal Surina to lobby the L-PRACGs to construct a joint governmental framework with the Prime Committee. The Congress of L-PRACGs is founded.
146	The Islander Tolerance Act creates the Dogmatic Opposition.
150s	Teams working under Prengal Surina make startling advances in the control of gravity using maxims from the universal law of physics. Key members of these teams (including Prengal Surina) become the first board members of GravCo.
153	Par Padron is appointed high executive of the Defense and Wellness Council. He is nicknamed "the people's high executive" because of his actions to rein in the business community.
160s	The business of multi technology booms. By decade's end, most connectibles live within an hour of a multi facility.
162	Union Baseball adopts radical new rules to keep up with the times and to even the playing field among bio/logically enhanced players.

168	Death of the Bodhisattva of Creed Objectivv.
177	A coalition of business interests forms the Meme Cooperative to stave off the harsh populist reforms of Par Padron.
185	Death of Prengal Surina.
196	Libertarian rebels, funded and organized by the bio/logics industry titans, storm a handful of major cities in an attempt to overthrow the Prime Committee and the Defense and Wellness Council. Par Padron initiates martial law and puts down the disturbances.
200	The bio/logics industry attempts to pack the Prime Committee with its appointees and paid lobbyists. Par Padron pushes through a resolution declaring that the people (via the Congress of L-PRACGs) will always hold the majority of seats on the Committee.
209	Death of Par Padron.
220s–230s	A time of great economic and cultural stability worldwide, dubbed afterward as the Golden Age. A resurgence in creedism results in the formation of the Creeds Coalition.
247	Birth of Marcus Surina.
250s	Almost all infants outside of the Pharisee and Islander territories are born and raised in hives. Life expectancies rise dramatically.
268	Creed Thassel is founded.
270	The first fiefcorp is established, and rules governing its structure are encoded by the Meme Cooperative. Most people see fiefcorps as a boon to society, helping the underprivileged gain skills and putting them on a track to social empowerment.

287	First successful tests of teleportation technology are conducted by a team that includes Marcus Surina. The extraordinary costs and energy involved have prohibited the widespread usage of teleportation to the present day.
290s–300s	The Great Boom, a time of economic prosperity, is ushered in, fed by the new fiefcorp sector and the promise of teleportation technology.
291	Lucco Primo establishes the Primo's bio/logic investment guide.
301	Birth of Margaret Surina.
302	Len Borda appointed high executive of the Defense and Wellness Council.
313	Marcus Surina dies in a shuttle accident in the orbital colonies.
310s–320s	The Economic Plunge of the 310s, a time of economic stagnation. Len Borda keeps the system afloat largely through the use of Prime Committee capital to fund research projects. Critics grumble about the return of the nation-state and centralized authority.
318	Rioting in Melbourne threatens the Prime Committee, but is put down by High Executive Borda.
327	Creed Thassel is nearly disbanded after a scandal caused by the drudge Sen Sivv Sor's exposé on its membership practices.
331	Birth of Natch.
334	Warfare erupts between the Islanders and the Defense and Wellness Council. Although the official "war" lasts only a few years, unofficial skirmishes continue to the present day.
339	Margaret Surina founds the Surina Perfection Memecorp, and the drudges begin to whisper about a mysterious "Phoenix Project."

351	The world economy officially surpasses its previous peak, achieved in 313, before the death of Marcus Surina and the Economic Plunge.
359	**Present Day.**

APPENDIX D
ON THE CREEDS

The creeds were founded with a noble goal in mind: to promulgate the spread of ethics and responsibility strictly through scientific and rational means.

HISTORY OF THE CREEDS

Organized religion had largely disappeared into the Pharisee Territories with the chaos and destruction promulgated by the crazed prophets known as the Three Jesuses in the early years of the Reawakening. Wanton destruction in the name of God by New Alamo and the subsequent splinter Texan governments contributed to this as well.

But with the rise of Sheldon Surina's science of bio/logics, many began to fear an intellectual imbalance. The great minds of the day traded horrified what-if scenarios about a society devoid of any moral compass. The atmosphere soon became ripe for a return to spirituality.

The cryptic hermit known only as the Bodhisattva filled that gap. He began wandering through Europe and Asia gathering followers in the early 100s, much as the Three Jesuses had done throughout the previous century. But the philosophy he preached about the search for Objective Truth was nonviolent, nonjudgmental, and extremely personal in nature. He allowed an administrative organization to coalesce around him almost as an afterthought.

Other organizations quickly took up the model that the Bodhisattva had put in motion. Some, like Creed Élan and Creed Dao, were old institutions that simply found in creedism a convenient structure suitable for modern times; others took inspiration from the Bod-hisattva and developed new philosophies that appealed to a wide body of followers.

ROLE OF THE CREEDS COALITION

The Creeds Coalition was founded in 237 as a means of formalizing the interaction between the large (and still growing) number of creed organizations. Most creeds participate in and fund the operations of the Coalition voluntarily. There are a number of creeds who have refused to join the Coalition and are thus not bound by its rules and regulations. But even those creeds that do not officially belong to the Coalition often recognize its authority because of its long history of good deeds.

The major functions of the Coalition are to keep interactions between the creeds civil and to act as a lobbying and advocacy group to the various government bodies. The Coalition also funds a number of minor creeds and engages in various philanthropic enterprises of its own.

To a lesser extent, the Coalition is assigned the duty of enforcing certain creed bylaws (such as the Objectivv truth-telling oath and the Conscientious pledge of resource preservation). However, considering how fearful the Coalition is of favoritism, its oversight is little more than a formality.

Leadership of the Creeds Coalition is an executive committee selected by all participating members, with membership tending toward heavy representation by the major seven (listed below). Chair-manship of the executive committee is a two-year commitment and is currently being held by the bodhisattva of Creed Enlighten.

One important bylaw of the Coalition is that none of its members are allowed to formally restrict devotees from pledging to multiple creed organizations. (In practice, however, some creeds *do* hold such restrictions.)

MAJOR CREED ORGANIZATIONS

While there are literally tens of thousands of accredited creeds in the Coalition's rolls, the number with any significant amount of influence is relatively small.

Creed Bushido (founding date unknown) was one of the products of the Autonomous Revolt. The creed was initially a martial organization whose aims were to preserve Japanese culture and tradition during a time of great upheaval. As the Reawakening got into full swing and the Creeds Coalition came into existence, the creed softened many of its stances and began incorporating the remnants of many other Eastern cultures into its rituals and traditions.

Creed Conscientious' (founded 322 YOR) goal is to conserve the world's computational resources. The creed is among the newest in the Coalition, and its membership is quite small (around twelve thousand). But increasing concerns about computational resources in recent years have brought the creed an abundance of favorable press and a disproportionate influence on Data Sea policy.

Creed Dao (founding date unknown), like Creed Bushido, also carries the torch of many of the ancient Eastern religious cultures. Some have likened its philosophies of peace, tolerance, and introspection to the teachings of Daoism and Buddhism. The creed tends to be very insular (if not downright secretive) in its beliefs, however, and therefore its tenets are not well understood by the population at large. The creed's color is bronze.

Creed Élan (founded as the Élan Society in 39), among the oldest and most venerable of the creeds, was originally known as one of the most generous and self-effacing. In recent decades, it has largely become the creed of the moneyed elite. And while the organization's critics delight in pointing out the hypocrisy of some of its members, Creed Élan still devotes far more capital to philanthropic endeavors than any other creed. The creed has no single leader, but is run instead by a consortium of major and minor bodhisattvas. Its colors are red and purple.

Creed Objectivv (founded 108) promotes the search for ultimate truth in the universe. Its members take what is known as the Objectivv truth-telling oath, where they promise not to lie and to devote their lives to seeking truth. Founded by a mystical figure known only as the Bodhisattva—the first creed leader to take that title—the organization continues to be run by a single leader. As of this writing, Objectivv membership runs in the low hundred millions. A good percentage of that number consists of "associate" members who are sympathetic to the creed's aims but do not pledge the truth-telling oath). The symbol of Creed Objectivv is a black-and-white swirl.

Creed Surina (founded 116) was founded by Prengal Surina and his companion Ladaru to honor Sheldon Surina's memory. The creed's official purpose is to promote "spiritual discovery and mutual enlightenment through technology," which most observers interpret as humanizing scientific progress. Some critics contend that such a goal might have been appropriate for the rampant Luddism of the early days of the Reawakening, but has lost its relevance. The creed has maintained a large membership (two billion) largely through the charisma (and money) of the Surinas. Creed Surina's colors are blue and green.

Creed Thassel (founded 268) began as a popular movement dedicated to the "virtues of selfishness" and run by the extreme libertarian philosopher Kordez Thassel. The creed's rituals were believed to be dangerous and mystical for many years, until drudge reporting revealed the mystique as something of a hoax. The Thasselians turned to a more conventional philosophy of hard-core individualism afterward, and the creed has been operating low-key ever since. Creed Thassel keeps its membership rolls private, but the drudges estimate its membership somewhere south of a million. The symbol for Creed Thassel is three parallel vertical lines.

MINOR CREED ORGANIZATIONS

Other creeds with significant membership rolls and some small amount of public influence include Creed Autonomous, Creed Enlighten, Creed Libertas, Creed Sacrificial, and Creed Tzu.

APPENDIX E

ON GOVERNMENT

The whole of humanity has never agreed on a single form of government, but with the so-called L-PRACG system of governance, it can be said that the race has largely agreed on a common *framework* for government.

THE L-PRACGS

After the collapse of the ancient nation-states during the Big Divide, people turned to locally organized civic groups to provide the basic services of government. Often these ad hoc groups came together to solve a particular issue and ended up taking on matters of security, trade, and justice by default. Basic principles varied wildly from culture to culture and place to place.

Eventually, as civilization built itself back up from the ravages of the Autonomous Revolt, civic groups began to band together. Larger groups had greater collective bargaining power and were able to specialize on certain aspects of governance. Thus was born the Local Political Representative Association of Civic Groups, more colloquially known as the L-PRACG (pronounced *ELL-prag*).

In modern society, L-PRACGs are responsible for the day-to-day services of government, as well as security, taxation, and regulation. Often L-PRACGs are organized around a central tenet (such as governmentalism or libertarianism), culture (Japanese, West African, Texan) or geographical area (the Shenandoah and Harper L-PRACGs). Other L-PRACGs use formulas or free-market tenets to determine the blend of services they provide. While some L-PRACGs are localized in one particular place, the vast majority are not.

Nothing prohibits citizens from joining more than one government at a time. (This freedom was in fact codified into law by the efforts of High Executive Toradicus in the year 145.) Most people today hold three or four simultaneous citizenships and rotate to new governments every few years. Likewise, in a free-market system, L-PRACGs are constantly shifting their policies and priorities to attract new members for their tax base.

It's not uncommon to subscribe to a local L-PRACG for basic neighborhood services; a vocational L-PRACG to streamline one's work life; and a personal L-PRACG that practices the tenets of one's particular creed or culture.

THE CONGRESS OF L-PRACGS

Founded in 143 through the tireless lobbying efforts of Prengal Surina and High Executive Toradicus, the Congress of L-PRACGs was intended to be an organization that could deal with the Prime Committee as an equal.

The Congress's main function has turned out to be the settling of inter-L-PRACG conflict. Given that there are tens of thousands of L-PRACGs spread throughout human space, the administrative aspects of coordinating laws and dealing with contradictions between them are formidable.

Most of the Congressional representatives are elected directly by L-PRACG citizens, but some representatives are still appointed by L-PRACG management. As of this writing, there are over 2,200 representatives on the Congress, headed by a single speaker. Given its large membership, the Congress tends to be slow to make decisions and often professes opinions far outside the mainstream of public opinion. This in turn means that the Congress generally has a difficult time commanding the drudges' attention.

Since the ascendancy of Len Borda to the head of the Defense and Wellness Council in 302, the Congress's power has been limited. Governmentalists loyal to Borda controlled the speakership and a slim majority of seats until very recently. In late 359, the governmentalist speaker was indicted in an embezzlement scandal and ousted in favor of radical libertarian Khann Frejohr. Boosted by this scandal, the libertarians recaptured the majority of Congressional seats as well.

THE PRIME COMMITTEE

The major governing body of the centralized government is the Prime Committee. However, since so many of the traditional functions of government have become the province of the L-PRACGs, the Committee is largely a legislative body and an umbrella organization to the various branches of centralized government.

The Prime Committee is divided into twenty-three voting and six nonvoting groups known as *bailiwicks*. Voting members of the Prime Committee include the bailiwicks of:

Congress of L-PRACGs (12 members)
Meme Cooperative (3)
Creeds Coalition (2)
orbital colonies (2)
Dr. Plugenpatch (1)
GravCo (1)
TeleCo (1)
The Vault (1)

Nonvoting members of the Prime Committee include the bailiwicks of:

Islanders (2 members)
Data Sea networks (1)
Pharisees and other unconnectibles (1)
The Prepared (1)
TubeCo (1)

The number of representatives on the Committee from business interests has always been a concern of libertarians. They charge that no government in the history of humanity has ever been so slanted toward the concerns of its business class; governmentalists counter that this slant in fact provides for a great degree of stability in what would otherwise be a very rocky system. In 200, High Executive Par Padron took action on the libertarian complaints by arranging the passage of a resolution decreeing that the Congress of L-PRACGs will always hold a one-member majority on the Prime Committee.

There is a growing movement by the libertarians for a nonvoting representative from the various groups of the diss. Many expect that this will be passed into law within the decade.

THE DEFENSE AND WELLNESS COUNCIL

The world's largest military and intelligence organization, the Defense and Wellness Council, was founded in 107 by the newly formed Prime Committee. Technically it falls under the jurisdiction and oversight of the Committee. Its single high executive and six lieutenant executives are appointed directly by the Committee.

In practice, however, the Defense and Wellness Council has been the dominant voice in governmental affairs for many years. Its research budget alone far outstrips that of the entire Prime Committee by many orders of magnitude. Not helping matters is the fact that the Committee has a history of appointing strong-willed, independent thinkers to the post of high executive.

The Council's peacekeeping officers have a complicated relationship with the tens of thousands of private L-PRACG security forces throughout human space. In years past, the Council's ubiquitous troops acted mostly as backup and support for private L-PRACG security; the Council's pledge of neutrality kept its officers distinctly above the fray of inter-L-PRACG conflict. Under Len Borda's tenure, however, the Council has moved away from its supporting role and become a force acting on behalf of the central government itself.

NOTABLE COUNCIL HIGH EXECUTIVES

Tul Jabbor (served 107–117), a well-respected military man, was the Prime Committee's first choice for the post of high executive. He served as head of the Council from its founding in 107 until his assassination in 117. Since the Committee did a poor job of defining boundaries in the Council's charter, Jabbor's aggressive, crusading style ended up defining the organization more than anything else. Jabbor's major accomplishments include the building of the Tul Jabbor Complex in Melbourne, the organization of the first central government army, the successful breakup of OCHRE's stranglehold on nanotechnology, and the setting up of governmental oversight for Dr. Plugenpatch.

Toradicus (138–147) continued the expansion of central government power begun under the reign of Tul Jabbor. He was largely responsible for persuading the L-PRACGs to accept Council and Prime Committee oversight. Along with Prengal Surina, he also convinced the L-PRACGs to form an umbrella organization (the Congress) that could deal with the Prime Committee as an equal. Toradicus's other major accomplishment was the Islander Tolerance Act of 146, which legitimized the Islanders' withdrawal from technological society and established the principle of the Dogmatic Opposition.

Par Padron (153–209) oversaw one of the world's major periods of technological change. During Padron's term, multi technology made the leap from theory to reality; practical gravity control allowed the colonization of Luna and the building of orbital population centers; and the bio/logics industry scaled to exorbitant new heights. Padron became known as "the people's executive" because of his decisive actions to limit the powers of the business community. The bio/logics industry, seeking to head off prosecution by Padron, formed the Meme Cooperative as a self-policing entity. Not satisfied, High Executive Padron cemented legislation decreeing that the Congress of L-PRACGs would henceforth always hold a one-member majority over the industry-appointed representatives of the Prime Committee. Unsurprisingly, Padron's actions led to great civil unrest and one of recent history's most vehement rebellions.

Zetarysis (229–232) was notable mainly for the excesses of her reign. Appointed by a deeply divided Prime Committee, she spent her three and a half short years in office conducting a pogrom against the diss and intimidating her enemies. It was not for nothing she was known as "Zetarysis the Mad." Her assassination by a member of the diss in 232 ended her tenure.

Len Borda (302–present) brought power back to the high executive's chair after a long series of lackluster officeholders. Given Borda's squabbles with Marcus Surina over teleportation early in his career, many felt that Borda would be a vehement antitechnologist. But after Marcus Surina's death and the subsequent Economic Plunge of the 310s, Borda became a champion of the bio/logics industry in general, and the fiefcorps in particular. His massive programming subsidies have been credited by many for lifting the world out of the Economic Plunge. Critics point to the stifling of civil liberties and dangerous expansion of the Council's military presence under Borda's rule, as well as the exponential increase in hostilities with the Islanders and Pharisees.

OUTSIDE THE DOMAIN
OF THE CENTRAL GOVERNMENT

A number of political entities exist that claim no fealty to the central government and do not follow its edicts. Among these are the Luddite government in the Pacific Islands, the numerous tribes and clans in the Pharisee Territories, the uncounted numbers of the diss, and certain orbital colonies and remote outposts beyond the reach of the Council's military forces.

Still, the Committee and the L-PRACGs do treat with these outside governments fairly regularly (see Dogmatic Oppositions and the Diss L-PRACG movement).

APPENDIX F
ON THE SIGH

The Sigh is the colloquial name for a group of autonomous networks devoted to sexual pleasure. Its usage rate among connectible citizens is paralleled only by the multi network.

The impact on society of such a system has been enormous. Sexually transmitted disease has become a thing of the past (though OCHREs and bio/logic programming had largely eliminated those threats anyway). Unplanned pregnancy is almost unheard of, and abortion has become exceedingly rare.

While the channels on the Sigh all rely on a common set of protocols and guidelines to function, each channel is a private and independent entity. Quality and user experience vary widely from channel to channel, and competition for innovative features rivals the competition among the bio/logic fiefcorps.

MECHANICS OF THE SIGH

In theory, the Sigh works the same way as the multi network. The user remains in a stationary location while sensations are broadcast directly into the mind via bio/logic neural manipulation.

In practice, however, the two networks work much differently. The Sigh is an entirely virtual environment that does not intersect with "real" space at all. Therefore its users are not subject to the strict rules of physics and mechanics that control the multi network. Users can project any type of body on the Sigh they desire, and rules of interaction are as varied as the imaginations (and Vault accounts) of its users.

Because the engineers behind the Sigh compete with one another and are not prone to sharing trade programming secrets, virtual sex is not nearly as "seamless" an experience as projecting onto the multi network. It's a rare channel that can claim complete verisimilitude in the act of sex.

Many, of course, see the separation between the real and virtual experiences to be the Sigh's greatest asset. Billions of users are content to trade realism for the benefits that only a virtual environment can provide. The uncomfortable aspects of sexual intercourse can be safely avoided in a world entirely governed by computational rules. The existence of a virtual environment for sensuality has also allowed certain relationships to blossom that might not otherwise have been possible, because of the constraints of nature, distance, or physiology.

So enamored are some of the Sigh's users of their virtual playground that hundreds of millions of couples choose to never have physical intercourse in the "real" world at all. Since sex is no longer a prerequisite for procreation, many couples decide to keep their love lives strictly online.

STRETCHING OF BOUNDARIES

Any environment used by billions of customers is bound to produce a wide array of legal, technological, and psychological challenges to society. The Sigh is no exception. Some examples follow.

Law. Long-held definitions of terms such as *rape* and *harassment* have undergone significant revision as a result of the Sigh. Is it possible for rape to occur in a virtual environment where the victim cannot be physically harmed and can log off the network at any point? Most L-PRACG courts say yes, but some claim no. Neither the Prime Committee nor the Congress of L-PRACGs has passed any definitive legislation on the issue.

Companionship. Because of the highly impersonal experience that certain channels on the Sigh provide, some users consider virtual sex to be closer to masturbation than intercourse. As a result, in many modern relationships it is not considered a violation of monogamy vows to have virtual sex.

Gender roles. The Sigh has brought the concept of alternative sexuality to new levels. In a world bounded only by the imagination, some choose to be neither male nor female, but some mixture or blend between the two. The artist Pullix Homer recently caused a stir by creating new and fanciful Sigh genders that interact in strange and sometimes startling ways.

Pleasure. Some scholars have decided that human sexuality is an unneeded intermediary step in the goal of achieving pleasure and have abandoned physical interaction altogether. Instead they have founded a new wave of bodiless "endorphin blast" channels, which many see as a future battleground between governmentalists and libertarians.

SOCIAL IMPLICATIONS

When the Sigh first moved from the laboratory into wide public usage (around the 280s YOR), many pundits predicted that virtual sex would be devastating to society. They imagined a world of users constantly plugging in to the network for a sensual fix, to the detriment of work, law, and creed.

Although the Sigh has created its share of addicts, it is apparent that the fears of the doomsayers never materialized. The economics of the Sigh prohibit users from spending too much time logged in; those for whom economics is not an issue often find moderation through strict creed and L-PRACG rules that strongly penalize addiction.

However, on the other end of the spectrum were those who declared the Sigh would bring about an end to social ills such as prostitution, sexual slavery, and rape. Unfortunately, these utopian predictions have not proven accurate either. While the Sigh might provide some would-be sexual predators with a place to vent their behaviors, it has undoubtedly inspired others in the real world to new heights of deviancy.

APPENDIX G

ON THE TRANSPORTATION SYSTEM

In the waning days of Earth's fossil fuels, many predicted that the lack of combustible fuel would cripple the world's transportation systems and bankrupt the world's economies. The truth of that prediction would never be tested, however, as the Autonomous Revolt occurred at roughly the same time as the last of the big oil wells ran dry.

Human transportation was not nearly as much of a challenge after the Revolt as the transportation of cargo. The civilizations of antiquity relied on intricate shipping, trucking, and airborne networks to keep goods and services moving. Without fossil fuels, these networks proved impossible to reconstruct.

The Reawakening (and Prengal Surina's universal law of physics) brought with it nearly inexhaustible sources of clean, renewable energy. This in turn gave rise to a number of transportation systems that greatly expanded humanity's options of getting from place to place.

THE TUBE

For the greater part of the Reawakening, the tube has been the dominant form of Terran transportation. Its tracks are ubiquitous throughout the civilized world, allowing travel to almost any spot on Earth at a fair price. In many cities, local tube trains cover almost as much ground as the ancient asphalt roads once did. Longer express routes run underground in dedicated tunnels that allow for faster speeds.

The tube's success is mostly the product of two technological advances: the development of so-called unbreakable steel, which allows for unobtrusive tracks that are extremely cheap to install and maintain; and the ability to control inertia, thereby enabling rapid starts and stops.

For many years, TubeCo was the darling of the financial world. Its influence was so pervasive in government that the company was given a seat on the Prime Committee itself.

Since the advent of affordable multi technology, however, TubeCo's fortunes have been on the wane. Local tube routes still have heavy ridership, but most fail to see the necessity of traveling long distances when they can multi instead. Expansion to Luna and Mars has not lifted the company's fortunes either, due to poor offworld planning and the exorbitant cost of shipping. (The ineptitude of the Martian tube system has even given rise to the popular phrase "as slow as a Martian train.")

The recent stripping of TubeCo's seat on the Prime Committee has lessened the company's prospects even further and led to chronic labor disputes. Many predict an imminent collapse.

HOVERBIRDS

Air travel has long been a staple of modern society, and the class of vehicles known as hoverbirds provides this service. Private hoverbird fleets run through and between all the major cities on Earth, Luna, and Mars. Specially outfitted vehicles make runs up to the orbital colonies as well.

Personal air travel has never really caught on among the masses. Given the fact that the tube is cheaper, safer, and almost as quick, hoverbirds have long had a reputation as a vehicle for the business class. Private ownership of hoverbirds is considered an extravagance that few but the wealthy would need or afford.

Hoverbirds do have an important advantage over the tube, however, in that they're not constrained to traveling where the tracks are. The typical hoverbird both takes off and lands vertically, allowing direct transport to all but the most crowded and confined locations. So businesses have relegated many of their shipping and transport needs to the hoverbird sector.

The Defense and Wellness Council has also made a heavy investment in hoverbirds, for obvious reasons.

UNDERGROUND TRANSFER SYSTEM

Faced with limited resources, the civil planners in the early years of the Reawakening struck on a pragmatic solution to their transportation issues. They would use the ancient sewers and data cable pipes to move cargo from place to place. Early underground transfer systems were rudimentary, often dependent on wind power, water power, and even manual labor.

But as technology progressed, so did the global underground transfer system. Heavy infrastructure investments during the time of Par Padron (late 100s YOR) brought the underground transfer system to the entire globe, where it has become one of the central government's strongest success stories.

In modern times, underground transfer has become a nearly seamless method of shuttling goods from place to place. The system is generally only used for local cargo traffic, given that there are much faster methods for transporting goods over large distances.

ORBICO

Interplanetary shipping has proven consistently resistant to economization, despite the best efforts of generations of entrepreneurs. As a result, the quasi-governmental agency OrbiCo has been given a virtual monopoly on transporting goods through space. (Transport of personnel remains a viable—though not wildly profitable—business, and OrbiCo competes against a number of smaller rivals in that market.) The agency is heavily subsidized by the Prime Committee and has never come close to turning a profit since its inception in 315.

Given the importance of interplanetary shipping to the offworlders in Luna, Mars, and the orbital colonies, OrbiCo has often been accused of taking bribes—or at the very least, of being very dependent on the whims of its political sponsors.

OrbiCo freight ships tend to be very utilitarian in nature. Bandwidth restrictions on interplanetary flights are such that networks like multi, the Jamm, and the Sigh are not accessible on OrbiCo ships (except when in port).

THE FUTURE OF TRANSPORTATION

Marcus Surina famously declared that teleportation would provide an end to the "tyranny of distance." Various multi network engineers have made similar declarations. And yet, three and a half centuries into the Reawakening, people still physically travel from place to place in large numbers.

Current trends indicate that Surina's words may indeed prove to be prescient, however. Declining ridership on the tube and the hoverbirds (and the still-dismal adoption rate of teleportation) point to a society that may one day live out its entire existence in virtual settings.

Conservation advocates such as those in Creed Conscientious warn that such an attitude can only lead to an eventual bandwidth crisis and universal disaster.

APPENDIX H

ON DARTGUNS
AND DISRUPTORS

MODERN WARFARE

The nature of warfare underwent a dramatic shift in the early years of the Reawakening. Improvements in OCHRE technology and bio/logic programming made it abundantly clear to battle tacticians that old-fashioned weapons were simply not up to the challenge of modern combat.

The new medical knowledge and the rapid-healing capabilities of OCHREs (not to mention advances in body armor) made constructing a lethal projectile weapon a much more difficult task. In such a world, even advanced biological and chemical weaponry quickly became out-moded.

Nuclear weapons programs were never restarted after the tumult and chaos of the Autonomous Revolt, in which several smaller nuclear strikes were executed. The death of the nation-state ensured that there were no large, well-funded organizations with the wherewithal and desire to construct atomic weapons. The advent of multi and the Data Sea made bombs increasingly irrelevant when enemies were scattered around the globe and rarely present in large numbers.

So combat tacticians of the Reawakening developed the dartgun.

DARTGUNS

The standard weapon of modern times is the dartgun. Much like their ancestors from antiquity, dartguns shoot thin, needlelike projectiles at great distances. But whereas ancient darts were often tipped with poisons and neurotoxins, modern darts are loaded with microscopic OCHREs containing self-executing black code programs.

Weapons programmers have grown remarkably proficient at creating OCHREs that can spread through the body and immobilize or kill an adversary within fractions of a second. Much of this is accomplished with controlled radio and subaether transmissions from the infecting OCHREs that interact with other machines implanted in the body. The complexity of the OCHRE system ensures there will always be loopholes for black code writers to exploit.

While it might seem like body armor could easily neutralize the threat of OCHRE-tipped darts, weapons engineers have become so proficient at creating armor-piercing darts as to render this strategy useless. Modern tacticians tend to focus on bio/logic defenses against invading code instead.

MULTI DISRUPTORS

Multi disruptors (often simply called "disruptors") were originally designed with one purpose in mind: to forcefully cut someone's multi connection. Before such weapons came into existence, there was nothing stopping an army from sending a multied intelligence agent into the midst of an enemy force. Such fears were also drastically slowing public adoption of the technology.

Common belief states that the Defense and Wellness Council initiated disruptor research as a way to safeguard the multi system. Having such weapons available, so the reasoning went, made seditious elements less likely to attack the multi system itself.

It has become public knowledge, however, that the Council has transformed the multi disruptor from a purely defensive weapon into an offensive one. Various drudge reports claim these advanced disruptors can actually inject programming code into an enemy's bio/logic systems, in the same fashion as an OCHRE-tipped dart. The Council has been loath to publicize or even admit the existence of these weapons, however, fearing that such actions might lead to widespread panic and abandonment of the multi system.

THE NEW WARFARE ACT OF 221

Probably the most significant piece of legislation to make its way through the government in the early 200s was the New Warfare Act of 221. This bill legalized nonlethal warfare and set the ground rules for nearly all conflicts that have followed since.

The bill essentially allows citizens to deploy nonlethal force in a wide variety of circumstances. As a consequence, private security has become a huge business, with every organization from creeds to bureaucrats to L-PRACGs hiring its own private force.

Proponents of the New Warfare Act say this legislation has drastically reduced the casualties of conflict and pushed opposing parties to discuss their grievances in a more civilized fashion. But detractors point to the thousands of private security forces with conflicting agendas who feel no compunction about shooting first and asking questions later.

The most controversial provision of the New Warfare Act actually requires L-PRACGs to leave security "trapdoors" in their members' OCHRE systems that are only accessible to the central government. The goal was to standardize weapons systems and prevent an escalating technology war. This provision drew (and continues to draw) public outcry and scorn, with libertarian activists calling it "legalized slavery to the Defense and Wellness Council." Few L-PRACGs to date actually comply with this law. Thus far, the Defense and Wellness Council has not sought to enforce it—although this may be because the Council's weapons systems are still effective enough to overcome most private programming defenses anyway.

ACKNOWLEDGMENTS

The author would like to thank the following individuals for their editorial contributions to this book: Lou Anders, Bruce Bortz, Cindy Blank-Edelman, Jerome Edelman, Deanna Hoak, and Philip Mansour.

For their contributions in publicizing and promoting his work, the author would like to thank: John Joseph Adams, Paul Goat Allen, Lou Anders, Matthew Arnold, Eric Beck, Rob Bedford, Carrie Blakeway, Darrell and Marsha Blakeway, Cindy and David Blank-Edelman, the good folks at Borderlands Books, Bruce Bortz, Tobias Buckell, Paul Cornell, Ellen Datlow, the other bloggers at DeepGenre, Michael de Gennaro, Thomas Doyle, Jerome and Barbara Edelman, Deborah and Steve Edelman-Blank, Kate Elliott, Marc and Kathy Estafanous, Nat Forgotson, Brent Garland, Denise Iger, Matthew Jarpe, Katharine Kerr, Mindy Klasky, Rick Kleffel, Mary Robinette Kowal, George Mann and the folks at Solaris Books, Philip and Erinn Mansour, Jill Maxick, Ian McDonald, Eugene Myers, Steven Oliverez, Cat Rambo, Paul Raven, Chris Roberson, Suzanne Rosin, Nick Sagan, Rob Sawyer, John Scalzi, the other authors at SFNovelists.com, Kevin Smokler, Tim Spalding and the folks at LibraryThing, Peter Watts, Andrew Wheeler, and Sean Williams.

A special thank you to everyone at Pyr, especially Lou Anders, Peggy Deemer, and Jill Maxick.

Final thanks go to Victoria Blakeway Edelman, who in addition to helping out with all of the above, made the author take out Ferris from this book too.

ABOUT THE AUTHOR

DAVID LOUIS EDELMAN is a Web designer, programmer, and journalist. He lives with his wife, Victoria, near Washington, DC.

Over the past twelve years, Mr. Edelman has programmed Web sites for the US Army and the FBI, taught software to the US Congress and the World Bank, written articles for the *Washington Post* and the *Baltimore Sun*, and directed the marketing departments of biometric and e-commerce companies.

His first novel, *Infoquake*, was nominated for the John W. Campbell Memorial Award for Best Novel. Barnes & Noble called the book "the love child of Donald Trump and Vernor Vinge" and named it the Top SF Novel of 2006. Mr. Edelman's short fiction has also been featured in the *Solaris Book of New Science Fiction, Volume Two*. He is a member of the popular DeepGenre and SFNovelists blogs.

Mr. Edelman was born in Birmingham, Alabama, in 1971 and grew up in Orange County, California. He received a BA in creative writing and journalism from Johns Hopkins University in 1993.

HOW TO CONTACT THE AUTHOR

E-mail:	dedelman@gmail.com
Web site:	http://www.davidlouisedelman.com
On Facebook:	http://www.facebook.com/p/David_Louis_Edelman/507439981
On LibraryThing:	http://www.librarything.com/profile/DavidLouisEdelman
On LinkedIn:	http://www.linkedin.com/in/davidlouis edelman
On LiveJournal:	http://david-l-edelman.livejournal.com
On MySpace:	http://www.myspace.com/davidlouisedelman